A Very Civil War is a love letter, and sadly a eulogy, to this once bucolic, jackdawed, Cotswold village, Little Rissington, where I live — always in the hopes that it will one day return to an earlier century.

Frankly, time travel can't come soon enough.

Special thanks to British History Online for their meticulously detailed and dedicated work on chronicling this beautiful land. I discovered the now vanished Court House in their magnificent archive. And particularly to Jonathan Blaney from British History Online and Dr Adam Chapman from The Institute of Historical Research for their affable assistance.

By the same author

Dark Lantern
Out of the Shadows
The Widow

A Very Civil War

CAROLINE ELKINGTON

ISBN 9798729746842

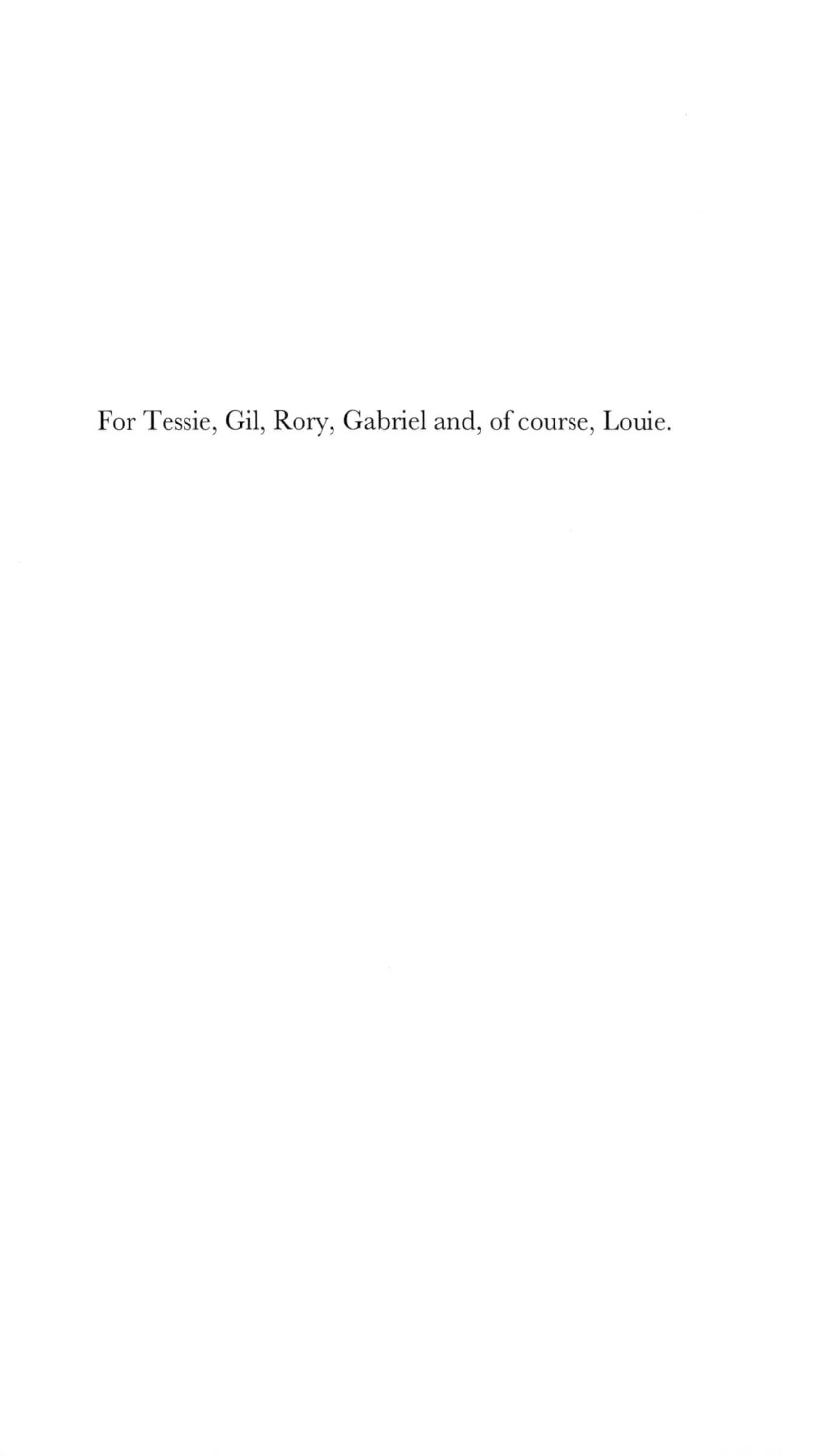

For Tessie, Gil, Rory, Gabriel and, of course, Louie.

One

"It must have been cool once upon a time."

"People don't say cool *or* once upon a time anymore, Con."

"Eat your breakfast before it gets cold."

"It says there's one just down by the church-gate."

"That's nice, sweetie."

"I'm going to look."

"*After* breakfast."

"K."

"What *would* be cool is if you read a book occasionally."

"Books, Con! Really?"

"Books will always be cool. And you have the whole of the summer holidays to read at least one."

"*So* boring."

"Gabe, must you be such a typical teenager?" Con sighed. "You've got six weeks to fill. There'll be lots of time for everything."

Gabe rolled his eyes, "*Auntie* Con, you're so old-fashioned. Like, some really old person from the really olden days."

"Don't call me auntie. That makes me feel extremely old. My aunts were permed and blue-rinsed."

"I don't even know what that means. Sometimes you speak in a dead language. Like Latin. Or Sumerian."

"Thank you. Your education is showing."

Gabriel uttered a sound which could have been a snort of either derision or agreement, it was hard to tell.

Con smiled at him fondly, "I've got things planned for us to do, you know? Being in the depths of the Cotswolds doesn't have to be deadly dull. Oh, for instance, there's a

Civil War re-enactment in Stow coming up soon. That'll be interesting. You like history, don't you Rowen?"

"Yeah, I suppose. Got a good teacher actually. But it'll just be a load of sad old people wearing fancy dress. A bit embarrassing."

"It'll be educational and fun."

"Proper death knell sounded there, Con."

"Philistine."

"Pass the pancakes, Gabe."

"*You* pass the pancakes."

Constance Harcourt eyed her two younger nephews with amused forbearance as she pushed the large dish of pancakes down the table towards Rowen, who forked three and transferred them to his plate before liberally drenching them in maple syrup.

A third nephew strolled absentmindedly into the kitchen, pausing on the threshold to take in the scene around the table and his eyes lit up, "Pancakes. Nice. Has anyone seen my phone?"

"It's on the sofa. Where you left it. Do you want coffee?"

"Please. Sorry I'm a little late. Got distracted."

"You're in a permanent state of distraction. It's your default setting. Sit down and have some breakfast."

"Thanks Con. Any plans for today? We going out?"

"Geocaching," replied Gabriel happily.

"That's like, prehistoric. Is that the best idea you've got? It's as old as The Ark."

"Trust you to put a damper on it, Guy."

Guy smiled, "You won't listen to me anyway. You never do. So, when are we going?"

Gabriel let out a whoop of delight, "Brilliant! After breakfast and Con's coming too."

"I am *not*!" said Con firmly. "I have no desire to traipse about staring mindlessly at my phone. I know zombies are all the rage in your odd little world, but I'd much rather not become one. I'd rather just go for a straightforward W-A-L-K. We can take Badger with us; he could do with a good long run after being cooped up in the car all of yesterday." The black cockapoo sleeping in front of the Aga, opened one cynical eye on hearing his name and looked at his owner but as she showed no signs of immediately leaving the house, he closed it again and drifted back to sleep.

"Okay. Deal," said Guy, "Happy to W-A-L-K Badge. At least he is loving and loyal unlike my brothers." He helped himself to some more pancakes and spread Marmite and maple syrup on them.

"Eww. You are so gross!" groaned Gabriel, making a disgusted face. "Why can't you eat normal food like a normal person?"

"Con, d'you think I could get some work over the holidays? Like in the pub? I could do with some extra money. University is going to be pretty costly and now Mummy is — a single mother, funds will be a bit short."

"I'll have a word with Abby at The Royalist and see if she needs any help. She's always busy at this time of the year. Hot weather brings in the tourists. And you've done some waiting before haven't you?"

"Yeah, I'm happy to do waiting or even dish-washing if that's what they need."

"I'll text her. Now, as soon as you've finished, clear the table and load the dishwasher and get your shoes on. We're going for a W-A-L-K."

"I just want you to look up from your phones every now and then and to take note of the real world. It's not a lot to ask. You're missing out on life."

"You're a Luddite, Con."

"Very probably but I see people walking down the lane with their eyes on their screens or chatting on their phones, not seeing the blossom on the plum tree or the red kites swooping over their heads or hearing the birdsong — it seems such a shame."

Rowen and Gabriel had dashed ahead past the old rectory and were racing each other to the bottom of the steep path which led to the church. At the bottom of the slope a wrought iron gate in a drystone wall barred the way; the merest trickle of a brook ran beneath the path on its way to join the River Dikler down in the valley. Constance had whiled away many a happy day as a child in that tiny stream, picking wild watercress and catching water-shrimp and sticklebacks in jars, building dams, and making dens in the pollarded willow which leant drunkenly over the water — when summers were baking hot and lasted forever and her only desire was to be either a Swallow or an Amazon or to find Narnia in the back of her wardrobe. Things were simpler then. Life was linear and you knew where you belonged. She felt sorry for modern children with their complicated, layered lives, where everything had to be photographed and recorded and captioned only to haunt you in later life; where technology made it easy for strangers to invade your world and destroy your self-confidence with some ugly words written anonymously from the safety of their bedrooms; giving them a temporary feeling of power over their fellow human beings. How sad, she thought, that modern day life had come to this. She knew she was old-fashioned and was glad of it. But sometimes she felt as though she were on the sidelines of a playing field, watching a very fast game of a sport she didn't understand and from a very great distance, as though through the wrong end of a telescope. She didn't feel connected, as though her roots had worked their way loose after years of endless battering by the winds. Rootless and yet firmly attached to her little handkerchief sized corner of England. The scents and sounds and sights of the place coursed through her blood and she could never imagine, in her wildest dreams, living anywhere else.

Rowen and Gabriel, unable to slow the impetus of their sprint crashed into the gate, laughing and out of breath. Rowen elegantly vaulted it and sped up the hill on the other side, where the path curved between the grassy shoulders of Church Field. Gabriel opened the gate and held it wide for his more sedate relations and the madly galloping dog, who within seconds had disappeared up the path after Rowen.

Having seen them through into the field he then fished his phone from his pocket and started swiping the screen.

"GPS says it's somewhere here, in the wall, by the bridge." Gabriel was peering closely at the old wall, sticking his fingers into nooks and crannies. "Aha! Got it. Well hidden!" He pulled a waterproof box out from between the stones, holding it aloft in triumph. He balanced it on top of the wall and opened it to reveal a cache of random objects: a toy car, some coins, a packet of stamps, a water pistol and a joke book. He picked out the water pistol and delving into his pocket brought out a plastic bag containing a mini pocket-kite which he put in the box. He then found a pen in his other pocket and filled in his details in the game log and returned it to the box.

"I'm not at all sure I understand the appeal of this," said Con quietly.

"A global treasure hunt? What's not to like, for a boy Gabe's age? A bit of an adventure, some environmentally unfriendly plastic, and a feeling of belonging to something. Just what he needs at the moment." Guy went to help his brother wedge the box back into the wall.

"Brilliant," said Gabriel, "Now can we play Pokémon Go?"

"Can't you just *walk* and enjoy the scenery?" asked his aunt, shaking her head.

"If you would just be more open to things you'd get so much more out of life," replied her youngest nephew.

"Come on, Con, we'll show you how to play," and they proceeded to try to explain to her exactly how the app worked. She pretended great interest and received an approving look from Guy. After a few minutes Gabriel had loaded the app onto her phone and was encouraging her to find the little cartoon monsters hiding around them. She gamely entered into the spirit of it while wishing she was slightly less inhibited and reluctant to delve into technology and all that it entailed. She had never enjoyed any kind of sport which involved either risk to life and limb or humiliation; she had been born without a competitive bone in her body and could care less if she had more monsters in her *Pokedex* or had remembered to get a *Pokeball*. It was like learning a new language but at her advanced age of thirty-four it was proving to be a struggle.

Gabriel was excitedly talking about *Lucky Eggs*, *Razz Berries,* and *Lure Patches* and his fingers were flying over the keyboard on his phone, sliding and clicking, while Con tried to keep up. Eventually her brain reached overload and she began to wonder what to give them for supper, wondering if they'd prefer Tacos or Spaghetti Bolognese.

"Con! You're not *listening*! I just said about *Caterpies* and you said that might do for supper! Look! See? There's a *Pikachu* on your screen. That's your first capture. Now, see if you can find more."

Con caught Guy's sympathetic glance and bent her head over the phone as she had seen others do. After a few minutes she managed to successfully capture another odd little character and was rewarded with a bone-crushing hug from Gabriel, which, she supposed, made the intense boredom worthwhile.

After half an hour of obediently following their confusing instructions, her neck started to ache, and her eyes were having trouble focusing on the screen. God, she thought, being old is very tiresome.

Rowen was throwing a ball for Badger and the two of them frolicked boisterously in the fields surrounding the church, Badger a dark, panting blur and Rowen laughing loudly at his antics. Rowen always laughed loudly — he was a loud and vibrant creature, full of nonsense, and affectionate to a fault. He was also oddly diffident and inclined to cover it up with excessive chatter and manic activity. He had caught her artistic streak at a very young age and was now a keen and talented photographer.

The little church stood away from the village to the north, circled by meadows and fields and woods, with a genteel view of the Windrush Valley and, somewhere beyond the typically rolling Cotswold hills, the refined Regency town of Cheltenham. Local myth had it that the village of Little Rissington used to be next to the church but was moved across the brook to the adjacent hill when the plague struck, the villagers being convinced that crossing running water would save them from death. All the village had amounted to in those days was a few cottages and some mysterious fourteenth century house called the Court House, which, according to legend, had probably been demolished during the Dissolution of Manorial Estates sometime in the seventeenth century. Little Rissington was basically still not much more than a farming village with no pub and no village shop anymore. One generally went through it, very speedily, on the way to somewhere else.

Constance Harcourt had lived in the village since her parents had moved them into their Great Aunt's old home some decades ago. To say she was a stick-in-the-mud would not be an exaggeration. Her family used the old farmhouse as a base at various times; it was the heart of their small family and had been since the forties. There were now several generations buried in the churchyard and her older sister, Tova had been married there, all three nephews christened, and one Great Aunt scattered in the middle of a wild summer storm. Con had attended the village school before being packed off to a nearby convent to finish her education; it had not been a salutary lesson for anyone involved. Nuns, she discovered, were an inflexible bunch on the whole, with one notable exception, her art teacher, an elderly, taciturn nun who had encouraged Constance to concentrate on her art and had lived long enough to see the first children's book she'd illustrated.

Con went through the little wooden gate into the churchyard and sat down on the bench beside the porch from where she could idly watch the boys doing what boys do. Gabriel was head down, eyes on his screen, Rowen racing Badger across the meadow, and Guy, sprawled on the grassy bank beside the path, reading a book he must have had stuffed in a pocket. She smiled to herself glad that the reading bug had caught at least one of them and thought that even if there were an earthquake, right in the middle of Church Field, Guy would remain happily in his own world until someone mentioned lunch.

Gabriel looked up from his digital universe and yelled to her, "Keep looking, Con! Bound to be some in the church-yard!"

Con sighed and reluctantly opened the app again and tried to remember how to use it; all the careful instructions seemed to have faded away already. She randomly pressed the icons on the screen and watched without much interest as something started to happen, a landscape appeared, the fields, the churchyard, the path. A badly drawn cartoon world. She looked up at the beautiful, tangible real world around her, the soft lush greens and bleached ochres of the meadow, the darker shadowed viridian of the wood bordering Church Field and the hazy cobalt blue of the sky above. And the glorious scents rising from the ground as the earth warmed up in the early August sunshine. She closed her eyes and breathed it in.

The screen made a little insistent hissing noise. She ignored it. She listened instead to the sharp cry of a buzzard, soaring high above the church, its broad wings quite still as it lazily circled. How amazing that must be, looking down on our miniature world and not have to worry about making supper.

The screen hissed again. A sort of electronic crackle.

She opened her eyes and looked at it. In the middle of the screen was a dark shadow, broken into jumping jagged lines, its edges zigzagging excitedly.

"Gabe?" she called, "I think I have something! Like a ghost with interference. What do I do now? I've forgotten."

Gabriel was already running, pretending to dodge imaginary rugby opponents and scoring an impressive try just by the gate.

He threw himself down onto the bench and grabbed her phone. "What *is* that? Weird. I think your phone is glitching. Wait, I'll just reboot." His nimble fingers danced over the screen and for a moment it went dark and then lit up again and he reopened the app. "That's well weird, Con. It's still there. Did you drop your phone?"

"I most certainly did not. I'm not careless with my possessions like some people."

Gabriel frowned at the screen, "Maybe there's something wrong with the app. I'll check online." More tapping and sounds of disgruntled confusion from an annoyed teenager. Con watched a dandelion clock drift by. Her nephew shrugged expressively, "My mate says there's nothing wrong his end and there's no sign online of any global problems with it. It's just you, Con!"

"Well, isn't that just my luck. Technology and I are always at war. Oh, look, the shadow's mutating." She pointed at the hazy shape which was now coming more into focus. "It looks like — a person."

Gabriel put his head close to hers and they stared hard at the emerging outline.

As they watched, a twitching form appeared against the cartoon landscape. It crackled and fizzed.

"We must have a crossed line," said Con, squinting hard at the image.

"Crossed line? What's that?"

"Someone else's call on our phone line — at the same time. Used to happen a lot — in the *olden* days."

"Did you even *have* phones?"

"Oh, very funny."

"It seems to be growing."

"Perhaps we should — ?"

"Why is it like, *real* when it should be animation? And — why is it wearing some sort of weird freaky costume?"

"I have no answers for you. It's *your* game, I'm just a bystander in this. What's it doing now?"

"No clue. Huh. I think it's a girl with long hair. Oh, and a — *beard*! What the — ?"

"Perhaps we should just turn it off. I'm not sure I like this. It's a bit disconcerting."

"Nah. Let's see what happens. It's sick."

"I do wish you wouldn't use that expression. It's revolting."

"Says the woman who still uses *Lawks* as a swearword!"

Con laughed and looked around to see if she could still see Rowen and Badger.

She started and let out a small squeal when she found her view blocked by a large, looming shape, hovering right in front of her.

"Gabriel! *What the hell*?!"

Gabriel looked up from the screen, "What is *that* — ?" He scrambled to his feet, "*Con!* Look out!"

The amorphous shape was shifting, its edges fragmenting and between the shattered pieces, Church Field and the village beyond were still clearly visible. Gabriel slid himself between the strange mirage and his aunt. "Maybe you should run, Con! This is crazy!" He pushed his hand forward, towards the flickering figure and watched in amazement as it disappeared into what looked like a shimmering heat haze.

"Rowen! Guy! Come quickly!" yelled Constance at the top of her lungs, panic rising.

Rowen stopped rolling with Badger in the long grass, leapt to his feet and immediately sprinted towards the church, helpfully followed by the now very overexcited dog. Guy turned the page of his book.

Badger arrived first and went into a mad frenzy of barking, circling the shadowy intruder, his hackles up and his eyes showing the whites.

Rowen grabbed him by the collar and hauled him away. "Con! What *is* that?! Get away from it! Gabe! Come over *here*!"

Gabriel was carefully examining his hand which he'd removed from the centre of the ghostly apparition's midriff, looking at it as though it might be melted or on fire, and then he backed away, pulling Con with him.

"*GUY!* Get your arse over here!" bellowed Rowen, in a voice that would have carried to distant galaxies.

Guy slowly unfolded his long legs and rose to his feet, with his nose still in the book and began to stroll up the path in a leisurely fashion. "Coming," he said dreamily.

Gabriel was still holding on tightly to Con, whether to protect or for protection, even he wasn't quite sure. Badger's legs were stiff with rage as he snapped and snarled at the constantly shifting penumbral cloud. He had decided that whatever this thing was, it was menacing his family and it deserved his undivided attention.

Then, just as suddenly as it had appeared, it started to lose its strength. The edges melted. The snapping, firecracker sounds faded. As Guy reached the gate, the spectral image disappeared.

Two

Guy was listening to his family all talking at once and Badger growling at empty space. He looked from one to the other and could clearly see that they all believed what they were telling him. Con was looking a little pale and Gabriel was fidgety with excitement. Rowen was trying to calm the dog and was unnaturally quiet.

Guy sighed. He felt he wasn't really cut out to play the role of father, but they were all looking at him in that way they had sometimes, like he was some sort of problem solver. He had no desire to solve anyone's problems, he just wanted to drift along in his dreamworld, undisturbed by his feral relations and their tiresome demands on his time.

"So, you're saying you saw a Pokémon ghost? A ghost in the machine. Funny."

"Not just on the screen Guy! It was *here! Actually* here. In our space. Like, *here.*" Gabriel gestured wildly to the spot where they had seen the awful vision. "Wasn't it Con?"

Con nodded, "Gabe's telling the truth. There was *something* here. First on the screen and then right here in the churchyard. We think it was sort of human-ish."

"You know that's not possible, right?"

"Yes, Guy," patiently. "I am fully aware that all three of us and Badger are suffering from some sort of mass hysteria. What else could it be?"

"How am I supposed to know! I didn't see it."

Rowen was looking thoughtful, "Honestly, I'd think we were all hallucinating if it weren't for Badger. He saw something. Look at him. His hackles are still up." The dog growled low in his throat and did a little yip of a bark as though to confirm his concern. "Dogs see stuff we can't. Or, at least, they're aware of things beyond our limited imaginations."

"I can see that. I can see that you're all — disturbed. But — it seems to me that whatever it is — was — it has moved on to pastures new. Maybe two parallel planes momentarily touched and what you saw was two different realties bleeding from one plane into another."

There was complete silence.

Guy laughed self-consciously.

"Jeezus," said Rowen, on a breath, "You don't think he's right, do you, Con! I mean, what else could it be? The app picked it up and maybe created a portal — "

Guy rolled his eyes, "I was *joking*. This isn't Doctor Who!"

Con was staring into the middle distance, a frown marring her forehead, her pale green eyes reflecting the brilliant sky. "That costume — it was familiar. I couldn't see it clearly but — " Con shrugged, "I think it was a Civil War uniform."

"Ha! It was very realistic!" exclaimed Gabriel.

"So, a crossed line with a Civil War re-enactor?"

"The Sealed Knot."

"The what?"

"Enthusiasts. Reliving the Civil War in full costume and with weapons. They sort of live it for real. I'm going to take you to see one of their displays in Stow. It's great fun."

"Sounds — thrilling. Can't wait. But why are they invading our phones? Laying siege to our technology. It doesn't make sense. I mean, is it even technically possible?" asked Gabriel as he switched on Con's phone again. All the children knew her passwords because they didn't trust her to manage her devices and because they wanted to use her account to buy things.

"I think you're ignoring the salient point here, my love. It wasn't *just* on my phone — it was actually here. In front of us. Not quite tangible but visible — in our personal airspace."

"True." He clicked icons, tapped out passwords and waited. The app stirred into life. "Here we go. Let's see if everything's back to normal now."

Three dark blonde heads and one chestnut one leant in to get a better view.

Nothing happened.

Badger began to growl low in his throat.

The four heads looked up at him. He was facing away from them, looking towards the gate. At something between him and the gate.

"Oh, bloody hell," said Con.

Rowen advanced towards the figure, now, still hazy around the edges but otherwise as clear as day and staring at Constance impassively. Rowen, stretched out his hand, "Er — how do you do? My name is Rowen. I'm from Planet Earth."

"Rowen!" said Guy, laughing.

"Are you from The Sealed Knot? Like, a re-enactor? That's a brilliant costume. Really authentic. Loving the sword, mate. Ever used it for real?"

The "re-enactor" frowned. Then reached out his hand. Rowen took a step forward.

"No! Rowen! Don't!" shouted Con. She sort of bumped Rowen out of the way, and standing in front of the re-enactor, stuck her hand out.

The man, tall and powerfully built, was dressed in a buff coat, a broad dark green sash tied at the waist, claret breeches, buff leather hose boots; his dark curly hair was worn long to his shoulders and he had an artistically sculpted Van Dyke beard and moustache. Con thought he was pretty dashing in a rough-hewn sort of way.

Their hands drew closer and then met. As skin touched skin, he seemed to shiver, and his outline frayed a little, but he held onto her hand and his grip was remarkably firm.

"You know, I'm not entirely convinced that he's from The Sealed Knot, boys. I have a feeling that things just got a little bit weirder."

"Looks like a Cavalier to me. All that face fungus and the frills," said Gabriel.

"Actually, they all dressed pretty much the same unless they were proper religious fanatics," said Rowen, whose favourite subject was history. "So, he could technically be either."

Con looked down at her hand which was still held by the apparition. Her heart skipped a beat. Her fingers were transparent.

"That's — peculiar," she murmured.

"Con! What's happening? You look like you're *dissolving*!" yelled Gabriel.

Rowen leapt towards the pair and grabbed his aunt by her free arm. "Quickly! Hold onto her!"

Gabriel dived forward like he was tackling a rugby opponent and Guy followed, they held onto anything they could. Badger started yipping aggressively, weaving in and out of their legs, trying to nip at ghostly ankles.

Then suddenly, Con and the re-enactor had gone.

There was no puff of smoke just a shimmering heat haze and an electronic fizzing sound coming from her phone, which lay abandoned on the grass.

The three boys collapsed onto the springy turf and stared blankly at each other.

Nobody said anything for a moment. Badger seemed to have regained his composure, throwing himself down in the shade of an ivy-covered tombstone, panting noisily.

"Any ideas, anyone? *Anyone?!*" said Guy unsteadily.

"Go after them? Call the police?" suggested Rowen.

"*Hello*! How are you going to explain that our aunt has been kidnapped by a — spectral Civil War re-enactor? They'd laugh in your face and make you take a breath test."

"We could follow her and get her back?"

"Maybe it's like Narnia and she'll pop out of a wardrobe somewhere."

"Good. I like your thinking, Gabe. Any idea *which* wardrobe? And will it make a difference that she didn't disappear *into* a wardrobe?"

Gabriel shrugged.

"Badger obviously thinks they've gone. Like, proper gone. No loitering in the ether," said Rowen thoughtfully, "Dogs know stuff."

Guy looked pensive for moment, "I think we'd better call Mummy. She'll know what to do. We can't deal with this by ourselves. It's well beyond our remit. We need a wiser head." He pulled his phone out of his pocket and punched in some numbers. He listened to the dial tone. A woman's voice answered.

"Mum? We've got a bit of a problem."

Constance looked down at her hand, which was still being held by the re-enactor. It was no longer transparent, which she thought was probably a good sign.

The re-enactor was looking down at her with a puzzled frown between his dark brows. She tugged her hand out of his and smiled up at him. He was built on the lines of a great oak tree, tall and broad. He was, as her sister was inclined to say, no oil painting, verging on ugly, his eyes heavy-lidded and sleepy, his nose long but had obviously been broken at some point, his mouth thin and stern.

"Hello?" said Constance tentatively. "That was odd wasn't it? I feel rather peculiar now — like I've been on a fairground ride for too long. A bit sick and my head is spinning."

His hard grey eyes narrowed, "I beg your pardon, Mistress but I do not understand."

"Oh, me neither! I can't think what happened. The boys and I were just playing Pokémon Go and there was some sort of technical disturbance — the signal, or something, I expect — or the server — I'm never quite sure which — "

He held up a large hand, "No, I fear I must interrupt you as I am still finding it difficult to understand what you are saying," said the re-enactor.

"Oh, I'll get the boys to explain. I'm really not at all *au fait* with the stupid game," and she turned back to the church.

Her eyes widened and her jaw dropped. "What the — ?" she breathed, "Where — ? Guy? Rowen! *Gabe!*" She stared at the church. "I don't get it. Where are they? And why does the church look like *that*?"

"Look like what, Mistress?"

Constance took a step towards the church and tried to take in what she was seeing. "It's shrunk. Where's the rest of it? And where the hell are the war graves and the war memorial?"

"Again, I am afraid you are speaking in tongues, yet, given what I do understand, your language is of the sewer and offensive to my ear."

Constance turned back to the re-enactor, "Huh. You're really staying in character aren't you! Perhaps I should introduce myself. I'm Constance Harcourt and you are — ?"

He bowed, "Colonel Sir Lucas Deverell. Parliamentarian."

"Ah, Roundhead. Rowen was right. He said they didn't all have shaven heads. I like the long hair — which is probably why I was always a Royalist fan, bit of a hippy — they looked so debonair with all their lace and feathers. Also, always loved The Three Musketeers. Great characters."

The man claiming to be Colonel Sir Lucas Deverell fixed Constance with a narrow-eyed glare, "Roundhead? I should be careful if I were you when you use such insulting terms — not everyone is as forgiving as I am."

Constance laughed, "I must say I'm impressed with your dedication to your role. Do you keep it up when you're at home with the wife and kids? Like a method actor?"

Lucas Deverell ran a large hand through his dark hair, leaving it tousled and shook his head, “You make no sense, Mistress Harcourt. Are you for the King or Parliament?”

“Oh, well, as the saying goes — the Cavaliers were wrong but romantic and the Roundheads were right but repulsive. I’m torn between my wayward heart and my conscience.”

“Repulsive?" said Lucas Deverell. “You are a Royalist then.”

“No, I don’t think so. Although it must be argued that the Queen does do a damn fine job. In the olden days I think my shallower side would have been eventually overridden by what was morally right. Anyway, I must go and find my nephews, they’ll be wanting their lunch by now.”

“Those boys? I think you have left them behind. In the other place.”

“*Other* place?” Constance looked around at the church again. Her breath caught in her chest and she was hit by an inexplicable wave of homesickness.

Something really wasn’t right. There were far too many trees, actual woods nudging right up against the fields on all sides and all the grubbed out wild hedges had been reinstated. The east side of the churchyard was no longer bristling with regimented lines of plain white war graves and watched over by the enormous sword-shaped memorial. The church was truncated, the nave shorter in length and the stone walls less weather-beaten and mossy. And there were elm trees. Many elm trees, their distinctive shapes bringing a misty tear to Constance’s eye as she recalled how the Cotswolds had once looked before the devastation of Dutch Elm Disease, even though she was too young to remember it first-hand.

It was like being in a dream where everything was familiar and yet altered in some way. Constance began to feel even more queasy.

“The boys — ” she whispered almost to herself.

"As I have already alluded — they no longer seem to be here. It appears they have remained in your original place while you have somehow crossed over into mine."

"Crossed over?" Constance was aware that she was sounding a bit slow-witted. "You mean — you *can't* mean — that this is not — that this is — a different *time!* That's utterly ridiculous."

"Well, what year of our Lord is it?"

"20… 20?" Constance said hesitantly.

"Twenty? What do you mean, twenty?"

"Oh, I mean it's… um, goodness, how can I put it? It's 20 years into the twenty-first century.

Narrowing his eyes, he scrutinised her for a moment, "You mean to say you have slipped back over three hundred years?"

"If this is the 1600s," she ventured, "as it seems to be from your outfit. So, what year is it?"

"It's 1646, and I will admit that I am as confounded as you seem to be. But, being a rational man, I can find no other ready explanation for your being here than you have somehow crossed over. God's works are a mystery. Who are we to question His judgement? And, if it is any comfort, your nephews looked as though they might be intelligent young men — I think they will survive."

Constance thought for a moment, "Yes, you're right, they're smart. They'll phone — call — Tova, my sister. She'll take charge even if she doesn't understand what's going on. It's what she does." Her face crumpled, "But, how do I get back home?"

The burly soldier looked distinctly uncomfortable, "We will find a way. If there is a way *across* — there must be a way *back*." He looked at her rather oddly, "Come, we had better make haste. It would not do for you to be seen wearing such unsuitable clothing — you might be mistaken for a — a lady of disrepute."

"Nicely put. Thank you. This is considered quite a — modest dress where I come from."

"Is that so?" said Lucas Deverell, frowning darkly. "I think, in that case, you are better off here."

Constance laughed and, unable to think what else to do, followed him across the churchyard. She noticed he had a slight limp, as they passed along the grassy path towards the north side of the church. Somehow, she wasn't surprised to see there were differences everywhere she looked: tall trees grown small, fields made extra wide for modern machinery now a smaller patchwork, edged with hedgerows. Gravestones she remembered as falling down and moss covered, now sprucely new, and where the Kissing Gate had stood for a century, just an untidy gap in the hedge. Looking out across the Windrush Valley, Constance could see no business parks or the urban sprawl of Bourton-on-the-Water stretching its ugly fingers out across the vale. There was the odd rooftop and curls of smoke coming from chimneys, despite the August heat. She wondered what nearby Cheltenham looked like now before the elegant Georgians had made their mark on it. Her companion turned right out of the churchyard and strolled away down the lane heading east towards Bobble Hill. He glanced over his shoulder at her, "This must be strange for you," he said, almost apologetically.

"I will admit it is a trifle unsettling. I recognise the lay of the land, but things are much altered — or *not* altered, I should say. It's hard to keep my bearings. Where are we going?"

"To my home. Just along here."

If Constance's bearings had been struggling before, they now positively threw up their hands in despair.

Where there had only been a muddy farm track and straggly hedges of sloe trees and brambles and beyond, fields of barley, there was a well-tended drive bordered with high hedges that had obviously once been neatly clipped and she could see the tops of some splendid specimen trees. Halfway up the lane Lucas Deverell turned into a recessed entrance and they were met by majestic double gates of wrought iron, supported by impressive stone pillars, with the word "Court" woven into the ironwork of one gate and "House" into the other.

Beyond the gates Constance could see a glimpse of topiary and walls topped with stone statues, a parterre, herb garden, and even a small orangery built against a high south-facing wall. She could also see that the garden had been severely neglected. Lucas Deverell swung the gate wide and bowed her through with a small flourish. As she drew closer still, she could see ivy growing where it shouldn't, and stones fallen from the walls; the topiary was in need of a good pruning as the shapes were becoming blurred.

"It's beautiful. Magical. I never even knew there had been a manor in this part of the village."

He stopped in his tracks, "It no longer exists then?"

She could have bitten off her tongue. "Oh, I'm so sorry — I shouldn't have mentioned it — so stupid of me."

"No need to apologise. Nothing lasts forever. The garden, I am afraid, is much in need of a good gardener. My estate steward and I have been away for a long time and there has been nobody to keep an eye on things."

"Where have you been?"

"The war, of course. The Siege at Gloucester in '43 and then the Battle of Lostwithiel last year. I have not had the chance to return home until the end of last month."

"No wonder the garden needs attention. Were you at Naseby?"

Lucas Deverell met her eyes, "You have heard of it? No — I was badly injured at Lostwithiel and had no choice but to leave the house and gardens to their own devices. But I had to return because my younger sister was forced to send my children home when her husband was killed at Cropredy. She was unable to cope."

He was skirting along the path to the front of his house, his boot heels crunching on the gravel and Constance was trying to keep up and ask questions at the same time, when he turned abruptly to her, "So, who won?"

"Who won the Civil War?"

"I mean, who won, the Royalists or us?"

"Well, in truth, with hindsight, nobody did."

With that, he crunched on through the gravel, leaving Constance wondering what to make of his lack of surprise.

"So, you're married?" she called after him. "How many children?"

"Widower. Girl and a boy," he threw the information over his shoulder as he sprang up the sweep of steps, two at a time.

Constance stopped at the foot of them to take it all in. She was having difficulty processing everything. The cogs in her brain were slipping and information was getting tangled.

The fourteenth century Court House was built in the local honey-coloured limestone; it was gabled, with double arched, leaded windows, and an arched door. It was not in the least ostentatious and seemed to grow naturally from the ground as though it had been sown there. Constance fell in love with it the moment she laid eyes upon it. When she reached the top of the steps, she stopped to look out across the walled gardens to the rolling hills beyond and couldn't believe how many times she must have walked across this perfect slice of heaven with Badger at her heels without ever knowing what had once been there. It gave her goosebumps.

"Come!" commanded Lucas Deverell from the doorway.

Constance, recognising the voice of authority, surprised herself by obeying.

Three

Constance had a tantalisingly brief glimpse of what must have been the Great Hall as they quickly passed through it. The Hall was wainscoted in linen-fold panelling, the ceiling was arched with oak beams, there was a massive carved stone fireplace and broad oak plank flooring. It wasn't one of those baronial halls that could house several clans all at once; it was a comfortable size and would have been the perfect setting for a modern country wedding.

Her companion opened the door for her and ushered her into a much smaller, cosier parlour. Panelled and plastered and hung with brightly coloured tapestries, it made Constance think of a BBC historical drama and she had to give herself a mental shake to remind herself that she was actually here. Lucas Deverell gestured to a chair and waited until she was seated before perching on the arm of another chair. Almost immediately a liveried footman arrived at the door. He studiously ignored Constance.

"Ah, Oates, there you are. We would like some refreshment and please send Mistress Fitch to me at once. That will be all."

Oates bowed and backed out of the room closing the door.

"Mistress Fitch is my housekeeper. She will be able to assist with your — attire. We are a little understaffed at the moment as I had to greatly reduce our numbers while I was away. And the war has taken many a good man, both servant and master. You will find the house is not run as it should be."

Constance smiled, “I don’t suppose I’ll notice. We don’t really have servants. Not like this.”

“That is — interesting. How do you cope with the running of the household?”

“We do it ourselves. Mostly. Some very rich people have help in the house but on the whole, we have — oh, um — machines? Devices? Tools?”

“And who works these *devices*?”

She laughed, “This is going to be very difficult to explain! They run on something called electricity — which is a power — energy — anyway, how can I — oh, like if you harnessed lightning and used the energy it creates to drive an engine — no, say a cart! You wouldn’t need a horse. There! Do you see?”

Lucas Deverell was watching Constance from beneath his hooded lids, “I think we shall have to agree to leave a good deal of your former life a mystery. I did observe however some peculiar lanterns that you and your nephews seemed to find enthralling, staring into the light like baffled moths.”

“Those are… well, they can be used for seeing and talking with people who are somewhere else and that’s how we found you. You appeared on mine… in mine… through mine, oh, I don’t know — anyway, there you were like a sort of ghost. You could say that they have taken the place of actually calling on people and seeing them in the flesh… giving them a hug. I don’t like them very much — they’re useful but distracting. Again, very hard to explain, I’m afraid.” Constance frowned at him, “I must say you’re being remarkably sanguine about me just appearing like this. If I were in your shoes I’d be running around like a headless chicken. Mind you, maybe I *should* be. I’ve just dropped out of my life. It’s like a dream — except it’s real and weirdly familiar. Good grief, I have no idea what the appropriate response is at times like this.”

“I have always been of the opinion that it is a waste of time to allow yourself to become overwrought by things you cannot govern. When you have fought in a bloody battle or two you begin to realise that it is more down to good fortune than good sense whether you survive or not - and in life it is much the same. I find that being pragmatic serves me better than being, as you say, a headless chicken. Also, I believe there are higher powers at work and that means anything might be possible. I think my father would have told me to trust my instincts and that is what I am doing."

"Of course, being a Parliamentarian you're probably a Puritan? Pious and virtuous. A rarity in my world. It's confusing though as your hair isn't shorn but my nephew, Rowen said you all dressed alike anyway. Although I must admit that my knowledge of history is unfortunately nowhere near as good as his. He was the one who was about to shake you by the hand."

"A brave fellow then and well-tutored," he said approvingly.

"Indeed."

"We must consider how we are going to explain your presence here. The servants will take my lead and are unlikely to question your sudden appearance openly, but the children will be curious and will desire a reasonable explanation. If we are not careful you will be burned at the stake."

"*Burned* — ? Good god. Barbaric! But I do see your point — that's something I hadn't yet considered, having only been here for five minutes. And it's nice of you to suggest I might stay, but I really can't just drop in on you like this without any warning — . No, I must — ", she trailed off.

"Precisely," he said firmly, "There is nothing to be done. The Lord has seen fit to choose me so who am I to question His motives?"

"Well, I suppose I'm not in any position to argue with you. Besides, it would be churlish and — frankly foolhardy of me to refuse your offer. You've saved my bacon." she said, "So, of course, yes, how to explain my sudden appearance? What about a victim of the war? Made homeless when my village was razed to the ground by the troops. Or perhaps a distant relation come looking for shelter? An outcast.

Thrown out by her overbearing relatives for some misdemeanour? Or, what about a new governess for the children to help with their studies?" Constance glanced out at the garden, "Or — ", she paused for breath, "A gardener, come to help you restore the grounds. I'm quite good at gardening."

"A journeyman."

"Well, that's a little insulting. I'll have you know I have some serious skills!"

"I apologise, I had not intended any insult, Mistress."

"Oh, don't worry! None taken."

"I must say you have a powerful imagination, Mistress Harcourt."

"Oh, please, call me Constance or Con. Mistress Harcourt is such a mouthful and so formal!"

"I think not. That would be overly familiar."

"Ah, yes, how unthinking of me. This is going to be a steep learning curve. Luckily, I have watched a fair few time travel and historical series, so I know how to go on."

He fixed her with an impassive stare. "Speaking in tongues," he said slightly irritably. He was quietly fascinated watching her expressive face but the words that came out of her mouth were perplexing and he was finding not being in command of the strange situation exasperating and he was beginning to feel a little short-tempered. He was not a man who found relinquishing control easy or natural; he was used to commanding a regiment of horse, his orders obeyed without question.

"I will do my best not to confuse you with terms you cannot possibly understand," said Constance kindly but saw that even that statement had somehow struck a raw nerve. His already rigid mouth grew harder and she thought to herself that he was basically an unreconstructed chauvinist and realised she would have to tread lightly. It wasn't his fault, of course; he was a product of his time and the protracted violence and uncertainty of the life he was living was bound to have long-term effects.

The manservant, Oates, returned at this moment, bearing a tray with a pitcher, tankards, and plates of food. Constance realised that she was very hungry and thanked him. He flicked her a startled glance and backed hurriedly from the room.

Lucas Deverell was glowering at her.

"Oh, no need to explode! I know what's bugging — concerning you. I shouldn't have thanked him. It's just not *done*. I'm afraid that little idiosyncrasy is going to be hard to iron out, not that I'll be staying long enough to do any ironing. We are a very polite nation, on the whole. And we say sorry a lot too. So, sorry." She beamed up at him, her eyes dancing with amusement.

His face relaxed a little, "How perspicacious. Exactly so." He gestured to the laden tray.

Constance nodded, "You would like me to dish up. I'll do my best." She filled the tankards from the pitcher, noting with interest that she was about to drink some kind of flat ale for tea and handed him a plate of pickled eggs, cheese, bread rolls, and a deliciously rustic-looking gooseberry tart. Her mouth was watering but she was determined not to offend her host again by taking food before he was served. She chuckled inwardly, thinking about what her enlightened friends would have to say about him and his quaint belief system.

They ate in silence for a few minutes, Constance trying not to gobble her food. She took a tentative sip of the ale and couldn't help her face puckering with distaste. It was sour and flat, and she was pretty certain that she would never acquire a taste for it.

"You find the ale unpleasant?"

"It's unusual for me to drink alcohol at all, let alone in the middle of the day and I think modern tastes prefer a sweeter brew."

"What do you drink then?"

"Tea, coffee, water, all manner of bottled drinks — none of them good for you, which is ironic. There's so much sugar in them — " she trailed off as there was a knock on the door.

The lady who entered the room dropped a brief curtsy and looked from her employer to his guest. She ran a coldly expert eye over Constance, who was wearing an ankle-length summer frock made of some pretty floral material which floated gently when she moved. The new arrival returned her eerily unblinking gaze to her master.

"Mistress Harcourt, this is Mistress Fitch, my housekeeper." Turning to the housekeeper, "Mistress Harcourt is a cousin of my wife's, she has been made homeless by the war — troops razed her home to the ground, leaving her with nothing but the clothes she stands up in. Which, as you can see, are not at all appropriate for — for a lady of her status."

"Barely suitable for a dairymaid, sir," muttered the housekeeper darkly. She was small and wiry and wearing a sombre black gown enlivened only with a linen kerchief crossed over her chest and tucked into her waistband and a severe white coif covering her greying hair.

"Mistress Fitch. You forget yourself," said Lucas Deverell in a dangerously quiet voice.

She bobbed another curtsey and mumbled an apology of sorts, but Constance felt it didn't ring true.

"Some clothes are required for Mistress Harcourt. You will find something, no doubt, amongst my wife's belongings." This request brought a sullen look to the housekeeper's already sour face and Constance couldn't help feeling a little uncomfortable.

"Yes, Sir Lucas."

"And see that the Green Bedchamber is made fit for use. Mistress Harcourt will be staying with us for a while until she is able to find alternative accommodation."

After she had gone, Lucas Deverell took a long drink of his ale and placed the tankard down with something of a snap.

"Mistress Fitch came with my wife having been with her since childhood; she was utterly devoted to Esther and perhaps now is understandably resentful of anyone interfering with her memory."

"That makes perfect sense," said Constance, "What happened to your wife?"

Lucas Deverell stood up and moved to the window overlooking the garden. "She had always suffered from indifferent health and the second child proved to be too much for her. She died in childbirth."

"God. I'm so sorry. How awful. How long had you been married?"

"Three years. We married late. We were both six and twenty. It was — an arranged marriage. Frances was our first born and Benedict came two years later. Because of the war, they have been living with my sister Ursula, in Banbury but her, husband, Jacob was killed at Cropredy Bridge last summer and I was injured not long afterwards at Lostwithiel. They have only just been returned to me."

"That must have been very hard for them."

"Their fortitude can only have been strengthened by their experiences."

"Gosh, that's a bit harsh. I mean, even for those days — *these* days."

"They have had a privileged upbringing. I think you will find they have nothing to complain about. Ursula has been a good aunt to them — almost a mother."

"But — *not* a mother," said Constance softly.

Lucas Deverell's face hardened slightly, "They have wanted for nought. An uncle and aunt who doted upon them, having no children of their own and a life without hunger or sickness."

Constance fixed him with what Guy would have called her steely glare, "I suspect that we're not going to see eye to eye on this. You see children who have been handed everything on a silver platter and I see two innocents who are as good as orphans, foisted on relations they didn't know very well and abandoned by their father who was then seriously wounded in battle. So, they never really knew their mother, they've lost their uncle, and, in reality, they also lost you, I imagine, for some years — to this terrible war. Doesn't sound such a privileged life to me."

"You are very forthright in your opinions, Mistress Harcourt. I am beginning to suspect that you are unwed."

Constance let out an unladylike guffaw of laughter, "Are you trying to tell me that I need a husband to keep me in line? That is just so prehistoric, it's not even funny!"

"A husband would be able to discipline you and help you understand where your duty lies — "

"Oh, *would* he now? You mean he'd box my ears or put me over his knee and beat me until I became more *biddable*? This I would really like to see! Oh, I wish Guy were here to witness this! He would be outraged. He's what we call extremely politically correct and won't let anyone get away with saying anything that might be construed as being offensive to any other human being. You could say he was immensely diplomatic. You, I fear, would fail all his rigid tests."

Lucas Deverell took a deep breath and Constance felt he was only just managing to contain what promised to be an impressive temper tantrum.

"I think perhaps, Mistress Harcourt, it's time for you to be shown to your bedchamber so that you can change and have a rest before supper. I shall send for Mistress Fitch." And without waiting for a reply he strode, with his halting gait, to the door, wrenched it open and bellowed for poor Oates, who was lurking just outside in the hallway.

Constance stood waiting behind the carved screens that sheltered the Great Hall from draughts and suddenly she pinched the flesh on her arm hard enough to make herself yelp in pain.

No, she wasn't still asleep and having a weird dream; her arm was now throbbing.

Lucas Deverell looked down at her and she saw the glimmer of a malicious smile in his sleepy eyes. "I am sorry to say that we are both wide awake," he remarked.

Four

Constance sat on the edge of the ridiculous bed and admired the hangings and carvings with a jaundiced eye. The Americans would just love this, she thought; they'd be snapping away with their iPhones and posting it all onto Instagram or Twitter.

"Well, Toto, I have a feeling we're not in Kansas anymore," she said and began to laugh a little hysterically.

Mistress Fitch came into the bedchamber carrying a pile of clothing in her arms and Constance couldn't help a slight lifting of her spirits as she sensed some retail therapy was imminent. The housekeeper laid the gowns reverentially onto the bed, stroking the creases away with a loving hand. She then left the room again and a few minutes later returned with another armful of petticoats and bodices.

"Goodness, how beautiful," said Constance. "Do you think they'll fit me?"

"The lacings can be altered," responded the housekeeper tersely. "You must take off that — *garment* you are wearing, and I will help you dress. We have no lady's maid here at the moment."

"I'm so sorry to be such a nuisance."

Constance stood and unbuttoned the front of her dress, then took her arms out and let it drop to the floor. Mistress Fitch watched, hands on hips, her lips pursed in disapproval.

"What is *that*?" she asked, staring incredulously at Constance's underwear.

Constance looked down at her front, "That, is — a new fashion in — London. It is called a brassiere, worn instead of

— stays. And these, are knickers — all the rage in Paris at the moment apparently."

"They look most unwholesome. Take them off and you will wear this instead." She held up a plain looking chemise which Constance thought looked horridly shapeless.

However, she did as she was told and removed both her bra and her knickers. Trying not to be self-conscious about her nakedness and wondering what the housekeeper would make of her tan-lines, she allowed the chemise, with three-quarter length sleeves, to be slipped over her head. It actually felt quite nice, liberating and airy. Then a roll of padding was tied around her waist, followed by two linen petticoats, each one adding considerably to the bulk about her hips, which she wasn't too pleased about. Finally, Mistress Fitch chose a soft grey green satin petticoat and slid that over her head and tied it around her waist.

This was followed by white stockings and plain tied garters, a whale-boned bodice with a pretty peplum on her hips, a short stomacher behind the lacings and lacy sleeves to her elbows. Mistress Fitch seemed to take great pleasure in pulling in the lacings very tightly until Constance found it quite hard to breathe easily. The housekeeper tucked the laces into the top of the bodice and then told her to sit down on a stool in front of the looking glass.

"Your hair has already been curled?" she asked.

"It's naturally curly."

"That will save time. Although, it is far too long. I will have to cut it."

"Oh. That will be novel. I've always had long hair."

The housekeeper took no notice and began to trim the long curls with some dangerous looking silver shears. When she was satisfied with the result, Constance peered down at the auburn curls on the floor and quietly mourned the loss but managed to remain silent. The housekeeper then briskly wound her hair up into a tight little bun at the back, allowing a gathering of curls to frame her face on either side. Constance thought it looked quite becoming but it felt really strange; the back of her neck felt very cold and exposed. She studied her reflection and tried to picture herself in a Van Dyck painting but couldn't quite picture herself standing so pale and unsmiling or looking with such devotion at her husband. She smiled to herself; she was bronzed by some unexpected July sunshine and she didn't think she could provide the required look of adoration even for long enough to sit for the portrait.

Lastly, the housekeeper arranged and pinned a simple lace collar around her shoulders which covered her décolletage and made her look far more respectable. Mistress Fitch nodded, "There. That will do. We do not have access to my lady's jewellery, or I would have dressed your hair with her pearls."

"Thank you very much, Mistress Fitch. You have done an excellent job."

"I am just doing as Sir Lucas says. No more. Will you take a rest now, Mistress Harcourt?"

"Thank you, no. I shall go downstairs and explore the house and garden."

"As you like," said the housekeeper stiffly, clearly disappointed not to be rid of her charge for a while.

As she walked along the wide corridor, Constance swished her skirts around her, enjoying the sound of the material moving and the very unaccustomed feeling of air circulating around under the skirts. It was oddly liberating. She skipped a few steps and then practiced walking in what she thought was a suitably sedate fashion, her head held high. She found that if she took very small steps it appeared as though she were gliding like a swan. She walked the whole length of the Long Gallery and when she reached the end she looked out of the diamond-leaded windows onto the garden below. It must have been really quite impressive in its heyday, before neglect had begun to rewild it. Nature was edging stealthily in from the fields bringing wildflowers and meadow grass and moles, which had left their destructive rows of volcanoes across the lawns. Tree branches lay where they fell, shrubs and hedges, free from regular shearing, were returning to the wild with unbridled enthusiasm. Constance rather liked it this way but realised that it very much went against the horticultural fashions of the day. She watched the jackdaws chase each other in and out of the wood and was about to continue on her way when she heard the sound of shrill voices.

Along the long gravel path ran two children, a boy and a girl. Both were dressed in exact replicas of adult costumes. It looked like they'd escaped from a fancy dress parade. The boy, who was chasing the girl, had a wooden sword and was brandishing it above his head as he ran, clearly pretending to be some kind of soldier. Just as they neared the house, the girl tripped and fell in a cloud of blue silk and the boy, instead of stopping to help her up, started stabbing at her with his sword. The girl cried out and kicked her legs out at him trying to fend him off.

Constance started to run along the gallery; then realising that her skirts were in her way she hoisted them up and sprinted. She raced down the broad, shallow stairs and swung through the Great Hall and out into the garden.

She reached the children just as the girl had begun to cry and the boy appeared to be going in for the kill. She swept up to them and snatched the sword from his hand rendering the small fellow speechless with fright. She then reached a hand down to the girl and hauled her up.

"Well, I must say this is a fine way to introduce ourselves! You must be Frances and you, you young scoundrel, must be Benedict. I am Constance Harcourt, a cousin of your mother's."

The children had suddenly become unnaturally still, their eyes wide and their mouths clamped tightly shut. They were both staring at the ground and avoiding looking at each other or Constance.

She stuck out her hand to Frances and the girl cautiously shook it but then tucked the offending hand behind her back.

Benedict took Constance's hand and with a little bow, obviously learned from his etiquette master, he dropped a light kiss on the back of her fingers.

"Well, that was very nicely done," remarked Constance. "Now, who can tell me what the fight was about?"

Neither said anything, keeping their eyes firmly on their feet but she noticed a guilty flush steal up over Benedict's cheeks.

"Benedict? Have you anything to say for yourself?"

He shook his head, his mouth taking on a mutinous look.

"Frances? Do you have any idea why your brother was trying to murder you?"

Frances stole a glance at her young brother, "No, Mistress Harcourt. It is a mystery to me. You never know when he will attack. He does not need a reason. He just always seems to be in a disagreeable mood — ever since he came out of long-coats."

"That is most unfortunate. I wonder why? You will probably find that something has upset him. Perhaps someone has said something he doesn't like. Or he is feeling neglected or persecuted in some way. I often find with my nephews that it can be the smallest, most unforeseen slight that plunges them into a bad mood. And all it takes is a sincere word of apology to mend the situation."

Benedict scuffed the gravel with the toe of his shoe and glowered, reminding Constance very much of his father.

"Well, never mind for now. Perhaps we can solve this tiresome problem later."

Frances, a tall girl with dark blonde ringleted hair and wide-apart blue eyes, frowned at Constance, "Where have you come from, Mistress Harcourt? I have never heard tell of any of my mother's relations. I thought she had none."

"I am a very distant cousin," lied Constance uncomfortably. "We never met."

Frances raised her eyebrows in faint surprise, "Father has never mentioned you before. I would have remembered I am sure. It is most odd. You certainly do not look like the painting of my mother in The Long Gallery."

"Cousins rarely look alike," said Constance knowledgeably. "I don't even look like my own sister."

"You have a sister? What is her name?"

Thinking that one should never stray far from the truth when inventing stories Constance replied, "Tova."

"What an unusual name. I think I would have remembered that too. How interesting," and she shot Constance a sly look from under her pale lashes.

Constance, starting to think it would have been better to have left her sister and her nephews out of it, wondered if it was too late to backpedal a bit.

Frances suddenly walked off along the path without a backward glance leaving Benedict shuffling his feet awkwardly.

"I don't suppose you would care to show me around the garden, would you?" asked Constance.

He peeked up at her from his father's grey eyes and smiled. "I could show you my fort?"

"That would be splendid. I do love a fort."

"Come this way then," he said, flying off at speed between the ragged topiary hedges.

Constance ran after him, her skirts bunched up around her knees.

"Wait for me!" she shouted after the fleeing figure. She saw a flash of amber silk as he disappeared into the undergrowth at the far end of the garden. By the time she reached the spot, he had completely vanished. She pushed her way through the bushes, leaning against the trunk of a tree to disentangle her petticoat from a bramble.

"Benedict! Where are you? Yoo-hoo!" She worked her way deeper into the shrubbery, searching for him. "Benedict! You're very clever! I can't find you. Is it an invisible fort?"

She heard the ghost of a laugh and stopped in her tracks.

She looked around and could see nothing but trees and bushes. Then, another snort drifted down to her and she looked up into the canopy of a large oak tree just above her.

There, cleverly built into the muscular branches of a magnificent oak, was a tree house with castellations and a flag hanging limply from a flagpole.

"Found you! How did you get up there?"

"There is a ladder on the other side. Come up and see."

Constance skirted the huge tree trunk and found the sturdy wooden ladder. Without even questioning her actions, she tucked her skirts into her waistband and with some difficulty scrambled up the ladder. She was seriously out of breath by the time she reached the platform and squeezed through the child-sized door.

Benedict was sitting on an old straw-filled mattress looking self-satisfied. "My grandfather built it for Father when he was a boy — he used to hide up here to escape his tutor. He does not know that Oates told me about it and then I found it. I come here when Frances is being vexing. You must never tell her about it. Promise?"

"I swear, on my honour."

He gave her a look of grudging respect, "That is a good oath for a girl."

"Why were you threatening Frances with your sword? Had she annoyed you?"

"She always annoys me! She told Father that I had taken his flintlock and fired it at a squirrel. Father beat me."

Constance tried not to look too shocked about the child abuse, remembering to look at it from the other end of the telescope. "I am not surprised he was angry. You could have come to great harm. The pistol might have misfired. It is not a toy. Your father was only trying to teach you a lesson about safety."

Benedict's eyes narrowed and his mouth twisted, "I might have supposed that you would take his side!"

"I am not taking anyone's side. I expect he was frightened — "

"My father is *never* frightened of *anything*! He is a very brave soldier and has fought many battles. Uncle Jacob told us."

"I am sure that is so, but if you think somebody you love might be in danger it can make you very angry and you want to impress upon them that they must change their ways before they get hurt."

"You sound just like Aunt Ursula. She was forever scolding me for doing bad things, but she always said she did it for my own good."

"I expect she did. She must love you very much."

"We were sent away because Father did not want us," said Benedict sullenly.

"I don't believe that. I think he needed to know that you were as safe as you could be while he was away doing his duty. If he hadn't loved you, he would have left you here with the servants."

The boy eyed Constance with disbelief and she resisted the urge to reach out and ruffle his long dark hair.

"We had better get down from here now before someone comes searching for us. If you go first, I will follow."

Benedict agreed and manoeuvred himself onto the ladder and was down it in a trice, as agile as a monkey.

Constance swung herself onto the first rung and started to carefully descend; she always felt she might have been a cat in a previous life because she never had difficulty climbing up something — it was coming down which usually presented the problem. She was just feeling for the third rung with her foot when she realised that her petticoat had become caught on the top of the ladder, wedged tightly between the bars of wood.

"Oh, damn," she muttered to herself, "Benedict? I seem to have got myself in a bit of a pickle. Can you help please?"

There was no answer. She cautiously peered over her shoulder and saw that her companion had deserted her.

"Oh, bloody brilliant."

She clung on for a while, wondering what to do. She tried calling for Benedict again but there was no response. She tried ripping her petticoat, but it was too difficult with only one hand free. Eventually she yelled for help to anyone who might be listening.

About ten minutes passed and she was beginning to despair when she heard a noise at the bottom of the tree.

"Benedict? Thank goodness, you've come back. I am well and truly stuck!"

"What the hell are you doing up there?" growled Lucas Deverell.

"Looking at the bloody view! What do you think? Honestly, what a stupid question."

"You curse like a foot soldier, Mistress Harcourt. It is not seemly."

"Oh, pooh to your seemliness!" snapped Constance, pushed beyond her limits.

"I am coming up. Kindly remain still and do not struggle."

She felt the ladder sway and give as he put his considerable weight onto the first rung. "Oh, it'll break! Do be careful!"

"It will *not* break. My father built it to last and it will probably outlive us all."

He kept climbing until he was just below her and then he squeezed up as far as he could until he could reach the folds of her petticoat and whilst holding her steady with one arm, he ripped the petticoat free. The violence of the movement made Constance lose her balance for a second and he put his arm about her to steady her.

"Now, we are going to climb down. Do not look down and do try not to panic. I will not allow you to fall."

Constance found that the previously irritating inflexible note in his pleasant voice was quite reassuring in a crisis and she was able to do as she was told without argument and very soon found herself safely back on the ground.

She breathed an enormous sigh of relief, "Thank you so much. I was really stuck."

Lucas Deverell cast a frowning glance at her disordered clothing, "You had better rearrange your petticoats Mistress Harcourt before we return to the house."

She looked down and made a sound like an infuriated kitten and quickly began to pull her now shredded petticoats back down over her knees. Then, just when she thought it couldn't get much worse, she suddenly recalled that she was only wearing a chemise under the petticoats and realised he had probably had a very good view of her thighs.

"Well, you might have *said* something! Or looked the other way. I thought you were supposed to be such virtuous gentlemen. I have to say that I find your morals questionable."

She thought he might have smiled but she wasn't sure.

"A gentleman would keep his own counsel and not shame a lady," he said quietly.

"Is that so? Well, I hope you're satisfied! I have been here less than a day and I have already been thoroughly humiliated! I wonder what you have in store for the rest of my stay!"

"Time will tell."

Constance rolled her eyes and flounced away through the shrubbery as fast as she could.

Five

Constance calmed herself by returning to the Long Gallery to look at the paintings. It was like having her own private portrait gallery and she took her time examining the works in detail. She had been to art school and trained as a book illustrator so to be able to study them at her leisure was a real treat. Eventually she stopped fizzing with wrath and embarrassment and was thinking only about brush-marks and glazing techniques.

In the middle of the row of monumental paintings were the ones of the immediate Deverell family. She supposed it was a bit like having photographs stuck with magnets to the fridge.

There were the impossibly angelic looking children in a double portrait set against the familiar Arcadian landscape; Frances, in a gown of turquoise satin, seated and Benedict standing behind her, his hand resting affectionately on her shoulder. Constance wondered how much bribery it had taken to get them to pose like that.

Then, their mother, Esther, a softly sensual portrait of a very young flaxen-haired woman in a golden silk gown, strings of pearls threaded through her hair and more draped about her neck. One pretty hand was resting palm upwards in her lap, holding a rosebud and the other, elegantly drawing attention to her décolletage. Her eyes were blue like her daughter's, wide-apart, and almost childlike in their innocence. Her mouth, a perfect moist rose-petal pink, a secret smile lifting the corners. Her skin was so pearly white it seemed almost transparent like the finest porcelain and her hair glinted as though just washed in some magical elixir.

She seemed so alive that Constance couldn't imagine that she no longer breathed.

She moved on to the next painting, an enormous canvas by the Dutch painter Peter Lely, which pictured Colonel Sir Lucas Deverell, in Parliamentarian uniform and gleaming breastplate, leaning nonchalantly against an incongruous Greek pillar, hand resting on the sword at his hip and his brooding grey eyes frowning impatiently at the painter as though he had more important things to do; he was obviously not happy to be wasting his time posing. Constance cocked her head to one side and contemplated this frozen moment in time. He really never could be called handsome, she thought; he had the look of a rugby player about him, much battered about the face, his nose having taken the worst of some powerful punches. His grey eyes were his best feature, cool and calculating, and yet sleepy, with bulges beneath them that made Constance suspect he might be concealing a sense of humour somewhere beneath the layers of grief and soldiering; her mother would have called them "bedroom eyes".

He was tall and broad shouldered and would always look his best in uniform, the breastplate just served to accentuate the width and strength of his chest and even the foppish length of his dark hair was unable to disguise the sheer physicality of the man. She could imagine him being mesmerisingly commanding on the battlefield and at the same time knew that these fine military attributes would make him an unforgiving father and husband.

She found she was reluctant to turn away to the next painting but managed to tear her eyes away and found the next portrait was of a couple: a beautiful girl with perfect cheekbones, sable brown hair and an elegantly indolent air and, holding her hand lovingly to his breast, a fine-looking, slender young man with kind eyes. Constance knew immediately that this was Ursula Deverell and her late husband Jacob. She looked closely at the title cleverly inscribed as though embroidered on the draping behind them and saw that it was Sir Jacob and Lady Ursula Prideaux of Banbury. It had been painted before the beginning of the war when they were both so full of life and hope, their lives stretching ahead of them.

Constance made a little sound of fury and quickly moved to the next paintings before she started getting too misty-eyed.

Another large canvas depicted an older couple, the lady sitting in a cloud of oyster satin and the gentleman standing beside her in some kind of severe dark robing. The title announced them as Sir Walter and Lady Cicely Deverell, and Constance thought that they had a rather intimidating air about them and that they were surely Lucas Deverell's parents. He looked as though he was a man of steady, if redoubtable, character, perhaps a little too serious at times and his wife looked as though she were only barely containing her high spirits long enough to complete the sitting — but she had the look of a woman who would not be crossed.

Having admired the collection and viewed the garden she was rather at a loss. She decided it would be a good idea to go and find someone to give her some direction, so she drifted downstairs and into the Great Hall, hoping to find some company.

The hall was empty, so she headed off to explore the rest of the ground floor. At the back of the hall, she found a door behind another screen which opened into a small courtyard in the centre of the house. A rill was cut through the paving and spring water neatly rippled across the courtyard into a circular shallow pond in the centre and then into underground channels that disappeared under the walls of the house. More inner doors led into the back section of the building and when she peered through the windows, she could see kitchens and a dairy and spotted a couple of servants hard at work.

She quickly returned to the hall and wandered into a parlour she hadn't seen before, on the right side of the building. It was larger than the one she had been in earlier; it was lined with bookshelves and smelled strongly of leather and beeswax polish. She had taken several steps into the room before she realised it was occupied.

"Oh, I'm sorry. I didn't realise anyone was in here," she said.

Benedict looked up from his work and carefully laid down the quill he was writing with. "I am glad of the interruption," he said, "I am finding my lessons very taxing, but I am told they are necessary."

"Yes, I guess so - if you're planning on going to university."

"Precisely. I want to go to Oxford and then join the army."

"You want to be a soldier?"

"Of course."

"You could study law or medicine."

"Naturally, I shall study law and then leave Oxford and enter the Inns of Court — Lincoln's Inn, like my father; but *then* I shall join the army. I am quite determined."

"I can see that. And what of Frances?"

He shot her a puzzled look, "Why, she will marry, of course."

Constance bit back the retort that came immediately to mind and said calmly, "Is that what she wants?"

Another surprised look, "Of course, she wants a good marriage!"

"Does she not have lessons with you?"

Benedict laughed, "Lessons? Good heavens, that would only make her an unruly wife, as you must know — if I may be so plain spoken, cousin."

No, thought Constance, don't *say* anything! Keep your modern ideas to yourself, he won't understand — yet.

"I don't believe education would be wasted on anyone. I think it is very important in order to improve civilisation."

"You sound like you have been schooled, Mistress Harcourt. Do you read?"

"I read *and* write. I have had the benefit of an excellent education."

"But, on the other hand — you are quite old and not yet wed."

"That was a matter of choice. I chose not to marry because I love my work."

"Your *work*? You mean looking after your parents' house?"

"No, I have my own house, and I illustrate books."

A look of amazement mixed with disdain crossed his face, "So, engraving and etching. That is a curious thing for a female."

Constance sighed, realising that she was not going to win this battle in the first skirmish. She would do it by stealth, wearing him down like water dripping on a stone, if she had time. One day she would persuade him that she was right and that his father's notions were outmoded and even dangerous. That's if she was here long enough to make a difference.

"You have a tutor?"

"Yes, Master Valentine de Cheverell. He was lately a student at Oxford and is now tutoring me. He has gone for his afternoon walk."

"What lesson are you learning today?"

He screwed up his face, "Greek history. It is very tedious. I really have no interest in it at all."

"I can imagine that it might not appeal to such an active young man as yourself. Although, as you no doubt know, the Greeks were famous for their formidable soldiers — the Spartans and Alexander the Great, who was a mere boy when he started his campaign to rule the world. You can learn a lot from ancient history. But I think the idea is that you can discover how Plato or Homer or Virgil have influenced our thinking today."

Benedict was staring at Constance with incredulity and seemed to have lost the power of speech.

"Yes, indeed," said Constance with some satisfaction, "It's probably a good idea not to look down upon people until you are sure of your ground. Now, where will I find your sister?"

Benedict pointed mutely in the direction of the Great Hall.

"The other parlour?"

He nodded.

Constance knocked politely on the door and entered when instructed. She found Frances sitting dutifully at her embroidery frame, making tiny stitches in a sampler.

She stood beside her to look at her work, "That is so beautiful, Frances. So delicate and such lovely colours. Do you enjoy needlework?"

The girl glanced up in surprise, "Enjoy? I would rather poke myself in the eye with the needle!"

Constance laughed, "I think I would be inclined to agree with you! I can think of nothing worse than labouring all day on anything so minute and time-consuming. There must be things you would rather be doing?"

The needle flashed in and out of the canvas, stabbing the material with marked violence, "Oh, yes, I would much rather be preserving fruit or picking and arranging flowers! So much *choice*! Only Benedict is allowed to do as he likes."

"Well, you may take comfort that he doesn't seem to be very happy either, studying Greek history. I tried to persuade him that it would be useful one day, but he was not convinced." Constance went to sit on the window seat and looked out at the garden. "Perhaps, when you have finished your work, you might like to accompany me for a walk to the church?"

The needle paused, "I would like that, but — "

Constance smiled, "I thought some fresh air might be good for us and to be perfectly honest I am a little bored having nothing to occupy my time."

"I suppose it would be all right," said Frances with a slight shrug.

"That is just splendid. I will wait here for you, then."

Frances tucked the needle into the canvas and rolled a skein of blue thread up and placed it carefully in an inlaid walnut box on the table. "I am ready now. Nobody cares what I do anyway, just as long as I do not interrupt them with my *nonsense* or interfere with their important business. I have no tutor or companion to make a fuss. Father is always too occupied with mending the estate and helping the poor." She didn't sound as though she thought very much of the deserving poor.

"He must have so much to attend to after being away so long. Everyone will want some of his time and will be demanding his advice about the most trivial matters. I am quite sure he would much rather be with you and Benedict."

Frances pursed her lips, "How little you know him, then. He has no desire to be encumbered with children he barely knows. He would prefer the company of his troops."

"I think you're being a bit unfair. He is bound to be altered by his experiences and losing your mother so young and now your uncle; anyone would find adapting to their old life onerous but ultimately his love for you and Benedict is what will keep him fighting for what he believes in. I think his main aim is to keep you and your brother in a world that is safe."

"You are a romancer, Mistress Harcourt."

"You have a good knowledge of English, Mistress Deverell. I suspect you like to read."

Frances's cheeks flamed, "I — I sometimes like to sit with Benedict when he is having his lessons — and I listen."

"How resourceful of you. Stealing knowledge from the unsuspecting men. I have a very strong feeling, Frances, that you will amount to something special one day."

The flush deepened and the girl modestly cast down her cerulean eyes but not before Constance had seen a flicker of satisfaction in them.

"Shall we go? Should we tell anyone we're going out or ask for someone to accompany us?"

"How very antiquated of you! I am often out by myself without anyone even noticing," replied Frances loftily.

They crossed the Great Hall and stepped out into the low evening sunshine.

"Is that wise when the war is not so very far away from here? There could be soldiers roaming the countryside."

Frances skipped down the steps to the path, "They would not dare to hurt me. My father is a Colonel in the Parliamentary Army — he could have them shot."

The sun still held some warmth and Constance turned to allow the rays to reach her face.

Frances, observing, said, "You have already been too much in the sun. I should have brought you a parasol lest you end up with skin like leather!"

Constance smiled at this and together they walked through the garden and down the lane to the churchyard. It was as they were approaching the church that her eyes were drawn upwards to the clear summer sky and noted with a slight shock that there were no con trails from airplanes and nowhere could she hear the sound of cars or lawn mowers. For a moment her heart thudded unpleasantly in her chest and her mouth went a little dry.

Frances danced ahead of her across the soft mossy grass and Constance watched her, fascinated, unable to help comparing her to girls she knew of her age. At fourteen she was just hovering on the cusp between childhood and womanhood and it didn't matter what time you were from; adolescent girls would always be a great trial. While this child had no mother to advise her, not even a devoted aunt now to guide her, and with her father distracted by other business, she would very much depend on her own self-belief and self-reliance, of that there was no doubt.

Constance was looking at the church and trying to place what had not changed. It was like a game of spot the difference. The main variance was the colour of the stone; it was newer, there was less moss and lichen, and the building had not been lengthened or altered. It was quite disturbing. She found an old tomb which had been covered in ivy when she'd last seen it but was now clean stone and she perched on it to look out over the field towards the village and wondered what the boys were doing. She hoped that Tova would be with them by now and that her sister would be open-minded when listening to them explain her disappearance. Tova had a habit of being a bit obdurate.

Tears filled her eyes and she ruthlessly rubbed them away with her knuckles. It was pointless being anxious when there was nothing she could do about it. They were all stuck in their various places and would have to wait for the universe to change its capricious mind about their present situations.

Frances span in circles, her petticoats swirling, until she became dizzy and crumpled onto the grass. She looked up, her head still reeling and saw Mistress Harcourt impatiently dashing away tears. She wondered what might have made her so upset and angry. The whole situation was extremely puzzling; she did not know what to make of it. This odd woman suddenly appearing from nowhere with her strange opinions and manner and her father just accepting her presence as though it were perfectly normal. Frances was not happy about it, although it was quite pleasant to have someone other than men to talk to and Mistress Harcourt seemed to be quite sympathetic to her predicament. She might be useful if ever she needed an ally.

Six

Jackdaws were roistering in the church tower, cackling and flapping their inky wings in the sun, their rowdy laughter echoing off the ancient walls. Constance watched them and tried to fathom how many generations there would be before they were *her* jackdaws. It stopped her from fretting about what was going on in the other real world and how she would ever manage to return to it.

Frances came and sat beside her, slightly out of breath from her spinning. She cast a shy glance up at Constance and sighed lustily.

"Yes? What is it?" asked Constance, still observing the jackdaws.

"I was wondering," began Frances uncertainly, "whether you thought I might be able to learn how to write. Perhaps, you could persuade Father to allow me to have lessons from Master de Cheverell. I would really like to learn and then I could write letters to Aunt Ursula."

The jackdaws suddenly took flight, swooping and darting across the sky, tumbling down, feathers catching the light, raucously quarrelling with each other like drunks outside a pub.

"I think you should talk to your father; he may be more amenable than you suppose."

"He will just dismiss me. I asked him before and he said that I would have no need for writing."

"Did he indeed! What about — if I taught you? I am quite good at calligraphy and you have a lively mind and would be easy to teach," suggested Constance.

There was a moment's silence.

"Why would you do that for me? You do not know me."

Constance looked at Frances directly, "It would give me great pleasure! Besides, I need something to occupy myself because I'm used to being creative and I'm missing my nephews and my sister terribly already. I'll speak with your father if you like."

A slow blush crept up over the girl's cheeks and she beamed at Constance happily, "I promise I will work hard!" She then leapt up and pirouetted away over the grass again, laughing.

Constance smiled as she watched her twirl, hoping that her powers of persuasion would be enough to convince Lucas Deverell to relent. She had an uncomfortable premonition that he was going to be hard to cajole.

"Good evening, Mistress Frances!" called a light male voice. Constance turned and peering into the dazzle of the sinking sun; she could make out a figure strolling around the side of the church.

"Hail!" shouted Frances cheerfully, "Friend or foe?"

"Definitely friend!" came the amused answer.

Frances span across the churchyard to the stranger and circled him as though they were performing a ballet. When she finally came to a wobbly stop, the man made an elegant bow and they both laughed.

Frances suddenly remembered her manners and gestured to Constance, "Oh, Mistress Harcourt, *this* is Master de Cheverell, Benedict's tutor." Turning to the tutor, "Mistress Harcourt is a cousin of my mother's; she is staying with us for a while because she has lost *everything*!"

Constance rose and held out her hand to the young man, noting that he was rather beautiful, with a smile as dazzling as the sun behind him and large pale eyes that spoke volumes. She felt herself grow rather warm and hoped she wasn't blushing. Valentine de Cheverell took her hand and bowed over it.

"I am delighted to make your acquaintance, Mistress Harcourt. I assume that when Mistress Frances says you have lost everything, that it is due to this wretched war?" He slowly released her hand, but she felt he would have rather held onto it for longer and warned herself against encouraging any flirtation. He really was very engaging, in an earnest sort of way, but far too young. She guessed he must be in his early twenties if he had just left Oxford.

"It is, indeed. I was forced to beg Sir Lucas for shelter." Not so far from the truth, she thought.

"It is fortunate that you have family to turn to. If the fighting goes on, I expect I may be forced to join up. I have no desire to fire a musket in anger but — the choice may not be mine."

Frances pouted prettily, "I hope that never happens. We would miss you."

Valentine de Cheverell flicked Constance a speaking glance, "And I would miss you and your brother. I enjoy being here although Master Benedict is determined to make my job as challenging as he can."

"He was studying hard when I last saw him in the library. We had a discussion about Greek history, and he professed an interest in the subject."

Valentine de Cheverell laughed, "That does indeed surprise me! He seldom shows an interest in anything other than shooting whatever animals cross his path."

"He did mention a strong desire to join the army — where, of course, he would be positively encouraged to shoot things!"

"I am very hungry," announced Frances. "It must be nearly time for supper," and she skipped lightly off around the church.

"We had better follow her and make sure she doesn't get into trouble," said Constance.

The tutor smiled at her, "I believe life is going to be a little more bearable for having you here, Mistress Harcourt."

Supper was held in the Great Hall at a long refectory table and was served by Oates and Mistress Fitch, who looked as though such a menial task was very much beneath her.

Lucas Deverell was already there, standing before the empty fireplace. He looked up to see his daughter flit through the door like an excited kitten, followed by Mistress Harcourt looking very flushed and then, the tutor, de Cheverell, looking pleased with himself.

"You are late," growled Lucas Deverell. "I have been waiting for at least half an hour."

Frances's good mood evaporated, and she hung her head, "I am very sorry, Father. We went for a walk and forgot the time."

Constance frowned, "I also apologise, sir. It was entirely my fault; I had no idea that supper would be ready. It was such a beautiful day — "

"I am not in the least interested in the weather conditions. The food is going cold and I have more important things to do than wait around for you. You had better go quickly and wash."

Frances bit her lip and sidled over to a side table where there were bowls and urns of water and cloths for drying. Constance carefully watched what she did and then proceeded to do the same.

Frances then went to stand behind a chair and waited, while the tutor washed his hands. Lucas Deverell glanced crossly at Constance and gestured to the chair beside his; he then stamped across the hall and bellowed up the stairs for his son. Constance felt like giggling and had to severely control the urge, remembering that she had frequently been given detention at school for her inability to curb her laughter. She stood behind her chair and watched out of the corner of her eye as her host returned and abruptly said grace before dragging out his chair and thumping down into it.

At that moment Benedict came skidding into the room and came to a standstill in front of his father, eyes firmly on the floor.

"I will not tolerate this sort of poor behaviour, Benedict. Wars are won on punctuality. You will never make a good soldier if you are always late. Wash your hands."

Benedict mumbled an apology and dashed to the side table to wash.

Once the master of the house was seated everyone else sat and helped themselves to the array of different foods; savoury and sweets all together. Constance eyed the heaps of little roasted birds beside her place with some misgiving and wondered how she was going to break it to them that she was a vegetarian. She mimicked everyone's else's actions and congratulated herself on making a very creditable first attempt at dining in an alien era.

She took some bread, sage cheese, roasted parsnips and turnips, and what looked like scrambled eggs; it seemed a very strange mixture, like a buffet gone mad. When Valentine de Cheverell passed her a plate of grilled chops, she shook her head and passed them on to the head of the house.

He gave her a questioning look, "You seem to be avoiding the meats, Mistress Harcourt. May I enquire why?"

Constance grimaced, "I — I have a dislike of eating anything with a face," she admitted.

"Well, you will not last long here then. I have no wish to send you back to your home in a worse state than when you arrived. You had better try to overcome this strange fancy or you will fade away to nothing."

"Easier said than done," she muttered.

"This notion is some new fashion?" he asked, with a warning look.

"You could say that. It is the very latest thing — in London. You'll all be doing it before long."

"I sincerely doubt that," said Lucas Deverell firmly, "Man has always eaten meat."

"You may have noticed, sir, that I am *not* a man!" snapped Constance before she thought to hold her tongue.

Valentine de Cheverell smiled across the table at Constance, "I have certainly noticed, Mistress," he murmured.

Constance pretended she hadn't heard his provocative comment but saw his employer send the young man a look of thundering disapproval; the tutor blushed and looked down at his plate in some confusion.

An uncomfortable silence fell, and everyone finished their meal without engaging in any more idle chatter.

Eventually the ordeal was over, and Constance breathed a sigh of relief. She just managed to stop herself getting up to help clear the table and guiltily watched the housekeeper and footman do all the work. Another servant she hadn't seen before came in to tell them that he had lit the fire in the parlour, and they all adjourned to the other room.

Again, she was shown to a chair by her host and was very sorry when the children were sent to bed leaving her with just the two gentlemen to talk to. Glasses of wine were brought and a little dish of comfits which were so sweet they made her teeth ache. She sipped the wine daintily, knowing she needed to be very careful, having been told on numerous occasions that she was a cheap date.

The conversation naturally turned to all things war and although they obviously had opposing views on many aspects of the struggles, the tutor being something of a conscientious objector, they managed nonetheless to have a civilised discussion about the reasons for and against it and the hopeful outcome. They both agreed that the monarch was very much mistaken, but neither could concur with the other about which side would ultimately win the argument. Constance, brimming over with a wealth of knowledge on the subject, had to sit quietly fuming, unable to share with them all the facts she had learned in school about their stupid wasteful war. She could never forgive the wanton destruction of hundreds of beautiful, irreplaceable manor houses and ordinary homes, whole villages being wiped out, the tragic loss of young lives, and the sheer stupidity of fighting one's fellow countrymen over matters which ought to have been thrashed out over the conference table were, she allowed, religion not at the centre of the conflict

When there was finally a lull in the conversation, she stood up and made her excuses, saying that, as it had been a very full and exciting day, she was extremely tired and would like to retire to bed.

They stood and bowed and wished her a good night.

In her bedchamber Constance found a shapeless linen night-gown draped over her bed along with a most unbecoming nightcap shaped like a loaf of bread but with an embroidered band, which she flung onto the blanket chest in disgust.

She washed with water from the pitcher and was about to climb into her bed when the housekeeper arrived armed with a bed warming pan.

Mistress Fitch quickly and efficiently warmed the bed and was just backing out of the room when Constance thought of something, "Thank you very much for the nightgown and for warming the bed — I wonder — do you have such a thing as a toothbrush?"

"Of course," responded the housekeeper, "The master brought some home when he was last overseas. They are Chinese. I will fetch one for you."

After a short while she returned with the item and sullenly handed it to Constance. It was bone-handled and looked like the bristles were horsehair but at least it was a toothbrush; she would remember to ask for some salt tomorrow.

Constance thanked her profusely and Mistress Fitch curt-sied ungraciously and left.

Constance had no idea what time it was when she finally climbed into her wonderfully soft bed. She lay awake for a while thinking over the extraordinary events and worrying a little about the future. What will be, will be, was her last thought before sleep claimed her.

She awoke to the sound of a cock crowing and wondered what on earth was going on.

She opened her eyes and saw the canopy of the four-poster bed and with a painful jolt, remembered. Her heart did its familiar nervous flutter and she had to wait a moment for it to settle before she could even contemplate getting out of bed and facing the new day.

With all the prescience of someone who had cameras fitted in the room, Mistress Fitch arrived with fresh water and some home-made soap. She laid out clothes for Constance and made the bed; then much to Constance's discomfort, she helped her wash and dress and arranged her hair. It was just so alien to have someone at her elbow anticipating her every move; after a while she realised that it would be easier for all concerned if she allowed Mistress Fitch to take over and get the job done. So she sat still, with her hands clasped in her lap and did as she was told.

Breakfast was already on the table and Constance arrived in the Great Hall just as Frances flew into the room.

"Oh! Mistress Harcourt! I am so glad to catch you alone. I wanted to ask if we may start our lessons today? I was worried in case my father found you first and suggested things for you to do." She was quite breathless and eager for an answer.

"I'm sure that your father is far too busy to worry about entertaining me. Of course we can start today; I have no objections at all. In fact, I'd be delighted. But first I must ask his permission."

Benedict was the next to arrive, fearful of another rebuke from his father and he was followed by Master de Cheverell and close on his heels, Lucas Deverell.

Breakfast was another buffet with bread and cheese, meats and cake, and the customary ale.

Lucas Deverell, playing the part of perfect host, asked everyone how they were planning to spend their day and made polite comments. Their day seemed to mainly consist of Benedict being schooled and Frances being ignored. The tutor chatted amiably with Benedict about Latin and Science while Frances ate in smouldering silence. In a gap in the conversation Constance asked the Colonel what *he* was going to do.

He regarded her warily, "I am inspecting the beehives first and then the corn loft and after that I must visit with some of my tenants."

"That sounds very interesting, sir. Perhaps Frances and I could accompany you? I think it would be beneficial for her to learn about beekeeping and to see how the estate is managed. What better way to learn but from her own father?" Constance smiled benignly at him, knowing that he would probably be infuriated.

The grey eyes darkened, the mouth tightened, "If you think it would be valuable to her, I will, of course, allow it. I am leaving straight away after breakfast."

"Thank you, that's very kind and — fatherly. We will both enjoy it immensely."

She received a cold look for her pains and smiled at him innocently, for all the world seemingly unaware that she was ruining his entire day with her machinations.

Valentine de Cheverell raised his eyebrows and hid a grin because it was the first time he had ever seen his employer backed so neatly into a corner and give in so readily.

He watched the newcomer with interest, noting that she blushed easily when embarrassed or angry, that she chewed her lip when uneasy, and that she had a very fine pair of laughing green eyes. He wanted to gaze into them all day and tried his best to amuse her so that she would turn those eyes upon him.

Lucas Deverell brought breakfast to an abrupt close and rising up, informed Constance and his daughter that he would be leaving for the apiary in about quarter of an hour.

Frances and Constance sped upstairs to change their shoes and collect shawls and a parasol and within the allotted time they were outside on the steps waiting for Lucas Deverell.

He came striding around the house, his limp adding a slight halting rhythm to his movement but not in any way slowing him down.

"Come," he barked, as he passed them, "I am not going to dilly-dally waiting for you two to keep up."

Aha, thought Constance, he's not going to succeed at making this into an unenjoyable excursion. She cast a speaking glance at Frances who rolled her eyes. Then Constance poked her foot out from under her petticoats and revealed that she had exchanged the high-heeled and highly impractical shoes for her own white tennis shoes. Frances let out a little gasp of shock and clapped a hand over her mouth, her eyes brimming with laughter.

"Those are so *ugly*!"

"Yes, they are but I will be able to run to keep pace with your father. Come on, he's getting away!"

And they raced after him.

Seven

The apiary was on the far side of the wood, facing south towards the village. There were a dozen hives, or skeps, as Lucas Deverell called them. They were picturesquely woven from straw and each stood on a little wooden table. One could hear, from some distance the humming of the bees; it vibrated one's skin and hair. As they drew closer, Frances hung back nervously and her father slowed and turning to her said, "You must not show your fear. Be calm and make unhurried movements. Talk to them. They will only become angry if they think they are in danger."

Frances nodded but was looking a bit pale. Constance took her arm and they moved closer to the hives. Lucas Deverell tied a muslin hood over his head and went from hive to hive inspecting them. The bees took an intelligent interest in him but did not seem otherwise disturbed by his presence. He had bees resting on his clothes and some crawling on his hands, but he showed no sign of alarm.

"Father, do they not hurt you?"

"No, child, once you have been stung a few times it does not seem to hurt as much, and they become used to their keeper."

"I would not like to be stung, I think," said Frances anxiously.

"Keep your distance then and they will leave you alone."

Constance was examining the hives curiously, having only seen their like in books, "How does one retrieve the honey from these? I can't see how they work."

"That can be the difficult part. The keeper has to drive the bees out in order to get to the honey. Often the whole colony has to be killed."

Constance, who lived in a world where bees were becoming scarce, was outraged. "But that is insane. You wouldn't kill a herd of cows after milking them! You must redesign the hives," she declared, ignoring the warning signs of imminent censure and trying to picture in her mind's eye the only beehive she had ever actually seen, she continued regardless, "You could make them with removable wooden sections — with vertical wooden frames which provide the support for the combs and then you could save the bee colonies."

Frances was staring at her incredulously, "Mistress Harcourt!"

Constance cast her a reckless glance, "I *know* it would work."

Lucas Deverell's dark brows knitted together above his broken nose, "You have the advantage over me there, Mistress," he remarked pointedly.

Constance had the grace to look a little shame-faced, "Yes, I suppose I do. But if you acted on my suggestions and cared to make some improvements, I think I could draw you a diagram of how it should look."

He considered her for a moment, and she could see the battle he was having between his practical side and the alpha male who had been allowed to rampage unchecked for most of his life.

"I will consider it," he allowed.

Frances let out a small gasp and covered her mouth with her hand. This was obviously the first time she had ever witnessed her father giving ground in an argument. Constance tried not to look too pleased with herself. It was probably the first and last time.

Once the beehives had been inspected Lucas Deverell limped ahead and Constance and Frances followed.

"He *listened* to you," breathed the girl in astonishment.

'Well, I'm not sure he will actually acquiesce — he just didn't disagree with me immediately. I expect he's saving the scolding for when there's nobody to witness my humiliation. Gosh, he can certainly walk fast for someone with an injured leg! We had better scurry along."

Frances laughed, "You do use the oddest expressions. Scurry! Gosh! So amusing!"

They ran down the path through the meadow to where the wrought iron gate should have been, above the brook, but instead there was an old wooden farm gate, tied with some twine. Lucas Deverell didn't slow as he approached it, one-handedly vaulting over it and continuing up the hill on the other side. Constance thought it quite impressive for a man of his size nursing some kind of serious war injury.

Frances ran ahead and opened the gate, bowing as Constance marched through, reminding her of Gabriel doing the same not so very long ago.

"I will race you to the top!" she shouted and sprinted like a gazelle up the steep slope. Constance was not inclined to athleticism and unwilling to compete but was delighted to see that Lucas Deverell had stopped to wait for them on the crest of the hill.

The Colonel stood impatiently watching the two young women making their way towards him and thought how odd it was that his life should have taken such an unexpected turn. One minute he was on a battlefield bleeding from an appalling pike wound in his leg and then he was lying for months in a poorly run field hospital where he had the great good fortune to be nursed by an elderly midwife with some sound medical knowledge and here he was, nursemaid to his wayward daughter and a complete stranger who showed no respect for his position or beliefs. Frances rushed past him, laughing and he tried to recall when he had last seen her in such good spirits. Mistress Harcourt, looking somewhat pink in the cheeks, reached him and made a face.

"It's the added weight of all these damned petticoats, I can barely move and I'm dreadfully overheated!"

"You do look ready to expire. Perhaps you should have stayed at home in the cool."

A fierce look, "Never! I'm damned well determined not to sit around all day sewing samplers — I'd go stark raving mad."

"Come, then, you have made your bed, now you must lie in it. And, if you please, refrain from being so foul-mouthed."

Constance laughed and went to join Frances, who was waiting beside a stone dovecote, watching the pigeons bill and coo in their pigeonholes.

Constance recognised parts of the village, but other parts were just missing as though a giant hand had swept them all away leaving just a few random buildings behind. It made her feel rather peculiar and she had to stop for a moment and gather herself.

Lucas Deverell glanced over his shoulder at her, "Are you all right? I had not considered — it must be — very different?"

She nodded not daring to speak in case her voice wobbled.

He retraced his steps to stand beside her, "I cannot imagine what it must be like for you. How has it changed?"

Constance took a breath, "Everything is — newer, of course. There are far fewer buildings. No rectory, no bus shelter, no telephone kiosk — "

"Speaking in tongues, Mistress Harcourt," he said almost apologetically.

"I'm sorry. I suppose I'm a little shocked. It hadn't seemed real before — but *this* — this is hard to ignore."

"I have no doubt you will become used to the changes in time."

"Time? How *much* time? I don't know how long I will be trapped here."

Lucas Deverell raised an eyebrow, "Trapped. That sounds extremely bleak. It cannot be so very bad. It could be a good deal worse," he said, with the slightest smile, "You could be *trapped* with a Royalist family."

Constance chuckled, "Well, that is true but maybe they would have been less quick-tempered."

He noticed that her eyes lit up when she was amused, and he tried hard not to mind that she was laughing at him.

Frances, getting impatient, called out to them, "Come on! Stop dawdling! We have work to do."

"She is right. I must see several of my tenants today to see how they do."

"Well, by all means, let us vamoose!"

Constance was pleased to see a puzzled frown appear between his dark brows.

"As in, let's hurry up!"

They caught up with Frances and made their way around what would one day be a village of some size but was now barely a smattering of recently built cottages and barns, with a cider apple orchard in the middle of it.

Constance was feeling disorientated and deeply troubled by what she was seeing. She couldn't process the new information her eyes were providing and prevent her memory from trying desperately to fill in the pieces that some prankster had so capriciously removed. It was like the jigsaw puzzle that Gabriel had been given that had been half-eaten and then regurgitated by Badger.

Where the lane had once been edged with Cotswold stone cottages and farmhouses, there were now just fields and trees and the terrible silent sky. They were walking up a verdant track where in centuries to come cars would race through the village on their way to more interesting places. Constance could barely curb a desire to tell Frances not to walk in the middle of the road - it was so ingrained in her. Hold the boys' hands, keep Badger in check and on the lead, listen for that telltale roar of speeding vehicles charging up the hill, ignoring the speed limit.

She was surprised to see a small row of tiny cottages where later there would be an eighteenth-century farmhouse. They were made for hobbit-sized people, the doors half the size of modern portals.

They approached the first one and Lucas Deverell thumped his massive fist against the arched door. It was opened immediately by a small woman shaped like a dumpling, wearing faded russet brown petticoats and a dark grey bodice and a none-too-clean apron, a coif covering her hair.

Constance was surprised to see her face light up when she saw who her visitor was.

"Oh, Sir Lucas! I had 'eard you was 'ome. We never been so glad to hear such news. Be you come to see my Amos? He's sufferin' from a bout of sickness."

"May we come in and see him, please Mistress Carter?" asked Lucas Deverell gently.

She bobbed a curtsey, "Of course, Sir Lucas. This way, if you please," and she waved them in. Constance hung back, reluctant to intrude but Lucas Deverell ushered her into the cottage before him, so she had no choice. He had to almost bend double to enter the small room but was able to stand upright once inside.

The building was relatively new and surprisingly clean, sparsely furnished and quite well-lit, the sun streaming through the diamond-leaded windows.

Mistress Carter showed Constance to a hard wooden settle but when she bid Lucas Deverell to sit, he held up a large hand, saying he preferred to stand. Frances sidled in behind them and lurked by the door, looking uncomfortable, and then after a few minutes she slipped back outside, unnoticed.

In the corner of the room was a makeshift cot with an elderly man lying in it. When he saw the visitors, he made a brave attempt to sit up to greet them but was too unwell and collapsed back against the pillow.

"Sir Lucas, it be so good to see you, hale an' hearty. We were right worried when we 'eard the news from Reverend Woode. We thought all was lost but 'ere you be. Safe an' sound. Terrible times, sir, terrible times."

"Indeed, Amos. And not likely to improve any time soon, either. Sadly, it looks like the troubles will go on yet awhile. You do not look good, old man. Is there anything I can do to help?" asked Lucas Deverell as he sat on his haunches beside the bed.

"Nay, sir. I be all right. Just old age, that's all."

"We will see about that. I will speak with the apothecary when he passes by this week."

Constance was eyeing the old man from the other side of the room and flicking through what she knew of bygone illnesses in her mind. Her interest in vegetarianism had led to her reading and retaining a great deal about nutrition and health.

"Sir Lucas, please could I have a word?"

He glanced up in surprise, "Not now, Mistress Harcourt."

She sighed, "Yes, now. I might have an idea about what is ailing this gentleman."

He glowered at her, "Mistress — "

Constance sent him a swift and quelling look. He stood up and escorted her outside. "What *is* it? You should not interrupt — "

"Yes, well, I'm really sorry but I might have the answer to Amos's illness. I mean, obviously I'm not a doctor but I've been thinking and remembered that one of the simplest things to cure is scurvy. I believe he has the symptoms — his gums and his skin, you see? It's possible that all he needs is some fresh fruit and vegetables and offal. Vitamin C and iron."

Constance found she was being contemplated from hard dark grey eyes and found it disconcerting. "There's no need to get all uppity about it. There are going to be ways I may be able to help because of well — *you* know!"

He rubbed a hand across his eyes, and she thought about what he had been through and how tired he must be.

"What do you suggest?" he asked on a sigh.

"I happened to notice that you have some lemon trees growing in your orangery. Lemons contain Vitamin C — which is a sort of er — magical property in fruit and vegetables and wholly necessary for good health."

"There is no need to patronise me. I am quite willing to believe that you are in possession of facts that we do not yet understand. If you think it might work, I will supervise changes to his diet. In fact, I will make certain that all my tenants are given access to the right foods. Does that satisfy you, Mistress Harcourt? Perhaps you could make me a list?"

Constance beamed up at him, the sun glinting on her hair, picking out coppery highlights and making her eyes sparkle like green sapphires. "Indeed I could, Sir Lucas. If that remedy doesn't work, it will, at least, do no harm. And a well-balanced diet will improve other aspects of his health and make him more resistant to illness."

Lucas Deverell's mouth tightened but he nodded, "Yes, I can see that. There is no need to hammer the point."

"I didn't think I was," said Constance rolling her eyes.

"You have no respect — "

"I have plenty of respect actually — where it's due."

She grinned mischievously as his temper began to visibly fray, "I think you'd better go back to Amos. Frances and I will wait here for you and hope that you can calm down a little before attempting to bite my head off," and she turned away to join Frances where she was sitting on the grassy bank.

"I thought he would explode," admitted his daughter nervously.

"It'll do him good to realise that he can't dictate to everyone. I don't want to be cruel when he has been through so much, but it seems to me that he has become overly used to soldiers doing his bidding without daring to question him."

"He has always been like that, ever since I can remember," remarked Frances with a slight smile. "Although Aunt Ursula said that he was a very kind and loving child and quite shy. I suppose life has worn him down."

"I think he has forgotten how to show any feelings other than anger and disapproval. I suspect that his leg gives him some pain too."

"I heard Aunt Ursula saying that the surgeon wanted to amputate it, the injury was so bad."

Constance shook her head, "He'd have been forced to leave the army. Life would have been even harder to bear," and she tried to picture such a vigorous man being forced to use crutches to move about. "Thank heaven they thought better of it."

"He would not let them. He argued to let him keep his leg and they agreed in the end. Aunt Ursula said he must have made a terrible fuss, so they had no choice."

"I can imagine."

The door of the cottage opened, and Lucas Deverell ducked out into the daylight. He caught Constance's eye and slightly inclined his head which she took to be his way of acknowledging her advice.

He went from cottage to cottage, each time insisting on taking Constance with him. He talked with the tenants, some very elderly, some younger and still able to work and he offered them help and advice. Constance thought he was probably one of the better lords of the manor as far as his tenants were concerned. In many ways he seemed to be quite forward thinking.

After they had left the last cottage, Constance looked back at the odd little row of dwellings, "They're alms-houses, aren't they?"

He grunted agreement but kept walking.

"You had them built?"

Another grunt.

She and Frances exchanged a laughing glance before the girl ran on ahead of them.

"Where are we going now?"

"To inspect the corn loft and threshing barn and then home. You do not have to accompany me, you know."

"Yes, I know but I think it might be instructive for Frances to see what being Lord of the Manor entails. It may make her more understanding of your awful moods."

He came to an abrupt halt and turned sharply to her, "*Moods?*"

"Yes, you have an uneven temper and to be perfectly frank, I'm not in the least surprised, having heard a little of what you have suffered these last few years."

"I have no need of your thoughts on the matter, Mistress Harcourt."

"I do not mean to pry, Sir Lucas. I'm merely trying to help your daughter come to terms with a father who is often away from home and in considerable danger and therefore perhaps somewhat distracted when he returns. She needs to learn that patience is indeed a useful virtue."

He stood looking down at her coldly for a moment, "I am not sure I need you meddling in my business."

"Well, someone needs to help those children and I've nothing else to do at the moment. And before you suggest it, I am *not* sewing samplers!"

A reluctant smile tugged at the corner of his mouth, "I would never dare to suggest it. I would be far too — loath to disturb the peace."

Constance laughed, "Benedict says you're daunted by nothing."

"Benedict is mistaken."

As they walked back down the path towards the brook, Frances ran ahead, Constance tried not to look at the wooded area where one day there would be a large rectory with battlements and a fig tree. It made her skin prickle and she wanted to avoid the desperate feeling of emptiness which seemed determined to overwhelm her when she was forced to consider her predicament.

"What will be there?" asked Lucas Deverell.

"How did you — ?"

"You are deliberately not looking over there. It is quite plain to see."

"Oh. It will be an old rectory. The gardens slope down to the brook. The owner I first remember there was one hundred and three when she died and is — *will* be buried in the churchyard. We used to steal the figs from her tree."

"You stole them? Were you punished?"

"No, it was just considered something children did. It's called scrumping. If they caught us, they sometimes shouted a bit, but it was mostly in jest."

"Your time sounds very — lenient, it would not be so now. Perhaps this is why you are so ill-disciplined?"

Constance let out a hoot of laughter, "It's so funny that you should think that! My family think I'm very controlling and scrupulous."

"Things must be *very* different in times to come then."

They had reached the bottom of the hill and Lucas Deverell held open the gate for her to pass through. They had just begun to climb up the opposite slope when Constance stopped in her tracks.

"Did you say something?" she asked her companion.

"I said nothing at all. Did you hear something?"

Constance turned back to the gate, "I don't know. I thought —" She looked around at the woods on either side of the path. "No, it was nothing. My imagination running wild," and she continued on her way. She had only taken a few steps when she stopped again.

"There! Didn't you hear that?"

"I hear nothing."

"A sort of thrumming sound. Like your bees."

Constance walked back to the gate and stopped to listen. She cocked her head, "It's coming from — oh my god!" She lifted her skirts and slid down the gentle embankment to the drystone wall which bordered the bridge.

Lucas Deverell watched her as she ran her hands across the stones. He feared she'd gone mad. Her movements were certainly feverish.

"What are you looking for?"

"Wait! I think — *yes!* Oh, my giddy aunt! I don't believe it! It's *here*." She was tugging at the stones but not making much headway.

Lucas Deverell could stand it no longer and joined her at the wall. "Show me."

Constance pointed at something caught in a large gap between the stones, "That box! It's Gabriel's geocache! I just can't believe it. Can you get it out?"

"Despite the fact that I cannot understand most of what you are saying, I think I probably can." He forcibly removed one of the stones and dragged the box out. "Here you are. What the devil is it?"

Constance threw herself down onto the grass and held the box to her chest for a moment, just trying to breathe, then, fighting back tears, she opened it. Lucas Deverell sat down beside her.

One by one she removed the items from the box and handed them to her companion.

"Oh, the clever boys! This is totally genius! But how did they know? What made them — ? "

A photo of the boys with her sister, Tova and Badger. All grinning madly at the camera although it looked like Tova had been crying. A simple but illustrated medical manual. A First Aid kit. A small solar powered torch. A condensed history book. A notebook and pencil. Painkillers and antibiotics. A rape alarm. Water purifying tablets. And most importantly, a note.

Guy had written in his scratchy, artistic hand,

"Dearest Auntie Con!

Not sure if you'll get this but hell, laws are made to be broken, even the laws of the universe. I'm hoping for some Time-Slip connectivity! We're all okay. Mummy took it quite well although she did a breath test on us all - even Gabe! She cries a lot though. Dad got the meds. Rape alarm was Rowen's idea. We love you and want you back with us. Take care.

Hugs from T, G, R, Gabe, and the stupid dog."

"What is this?" asked Lucas Deverell.

"That's a rape alarm. It makes an ear-splitting noise if I'm in danger."

"Your nephews do not have a very good opinion of the men in the past then?"

"Women carry them all the time in my time. Just in case."

"That is a sad indictment of both our times." He looked down at the strange objects he was holding, "And this?"

"A kind of — lantern — powered by sunlight."

"And the little painting is of your family?"

"Yes," replied Constance, in a stifled voice, "It's called a photograph. It's not a painting but an exact likeness made by a machine."

Lucas Deverell said nothing.

"I must put the box back exactly where it came from. But I should put something inside it so that they know I found it."

He handed back the notebook and pencil.

She wrote, in a shaky hand,

"Thank you, Guy! Literally lifesaving stuff. Not sure how this whole thing works yet. Am safe with family of local Lord of the Manor - Colonel Sir Lucas Deverell - still in Rissy. Food okay and bed comfy!

Missing you all.

Love you, Con."

She folded it up and put it in the box.

"You are crying, Mistress Harcourt."

"Well, obviously I *know* that! There's no need to point it out. I do wish you wouldn't call me that, it sounds so stuffy."

He reached into a pocket in his breeches and handed Constance a silver shilling. "For the boys."

She turned it over in her hand, "Good grief. Look, it's Charles I!"

"Yes, it is unfortunate."

"Oh, they'll be tickled pink! Thank you." She put it inside the folded note and closed the box. Lucas Deverell took the box from her and jammed it back into the wall, replacing the stone afterwards.

"Come, we must be going. There is still much to do before we can go home. It seems that Frances has had enough and deserted us."

"I think she did very well, considering her lack of years."

"Frances is no longer a child. It is time she prepared herself for marriage and a family of her own."

"She's fourteen! She's too young to think of marriage. Gosh, in my time that would be considered a serious offence and would get a prison sentence."

"She can become engaged now but has the choice to end it later if it is thought not to be suitable. You understand that I am not a believer in the dictum that women are weaker vessels. I do not believe, despite the teachings, that women are inferior to men, morally, spiritually or intellectually. Physically weaker perhaps but in other ways the sexes are mostly well-matched."

"I'm glad to hear you say that, but I suspect that the common practice of not educating women has a great deal to do with those antiquated beliefs. If you were to level the playing field everyone would stand a chance. Elizabeth I proved… I mean Queen Elizabeth proved that, with education, a woman can fulfil the most demanding of roles; in fact, many of the most renowned world leaders in my day are women. And, as we're so opportunely on the subject, I would like your permission to give Frances some lessons in writing. She's very enthusiastic about the prospect and I think it would be beneficial to her self-confidence."

"Is this how you acquired your — er — "

"Impudence?"

"I have another name for it. I have no desire to see my daughter's good character ruined."

"Are you saying you think my character is ruined?"

His eyes met hers, "I have no way of knowing what your character might have been had you not been given lessons. Perhaps, though, if you had devoted yourself to your sewing — ?"

"Oh, very amusing, sir."

Lucas Deverell removed his dark green sash and placed all the geocache items in it and then slung it over a broad shoulder.

They walked in amicable silence up to the church and then past the Court House and down the lane to the corn loft and threshing barn, which backed onto Bobble Hill, facing out across the Windrush valley.

Lucas Deverell told her how his father, Sir Walter Deverell, had the barns built some forty years ago when he was adapting the estate in an effort to make it more productive. Constance then suffered a lesson on estate management, good animal husbandry, building repair, and managing estate tenancies. She was told that his estate steward, Mr Quinton Gittings, had been an absolute paragon of virtue while his employer was away but how, while he was recuperating, he had received a letter from Mr Gittings, stating that he felt that he could no longer delay the inevitable, that it was his duty to fight for his King, and consequently had joined up with His Majesty's troops — Mr Gittings being a staunch Catholic and Royalist. His employer had not heard from him since and feared that he had been lost in battle. Apparently, he had managed the estate with admirable efficiency and a firm but gentle hand. He had been unshakeably honest, a trait that was, according to Lucas Deverell, exceedingly rare in these troubled times.

Constance made a pretence of paying attention to his words as she wandered about enjoying the familiar smells of a hay barn, the dusty warmth that tickled the nose, the sweet taste of the hay in the air and the glittering dust motes which danced in the narrow shafts of sunshine filtering through the roof.

"You are not listening."

"Oh, I am. Being a female I can multitask — do many things at once. Quinton Gittings. Royalist. Honest and true. Animal husbandry."

"It is sheer luck you managed to recall anything I said at all," said Lucas Deverell blandly.

She laughed, "You might be right, in this case. What are we doing now? Is your inspection finished?"

"It is. Let us go home."

Home, thought Constance wistfully. Where *is* home?

Back at the Court House Constance found Benedict having yet more lessons with his tutor and Frances stitching away crossly in the parlour.

"You have been a long time," she said abruptly.

"Yes, I'm sorry, your father insisted on showing me some rather dull barns. Full of hay."

Frances smiled reluctantly, "He is very devoted to his barns."

Constance laughed, "Men are strange creatures."

"And yet he thinks women are the strange ones. Did you ask him about the lessons?"

"I did. He didn't exactly say yes but neither did he say no. So, I am taking it that he has given his permission."

Frances's face lit up. "Could we start right now?" she asked, casting aside her needle and thread with careless abandon.

Constance told Frances what they would need, and the excited young girl flew about gathering paper, ink, and quill and arranging them on the burr walnut bureau by the window.

As they found chairs and sat down together Constance was heartily thankful for the two terms she helped out at their village school as teaching assistant. She, at least, had an idea of how to start teaching Frances the basics of writing and her own calligraphy skills would help her mimic the beautiful script Frances would be expected to master.

An hour later, her pupil was happily shaping her letters in long neat rows, the feathery end of the quill swishing to and fro and the nib making scratchy sounds like a mouse in the wainscoting. Constance was able to sit back and observe whilst allowing her mind to wander a little.

She tried desperately not to do the what-ifs, where the idea of being stuck in the past forever sent her into a state of panic. The thought of never seeing her family again hit her like a body-blow and made it difficult to catch her breath. She had to push it away from her, tucking it out of sight and out of mind in the most remote recesses of her brain. She decided to just take her present existence a day at a time and not to worry too much about time at all, either abstract or real.

As she couldn't help her own family, she would do her very best for the one she had been so randomly grafted onto. The children were clearly in need of someone to take notice of them and guide them through the difficult times ahead. When she thought about what was coming — the battles and disease and political upheaval which would affect all their lives — she was afraid for them. She wondered if she should warn Lucas Deverell but couldn't help feeling it would do more harm than good.

"What do you think, Mistress Harcourt?" said Frances, pointing to a perfect line of looping Bs.

"Oh, my! They're a work of art! You have a natural aptitude for writing. I'm very impressed."

Her pupil couldn't help a little smile of self-satisfaction as she returned to her work. She realised that pleasing her teacher gave her a warm glow inside. This was a new sensation for her, and she found she rather liked it. Nevertheless, she was still not entirely convinced about the reasons they had been given for the sudden appearance of Mistress Harcourt in their lives; she realised that she had some doubts about her father's explanation.

They worked together this way for another half an hour and then Constance suggested that they should go into the garden for some fresh air.

Once out in the sunshine Constance found her mood brightened and she decided to see what she could do to restore the garden to something of its former glory. As she wandered around, she pulled up weeds, leaving them in piles to gather up later. Frances trailed behind her for a while but soon lost interest and when Benedict was finally released from his lessons, she seemed quite glad to see him and they raced off into the woods together.

Lucas Deverell had told her that he would be riding out to the more remote farms on his estate and would be away till late, so Constance knew she had the afternoon to herself.

Constance eventually went inside to find Oates to help her find some gardening tools. He greeted her request with a reproachful sniff and grudgingly led her to the stables which were situated behind the house. He left her to her own devices muttering something about the master not approving.

In a dark storeroom at the back of the stables she found what she was looking for and began by pulling out a wooden wheelbarrow and filling it with some beautifully crafted tools: spade, rake, shears, pruning knife, and watering can. Extremely satisfied with the outcome of her search, she wheeled her trophies around to the parterre in the front of the house. She caught sight of her green satin gown and thought it would not make her very popular if she ruined it on its first outing, so she ran up to her bedchamber to find something more suitable to wear. In amongst Lady Esther's clothes, she found a plain linen skirt and bodice in a faded forget-me-not blue and because she felt she would probably be getting a little overheated, she took off one of her petticoats, which had the effect of slimming down her outline a good deal.

She began by furiously weeding for an hour or so and then taking up the shears she made a start on cutting back some of the wilder shrubs at the back of the parterre which were in dire need of a severe trimming. She decided to leave the clipping of the box hedges to be done in the autumn - she wasn't counting on still being around - so any new leaves wouldn't scorch in the fierce sunshine. She raked the gravel, picked a big bunch of lavender which was covered in bees, deadheaded the roses, and promised herself that she would thin out the fruit on the apple and pear trees the next day. By this time, she was ravenously hungry and quite tired and went in search of the children.

She discovered them chasing butterflies in the meadow between the house and The Wilderness where Benedict's fort was. She could hear them laughing together and thought that there were few more delightful sounds in the world — *any* world.

She sat down on the grassy bank at the edge of the meadow and watched them for a while. Eventually when they were breathless, they came to throw themselves down beside her, panting and gabbling with excitement. They were like two boisterous puppies.

"We have missed dinner!" exclaimed Benedict. "We shall have to wait until supper now. I shall die of starvation! I could eat a horse."

"Mistress Fitch will be offended. She will make that awful face — like this!" And Frances did a very fine impersonation of the housekeeper looking disapproving. They all laughed and then were quiet.

"I really am *very* hungry," said Benedict fretfully.

Constance stood up and dusted down her skirts, "Wait here. I shall be back in a short while."

They watched her run towards the house and exchanged a glance. Frances rolled her eyes, "She is rather odd, is she not? Did you see how filthy she was? Her face all streaked with dirt."

"She looked like a serf," remarked Benedict lying back in the grass and closing his eyes. "I wonder where she has gone. Perhaps she has been out in the sun too long and become touched in the head."

Twenty minutes later they heard their peculiar new companion running back to them and lazily opened their eyes to see Constance, bearing a laden basket and grinning.

They sat up and looked on in amazement as she unfolded a cloth and spread it out on the grass and then laid out an array of food: some slices of meat pie, cheese, bread, chicken drumsticks, and a punnet of gooseberries and cherries.

"There," she said, "A picnic."

"Pick nick?" repeated Frances, "What is that?"

"A meal eaten outside — mostly in the summer, of course. Go on then, help yourself. I've brought some of that horrid sour ale too."

It took a moment for the children to gather their wits and begin to lose their inhibitions enough to take something to eat.

After a few moments they were tucking in with gusto and Constance observed them with satisfaction. After eating, she lay back and gazed up at the sky through half-closed eyes, at the little puffs of cloud and the buzzards soaring on thermals high above them. She waved to them.

"Who are you waving at?" asked Frances idly.

"The buzzards."

Benedict met his sister's eyes and tapped his forehead meaningfully.

From where she lay on the soft meadow grass, Frances could see their land spreading out all around them, the fields and the farms, the river and the barns. “Who owns the sky?" she asked.

“Interesting question,” said Constance. “God, perhaps. Or Mother Nature. Maybe it’s just at liberty — slave to no man.”

Constance felt drowsy after all her hard work, the food and the warmth of the sun. She put an arm across her face and drifted away into a half-asleep dream world.

The children fell silent. Bees hummed and birds chirruped.

Nine

She was awoken by the sound of someone approaching.

"So, this is what happens when the cat is away!"

Constance opened her eyes and looked up at Lucas Deverell frowning down at them. She sat bolt upright, a blush of guilty pink flooding her cheeks.

"Oh, I must have fallen asleep," she gasped, "We were just — "

"Yes, I can see. Eating outside like workers in the fields."

"Or Royalty. Queen Elizabeth enjoyed a good outdoor feast after a hunt apparently."

Lucas Deverell observed his children and their companion, taking in their flushed faces, tousled hair, and nervous expressions.

He sighed, "Is there any left for me? I missed dinner."

Everyone let out their breath and visibly relaxed as he made his considerable bulk comfortable on the ground. Constance handed him a cup of ale and a chicken drumstick, which he immediately sank his teeth into.

"Delicious. And so much tastier when eaten out in the fresh air." He eyed Constance over the chicken leg, "Mistress Harcourt, have you had some kind of accident?"

She frowned, "No, sir, I haven't."

"I thought you might have fallen in the pond," he remarked.

Benedict sniggered and Frances slapped his leg.

Constance put a hand up to her hair which was hanging in unruly wisps and curls and sticking to her hot, sweaty face. "Oh. I see. Do I look a fright?"

"A gentleman would never say so," he murmured.

"I have been gardening, you see? And it was very hot, even though I took off one of the *dozens* of petticoats one is forced to wear!"

"Mistress Harcourt!" said Frances, shocked to her very core.

"Gardening? We have hired hands to do that. There is no need for you to do it."

"I actually like gardening. Where I come from, it's very fashionable even in the highest circles."

"I have only your word for that. Here we like the staff to take care of the gardens. Next you will be doing the cooking."

She cast him a mischievous glance, "I do like to cook."

"I must insist that you let the servants do it or it will cause a scandal."

"I will attempt to stay out of the kitchen, as you insist."

"How did you manage to obtain the food?"

"You hadn't ordered me at the time to stay out of the kitchen! I asked the kitchen maid for the leftovers from dinner, which we all missed. It seemed a shame to waste it."

"Did you indeed! How enterprising. I wonder what Mistress Fitch will have to say about it."

Constance laughed, "I have decided to tell her that you very much enjoyed the picnic! That will hopefully appease her."

She was gratified to see an appreciative smile light up his grey eyes.

He finished his meal and emptied his cup of ale, with a slight grimace as it was the weak brew, then with a tired sigh, lay back on the grass. The children, seeing their father do so, followed suit and sprawled beside him.

Constance longed for a camera so that she could record this moment.

"Did you manage to see all your tenants this afternoon?" asked Constance, conversationally.

Lucas Deverell made a sleepy sound in his throat, "Mmm-hmm."

"That's good. Any problems?"

"Unnhh-uhh."

"Fascinating."

"Mistress Harcourt? I think Father is asleep."

"I think so too."

And so they spent the rest of the afternoon snoozing in the sunshine until they were disturbed by someone calling loudly in the distance.

Constance sat up and realising what a spectacle they must look quickly woke the others in bit of a tizzy. "Tidy yourselves! Someone's coming!"

The Lord of the Manor didn't open his eyes, "There is no reason at all why we should not be lying in the meadow enjoying this fine day. For goodness' sake calm yourself."

The voice grew closer.

"Sir Lucas! Sir Lucas!"

"Here!" he bellowed, without moving a muscle.

Mistress Fitch tottered into view, her face purple with the effort. Constance started to get up, but her companion hissed at her, "Sit!" and she sat.

Mistress Fitch arrived puffing and blowing and quite unable to form a coherent sentence for a moment.

"What is it?" asked her employer, testily.

"It — it be — Mr Gittings! They have brought him back. But he be injured, sir, badly injured!"

Lucas Deverell was suddenly on his feet and alert. "Where is he?" he barked.

"They put him in the Great Hall, sir."

For a man of his build, Lucas Deverell ran swiftly, long legs carrying him over the ground with speed and agility, despite his injury. Constance turned to the children, "Gather up the picnic and go back to the house. I shall see if I can do anything to help."

Constance picked up her skirts and ran, overtaking Mistress Fitch, who was now walking in a more sedate manner.

In the Great Hall there was a state of disorder; several surly men standing about, clutching their hats and muttering,

Oates looking affronted, a kitchen maid sniffling, and in the midst of them a stretcher bearing the injured man. Lucas Deverell had taken command and was issuing orders and within minutes the maid had been sent to find bandages, Oates had been told to supervise the preparation of a room for the patient and the grumbling locals had been thanked and sent packing.

Constance went straight to Mr Gittings and took a good look at him.

He was in a terrible state, his clothes torn and filthy, his long hair matted with dried blood. An older man, possibly in his late forties, his hair and beard greying, his cheeks sunken and his eyes hollow and the skin around them had been badly burned. Constance noted that he also had a rash, small red spots on the parts of his body she could see.

She turned to Lucas Deverell and caught his eye. He came to her side.

"Mistress Harcourt?"

"I must consult the medical book that Guy sent. Mr Gittings is extremely ill and it's not just from the wound, he has some kind of fever with a rash. My medical knowledge isn't anywhere good enough to know what this is. But I think the first thing will be to get him out of these clothes and bathed — if you could organise that? I'll be back in a moment."

He nodded and addressed Mistress Fitch who was standing nearby awaiting orders.

Constance sped upstairs to her bedchamber and finding the medical book, sat down quickly to skim through it looking for pertinent information. She found illustrations of rashes and after reading some of the symptoms described she decided that Mr Gittings had probably contracted typhus. She went cold with fear and continued to read. She retrieved the bundle of boxes that had come from the geocache container, four packets held together with a rubber band. Antibiotics. She found what she hoped was the right one, and some painkillers, and tucking the book out of sight into the waistband of her skirt and carrying the first aid kit, she returned to the Great Hall.

Two servants were carrying the stretcher out of the room and Lucas Deverell was giving instructions to Mistress Fitch on bathing and the destruction of his clothing; to be burned immediately.

He raised his eyebrows at Constance, "Gaol fever?"

She nodded, "Yes, typhus, I think. I've read about it and I think I have found how to treat it."

"There is no treatment, he is certain to die from it," said Lucas Deverell with awful finality. "According to the men who found him, he managed to tell them he had been injured in the battle then captured and imprisoned by Parliamentarian troops at Langport. They marched the hostages to Highworth and imprisoned them in the church; they had been there for some weeks when inevitably the fever broke out. Some of them engineered an escape and helped Quinton make the journey home, leaving him in the village."

"Poor man, how he must have suffered. But I have medicine — I'm hopeful it will help. Let me at least try, we have nothing to lose."

He considered her for a moment and seemed to be convinced by something in her earnest expression, "If you believe there is a chance — "

"First a thorough washing, head to toe, burning all of his clothes and a clean bed. He must be given these pills regularly. I will see to that. If we're in luck and he has only had the disease for a week or so, the medicine may work. I can't *promise* a cure, you understand."

"Naturally. Anything you can do for him — He is a good man, despite his misplaced ideals."

"Can you ask Mistress Fitch to bathe around his eyes? He seems to have some kind of burn injury."

"Accidental ignition of gunpowder I suspect — powder burns. He is a musketeer and explosions are common."

"The best thing according to the book, is to make a saline solution and wash the wounds with that. A quart of water needs to be boiled for five minutes and then two small spoonfuls of salt added, mixed and cooled."

"I will see to it."

"I must change my clothes and wash before I can go to him. I won't be long."

Later that evening Constance was sitting beside her patient's bed and wondering how on earth she was going to manage; she knew very little about medicine and, even with the help of the manual, Quinton Gittings's problems were manifold and probably incurable. He had been bathed and put into a clean nightshirt and his wounds had been cleaned and bandaged as she had instructed. She had managed to get him to swallow an antibiotic pill and after a period of coughing and severe chills, he was at last sleeping, albeit fitfully. According to the thermometer from the first aid kit, he had a temperature, but not high enough to warrant bathing him with tepid water yet. But she was monitoring him and consulting the book every few minutes just to make sure.

She hoped now that he had been ruthlessly scrubbed and his clothes burned that the lice which carried the disease would all be dead and gone. The conditions in the church where he and who knows how many others had been held must have been squalid and insanitary in the extreme; he was lucky to be alive at all. To have survived the march from Langport to Highworth and then imprisonment and the ill-treatment which had been meted out, his strength of character must be formidable.

She was concerned about his eyes though, a blast of gunpowder close to his face may well have done permanent damage to his sight. There wasn't much she could do now, until she was sure his condition was stable.

Lucas Deverell was in and out of the room all evening. Eventually, obviously having nothing left to occupy him, he settled down in a chair on the other side of the bed, his booted legs stretched out in front of him, his chin sunk onto his chest.

Constance thought he looked weary, "Why don't you go to bed? I'll stay with him. I am quite awake. I'll call you if there's any change."

He frowned at her, "Perhaps it is you who should go to bed. You have been busy all day."

She smiled at him across the bed, "We could take it in turns."

"A fair compromise. I will sit with you for a while though. I could do with some idle conversation."

"Are you calling my conversation *idle,* sir?"

"On reflection, probably not," he remarked wryly.

"I should think not!" said Constance crossly and then immediately lapsed into silence just in case her conversation was found wanting.

After a few moments her companion chuckled, "I am very sorry. I did not mean to offend you, I swear. I will attempt to improve my manners. You must find me very boorish. The army does very little for a man's ability to converse with ladies about genteel matters."

"No, I can imagine and I'm not blaming you. Although I don't know what makes you think that I wish to talk about genteel matters. I'm quite content to talk about almost any subject — apart from, perhaps, managing rent arrears!"

"I am beginning to suspect you found my barns rather uninspiring."

"I did not! They were — fascinating. Very fine examples of — farm buildings."

Lucas Deverell's mouth twitched, "I suppose I must be satisfied with that. My father was inordinately proud of them. He was always trying to improve the estate, to make the work easier for everyone."

"I saw the painting of him and your mother in the Long Gallery. Sir Walter looked as though he would have been a splendid Lord of the Manor — diligent and kind. Your mother looked as though she would be great fun to be with — vivacious; but I sensed she might have been quite firm?"

"Yes, she was. She ruled with a rod of iron and old-fashioned notions about children. They were oddly mismatched and yet had a wonderful marriage and loved each other devotedly. Ursula used to liken them to the sun and the moon. But even though they were so different, they needed each other and when he died, my mother was inconsolable. Father was the flying buttress to her exuberant cathedral."

"What a lovely idea. How perfect to love and be loved like that."

"You have never thought of marriage?"

"No, but that doesn't mean I haven't thought myself in love on occasion. According to my sister I have the worst taste in men and always choose the ones whose only reliable quality is their ability to let me down at the first opportunity. When you say that you and your wife had an arranged marriage — ?"

"Our families contrived that we should become engaged from our early childhood, so we always knew we were destined to marry. We liked each other. She was amenable and beautiful and — "

"Wealthy?" She couldn't help the slight curl of her lip as she said it.

"You are surprised that it should be an important factor in a union between two people? How else do you keep the houses and estates tenable so that the workers can keep their homes and livings? Everything is dependent upon the Lord of the Manor and his wife. If that structure fails, then many others will be victims of that foundering. We are all sustained by each other."

Constance sighed, "I see that. I understand the necessity of finding a way to keep the estate working and your tenants happy, but I am in favour of a romantic connection between husband and wife. Like your parents."

He gave her a sardonic look, "Theirs was an arranged marriage too."

She shrugged, "Well, I suppose with the law of averages at least a few of them will be lucky enough to find the right partner but I cannot help but think of all the poor people who have to live their entire life with someone they can never love. It seems heartless and I'd rather be alone."

Quinton Gittings stirred and muttered something. Constance quickly grabbed the beaker with cooled herbal tea in it and lifted it to his lips.

"Mr Gittings, try and drink some of this please. It will help you."

Lucas Deverell leant over the patient and helped ease him up into a better position so that Constance could pour a little of the liquid between his dry lips.

"It is time for him to have more medicine as well," she said.

Lucas Deverell took the beaker from her. She pushed a pill between her patient's lips and her companion managed to get him to take some tisane to wash it down. She had no idea if what they were doing was enough, but she supposed it was better than nothing.

"Just in case — something happens to me — you know — if — something *happens*! You have to keep giving the medicine until the packet is finished."

"I understand. What do you think might happen?"

"I don't know but I'm guessing that as we have no apparent control over whether I come or go — "

"That you might just — go?"

"Anything's possible. You and I have witnessed the impossible. You reached out your hand to us in the churchyard and I took it and that brought me here — *somehow*. It's known as a portal — from one time to another. But until now I thought it was just fiction or fanciful scientists with too little to do. You know, making things up because they're at a loose end?" She saw a look she was learning to recognise cross his face, "Speaking in tongues again? Sorry. There are theories put forward by the great thinkers of our time that one can travel into the past and the future. Of course, there are other great thinkers who say that it is absolutely impossible — that if you could time travel, there would be some evidence. I was in *their* camp — right up until a couple of days ago. Now, I think either the fanciful scientists were right all along or I'm going mad. It's a tough choice."

"That would mean that we were *both* mad and that does not seem likely to me. How would you explain the box in the wall?"

Constance shrugged, "I just have no idea. Really, my mind is tying itself into knots trying to work this all out. When I was a child, I read a book called Jennie by Paul Gallico — and the hero, a young boy, turns into a cat but it's because he's been in an accident and is unconscious. Maybe I'm ill and just don't know it. Perhaps, I'm lying in a coma in hospital."

"You seem very real to me," said Lucas Deverell pensively.

"It's astonishing what the human brain can do. I think it's best not to think about it, in case it does actually drive us insane. If it *is* a dream — it's a truly impressive one — but I shall be quite disappointed and sad."

"Oh, really? Why?"

"All that work I did in the garden would be for nothing!"

He laughed softly.

Ten

Days and nights passed, and a routine was established which allowed Constance and Lucas Deverell to each take a share of the nursing. Constance was surprised to find that despite his size, Lucas Deverell was quite adept at administering to his friend and had no qualms about what he was asked to do. His military training proved useful and his natural common sense meant that Constance was able to trust him to take over from her when she was unable to keep her eyes open any longer. They sometimes passed in the night without saying a word, just a polite nod or an exhausted half-smile had to suffice. Oates brought them sustenance to their own bedchambers, or they ate in solitude at odd times of the day in the Great Hall or parlour. The children flitted in and out of their elders' peculiar existence like pale little ghosts, realising that the adults in their lives were too involved with other matters to take much notice of them. Constance gave Frances the occasional writing lesson when she had the energy and encouraged the girl to practice her letters whenever she could, and Valentine de Cheverell continued to tutor Benedict and happily took them for walks across the fields to keep them out of everyone's hair.

Mistress Fitch was sullenly quiet but efficient and willing to do anything her master instructed her to do. Constance learned very quickly that she had to speak through Lucas Deverell to get the housekeeper to do anything. She was unable to even look at Constance without enmity leaking out of every pore. Constance supposed that it didn't help that she was forced to wear gowns which had once belonged to her mistress and were therefore a constant reminder of her devastating loss.

Every so often news arrived by a military messenger about the war and it intruded into their lives like the ultimate spectre at a feast. Lucas Deverell broke the seals on the letters and descended into moroseness which could last a few hours or all day depending upon the content of the letter. Having made a forlorn attempt to talk to him about what was going on and receiving short shrift for her pains, she would try to steer the conversation into less choppy waters. If she felt he really needed cheering up she would selflessly bring up the subject of barns. The third time she deflected his anger with this tactic he stopped halfway through his sentence about the correct spacing for stalls and fixed her with an old-fashioned look.

"Mistress Harcourt! Are you making a shameless attempt to divert me?"

Constance collapsed into giggles, "Damn! Found out!" It took her a while to stop laughing and she ended up lying partly on their patient's bed, wiping her eyes and hiccupping.

Lucas Deverell watched her with interest from beneath his sleepy eyelids.

"I am beginning to wonder if you are a typical example of a female from your time or if I have just been extremely unfortunate."

Constance made a faux-shocked face at him and then started laughing helplessly again, her face pink and her eyes sparkling.

Lucas Deverell smiled.

"It might be time for you to go for a stroll in the garden. But *mind* me — no gardening! Not even one weed. Just some gentle exercise and fresh air."

Constance wiped her eyes on her sleeve and pressed her lips together to keep the slightly hysterical high spirits in check.

She nodded, "All right, I'll go but call me if anything changes."

He promised that he would do just that and satisfied, she wandered downstairs and out into the brilliant sunshine which seemed to have come to stay for the summer.

She aimlessly meandered about the grounds, looking critically at the planting and imagining what she could do to improve it, mentally pulling plants and shrubs out and replacing them with more suitable specimens. She was passing the orangery when she heard a babble of voices on the other side of the high wall. She called out and in moments Frances and Benedict had arrived, followed, in a more measured manner, by their tutor.

They looked so hot that Constance wished she could get them into some cooler clothes — t-shirts and shorts; they were dressed like miniature adults, buried under layers of heavy fabric and unnecessary additions like collars and tight bodices.

As Valentine de Cheverell approached Constance he was already smiling broadly. She was looking a little dishevelled as usual and rather tired, but her face lit up at the sight of the children running towards her and he thought that when her eyes smiled, there was no better sight to be seen.

"We have been walking the fields and reciting poetry," he told her.

"Outdoor lessons. What a wonderful idea. Better than being shut inside on such a perfect day."

"How is Mr Gittings? Is there any improvement?"

"His fever seems to be on the wane and the rash is a little better but he's still very poorly and I haven't yet been able to examine his eyes properly. I fear they may be damaged. But I think it's encouraging that he has not succumbed to the disease, it shows great heart."

"He is certainly a man with a stout heart. Hard working and resolute in everything he does, not a man to waste words — perhaps a little reticent and hard to know but nevertheless a man with a good brain and sound common sense. Sir Lucas was very fortunate to have him for his steward; he could have had none better. I hope he fully recovers."

"Sir Lucas seems devoted to him. He must have been devastated when Mr Gittings left to fight for the King?"

Valentine de Cheverell shrugged, "You would never have suspected he was in the least put out by it. Although he was lying in a field hospital when he eventually got the news; on his return he seemed at peace with his steward's desertion. He told me that we had to follow our hearts or suffer the bitterness of regret until the end of time."

"Gosh, that's very profound."

"I think Sir Lucas has suffered a good deal of regret in the past and has not yet found a way to live with it peacefully."

Constance suddenly felt a little awkward talking about Lucas Deverell with one of his employees and turned to the children who were scuffing their feet in the gravel, making patterns.

"Frances! Benedict! Come here!"

They looked up guiltily and sidled over to her.

"Go over there. Sit down on the grass and take your shoes and stockings off at once!"

They exchanged a startled glance but did as they were told.

"Now, walk on the grass barefoot and marvel at the delightful sensation of cool grass between your toes," she commanded them.

Valentine de Cheverell's eyes were wide, and his mouth had formed a surprised O. He caught her eye and saw the mischief there and once again was smiling.

"Do I sense a misspent childhood, Mistress Harcourt?"

"Very likely. Certainly an enjoyable childhood. I cannot bear to see those two trussed up like chickens ready for roasting."

Valentine de Cheverell gave a shout of laughter, "Mistress Harcourt, you are incomparable! I have never heard the like. The things you *say*!"

Constance blushed pink and quickly turned away.

It was this moment Lucas Deverell chose to look out of the Long Gallery window on his way to find Constance.

He observed his usually reserved children tiptoeing cautiously across the grass, apparently barefoot and his son's young tutor regarding Constance Harcourt with something akin to adoration.

Somewhere deep inside his well-fortified heart he felt something stir. He wasn't quite sure what it was, but he didn't like it much. He watched as Constance Harcourt said something to his children and made them laugh and he watched as Valentine de Cheverell reached out and removed a petal from her auburn hair.

He rapped his knuckles slightly too violently on the window and saw them all start, suffering various degrees of guilt. Frances covered her naked feet quickly with her skirts; Benedict waved carelessly; the tutor looked wholly unperturbed and Constance Harcourt's beautiful face went a deeper shade of pink.

"I'm so sorry. I should have come back in sooner," panted Constance, having run all the way up to the bedchamber.

"It does not signify. The air will have done you good I am sure. I just wanted to advise you that Quinton rallied for a short while and even tried to speak. He seems to be improving a little."

"Oh, that's marvellous! The medicine must be finally doing its job." She bent over the patient and stroked back the long, grizzled hair from his forehead. "I wonder if we could look at the burns and see if they're any better?"

"Certainly. Will you take the bandages off?"

"I'll just wash my hands first."

Following the instructions in the medical book, Constance carefully removed the bandages and where they had become stuck, loosened them with some saline. She then cleaned the burns and when satisfied that she'd done her best, she glanced up at her companion and surprised an unguarded look on his face which made her forget what she was about to do. But no sooner had she seen it, than it was gone. So fleeting, she thought she must have imagined it. He had already looked away and was busying himself clearing up the used bandages.

Constance peeped at him from under her eyelashes but there was no sign of anything different, nothing that might explain the frisson that she felt just a moment ago. She just sensed some sort of sea change, a shift in his demeanour — nothing palpable, nothing nameable but enough to make her suddenly very aware of him.

They were cleaning up the mess they'd made in silence when Quinton Gittings groaned softly and lifted his hand a little way from the bed. Constance immediately went to sit beside him and held his hand in hers, comforting.

"Mr Gittings? How do you feel? Can you talk? Sir Lucas is here and will fetch you something to drink." The thin hand in hers twitched and she squeezed it gently. "I would like to look at your eyes, if you wouldn't mind? I need to see how they're faring after the blast." He returned the pressure of her fingers and she looked up at Lucas Deverell and smiled thankfully, feeling rather tearful. She sniffed and patted his hand then asked him if he could open his eyes.

She could see he was trying but she quickly realised that help was needed and reached for the saline again. After applying it carefully to the skin around his eyes and removing any of the residue that might be hindering movement, she asked him to try again.

This time one eyelid lifted, and a cloudy chestnut brown eye peered out.

"Oh, hello there! I'm Constance Harcourt. How do you do?"

Quinton Gittings frowned slightly, "Come — closer," he whispered.

She moved her face nearer to his, "Is that any better?"

He shook his head and closed the eye. "I cannot — see."

Constance looked up anxiously at Lucas Deverell, "Let us try the other eye, sir. Try to open it," she said encouragingly.

After a while he managed to open the other eye and Constance held his hand and leant over in the hopes that he might see her more clearly.

"I think — I can see a — shape," he spoke with great difficulty, as though every sound cost him dear.

"Splendid. That's a start. Now, close them up again and I shall put fresh dressings on your burns. You've done so well."

As she wrapped the clean bandages around his head, Constance found she was crying soundlessly, the tears sliding down her face and dripping off her chin onto the bed.

Then a large hand was pressing her shoulder, the weight and the warmth of it, an unexpected balm to her shattered spirits. The relief of hearing Mr Gittings speak and maybe see something, even if it was only with one eye, was too much. She hadn't realised just how much the last few days had exposed the raw nerves. She just managed to finish the bandaging and then turned and buried her face in Lucas Deverell's sash. He didn't move for a split second and then his arms wrapped around her and held her while she sobbed silently into his solid midriff.

A knock at the door made Constance gather herself and, with a regretful sigh, she moved out of the circle of Lucas Deverell's powerful arms and scrubbed at her eyes impatiently, sniffing and realising just how much she had been missing the enormous, rib-crushing hugs her nephews gave; the healing power of human touch could not be underestimated.

Mistress Fitch had come to tell her master that he was needed in the village because of some dispute about an unpaid bill and as Justice of the Peace he was required at the scene to resolve the matter.

He left saying he would return as soon as he was able, but Constance couldn't meet his eye for some reason and just nodded whilst diligently straightening her patient's bedclothes. Once he'd gone, she sat and stared into space for a while. She spent a good half an hour castigating herself and asking herself what the hell she thought she was doing. She muttered crossly, so distracted by her thoughts that she very nearly forgot to give her patient his medicine at the allotted time. It seemed to her that she was already beginning to forget who she really was. It was like being on holiday in a foreign land; it took a few days to acclimatise to the new country and its circadian rhythms and then it was so easy to end up going native and being reluctant to return to one's old life at the end of the sojourn. Or maybe she was being brainwashed by her gaolers. Except they weren't keeping her here against her will, they had taken her in when she was homeless and accepted her presence with equanimity - apart from the housekeeper, of course, who hated her.

Quinton Gittings stirred, and Constance shook herself out of the confused reverie she'd fallen into and resumed her nursing duties with rather too much gusto. She fussed over him, sponging him down and arranging pillows and asking after his well-being until eventually he caught her hand in his and held it.

"Nothing — is insurmountable," he murmured, his voice shaky and muffled. His mouth, which was all she could clearly see of his gaunt face, was faintly smiling.

"Oh, Lord, I'm so sorry, Mr Gittings. I didn't mean to disturb you. How selfish! It's just that I — "

"Showed — that you care."

Constance squeezed his fingers, "I was a bit overwhelmed and allowed it to make me — *needy*! Ugh. Awful. So mortifying. It won't happen again."

"Perhaps it — should."

"Really? Why?"

"Lucas is too much — the soldier."

"He *is* very inclined to be controlling."

"War will do that."

"He wasn't always like that?"

"Known him twenty years — since his mother — was alive. Always kind — "

"I think you should stop talking now. It's exhausting you. I am going to make you some nourishing broth." Her patient turned down his mouth and she laughed, "It will do you good."

Having asked Oates to sit with Quinton Gittings, Constance invaded the kitchen and taking no prisoners declared that she was going to do some cooking. The kitchen maid looked terrified and the cook, whom she'd never met before, flew off the handle and announced that nobody, other than her, had ever cooked in her kitchen and that wasn't about to change now.

Constance smiled sweetly at her and prepared to smooth ruffled feathers. "I will need your help, of course, Mistress —?"

"Peel."

Constance hid her smile, "Not Emma by any chance?"

"No, *indeed*! Agnes."

"Well, Mistress Peel, I have come to beg your advice because I have been told that there is no finer cook than you in the whole of this county."

The cook folded her arms across her magnificent bosom and gave Constance a narrow-eyed look, "And who told you that, pray?"

"Sir Lucas. He was very fulsome with his praise."

"Was he indeed!"

Constance could sense her weakening a little and pressed home her advantage, "Mr Gittings is finally showing some slight signs of recovery and I thought we might be able to make him some broth to build up his strength. And I do really love to cook and have been missing being in a kitchen."

"Mr Gittings is on the mend, you say? Well, that be the best news! He has been sorely missed. A good man and never a bad word to say about anybody." She looked Constance over with a critical eye, "What kind of broth?"

"I was thinking perhaps a bone broth with chicken, vegetables, and barley?"

The cook nodded, "Herbs. White wine."

"Perfect! That should do the trick."

Once allowed grudging access to the hallowed territory, Constance was extremely careful to show due deference at all times to the undisputed ruler of that kingdom.

Whereas normally Constance would have taken a ready-prepared chicken from the fridge, the quivering kitchen maid was dispatched to catch a chicken from the field by the barns and while they waited for her to return, they prepared the vegetables and chopped herbs.

Constance heard the chicken's last indignant squawk outside the kitchen and tried not to be mimsy about it. She had to get used to this way of life being red in tooth and claw and not think wistfully of tofu and out of season avocados and jars of peanut butter.

She picked herbs from the garden and pounded mace, peeled onions and watched as Mistress Peel brutally dismembered the still-warm chicken and put the pieces in a pan and put it to boil slowly with pepper and mace and a whole onion and barley. Her cheeks rosy from the heat from the fire and the energetic pounding, she pushed back her damp hair and looked with satisfaction at the results of their efforts. It was starting to smell quite good.

There was a slight kerfuffle outside the kitchen and then the door opened to reveal a none-too-pleased Lucas Deverell.

Her welcoming smile was ignored, "Did you manage to sort out the dispute?" she asked cheerfully.

He scowled at her, "I thought I told you — "

"Mistress Peel and I have been making bone broth for Mr Gittings."

"I do not care what you have been doing! Come with me now."

She made a face at him, "Oh, do get off your high horse! I was only helping a little with the cooking."

He marched to the door and held it open for her, fixing her with a look which made her hackles rise. She tossed her head and stormed past him.

"I thought I made it abundantly clear! I told you *not* to go into the kitchen!" he bellowed.

He had skipped past the dangerously quiet stage and gone straight into erupting volcano.

Constance was indignant and determined not to be cowed just because he had a very loud voice. She also guessed the attempt at amelioration in the village had not gone well but even so this still didn't give him licence to yell at her.

She stuck her chin in the air, "Please don't bawl at me as if I were one of your pikemen! We're not on the battlefield now!"

He took a deep breath, "More's the pity! I could have you whipped for disobeying orders!"

"Orders! Who do you think you are! Thinking you can order me about? I'm an independent free-thinking woman not a bloody serf!"

"Do not curse in my house!"

"Oh, for God's sake, you sound like Mother Superior! So Victorian! So, tyrannical!"

"You deliberately flouted my orders! If they find out about this in the village — my neighbours — !"

"What will happen? Will I be burned at the stake? For goodness' sake calm down. I just helped make some broth — I didn't murder anyone!"

"It may be all right where you come from but for the Lady of the — !"

Constance gaped at him, "*I beg your pardon*? Lady of the Manor? What the hell are you suggesting? "

He threw up his hands in despair, "I am saying that while you are here in my care, I am accountable for you. You are acting as the lady of the house and in that capacity you must behave appropriately."

"You have such stupidly old-fashioned notions!" She stopped, looked at him and suddenly started laughing.

"What amuses you, Mistress Harcourt?" he barked.

"Well, I'm being a bit stupid. Of course, you *are* old-fashioned! Bound to be. It's not *your* fault."

"I thank you, Mistress."

"Oh, *do* stop calling me *Mistress* so haughtily! I'm sorry I had the temerity to make some broth. I'm sorry I curse a lot. I'm sorry I'm such a burden to you. But you really must try to be less shouty when you're speaking to ordinary civilians. We're quite sensitive creatures."

Lucas Deverell looked down into her flushed face and felt the anger slowly melt away. She still looked agitated and spoiling for a fight, her eyes, those pale green eyes, were still alight with the thrill of their skirmish.

"You are like no other woman I have ever met."

She frowned, "Is that a good or a bad thing?"

He pressed his lips together, "I am not entirely sure yet," he admitted.

Eleven

By the end of that week, Quinton Gittings was sitting up in his bed and although his eyes were still bandaged, he was taking an interest in life, and especially the nurse with the smiling voice, who seemed to spend most of her day patiently sitting beside him, tending to his needs, feeding him and dressing his wounds. She chatted about the children and the village and what she was hoping to do with the garden and the weather, which seemed to have set fair, and the beehives and anything and everything except her past life and his old friend Sir Lucas. And all the while he thought there was something unearthly about her, something he couldn't quite put his finger on, the language she used, some of which, despite being a well-educated man, he could not understand; he thought it was more about what she did not say. He listened and wondered. When he asked her particular questions there was often a lengthy pause before she answered, and he tried to ask the type of questions which would build a picture in his mind of the woman who sounded like a lady of noble birth but sometimes laughed like a fishwife. Her hands were as soft as flower petals and yet she never baulked at helping him to wash or changing his dressings. She had given him some kind of medicine which he had never heard of before and if he had been a more suspicious man, he might have had his doubts about her intentions but there was something in her voice and the touch of her hand which gave him unquestioning confidence in her.

She sometimes sang fragments of songs which were unfamiliar to him and when he asked her what the song was called, there was a telling pause followed by an obvious untruth. The first time he asked she had replied without thinking, "*Meet Me on The Corner* by Lindisfarne." He knew very well that Lindisfarne was an island with an ancient monastery on it, but the song did not sound like any Gregorian chant he had ever heard. After that she was far more cautious with her answers and he was sorry for it.

She asked him what he liked to read and went at once to see if she could find something suitable in his employer's library. She returned triumphantly bearing The Tragedy of Mariam by Elizabeth Carye, and he could not help a wry smile as she struggled with the reading of it. Eventually she became used to the rhythm of the couplets and sonnets and performed it quite creditably, her voice soft and musical. During one reading session, he heard Sir Lucas enter the room quietly (but unmistakably him) and he stood by the door listening to her for a good while before leaving without saying a word. Quinton Gittings slowly built a narrative in his mind and, on that day, he added another interesting layer to what he was learning about his employer and the mysterious new addition to the Court House.

Every day his devoted nurse would remove the bandages and wash his burns and then they would go through the same performance each time — open your eyes — can you see anything? Never mind, perhaps next time. He already knew, he could sense it; he just did not know yet how little sight remained. He was prepared for the worst but knew that his companion was not. She was still clinging onto the forlorn hope that he would one day be able to see again. He could not say he was resigned to the idea of being blind but, as he should be, by rights, lying dead in that church in Highworth with the rest of his regiment he was grateful to still be breathing. He was by nature a man not given much to fanciful conjecture, but he would stake his life that there was more going on here than met the eye — even a blind eye. He listened carefully to the voices, paying attention to the manner in which things were said. He found he could now hear many more subtleties in the changes of inflection. It kept him occupied and helped him through the long days of his recovery.

When he deliberately steered the conversation to Lucas and their shared past, she fell noticeably silent, listening to every word as though her life depended upon them. He could *hear* her listening. He could almost hear her heartbeat increasing. Her breathing became a little shallower and faster. She did not move at all. When he finished telling the story, she would let out her breath in a sigh but say little that might mean she had to speak his name.

When she was resting, his friend came and sat with him and they talked about old times, reminiscing like two old men on the village green. Those days when they had both been so sanguine about their futures seemed like centuries ago, the war now standing foursquare between them and the agreeable memories they had once shared.

Lucas would discuss estate matters and ask for advice about any problems which had arisen. He talked about cows and hay and barns. He would mention the children and how quickly they were growing and how they were hiring a new forester to care for the woods and The Wilderness which had been sorely neglected these past two years. He said how he missed having a dog about the place; his last one, a deerhound, having succumbed to old age while he was away, and wondered if he should acquire another one when there was always a chance that he would have to return to his regiment at short notice. He thought the children might find a dog entertaining and good company while he was away, and it would also be added protection for the house in these troubled times.

Quinton Gittings listened. He knew his recovery from the typhus was miraculous and felt a strong pang of guilt when he thought about his comrades who had not even been lucky enough to die from a swift and efficient musket ball to the head but instead died a slow and miserable death from the wretched gaol fever. He gradually grew more determined that his second chance at life would not be wasted; he would find some way of making a difference so that the soldiers he had been forced to leave behind might, in some way, be able to find peace.

One day, he asked Constance Harcourt to tell him about her family, remarking casually that she had not yet mentioned them. The silence that followed ached like a broken bone. He was immediately sorry he had asked but the lack of response intrigued him and made him wait patiently while she tried to find some way to evade the subject. Her voice, when she began to speak again, was stifled and he inwardly reproached himself for being so Machiavellian. He was finding that idleness was a breeding ground for the baser instincts he had previously not acknowledged, and he began to wonder if he might have been a very different kind of man had he not had such a demanding profession.

Her answer, when finally it came, was unsatisfactory. She lightly touched upon her immediate family, her sister and nephews but even when gently pressed, was not able to enlighten him much more. He could hear the tears catch in her throat and wondered why she was separated from these paragons. Something was keeping them apart. The war. A division in the family. Something she obviously deeply regretted and caused her a good deal of sorrow and heart-searching. Something she was not prepared to talk about. Something that his good friend knew about and also would not discuss.

Then came the day when his bandages were removed for good and the condition of his eyes was finally revealed and acknowledged. And the moment he had dreaded arrived, not the loss of the sight in his right eye or the partial loss in the left, but the panicked sobs that erupted from Constance Harcourt. It was he who comforted and soothed and she who suffered for him. The wounds were healed on the outside and the loss of his eyesight could be born, with, if not ease, then at least serenity and he was convinced deep down that God must have a reason for afflicting him so. It was a trial he was determined to endure.

Constance gently unwound the dressings and held her breath. She had been putting this moment off and even now, she was debating with herself about the wisdom of uncovering his poor eyes. She had drawn the curtains, so the room was dimly lit. She had prepared him as best she could. She had called for Lucas Deverell to be present because she didn't think she could do it by herself without some solid moral support.

The last ribbon of linen fell away and after she had bathed his eyes again, he slowly opened them.

Constance quelled the urge to run away from her patient and the cruel truth. She knew as he looked about him that he was seeing nothing but ghost-like shapes. He smiled resignedly and shrugged. She wept. She tried not to, but the sounds just tore out of her and she could do nothing to stop them. There was no hand on her shoulder this time to calm her and no broad green sash to weep into. Lucas Deverell stayed resolutely on the other side of the bed.

She couldn't help but wonder if twenty-first century doctors might have been able to save his sight and from there, she made the logical jump to blaming herself for the end result of her care. She had grown fond of this stoical and quietly humorous man over the weeks and looked forward to each day spent with him. She could quite see now why Lucas Deverell was so devoted to him and realised afresh what a blow it must have been when his steward left to fight for the other side. The fact that he had been able to maintain the friendship despite their differences said a great deal about both men and their personal loyalties.

Quinton Gittings reached for her and she took both his hands in hers, "I'm so *very* sorry, I'd hoped — that given time to rest and heal that — " she whispered, distraught.

"Please, Mistress Harcourt, if you could but think of it this way, that I should be dead and buried by now if it had not been for you. And from under the ground, I could see nothing at all but darkness. At least now I can feel the touch of your hand, I can hear your laughter and although I may not be able to see you, I have the inestimable joy of hearing your thoughts. You cannot even begin to imagine how very grateful I am to you for these gifts. I do have one small request though," and he turned his face to Lucas Deverell, "I carry in my mind the memory of your ugly face, my dear Lucas and I would ask you to describe our companion for me, so that I may picture her a little more clearly."

Lucas Deverell's eyes met Constance's over the bed.

He frowned, "I will do my utmost, Quinton, but you know that I am not blessed with a poet's tongue. I am but a brutish soldier with a love of barns."

Constance grinned at him, her eyes warm and alive.

Lucas Deverell cocked his head and contemplated Constance, "She is a little shorter than Ursula and slight of build. Her hair is the colour of a ripe chestnut and it curls quite wildly — which I fear denotes what goes on inside her head. Her mouth curls at the corners and her teeth are very white. Her nose is straight and tips up a little at the end. I am afraid she often stays too long in the sun despite Frances reminding her that it is bad for the complexion — and is sadly burned by it."

"I am impressed Lucas! You are a poet after all. But you have not mentioned her eyes."

"Ah, yes, her eyes," said Lucas Deverell pensively. "They are palest green and dark-lashed and kindle in a magnificent fashion when she is angry and dance when she is amused. And — she blushes as pink as a rose when in a passion. Will that do? I suspect poor Mistress Harcourt is discomfited by the unwonted attention."

"Thank you, I can see her clearly now!" said Quinton Gittings, smiling broadly.

Constance, whose cheeks were delicately suffused with colour, patted his hand, "Thank you *so* much for that, Mr Gittings! That wasn't in the *least* bit uncomfortable."

He laughed, "I wish you would call me Quinton. Mr Gittings makes me sound like a schoolteacher."

"Only if you call me Constance!"

"It is a deal, my dear Constance. What a perfect name for you."

"I was named after an absolutely scandalous Great Aunt."

"However scandalous, she would have been proud, I think."

Lucas Deverell was lounging in his chair, legs stretched out in front of him, idly watching this exchange from half-closed eyes. He was relieved beyond measure that Quinton was on the mend and knew that without the miraculous intervention of Constance Harcourt, he would now be trying to come to terms with the loss of his best friend. But he found himself envying his friend's effortless manner with her and wished he could be that adept at putting her at her ease; he just seemed to have the ineffable ability to rub her up the wrong way. He had always been only too well aware that he lacked the necessary social skills to successfully pay court to a woman and had he and Esther not been betrothed when they were children, he doubted he would ever have married.

"I think, Quinton, we should try to get you downstairs tomorrow and then perhaps out into the garden. Despite what Sir Lucas says and Frances's constant scolding, some sunshine will do you good. We shall set up a day bed in the orangery so that you can convalesce."

"That sounds like an excellent proposal."

"And before we do that, I am going to have to beg Sir Lucas to shave your beard because you look like a veritable wild man! I can trim your hair and make you look a little more presentable in case anyone should pay us a call. You wouldn't wish to scare them away or frighten the children!"

"Indeed not! Shave away!"

Quinton Gittings felt rather pleased with himself. He may not be able to see anymore but he thought he was doing rather well with his clandestine little mission. It amused him to discomfit Lucas, who had always been so very sure of himself, so military even before he had joined the army. He was used to being in charge, to commanding regiments of unquestioning soldiers and not having to bother with the niceties. Quinton remembered his wife very well; poor Esther, so ridiculously lovely to look at but, to be honest, he had always found her a little insipid. A marriage which had always been doomed to fail right from the very start. Lucas had ignored her or bullied her and when the children came along, he had ignored them too and finally abandoned them. Of course, it was not entirely his fault, he had gone from university to the law courts and then into the army and learnt his manners either in the taverns of London or on the battlefield. Quinton knew the man beneath that belligerent protective layer and thought, although he was well-disguised, it was not yet too late to attempt a daring rescue.

And today he had discovered that the battlements were already showing signs of vulnerability.

The following day, washed and shaved and dressed in his own clothes fetched from his home, Quinton Gittings was carried out into the garden in a chair and placed regally in the orangery to enjoy the sunshine. Constance fussed over him, bringing blankets and possets and books to read to him and the children came to look curiously at him through the glass.

The smells that assailed his nostrils were myriad and for a moment he was overwhelmed by the sensations which seemed to bombard him, but Constance was suddenly there holding his hand and he took a breath and tried to relax. Even though he could no longer see, he was unused to the strong daylight and it dazzled him; he closed his eyes and leant back in his chair to enjoy the warmth of the sun on his face. Constance was humming and it sounded as though she was watering the lemon trees. He imagined her auburn curls shining in the sun and her green eyes reflecting the sky.

"What colour is your gown, Constance? I can hear it rustling."

She laughed, “It’s a kind of apricot — with pale blue ribbons and cream lace. To be perfectly frank it’s not really my kind of thing and I’m absolutely boiling in it! I’ve taken off both the petticoats but it’s still like being trapped in an oven! And whoever thought of stays should be severely punished!”

“Anyone would think you had never worn such a garment before.”

Silence.

“Oh, I’m sorry, Quinton, I’m prattling on like a half-wit. I’m just so very overheated that I can’t think straight.”

Quinton Gittings smiled, “Of course, dear girl, I perfectly understand. It is just that sometimes you sound as though everything is new to you and I wonder if that is because you have perhaps been living abroad?”

Constance tried not to panic. If she lied, the lies would escalate and come back to bite her; if she prevaricated Quinton would eventually start to suspect her of something nefarious. She was caught between a rock and hard place.

She bit her lip, “I have — lived in another — place and that might be why some things feel strange to me. But I will get used to them — in time.”

Quinton realised that his enquiries were causing some distress, so he changed the subject and began to discuss the unusually hot weather. He heard her little sigh of relief.

She found a lemon that had fallen from the tree and brought it to him. It smelt so sourly fragrant it made his mouth water and she promptly dashed off to make him a drink from it. He listened to her footsteps fade away and tried not to feel afraid of the quiet that descended, leaving him with only his thoughts to occupy him.

He closed his useless eyes and lay back in his chair to await her return.

Twelve

Lucas Deverell was in a good mood. Sir Thomas Fairfax had stormed Bridgewater and the town had surrendered. The message had arrived late one sultry afternoon and had considerably lifted his spirits. He ruffled Benedict's hair as he passed him, causing the boy to wonder what was wrong with his father; he praised Frances for her lettering which made her blush with pleasure. He then happily read some dreary essays by Sir Francis Bacon to Quinton who was recovering well and occasionally, if assisted by the support of a friendly arm, could manage to walk slowly around the parterre without becoming exhausted.

He told himself that he had merely chanced upon Constance Harcourt wandering through the meadow below the house and stopped to watch her from a distance as she drifted through the softly waving grass, her thoughts clearly faraway. She bent to pick some cranesbill and tucked them into her hair. She looked like Titania from a Midsummer Night's Dream. A thought struck him forcibly and his mouth tightened a little. Then, giving himself a mental shake, he limped across the field towards her.

"There is news! Fairfax has taken Bridgewater and taken a great many Royalist prisoners."

Constance, startled out of her reverie, looked up and saw him bearing down on her, his face wreathed in unaccustomed smiles.

"Bridgewater? Oh, dear. Such a harmless little town. How very sad."

"Sad! No! Do you not see? This is excellent news. It means we could win control of the West Country before long."

"Oh, but I was born in Somerset. It's such a beautiful place. I don't like to think of it strewn with dead bodies."

Lucas Deverell frowned at her in some confusion, "You were born — ? *Sad?* I am not sure you understand the full import of this! The quicker this is over the better for all concerned."

"Perhaps it would have been better if it just hadn't happened in the first place. If men didn't start bloody wars! If you weren't fighting your own countrymen! I mean, it's such a criminal waste. So many people died. And to what end? It all turns about again anyway and you're back to where you started. And it's not like it just ends here — it goes on and on for sodding years, tearing the country apart!"

Constance was suddenly aware that her companion's face had frozen into a blank mask.

"I — that is — oh, lordy. Just forget what I said. I'm sorry. Oh, Jesus."

He stared at her, his eyes dark, "Years? You say the war will last for *years*?" His voice was chilling.

Constance buried her now ashen face in her hands, "Please! Don't ask me anything else. It's best you don't know the truth. It might change everything for the worse."

"But with your knowledge we could save lives. We could stop the destruction — "

"Lucas! *Listen* to me! If we mess with history, we have no idea what will then happen in the future. Do you see? If someone who should be killed — isn't — and they live and then they kill someone who *should* have lived in order to make the world the way it is supposed to be — "

Lucas Deverell was silently trying to fathom the meaning of her words. He had an urge to try to shake some sense into her but instead took a step away from her and tried to calm his ragged breathing.

"So, you are unwilling to help end this?"

She made an exasperated sound, "You see, I don't really know how all this time stuff works. I don't see how the future can be changed, it's already happened — books have been written about it, films have been made— history cannot be unwritten — but — I'm scared that if I tell you anything, you won't be able to change anything anyway. Who would listen to you? How would you explain your argument? Oh, a strange woman time-travelled from the future and *told* me? You'd be pilloried or killed! Everyone would think you'd either gone raving mad or were in league with the devil! It would be too dangerous. I couldn't let you do it."

"Not let me do it? *Why?!* What can possibly be stopping you?"

Constance glowered, not liking this line of questioning at all, "I — I — you have so many people who depend on you. Frances, Benedict, Quinton, Master de Cheverell — "

"Ah! The *tutor!"* he exclaimed.

Constance looked at him in some astonishment, "What do you mean by that exactly?"

"He is young. He is handsome. And he is evidently besotted with you."

"Are you saying — ? You think — oh, my giddy aunt! You are *such* a blockhead! He's only about twelve years old for god's sake! You utter pillock."

At this he looked so shocked it arrested Constance in full flow. "Oh, what have I said wrong now?"

Lucas Deverell did not know whether to laugh or bellow at her some more.

"You surely cannot know what that word means, or you would not have said it."

"It just means idiot. Halfwit."

He could not help a slight twisted smile, "It refers to a part of a man's anatomy best left unmentioned — if you purport to be a gentlewoman that is."

"Oh," said Constance, slightly deflated, "It must have lost its original meaning over the centuries then." She shrugged, "This whole language thing is quite difficult. I didn't mean to be rude." She grinned sheepishly, "Well, I *did* — but not *that* rude."

Her face had regained some of its usual colour and when she smiled up at him like that, he found he forgot why he was angry in the first place and it incensed him that he was so easily diverted.

"Will you at least tell me — ?"

"I can't! Don't ask me. It's not fair. You have to understand — I *want* to tell you but I daren't." She reached out and gripped his arm, "It could have devastating consequences. I can't risk that. What if something we change here means that one of my relations dies in the future? What if, by our meddling, we prevent, for instance, Alexander Fleming, the inventor of antibiotics, being born? That could mean that Quinton would die."

She watched as the truth gradually dawned on him, as her words finally added up in his head.

"You see? *Consequences.*"

He nodded, "All right. I begin to see your argument has some merit. But is there nothing we can do — ?"

Constance looked away into the distance, a look of concentration making her frown, "I've just had a ridiculous thought. What if I somehow made a trifling change here that should show itself in the future?"

"How? For what purpose? What could you do?"

She suddenly smiled, "Well, I have no doubt that you will heartily object but what is here right now and still standing in the future?"

Lucas Deverell shrugged, "The church?"

"Exactly! The damn church! Where we first met. Where I crossed over. Where everything happened. The church!"

"But what will you do?"

She cocked her head, "Why, I believe a little graffiti is called for, don't you?"

"If I knew what — *graffiti* was — I might possibly agree."

"It's art, in a way. Scratching on, in this case, stone! Bloody brilliant!"

"I do wish you would not curse. It is just not — "

"Ladylike? Pooh to that! You really are an old fossil! Come on! We have some vandalising to do!"

"*Constance!*"

On the way to the church, they stopped to get a stone carving chisel from the stables. As they made their way along the lane Lucas Deverell considered the unexpected turn his life had taken. He liked a well-ordered life, everything in its place; he liked having control over uncontrollable things, he did not particularly enjoy this feeling that some capricious being had taken charge of his destiny. He seldom gave in to impulse, which made him a good leader; he carefully considered everything before acting; he was methodical and exacting. He never lost his temper on the battlefield because there was no cause: his troops listened and obeyed. This woman beside him seemed to have come from nowhere to disrupt his ordered life and turn everything upside down. She was a force of nature which he could not control. He wondered if anything would ever be the same again. He wondered if he wanted it to be the same again.

Minutes later Constance Harcourt had found a hidden corner of the church, on the north side of the tower and was scratching away on the inward facing side of a buttress. He was quietly disturbed by this wanton desecration of a sacred building but held his tongue.

When she had finished, she sat back on her haunches to admire her handiwork. "There, look! It'll hardly show once it's aged a bit." She smiled up at him," Oh, don't look so disapproving! It's a necessary evil."

Lucas Deverell peered around the corner to see the results of her endeavours. It was a small smiling face.

"It's an emoji," she said blithely, "It could only have been made by someone from the future. He'll know it was me."

He nodded, not understanding, "And now — ?"

"Now, I must go and write to Guy and hope he receives the message. It's all a bit in the lap of the gods."

Lucas Deverell retrieved the box from the wall and Constance sat down on the grassy bank to open it. She seemed delighted to find that her last note and the silver shilling had gone and happily began to scribble a letter to her nephew on the notepad.

"Dearest Guy!
Urgent! Go to church and look on inward facing wall of buttress on northside corner of tower and tell me if you see anything carved there. Trying to prove something. Hope all well. I'm fine.
Love to all."

She put it in the box and her companion replaced it in its hidey-hole.

"I didn't feel anything spooky this time. I wonder if that will make a difference," she pondered aloud. "Anyway, that's all we can do for the time being. We should probably go home and make sure the children aren't tormenting Quinton."

"He's made of pretty stern stuff, that fellow. Home, it is though."

"Home," said Constance, "How odd."

"Odd? Why?"

"To consider it home. It's as though I'm being disloyal."

"Surely one can have more than one home?"

"Home is where the heart is," laughed Constance but then wondered why she was laughing and frowned, "I'm starting to feel a bit divided and it's unsettling."

"That is understandable. Come along, Mistress Harcourt, let us go and rescue the children from Quinton's tongue lashing!"

Constance pursed her lips, "You called me Constance earlier so don't you dare go back to addressing me as though I were an elderly dowager with gout and a hump!"

Lucas Deverell chuckled, "Then you must call me Lucas."

"Grand. So be it."

Constance spent the rest of the afternoon and evening entertaining Quinton Gittings, teaching Frances how to spell some simple words and hoping Guy remembered to occasionally check the geocache box. He was inclined to be a bit forgetful, but she was certain Rowen would remind him or check it himself. She had no idea how long she should wait before checking the box again herself. She wanted to sit beside it and just stare at it, hoping to see something happen. She didn't know what strange forces were at work and was afraid that if she kept disturbing the box, she might disrupt the energy and then the whole damn thing would just stop working and she'd be stuck here forever, unable to contact her family.

As Lucas limped into the room at that point her thoughts became confused and she found herself wondering about his arranged marriage and how Quinton had hinted that he was not ideal husband material.

Lucas had brought his friend a glass of brandy to fortify him. Constance observed with interest as he threw himself into a comfortable chair and prepared to take a sip of his own drink. He caught her enquiring look, the quizzical eyebrow, and muttered, "Oh, good God," crossly. He rose, handed Constance his glass and left the room.

Quinton Gittings looked puzzled as he tried to work out what he had missed. "Teaching my friend some manners, eh?" he said, hazarding a guess.

Constance giggled, "Just trying to get myself a glass of brandy. I don't see why the gentlemen should have all the fun."

"I fear poor Lucas has been too much in the company of soldiers and farmers and has had very little to do with more refined human beings. His knowledge of the fairer sex is unfortunately limited to a wife who was naught but another kind of servant to him and a daughter who is all but a stranger. I think you are come as a rude awakening for him."

"What about Ursula? Are they close?"

"As close as one can be when he was mostly away at school or university or the Law Courts and then the army.

He has lived his life a good deal away from home and Ursula married young and moved with Jacob to Banbury. They see very little of each other, more's the pity. She would have been a good influence upon his character. She is strong-willed but kind and I have no doubt has been a fine and loving aunt to his children. She took them in and treated them as her own. It is a terrible shame that she is now alone with no children or husband and so far away from her remaining family."

"Perhaps she should come and live here then?"

Quinton Gittings was about to say something when the door opened, and his friend came back into the parlour.

"We were just remarking, Lucas, on how fortunate the children are in having Ursula for their aunt."

Lucas sat, stretched out his legs and took a swig of his brandy, "They are indeed, and I can never thank her enough for how she took them in without demur. I only wish — "

"As do we all. Jacob will be sorely missed. Constance suggested that Ursula should come and stay here. In these troubled times it might be a way of keeping everyone safe? All under one roof."

Lucas fixed Quinton with a morose stare, "She wouldn't leave Banbury and the house they shared — the memories — "

"Oh, I think she might if the children wrote to her and *begged* her!"

"Oh, perfect!" said Constance happily, "It would be a good reason for Frances to practice her lettering. And it'd be nice to have another female about the place. Frances and I are sadly outnumbered."

Lucas appeared deep in thought, his chin sunk onto his chest, "I suppose it would be sensible especially as I could be called up at any moment."

Quinton heard the startled intake of breath from Constance and smiled inwardly.

Lucas continued, "My injury is no longer as debilitating so if I am needed for the next push, I will have no choice but to re-join my regiment. I have been on furlough."

Constance felt her chest constrict and her stomach lurch in an unfamiliar and not very pleasant way. She swallowed and tried to speak but no words materialised, so she fell silent and knocked back her brandy rather too fast. It went straight to her head and she started to feel a little giddy. Not noticing the beginnings of inebriation, Lucas refilled her glass from the bottle he had brought with him and she made no complaint. She suddenly rather fancied being irresponsible and carefree.

"Brandy is quite an intoxicating beverage," Quinton murmured.

"Thank you, dear friend for pointing that out, I would never have known otherwise," said Constance, slightly slurring her words.

"She's going to have the devil of a head tomorrow," said Quinton.

"Serves her right," responded Lucas callously.

She snorted and tossed back the rest of the brandy.

Constance looked up at the long flight of stairs and burst out laughing.

"No way, José! I'm not going up there! I'll sleep down here tonight, if you don't mind!" and she turned to go back to the parlour, but her legs buckled under her and she toppled drunkenly.

Lucas Deverell growled, swept her up into his arms and without too much difficulty bore her up the stairs to her bedchamber, where he deposited her unceremoniously onto her bed.

"Now, stay there!" he barked at her as he lit some candles and then searched her linen press for some kind of suitable nightwear.

Constance giggled and curled up on the bed. Nobody had ever bodily picked her up like that before and the ardent feminist in her deplored her unforgivable desire to have it repeated. At once.

Lucas threw a shift onto the bed, "Put that on and get into bed."

She beamed up at him, her eyes half-closed, "No. I don't want to."

"I will call Mistress Fitch to come and tend you."

"I'll scream if you do. She *hates* me."

"You are being absurd. Oh, for God's sake, Constance, stop that!"

Constance was sitting up and struggling to get off the bed. "I'm leaving," she said, "Nobody wants me here. I want to go home. To my real home. To my family. I miss them."

"Of course you do. It is only natural, but you cannot leave. You know you cannot. One day you will be able to, I'm sure. Until then will you please just do as you are told!"

She sniffed, "All right, you big bully. But I'll need help — "

Lucas Deverell muttered an ugly curse under his breath and wondered why it was easier to command a regiment of disorderly soldiers than manage this one infuriating woman.

He pulled her to the edge of the bed, but she started to lean a bit, so he wedged her with his knee, then wrangled her out of her bodice, while she laughed helplessly. He then twisted her around so that he could reach the lacings at the back and clumsily unlaced her stays, which he pulled up and over her head. She immediately flopped backwards on to the bed and started singing loudly. He looked down at her for a moment and considered calling for the housekeeper, but Constance was right, she did hate her, so he valiantly battled on. Next the skirt came off and he was a little shocked to find she was only wearing a shift and no petticoats underneath.

"Where the hell are your petticoats?"

She hooted with laughter, "I took them off! I was so damned hot!"

Lucas took a deep breath, "You are a strumpet, Mistress Harcourt. God knows what Mistress Fitch would make of it. She would think you irredeemably depraved and probably call a priest to deal with you! And *where* are your shoes?"

"I left them in the garden."

"In the — ?"

"You sound — sooo — pompous," she said and hiccupped loudly.

He ignored her and knelt to take her stockings off. He was just thinking how odd that he had never even done this for his own wife when Constance started to drag the shift up over her head. "No! Constance, do not dare — !"

She peeped at him through an armhole, "Oh, do *you* want to do it?"

Lucas groaned and pulled the garment back down. "Just wait a moment. I will shield you with your skirt while you take it off and put this clean shift on."

This they somehow managed to accomplish without compromising her honour, although Constance seemed to find the whole thing hilarious and giggled throughout.

He had just managed to get her decently dressed and was tucking her into bed when she reached up and threw her arms about his neck, pulling him close.

"Constance, what are you *doing*?"

"Oh, my god! Are you going to tell me to *unhand* you? That would be hysterical! *Unhand me, Mistress Harcourt!*" she mimicked his voice and then peered up at him blearily, "I just wanted to thank you," and she pressed a soft kiss upon his surprised mouth, pulled away, looked at him from sleepy laughing eyes and then kissed him again. She promptly fell asleep in his arms and he gently lowered her back against the pillows.

He watched her sleep, her mouth slightly open, her curls in disarray about her flushed face, one hand tucked up against her cheek and he hoped to God that she was afflicted with the world's worst headache in the morning. After this night's work, she deserved to suffer.

He pulled the covers over her shoulders and could not resist dropping a kiss on her forehead.

"Goodnight, *doxy*."

And he quietly left and shut himself in his bedchamber, where he sat on the edge of his bed, head in hands and waited for the aching to stop.

Thirteen

Lucas Deverell looked up hopefully from his breakfast to observe Constance entering the Great Hall. To his huge disappointment, she looked to be in good spirits. In fact, she looked positively radiant. She was a little late but apologised, saying that it had taken her a while to find her shoes.

He cast her a look of disbelief, having been certain that she would not only be rendered useless by, at the very least, a thumping headache but that she would be covered in shame after recalling her appalling behaviour. She seemed to be suffering none of the afflictions he had wished for her but, in fact, had apparently forgotten the whole evening.

Constance forced herself to smile at Lucas and she greeted everyone with enthusiasm and ebullient good humour. She then devoured a hearty breakfast, despite the fact that her stomach was rebelling, talking all the while about her plans for the day and never once letting the conversation wane. Lucas eyed her with first, astonishment and then grudging admiration; she must have a head like an ox, he thought.

Constance was trying to ignore the painful throbbing in her temples and the mortifying memories which had unfortunately not been obliterated by her hangover. She envied drunks who could recall nothing of their poor behaviour while intoxicated, how liberating that must be. Every time she thought about the events of the previous evening, she suffered a hot flush. Tova would be rolling her eyes and giving her a lecture about alcohol being a poison for some people and asking why she insisted on drinking when she knew that she always ending up regretting it. And she would be right.

Lucas surreptitiously studied her face looking for any sign of recollection but saw only a woman who had clearly forgotten that she had brazenly kissed him whilst in a state of partial undress. He shook his head and tried hard not to think about the sleepless night he had spent attempting to block it from his mind. A task he had found difficult. When he had finally managed to sleep, his dreams had been filled with images which were now seared into his brain. He rubbed a tired hand over his eyes and thought wistfully of the simplicity of battle — kill or be killed. Here, he was out of his depth and up against someone who did not know the rules and, even if she did, would laughingly refuse to play by them and, who played a game where she also had an unfair advantage.

Quinton Gittings caught a ripple of tension in the air and wondered what had happened last night after Lucas had escorted him safely to his room and then left him to go and rescue Constance from the consequences of too much brandy. He could hear false jollity in her voice, and she was chatting without pause. His friend was quiet, which was not unusual but there was an air of simmering emotion and he dearly love to know how the evening had concluded for them both. He suspected, reading between the lines, that it had been embarrassing on her part and frustrating on his. And this made him chuckle to himself with the kind of childish glee he had not enjoyed in a long while.

Frances was aware that her father was in a strange mood, he had been almost jaunty yesterday but today he was distracted and subdued. She had had a small demonstration of how it would be if he had been a more attentive parent and found that she liked it and wanted more. The warm glow instigated by his praise had stayed with her all day. And when she had her next writing lesson, she tried extra hard to make the loops and curls as beautiful as she could. She wondered why Mistress Harcourt was so extremely talkative today although it was nice to listen to her pleasant voice filling the usually quiet corners of the Great Hall. Mr Gittings seemed quietly amused by something which she found odd because he was blind, and she could not fathom how he could find anything to laugh at now he was so impaired. On the other side of the table was Benedict's tutor, who was, as usual, engaging her brother in a very dull conversation about Greek gods but at the same time he was managing to listen to and join in with Mistress Harcourt's rambling discourse. He laughed too loudly at her quips and agreed too keenly with everything she said. Frances thought he was being remarkably immature, and it was very obvious to her that he had a bit of a passion for her. Frances thought it quite revolting when adults behaved so stupidly — it made her pity them. She curled her lip and ate another large mouthful of ham. She would *never* act in such a demeaning manner.

Valentine de Cheverell thought that every word that dropped from Mistress Harcourt's lips was gilded and encrusted with diamonds and pearls. She seemed keen this morning to capture his attention and he was more than willing to give it. He thought she was finally beginning to appreciate that he was not just a callow youth with no prospects; that he had wit and wisdom and would be able to keep her amused and cherished for an eternity. He was considering penning an ode to her eyes.

Constance wished that Benedict's guileless young tutor would stop gazing at her as though he wanted nothing more than to gorge on her right there at the breakfast table. He really should learn to disguise his feelings so that he didn't become a laughing stock. And, if his employer's smouldering expression was anything to go by, he should be wary of imminently losing his position.

Eventually the meal was over, and Constance took Frances away to give her a lesson in the parlour but just as she was leaving, she turned back to Lucas who was still standing beside the table waiting to help Quinton.

"Lucas, I was wondering if it would be all right if Frances and Benedict wrote to Lady Ursula?"

He looked up and nodded, "Of course. Even if she refuses to come, she would be delighted to receive communications from the children."

Constance thanked him and then Quinton's unsteady progress caught her attention, "You know, a walking cane would be a good idea for Quinton and then he could feel for where the furniture is and have some support and be able to whack the children too if needs be!"

Before Lucas could say it was a good idea, she had gone, and he was left staring at the closing door.

Quinton smiled, "She is going to give some poor fellow a mighty hard life when she finally decides to marry. He will be run ragged."

His companion grunted and informed him shortly that he would go at once and find him one of his father's old walking canes.

The parlour was too stuffy, and Constance suddenly decided to take the lesson outside. Frances questioned the wisdom in this and said the paper would flap and the ink would dry too quickly. Constance just laughed and said there were other ways to make letters.

They reached the small pond at the end of the garden, much neglected but still containing some water and with a flat stone edging upon which they sat down, and Constance handed Frances a thin twig.

"There's your pen and here is a large inkwell full of slimy green ink. You're sitting on your paper."

Frances laughed and dipped her pen into the water and traced a beautifully formed F onto the stone. The sun almost immediately dried it up so she drew it again. The lesson flew by and Constance said that as she had done so well that they would begin to write the letter to her aunt that evening when the heat had died down enough for them to be shut inside.

"This weather is ridiculous. I wonder, will it ever break? It reminds me of childhood summers we spent on the coast, where you had to race to get to the water because the sand was so hot it burnt your feet."

Frances gave her companion a questioning look, "You were allowed to run barefoot — on the seashore?"

Constance gulped, "Only when our mother wasn't looking! Father was very lax in that way and let us run wild but if Mother saw, we were in trouble. She was very particular and liked us to behave properly at all times." This much was true, she thought, but chided herself for the slip-up. She would have to be more careful. It was limiting though; she wanted to share her previous life with the children and tell them about her sister and nephews, but she didn't dare in case she said something careless and caused Frances to start questioning things.

After the lesson they wandered down to the meadow below The Wilderness and sat in the long grass. Constance took her shoes and stockings off and stretched out in the sunshine. Frances looked at her enviously then laughed and followed suit.

After a while Constance sat up and began to gather wildflowers and fashion them into a coronet, which when she'd finished, she placed on Frances's hair and took a mental snapshot of her.

"Come on, I'd better go and see if Mr Gittings needs anything, I expect your father has gone out to do estate business and just abandoned him to his own devices."

She found her stockings and shoes and just then, voices drifted across the hill to them and she turned to look towards Wyck Rissington.

She could just make out a small group of men making their way across the fields in their direction. She and Frances scrambled to their feet and watched as they approached.

'I think they are soldiers," said Frances.

"I think so too. But we have no way of telling which side they're on. They all wear the same kind of uniforms."

"What should we do?" asked Frances nervously.

At this point one of the soldiers called out, "Good afternoon to you, ladies! Be we on the right track for Oxford?"

"You are a little off target," replied Constance, "You're headed south! You need to head south east for Burford."

They kept on walking steadily and Constance saw them exchange some looks she didn't quite like. She had to get Frances away from there. "Frances, you're really fast. I want you to run like the wind and find Oates and Master de Cheverell and anyone else and tell them the soldiers are here. Tell them to guard the house."

"I cannot leave you — !"

"You can. Go on, *run!*"

Frances picked up her skirts and flew away up the field.

"Oi! Where she be goin'?" yelled one of the men.

Constance started to back away and wished she'd put her tennis shoes on. She wanted to give Frances long enough to get to the house, hoping to delay these men before they had decided on a course of action. They appeared to have been just passing by, but she had a really bad feeling. If they were going to Oxford, it was probably to join up with the Royalists troops garrisoned there.

She kept slowly backing. "You need to be heading *that* way," she said pointing off in the general direction of Burford.

One of the soldiers laughed, "I think we be goin' to be a bit busy for a while, ain't we lads!"

Constance turned and ran.

She was no athlete, especially in a long heavy skirt but fear gave her some impetus and she took off like a startled gazelle. There was a volley of shouts behind her and the sound of thumping feet in the grass.

She had just made it to the edge of The Wilderness when a flying tackle brought her down.

The wind was knocked out of her and she couldn't catch her breath.

"I got her lads!" her assailant shouted and pinned her down on the ground. The three others circled, laughing and egging him on, and although she had begun to fight back in earnest, she knew she didn't stand a chance; all she could hope was that she could delay them long enough to give everyone at the house an opportunity to arm themselves.

"Get her skirts up. Go on! Let us have a go! It be months since I 'ad any."

Constance kicked out and managed to smash one in the groin, sending him reeling. She felt rough hands groping her breasts and her petticoats being dragged up around her waist. She closed her eyes and gritted her teeth.

Then a shot rang out.

One of the soldiers staggered backwards, a look of mild surprise on his face, a gaping wound in his cheek spurting blood; he fell to the ground, stone dead.

Then, a heartbeat later, the butt end of a musket demolished another soldier's head.

The final two men took off and ran straight into the newly hired forester steadily pointing a musket right at them, they careered to a halt and put their hands up in surrender.

Constance felt her skirts being tugged gently back into place and someone lifting her.

"I'm fine. You can put me down. I can bloody walk! Are they all dead? I hope they're all dead. Bastards."

"Two dead. Two going to regret what they just tried to do," said Lucas Deverell roughly. "Richard is handy with a musket. He was a soldier before he took up forestry and Oates is wielding my sword as though he were born to it!"

"Good. On second thoughts I feel a bit peculiar you'd better not put me down."

He made a sound halfway between a groan and a laugh.

"Is Frances — ?" she asked.

"She is fine. Out of breath and scared — but fine."

Constance put her head on his shoulder and gave herself up to the delayed surge of terror she had felt and started to tremble uncontrollably.

The solid arms around her tightened their grip as he limped back to the house with her.

"You're making a bit of a habit of this fireman lark," she remarked into his neck.

"Speaking in tongues, Constance. Be quiet."

The Great Hall was cool and shadowy, and Constance took a deep breath and tried desperately to steady herself. She had been deposited into a chair and Lucas Deverell was bellowing for his staff.

"Do you have to shout so loudly?" she asked tremulously.

"We need Mistress Fitch. Where the hell is the woman?" he shouted, and Constance covered her ears.

"You sound like a Vogon. So shouty and rude."

He took no notice of her, "We need a woman to care for you."

"I'm all right. Nothing *happened*. And I certainly don't want *her* looking down on me with that — awful sour face!" She sniffed, "I think I'm just a bit in shock, you know? I'll be fine in a minute. Honestly. Just calm down, *please*."

She looked up at him and he saw how pale she was, and he dragged his hands through his hair in frustration. He had no idea what to do for the best. He had seen everything in his soldiering life, all kinds of deaths and every atrocity man could inflict upon his fellow human being and he thought he had lost his ability to feel anything. When his young daughter had flung herself into his arms, panting and crying and trying to tell him something so urgently and incoherently, he had in an instant become that officer, calm and in control. The armour of authority. As Frances was telling him that Constance was in the meadow with soldiers, Lucas was already preparing his musket and quickly marshalling Oates and sending for Richard and limping steadily towards the meadow.

But then he saw. He saw the soldiers crowding around her on the ground and the years of discipline and training just vanished like smoke — As he raised the musket to take aim, he found he was shaking. He had meant to shoot the soldier right between the eyes but had missed and the musket ball had exploded his cheekbone instead. Then just pure white-hot rage had taken over and a crushing blow from the butt end of his musket had taken the next one down. He would have cheerfully slain all four had Richard not arrived at that moment.

He now had two bodies and two prisoners, a deeply distressed daughter and this remarkable woman who was denying with her words that she was affected by the violence she had suffered, while her eyes were telling him a very different story. He was torn. Soldier, father, enemy — friend? Which was he? He was losing himself in a world he was finding increasingly difficult to understand.

"I must thank you for sending Frances out of harm's way. She was spared the sight — and to warn the household — "

"Don't."

Tears were sliding down her face. "I was so frightened they would — she's so young — ", her face crumpled.

"Constance — for God's sake!"

"I'm so sorry, but if we hadn't been in the meadow — if I had given her the lesson in the parlour as I should — "

Lucas squatted down on his haunches, took her hands away from her face and held them, "The soldiers are to blame, not you. I don't think you realise how much you have helped Frances already — she is a changed child. And I cannot imagine how things would be without you here — you have made such a difference."

"I think I've ruined your life. It was all perfectly ordered before I came."

"Yes, it was," replied Lucas with a crooked smile, "And now it is in complete disarray and the children laugh more. Quinton seems happy that you are here and Master de Cheverall, well, he is in ecstasy, his head bursting with poetry and his heart full of song."

Constance laughed through the tears, "And you?"

"I am slowly becoming reconciled to the lack of discipline and order. Although, I must admit that I am not yet used to the increased levels of anxiety."

"But you have fought in battles!"

"And, yet somehow I find life at the Court House more fraught with danger and stress." He released her hands and stood up, "I am not entirely sure I was cut out for such a challenging home life."

"So, you'll be glad to return to the army then?"

"I shall welcome the peace and quiet," he said with a dry chuckle.

Constance smiled and then, unable to contemplate him leaving, she buried her face in her hands again and started to cry in earnest.

"Oh, damnation!" exclaimed Lucas, "I wish to God that Ursula were here. She would know what to do."

The sobbing continued so he limped quickly out of the Great Hall and returned a few minutes later with Quinton Gittings in tow.

Quinton hearing the uncontrollable weeping coming from Constance, found his way at once to her side and enfolded her in a firm embrace. He held her so, until the crying had subsided.

Lucas Deverell watching this, felt a twinge of some emotion he was reluctant to name and turned on his heel and left the room.

Fourteen

Quinton Gittings sat with Constance until she was able to talk coherently about what had happened and then he listened as she described every moment in stark detail. He allowed her to talk until she was spent, and the tears had dried on her cheeks. He then gently suggested she go upstairs and tidy herself and come back for supper which would soon be on the table.

She thanked him profusely and gave him a warm kiss on the cheek, which, he thought to himself, should perhaps, by rights, have belonged to Lucas but his stupid friend, as usual, had made such a hash of everything that Quinton was reaping the rewards.

Constance was sitting on the edge of her bed, thinking.

She'd stopped crying at last and was feeling empty and blank, as though her head were full of static mist.

Talking about it had helped. Quinton was such a good listener; she suspected he had always been so and that it wasn't just because he had now lost one of his other senses. He cared deeply about his friends and was loyal and trustworthy. Lucas Deverell was trying hard, but he had all the finesse and tenderness of a taproom full of rugby players.

She didn't know how she felt about what had happened; the sudden violence had stunned her both mentally and physically and although she had always advocated fighting back if attacked, when it actually happened to you, there was a void, a time when your body froze, and your brain felt nothing. As though time stopped. By the time you woke up it was too late.

She felt she could have given a better account of herself; she was disappointed that she hadn't been able to fight back. She kept replaying it in her mind and was unable to escape the fact that if Lucas, Oates, and Richard hadn't arrived, the outcome would have been unthinkable.

A timid knock on the door interrupted her dark thoughts.

Frances peeped around the door, "May I come in?"

"Of course! Come and sit by me. I could do with some female companionship."

Frances flushed with delight, "I would have come earlier but Father said you were still very upset and should not be pestered."

Constance took the girl's hand in hers, "You could never pester me! You know, Frances, you were splendid today. If it hadn't been for your fast feet — "

"I know what would have happened, Mistress Harcourt. I have heard what soldiers do and I know you were saving me from them."

Constance enveloped the child in her arms, and they clung onto each other for some time. When they separated, Frances was puffy-eyed and sniffling.

Constance wiped away her tears, "I wish you would call me Constance! Mistress Harcourt makes me sound so very *old!*"

"But it would not be seemly!"

"Oh, pooh to that! Think of me like an aunt. Like Ursula. Please?"

Frances nodded happily, "Constance. It is pretty. And suits you. You *are* constant. You will stay, will you not?"

Hearing the question she had feared, Constance's heart quailed, "I cannot predict what will happen sweet thing, but *whatever* happens I will always do my utmost to find my way back to you. I promise. I want you to remember this — I will *always* be thinking of you and trying to find you again."

Frances looked long and hard into Constance's pale green eyes and nodded, believing her.

Constance made herself go down to supper even though she wasn't hungry and didn't really want to face anyone. Frances escorted her, holding on tightly to her hand. When Constance saw Oates standing in the Great Hall, she went to him and put her hand on his arm and thanked him for having brandished a sword so heroically. He stammered a startled response and later repeated her words verbatim to the kitchen staff with glowing pride, forever after, her faithful slave. Mistress Fitch, for once, kept her own council realising that this might not be the moment to cast aspersions on the conniving harlot.

Everyone was a little too chatty, a little too normal, trying a little too hard — although Valentine de Cheverell was pale and silent and could not meet her eyes. Eventually she had to say something to ease the tension.

She stood up, "I just wish to thank you all for having been so very kind to me. Today is not a day I want to remember for obvious reasons but the one thing I will remember is that you came to rescue me and fought for me. I must remember to thank Richard tomorrow as well. So, to Frances and her fleet feet and brave heart, Lucas for his shooting prowess and *terrible* temper, Oates for his redoubtable swordsmanship, Quinton for his listening skills and sensible words, and finally Valentine for bravely staying behind to protect everyone in the house. You are all my heroes, warriors one and all!" and she raised her glass and drank a toast.

"I hope that is milk," murmured Lucas dryly.

As everyone left the Great Hall after supper, Constance caught up with the tutor and gently persuaded him to look her in the eye. He blushed.

"Someone had to remain behind to protect the children. I'm glad it was you, Valentine. I knew you would have defended them to the death!"

He took her hand and raised it to his lips, "I only wish I could have been the one to save you. I would do anything for you, Mistress Constance."

Constance gently withdrew her hand and smiled, "I know, and I am eternally grateful that Frances and Benedict were in such good hands. None better."

Lucas Deverell coldly observed Valentine de Cheverell making an ass of himself and thought how very typical that Constance should have seen the boy was feeling he had let her down by not dashing to her rescue and she had gone to reassure him.

Quinton arrived at his side, his newly acquired cane tapping the floor, "It is almost as though she has a sixth sense, is it not?"

"Indeed," replied Lucas, "Like you, my friend!"

Quinton laughed, "It would not do for *both* of us to be blind!"

Lucas gave him startled glance, "Are you suggesting — ?"

"Oh, yes. *There are none so blind as those who will not see.*"

"Trust you to throw quotes at my head! What is it that you think I am missing?"

"Oh, so very much, Lucas, so *very* much. And mostly it is your damnable pride getting in the way and your unfounded belief that everyone would be better off without you."

"You are talking nonsense. It must be the blow to the head you suffered."

"Ah, Lucas, I do hope that you see the truth before it is too late. *Time and tide wait for no man.*"

"Perdition! Spare me the damn prosing, Quinton!"

"I realise that it is not my place to say so, but I think it is time you had some gowns of your own, Constance," said Quinton, as they sat comfortably in the parlour. "There is apparently a very creditable local seamstress you could ask to assist you."

Constance was sitting at the writing desk with Frances attempting to pen a letter to Lady Ursula, begging her to come to the Court House; Frances was copying Constance's letters very ably, her tongue sticking out between her lips in avid concentration.

She looked up at the mention of new dresses, "Oh, yes! Nobody should have to wear second-hand clothes. She would look lovely in red or green, would she not? Mother's colours do not suit her as well. And the gowns are a little big and unfashionable now."

Constance was loath to have money wasted on clothes she may not be needing for very long even though the idea was enticing.

Benedict, who was reading a book, curled up in a chair in the corner of the room, snorted, "Gowns!"

"What are you reading Benedict?" asked Quinton.

Benedict didn't look up, "The Man in the Moone."

"What is it about?"

"A Spanish man called Gonsales, flies to the moon pulled by wild swans — or they may be geese — and finds giants called Lunars but becomes homesick for his children and returns to Earth."

Constance's and Lucas's eyes met across the room and, even though she smiled at him, he read in hers a desperate sadness which made him feel utterly powerless.

Benedict continued, "It is a very strange story and difficult to read but Master de Cheverell wishes me to study it. He says it is about more than just a journey to another place; he says it is a way of finding fault with your own country without doing it openly and being punished."

"It sounds most unusual. Have you read Don Quixote yet? There are valuable lessons to be learned from that book too. About misplaced chivalry and a man who says, "*I know who I am!*" Although he is terribly mistaken, and his noble quest is just a fool's errand. A knight errant accompanied by his wise and faithful companion. It is both witty and tragic."

Lucas laughed, "If what you are so obviously alluding is true, you must be Sancho Panza then, dear friend?"

"Well, I am certainly not the idiot who jousts at windmills!"

"No, you are the idiot who *follows* the idiot who jousts at windmills!"

Quinton chuckled, “And fair Dulcinea? Who might that be, I wonder?”

Lucas Deverell eyed his steward with wary amusement, “Are we talking about Dulcinea or Aldonza Lorenzo?”

Quinton shrugged expressively, “That is up to the fool with the lance. He cannot have it both ways. He needs to make up his mind — is it to be windmills, the impossible dream of perfect Dulcinea or the bawdy reality of Aldonza.”

The smile faded from Lucas's eyes, “Did he not, in the end, choose death and, in renouncing his chivalrous self, did he not also renounce the fair but imaginary Dulcinea?”

“As I have already mentioned, Don Quixote was a deluded fool,” said Quinton.

Benedict rolled his eyes, “Perhaps I *will* read that book next,” he announced, “Although Don Quixote sounds even more mad than the Spaniard and his geese — or swans.”

Constance looked up, “I think, on reflection, I would rather be compared to Aldonza; at least she worked for a living albeit as a — lady of the night. I would rather that than have my eyebrows described as *rainbows*!”

The two gentlemen fell silent.

“You have studied Don Quixote?" asked Quinton Gittings after a moment’s pause, trying and failing to mask his surprise.

“Well, we read it at school although not in the original Spanish I must admit, and I wouldn’t go so far to say I *studied* it!”

There was a weighty silence. Lucas cleared his throat.

Constance fixed them both with an aggrieved look which only one of them could appreciate. Then catching Lucas's warning glance, she sighed and turned her attention back to Frances and her lettering.

“We must tell him, Constance. It is the only course of action. Otherwise, he is going to suspect us of being duplicitous and that I could not tolerate. He was ever a perceptive man and removing one of his senses has emphasised that ability not diminished it. He is already aware that something is awry."

"It isn't something you can just slap down into a conversation! He'll probably think we've lost our minds. What do we say? I mean, here's a nice glass of ale and oh, by the way I'm from the future? Do your lot still burn witches?"

"My lot?"

"Puritans."

"You do know that I am not a Puritan, do you not? I am for Parliament and I happen to be a Protestant. Quinton is a Catholic and supports the King. Neither of us is extreme in our religious beliefs and are only got involved because it was forced upon us. If we had had the choice, we would be farming the land and caring for our dependents."

"Oh," said Constance, whose grasp of the distinctions between the many and varied religions was poor at best. It seemed to her that each one was not much different to the next and that their members were fighting over the most trivial differences like whether stained glass windows were a good thing or not. "If you're not an actual Puritan does that mean that you're still religious — you know, like church every Sunday?"

"Of course, in ordinary circumstances. The war means that our usual behaviour has had to be modified somewhat. Do you not go to church?"

"Jeepers, no! There are still, sadly, all kinds of fanatical religions, in my time but there are also a great many atheists and agnostics and kind-hearted Jainists and those who drift about with flowers in their hair — "

"Like you."

Constance laughed, "I *am* basically a hippy — which is someone who believes in Mother Nature and — " She was about to say 'free love' but thought better of it as she didn't fancy explaining that concept to a man with such a strict moral code. And, anyway, she wasn't sure that she believed in free love herself. She had often thought herself to be a little bit puritanical. Tova had always considered her to be strait-laced. And now she found herself trapped in the Land of the Strait-Laced and it turns out she's actually more permissive than she thought.

"So, will you tell Quinton?" asked Lucas. "I am not sure I have the ability to explain."

"All right but I don't know how we're going to convince him —"

"We cannot even show him the books and the sun lantern to persuade him."

Constance gave him a curious look, "What convinced you?"

"I saw you there, with the boys. To start with I thought you some sort of phantom but when I touched your hand, I knew. But he cannot see so — "

"I'm going to have to convince him with words alone."

"You have me to support you."

'That's a comforting thought. He could never accuse you of being fanciful."

"Should I be insulted?"

"You're a stolid man of your time, Lucas Deverell. No insult intended. Actually, I think you're quite a liberal, which is a good thing, in my opinion."

"That gives me hope."

"Although, your temper can be a little uncertain."

"For which I can only apologise. I would like to blame the Army, but I fear I could be a disagreeable child. Ursula will tell you, I am sure."

"Oh, I do hope she will come. I long to have a woman to talk with."

"I will send the letter by messenger tomorrow. As long as he is allowed to pass with no incident, we should have an answer within a few days. Banbury is not far. A mere forty miles."

Constance was suddenly struck by an unpleasant thought, "But, what if Lady Ursula doesn't like me? She might take against me like Mistress Fitch!"

"That is just not possible. Under the austere exterior, my sister has a very amiable nature and although she can be quite forthright at times, she is, on the whole, warm-hearted. And you are — very easy to like," said Lucas Deverell with a puzzled frown, as though he had at that moment acknowledged something to himself and found it was not at all what he had expected.

"Gosh! Thank you. That's very — nice of you."

"So, when shall we broach the matter with Quinton?" asked Lucas desperate to change the subject.

Constance flicked him a thoughtful glance, understanding that something had spooked him; he had shied like a skittish horse.

"I suppose the sooner the better?"

After breakfast the following morning Quinton Gittings was sitting comfortably in the parlour enjoying a nice cup of chocolate when the world as he knew it came to a shuddering standstill. It seemed to him that one minute the earth was spinning in one direction and the next it had stopped and taken an entirely different course. He credited himself with being possessed of an enlightened mind and was fairly certain that he was not easily shocked or dismayed but as Constance spoke, he felt that certainty wither away. He wished he could see her face, he felt sure if he could look into her eyes, he would be able to see the truth and accept whatever that truth might turn out to be.

He allowed her to talk without interruption whilst in his head arguments were being made and counter-argued and summarily discounted. He noted that her voice was a little tremulous and that she was choosing her words with unusual caution. He also noted that she sat very still as she spoke, her usually expressive hand movements were being held in check, he could feel it. He was pretty certain that those hands were clasped together tightly in an anguished knot. This confession was costing her dear. He had grown to like her, nay, even love her, like a sister and he had no wish for that to change. He could count the members of his own family on slightly less than one hand: a brother he had not seen these last ten years, a doddering and disobliging uncle hidden away somewhere in the wilds of Yorkshire, and some distant cousin he could recall meeting at his father's funeral when he was a mere stripling and had never seen since. For all he knew he was the last of his branch of Gittings and the very last to carry the name. He was therefore even more reliant upon his dear friend and this extraordinary woman who had, apparently, come to them from another time.

Her words faded away. There was a tense silence.

"Quinton?" said Lucas gently, "It is the truth. I would lay my life on it."

And so, his world was turned upside-down and inside-out.

Fifteen

He felt two pairs of eyes looking at him. He sensed their concern and oddly, palpable fear. If ever there had been a moment when he regretted that damn firing pan blowing up in his face, this was it. He could just make out the bulky shadow of Lucas Deverell against the window, like a large brooding storm cloud. And closer to him, the blurred pale oval of Constance's face.

He knew that the words he said next would be some of the most important and life-altering words that would ever leave his lips.

"I cannot truly fathom what you are telling me, Constance — it is far beyond the limited scope of my poor brain. But I have felt for some time that there was something singular about you and your sudden arrival at the Court House, but I have not been able to even guess at what that might be. There is, for instance, the unusual way you talk, the words you use and your knowledge of medicine and literature; these things first alerted me to there being some inexplicable difference but never in my wildest imaginings did I think that the answer would be so — far-fetched. And yet, after listening to Benedict last night, talking about his book — I see that there are erudite men in this world who have impossible dreams. Like Don Quixote with his windmills and mad obsession with Dulcinea — who was but a figment of his imagination and the Spaniard and his wild swans. Perhaps there are things which we cannot fully understand. After all, we believe in a God we cannot see. *"There are more things in heaven and earth, Horatio, than are dreamt of in your philosophy."*

"Hamlet," said Constance quietly.

"There. That is what I was alluding to. You know too much even for one of those rare bookish females. And the medicine?"

"Antibiotics — they're widely used in my time largely because of the work of Alexander Fleming at the beginning of the 20th century. They have saved millions of lives."

"Including mine."

"Yes, thankfully. I know none of this makes any sense, Quinton, but it was Lucas who brought me here. There was some peculiar connection with him which broke through some barrier between our worlds. My nephew Guy would have an explanation, I'm sure — a very lengthy one! To be perfectly honest I'm not sure I believe it myself!"

Quinton Gittings raised his eyebrows, "I think we had best leave the mechanics of the travelling itself to Guy and try to deal with the results. Which is you, dear Constance, *here.* That is real enough for me. And the fact that Lucas, one of the least imaginative or impressionable men I have ever known seems to be convinced, then — I must be too."

Lucas managed a laugh, "I will tolerate these unjustified slights upon my character if it means that you have not consigned us to the Devil."

"The Devil cannot have you yet awhile, dear fellow. Not until I have discovered the reason behind all of this."

"Ah, yes, there must *always* be logic. This is why I employ you as my steward, of course - your unfailing quest for rationality."

"I thought it was because nobody else would work for someone with such a volatile temper."

Constance, watching this exchange, felt it was probably just papering over the cracks but at least the two men were able to talk light-heartedly with this all out in the open. She had feared that Quinton would allow the austere and fastidious side of his nature to overwhelm his lifelong friendship with Lucas. It seems the long-standing attachment could withstand not only their political and religious differences but also the intrusion of a headstrong time traveller into their previously well-managed lives.

"So — you are prepared to believe us?" she asked tentatively.

Quinton smiled, "Looking at it dispassionately, which is how I tend to look at everything, I see that you are both convinced that this is true and because I have deep faith in my circumspect choice of friends, I must admit that I am ready and willing to believe."

Lucas and Constance looked at each other across the room, both relieved and surprised and, after all the explaining, at a loss for words.

"Am I to suppose that we are now awaiting a response from your nephews about the desecration of the church?" said Quinton.

Constance made a face at Lucas, "I promise that given a few years you will not be able to see the carving at all unless you know where to look! It will be very hard to spot. It was a necessary evil. I will go and inspect the virtual postbox later to see if there has been an answer. And I will also find Richard to thank him for his timely and brave intervention."

"You will find him just down past the bridge; he is clearing in Henever Wood. He has been, until recently, a journeying woodsman but I am employing him permanently to restore the estate woodlands. Take someone with you for — "

"A *nursemaid*!" Constance rolled her eyes. "You're not going to insist on a permanent bodyguard, I trust?!"

Lucas scowled at her, "There may be other soldiers roaming the district. You must be more careful — "

Constance bit her lip, "Oh, I all right. But I can't take Oates or the children because of the, you know — *box!*"

Lucas sighed, "Of course. I had not thought about that."

"I would offer to escort you, Constance, but it would be a case of the escort needing to be escorted," said Quinton with a wry smile. "I think you had better go with her, Lucas. You would provide ample support if needs be."

"As ever, Quinton, a reasonable solution."

"But I don't want to be a nuisance and take you away from your work," said Constance slightly irritably, thinking it would have been nice if Lucas had offered to take her instead of being persuaded by his friend.

Lucas crossed the room and stood looking down at her, a mischievous smile sparking his grey eyes, "I cannot think why I did not offer to take you in the first place. My mind must have been elsewhere. It has been a trying morning."

Constance gave him an old-fashioned look, "It seems to me that you are very easily tried then. As my mother used to say, *Manners maketh man.* Yours have been sadly neglected and need some tender loving care, not unlike your garden."

"I will make a concerted effort to improve them just to please you," he replied cheerfully.

"It's probably too late to change them," said Constance bitterly.

They approached the wall by the brook and Constance stopped a little way off, "I don't hear anything. It's completely quiet."

"That might not have any bearing upon it."

"I know. I just — "

"I will open it and then we will know."

"No! Let's do it on the way home. I just feel something's not right at the moment."

"All right. Let us go and find Richard, then."

Henever Wood sloped down the hill, the trees clinging to the fiercely sloping flanks; the innocuous looking brook had over time cut a steep gully into the hillside, making the terrain on either side of what was basically a ravine difficult to negotiate. Constance had played in the woods as a child and picked the bluebells and snowdrops that grew there but it was easy to miss your footing and slide down the treacherous banks ending up knee-deep in the icy water. She found that hampered by her skirts she only had one hand free to hold onto branches and tree trunks to steady herself, so when Lucas Deverell proffered a large hand to help her, she was grateful for it and grasped it quite firmly and without argument.

"I'd forgotten just what an ordeal this could be! Not for the faint-hearted. I was a lot younger and a good deal more reckless when I was last in here," she gasped, as she slithered from one tree to the next. Eventually they reached the little brook carving its relentless way down into the valley, more of a gorge than a stream. The water chuckled happily but Constance could remember being caught in it for a very stressful and uncomfortable hour before rescue came, so she knew its merry song was but a masquerade, concealing a darker side.

A bonfire burned steadily in a clearing, where the tangled and disordered undergrowth was being carefully ordered by a stocky young man wearing a leather jerkin, his dark blonde hair caught back in a ponytail, a battered black tricorne jammed on the back of his head and a short clay pipe clenched between his teeth. He stopped working as they drew near and doffed his cap.

"Constance, this is Mr Richard Thorne, our new forester. Richard, this is Mistress Harcourt, a cousin of mine.;"

Constance instinctively stuck out her hand and, after the briefest hesitation the young man, wiped his hand on his grubby breeches and shook her hand firmly. She beamed at him, thinking what a very attractive man he was, blue-eyed and with a broad grin; then she remembered that he had seen her during the attack by the soldiers and felt the colour creeping up over her cheeks.

"Good afternoon, Mr Thorne, I wanted to come especially to thank you for your timely intervention yesterday. You were terribly brave."

"Afternoon, Mistress Harcourt — Sir Lucas. Happy to oblige, Mistress. Only sorry I was not allowed to shoot them."

"Me too! Except I'm not allowed to say that apparently! I understand you were a soldier until recently? It must be a great change to be working in the woods."

"Aye, Mistress. I was a forester before, but the war put paid to that and then a musket ball put paid to my soldiering."

"I am so sorry. Do you miss the army?"

A quick glance at Lucas, "I miss serving under Sir Lucas, Mistress. We had some times I will never forget but also times that stop me sleepin' easily these days."

"I cannot even begin to imagine what you must've been through but I'm more than glad that you survived and that you know how to wield a musket so expertly."

"I am too. Those two soldiers have been handed over to our local militia and will be harshly dealt with I am sure."

"Oh, I did wonder — ," said Constance, "At least they cannot go on and hurt anyone else."

"True, Royalists have a bad reputation for pillagin' — and other such things."

"Well, we will not keep you, Richard," said Lucas Deverell. "Mistress Harcourt was insistent that she wanted to thank you personally, even though she was forced to endanger life and limb to do so! I shall now see her safely back up to the village. Come, Constance."

The return journey was tortuous and had it not been for Lucas having a very firm hold on her, she would have slid on her backside all the way down to the gully several times. At the top of the ridge, he released her hand and for several minutes she felt completely bereft and wondered how she could engineer the situation so that he would have to hold her hand again. She then admonished herself and tried hard to persuade herself that it was just a passing fancy brought on by the predicament she found herself in: sheer loneliness and a longing for her family. Why she should be developing any kind of emotional attachment to such a tiresomely chauvinistic Neanderthal, she had no idea. If one happened to catch sight of his face at the wrong angle, his broken nose became difficult to ignore and looked as though he had been at the bottom of many collapsed rugby scrums, but she then argued that when he looked at her from under his deep, lazy eyelids, with that glint in his eye, she felt a little flutter in her chest which made her wonder whether travelling through time had fried her brain. He would certainly not have fared well under Guy's close scrutiny; he would have been very firmly put in his place and given an emphatic lecture on political correctness. Although, thought Constance, with a wry smile, Guy would certainly have approved the long hair and lace collars and cuffs.

As they made their way along the path through the woods, Constance couldn't help remembering other times in that place: climbing trees and building dens, picking cobnuts and damsons and sloes for sloe gin. Such ridiculously innocent times compared with these days and they seemed so far away, no more than a dream. What was happening to her? Her real life was fading, becoming bleached by the sun, so that she could no longer see the true colours and tones; like one of those old Kodak photos in the family album, turning orange with age and then slowly vanishing leaving just ghostly outlines and a smudge of unrecognisable shadow.

As they reached the bridge over the brook, Constance felt a sudden chill run down her spine. Her skin prickled and the hair at the back of her neck stood on end.

"Lucas!" she whispered and grabbed his arm.

He looked down at her from quizzical grey eyes, "What is it?"

"I think — I can feel something in the air."

As they drew closer to the wall, the feeling became stronger and Constance was pulling Lucas along, "It's really buzzing! Quickly, get the box out!"

Lucas prised the container out of its secret place and handed it to her.

Sitting on the bank, she unclipped the lid and opened it.

The strange feeling became like a throbbing pulse in her head, she thought this is what tinnitus must feel like. It was actually painful and a little scary.

Inside the box was a letter, more photographs of the boys, Tova and Badger, and some close-up photos of some lichen-covered stone. These Constance peered at closely.

"Nothing," she said with satisfaction. "Absolutely bloody nothing! Look!" She thrust the photographs at Lucas, who took them and examined them.

"So — remind me — this means — ?"

"This means that I can't mess up the future! This is bloody brilliant! I can't kill my own great-grandmother by doing something stupid with the timeline. Although, it also means I can't alter the future in order to benefit anyone either. So, by saving Quinton I haven't changed anything that has already happened. It's sort of a mixture of relief and frustration. Part of me *longs* to meddle and change the bad things — I can, but it won't make a *lasting* difference. It won't alter history. What will be, will be."

Lucas nodded, "I think I am beginning to understand. We can be influenced by the future, but the future cannot be influenced by us. Is that about the crux of it?"

"By George, he's got it!"

"Who is George?"

Constance laughed, "Never mind, it's just a quote from a — film — no, never mind. Some things aren't worth explaining."

Constance quickly wrote a note telling the boys how the antibiotics had saved Quinton and how Guy would have laughed to hear her trying to explain time travel to a gentleman from the seventeenth century and how much she was missing them, and she put it in the box and Lucas returned the box to its hidey-hole and they stood for a moment just staring at it as though they expected it to disappear in a puff of smoke.

"I can still hear something but it's getting fainter now, it's like your bees, a sort of deep thrumming sound but at the same time it seems to disturb the air, causing ripples," said Constance as they made their way back to the house. "I thought Mr Thorne was really nice."

Lucas grunted.

Constance smiled, "A very likeable fellow."

Another grunt.

Constance laughed.

"Such kind blue eyes and an adorable smile!"

Silence.

She chortled to herself and then caught sight of the dark look on his face.

"I'm only *joking*! Jeepers! Where's your sense of humour?"

"As you keep so charmingly pointing out — I do not have one."

"Oh, my! Is it because he was your subordinate in the army?"

"He was my Sergeant Major and very competent he was too."

"How was he injured?"

"Musket ball to the back of the head. They couldn't remove it all, so he has some still lodged in his skull. But it means he was discharged."

"That's awful. But kind of you to take him on as forester."

"Not kind at all. I would have been a fool not to employ him. He is damn good at his job. And he was a very fine soldier. Brave and resourceful. He was with me when I was injured, got me to the field hospital, never left my side, and then brought me home."

"I must remember to give him a big hug next time I see him."

"Constance!"

"I'm just saying that I'm grateful he saved you! Calm down."

Lucas Deverell glowered down at her, his temper fraying at the edges. It was as though she were goading him on purpose. He had no idea why some of the things she said were so provoking, but he found it difficult to stay composed when she seemed determined to nettle him. She cast him a mischievous glance from her lively pale green eyes and he took a deep breath because he was not used to anyone mocking him. It had come as something of a shock to him that anyone might find him ridiculous or that he would mind so much that any female, especially *this* female, found him to be laughable when he had shown his mettle by leading men into battle. He felt he deserved some respect but this woman, this maddening, captivating, impossible woman seemed to think he needed constantly reminding of his defects.

Constance sighed, seeing him gallantly fight the urge to shout at her; she suddenly felt ashamed that she should have teased him when he really knew no better. It was as bad as baiting a poorly trained Rottweiler and expecting it to understand your reasoning.

"Oh, my giddy aunt, I am *so* sorry, Lucas! I'm used to being with three really annoying boys who tease each other all the time. I shouldn't be such a malicious cow."

She looked so concerned that his outrage immediately abated.

"No, *I* am sorry that I am so irascible. Ever thus, I am afraid."

At this point they were strolling through the gates of the Court House and were surprised to hear a babble of voices coming from the front of the house. Constance glanced up at her companion nervously, "Now what? You don't think it's soldiers — ?"

"Even if it is, I am here and I will let no harm befall you. I swear."

She found her hand being firmly clasped in his and said a silent thank you to whichever friendly god had arranged that.

They approached the house, and the babble became louder, until they were nearly at the steps where they could see a rider in a dusty army uniform, slumped on an exhausted horse, being fended off by Oates holding a wavering musket, a stableboy with a rake, two kitchen maids, and the cook, all talking at once.

Constance's heart sank. She thought she knew what this was about. She tugged on Lucas's hand and tried to stop him heading towards the inevitable.

He stopped and frowned at her, "It is just a messenger."

"I know. But he's in uniform."

"Yes, I can see that. Why are you so frightened? Is it because of the soldiers — ?"

"No, you big idiot! He's come to make you go back to the army."

"We knew this day would come. I am prepared."

"Well, bully for *you! I'm* not!"

"But, Constance, I have no choice. I must go. They will need all their commanders for the last push."

Constance bit her lip, hard. She mustn't say anything. She must let him go and fight this futile first war not knowing that there are two more to come in quick succession. Not knowing the outcome or the appallingly high body count.

She closed her eyes and let go of his hand.

Sixteen

Constance watched impassively while Lucas dispersed the maids and the cook, carefully removed the musket from a quivering Oates and told the stableboy to put the rake back in the stable before he hurt someone with it. He then had a stony-faced discussion with the messenger, who handed him a letter which he opened and quickly read and only after he had folded the paper up did he glance up at her. Their eyes met and Constance knew.

She hadn't moved since they'd arrived back at the house. She seemed rooted to the spot. Her eyes not leaving him. As though by sheer force of will, she could make him stay.

He came to stand beside her.

"It is time. They are amassing the troops in the West Country and need everyone."

"When?"

"Now. I have orders to leave immediately."

Constance could feel her heart rate accelerating and a wave of panic washed over her. She was to be trapped in this place with a couple of children, a bunch of random servants, and a blind man, in the middle of a bloody civil war. She realised she had only managed to keep her cool so far because of the presence of this man beside her; he had held everything together and provided the stability she needed to keep the overwhelming anxiety at bay. She had managed to hold herself together because he provided her with stable support, like a sturdy drawbridge or a muscular Rottweiler. Without him she would be vulnerable on all sides.

He was trying to read her face, "Ursula will hopefully be here soon. She will help. You will have companionship and she knows how to manage the staff. You will like her. She is nothing like me, I promise."

"I am used to you now," said Constance in a suffocated voice. "I don't think I can do this alone."

"You will not be alone. Quinton will guide you and Ursula — "

"They're not *you!*"

"Constance, you have to understand, I do not have a choice. I *must* go. Fairfax has been at Sherborne Castle and Prince Rupert is holding Bristol."

"I don't give a flying fuck about Fairfax and bloody Bristol! I want you to stay here!"

"You are being unreasonable. And unladylike — "

"I know but I'm under a good deal of stress," she said sulkily.

"I must go and see to things before I go. Quinton, the children — "

"Oh, fine! Go on. I really don't give a damn."

He stared down at her for a long moment, but she refused to meet his eyes, knowing that she was being childish and making his departure even more traumatic.

"Very well," he murmured and turned on his heel and walked away from her.

She watched him go and wanted to run after him, but her legs wouldn't budge.

Lucas Deverell was troubled. Never before had he thought twice about abandoning his family and heading off to war. Leaving his children with his sister and brother-in-law was the nearest he had come to having a crisis of conscience over his role as a father. His duty to his country was paramount. He had always been certain that his choices were made for the right reason. Now, as he sought out his friend Quinton Gittings to tell him the news, he was questioning his decisions and seeing those angry green eyes baldly accusing him of dereliction of his duty as head of the household. He was suddenly aware that he was reluctant to leave. Quinton was, as expected, sanguine about the prospect of being in charge of the family for an unspecified amount of time and promised to do his best to help Constance in the months ahead. The children were less amenable: Frances, who would have usually cast her eyes to the floor and said nothing, flew into a fury and informed him he was a terrible father and that he was not to be surprised to find them all dead in their beds on his return, and Benedict confounded him by bursting into noisy sobs.

He looked at them in utter astonishment. This was not how he had imagined his departure. It was usually brief and well-ordered, and he was able to put them out of his mind the moment they were out of sight.

He had no idea how to cope with this onslaught of emotion so he did what he thought Constance would have done — he gathered them both up into his arms and embraced them. Frances stopped her tirade and Benedict's tears started to dry up. He promised faithfully that he would be back as soon as he could and made them swear that they would help Quinton and Constance and Aunt Ursula run the estate while he was gone. He made a particular point of instructing them to take especially good care of Constance as she had no family of her own close-by.

He then talked to his staff, all gathered in the Great Hall to see him off and reminded them that he expected them to behave exactly as though he was still there and in charge. Afterwards, he took Mistress Fitch aside and told her that he was depending upon her to make sure that everything ran smoothly and that she was not to forget where her duties lay. Mistress Fitch bridled but managed to keep her tongue between her teeth.

Lucas then went over to Oates and told the delighted footman how highly he regarded him and that he was to guard the children and the womenfolk with his life. Oates was only too happy to agree, seeing himself in his mind's eye as a sort of Saint George.

Valentine de Cheverell was also more than ready to promise to lay down his young life for Mistress Harcourt and the children and swore that nothing on earth would make him abandon his post.

He found Richard Thorne in the stable yard and told this redoubtable young soldier that he could only leave to do his duty because he knew the forester was at hand to protect his family. He also, in as roundabout way as he could, warned Richard that some people could be headstrong at times and might need gentle persuasion to steer them away from a dangerous course.

The forester nodded, "You mean Mistress Harcourt, sir? I will do my best."

Lucas smiled, "Very astute. Although you did not hear it from me!"

"I take your warning, sir."

The stable lad had strapped his bags and weapons onto the saddle and brought the horse around to the front of the house. The messenger having been given refreshment and a short while to rest his weary bones, was waiting impatiently.

Lucas had changed into his full uniform, with breastplate and sash and thigh-high boots. He looked around the small knot of his friends, family, and staff and could see one face was missing. Where the hell was she? He had no time to search for her for the messenger was restless to start their journey. He let out a string of curses and damned all women, but particularly this one, to perdition.

He mounted up and wheeled his horse away towards the gates.

"Damn her!" he muttered darkly and pulling the horse up angrily, he turned in his saddle to look back over his shoulder.

There she was, standing to the side of the small gathering, her face pale and her eyes on him.

He threw himself from his horse and strode with his halting gait back to her.

Her eyes widened and she took a step away.

Lucas Deverell swept her up into a crushing embrace, her feet came off the ground and he roughly kissed her open mouth until she kissed him back. He then deposited her back onto the ground and stood staring down at her.

"Be here when I return," he said hoarsely, and he turned away and within seconds was galloping away down the lane.

They listened to the sound of the hoofbeats thumping away into the distance, like a fading heartbeat, and then slowly dispersed back into the house; the tutor escorting Quinton back to the parlour and Benedict following, sniffing miserably.

Frances quickly dashed to Constance's side and put her arms about her trembling body. She buried her head into her shoulder and wept.

Constance was still staring at the last place she had seen Lucas, by the gates, a last brief glance over his shoulder and he was gone. She could still feel his mouth on hers and the hard metal of the breastplate against her breasts. She would probably be covered in bruises in the morning. How bloody typical of him not to think that she would be crushed against the hard metal! How careless of him to kiss her in front of everyone! How would they react to such a show of unbridled passion? And then to just *leave* her to deal with the fallout! Typical! Oh, god but she wanted him back! Ridiculous man! Why had he waited until the last minute to kiss her? He had had plenty of opportunities. She almost stamped her foot in frustration. Then she slowly became aware that his daughter was clinging to her like a drowning kitten clings to a passing twig.

"Frances," she whispered because her voice seemed to have disappeared, "He'll be back. I know he will. He *must.* I cannot live — "

Frances raised her head, "He kissed you very *thoroughly!*"

Constance gave her a watery smile, "He did indeed. I shall be having words with him about that in good time! In front of all the staff! In front of Mistress Fitch! I am already no better than a harlot in her eyes. Stupid man."

"He has always been a bit lacking in understanding. Will he be all right, do you think?"

"He damn well better be! I have things I need to say to him!"

Frances laughed and gave Constance another quick squeeze before letting her go.

Lucas Deverell berated himself all the way down the hill and into the valley. How could he have been so stupid? To kiss her like that in front of everyone! To create such an unseemly exhibition! What had he been thinking? And then to just leave her to face the consequences by herself. What a complete fool. She would never forgive him. But then he thought, bullishly, she *had* kissed him back quite ardently; in fact, he had been quite taken aback by her response, so he had hopes that she might not have been entirely averse to his advances. God in heaven! He did not want to leave her. He must have uttered something aloud because the messenger asked if he was all right.

His biggest regret about the whole shambles was having worn his damned breastplate. He realised when he had embraced her that not only would she have been extremely uncomfortable, but he had missed out on the feel of her body being pressed to his. It took several miles of hard riding to dampen his ardour.

Constance went straight to the parlour to find Quinton. She needed to talk. She wanted to discuss her feelings with him. She was bursting with a desire to share her raw emotions with anyone who would listen, and Quinton was such a keen listener. Frances had gone up to her room to find her shawl and Constance wanted to just let the words fall out of her so that she could relive that last moment.

Quinton Gittings heard her footsteps approaching hastily and she flew into the parlour as though fired from a cannon.

Only then did the impetus seem to dwindle and she slowed to standstill in the middle of the room.

"Quinton, I — "

He waited.

She took another step. "I — "

He smiled benignly at the soft blur of her.

He heard her throw herself into the chair beside his and sigh deeply.

He said nothing. She made a fretful sound and tapped her foot restlessly.

"Honestly! Can you credit it! He — *kissed* me! In front of everyone! Stupid oaf!" she finally exclaimed.

"Yes, I know," said Quinton, "I heard what they were saying around me. Apparently, it was quite impressive. Typically decisive."

"Actually, a bit bloody late, if you ask me!"

"That is also typical. But, when he finally makes up his mind to do something, it can be a wondrous sight to behold."

"I'm glad you *didn't* see it. You'd have been shocked. I doubt Mistress Fitch will ever speak to me again. She already thinks I'm in league with the devil. This will surely confirm her worst suspicions."

Quinton laughed, "Yes, I am afraid you may be right, she only ever loved one other and that was Esther. Devoted to her. In her mind I feel she still hopes Esther will one day be back and she is saving Lucas for her. And, you know, I would *not* be shocked. I am happy to know that Lucas has finally let down his guard enough for someone to sneak underneath it. He has had those enormous fists up for so long now I thought he had forgotten there was any other way."

"But why did he have to wait until the very last minute so that I didn't have time to tell him — ?"

"Tell him? How you feel? How *do* you feel, Constance?"

A slight pause and another sigh, "It's so complicated. I don't even know myself really. I only know that I want to be with him. I want those big stupid arms around me. I want him to look at me from those sleepy eyes and — well, you know!"

"Yes, I do. You know he has been behaving very out of character for some while now — since you arrived so precipitously into our lives. I have never known him to be this unsure of himself. Or — so contented to just be here at the Court House; usually he is champing at the bit to get away. Anything rather than having to confront his emotions or deal with human frailty in all its naked frustrating glory."

"I've *ruined* his life," said Constance mournfully. "I've taken a perfectly good Roundhead and broken him."

A choke of laughter escaped Quinton, "He was broken *before* you came! You have found some of the missing pieces and fitted them back together. Given time I truly believe that you could make him whole again."

Constance put a hand over her mouth to stifle the sobs that wanted to come tearing out, "What if I haven't *got* time? What if I'm forced to go back? What if he gets — *killed?*"

"You cannot live your life in a state of foreboding, my dear girl. We cannot predict what will happen and it is just as well because otherwise we would be too scared to do anything. Now, all we have to do is keep this family together, to make sure the estate does not go to rack and ruin and pray that Lucas will come home soon."

She sniffed forlornly and wiped her face on her skirt. "I know you're right, but it's come as something of a shock to me. I never expected to fall in love with someone from another century or with someone who is so bloody-minded and politically incorrect. It really makes me wonder if I didn't suffer some sort of brain damage on my way here."

"Fall in love? You love him?"

"Unfortunately, I think so."

"Well, then it's imperative that we all find a way to survive because, although I do not think he realises it yet, Lucas is in love with you too."

Constance did all that was necessary to make sure Frances and Benedict knew that they were going to be nurtured and not abandoned and she quickly established a routine where everyone understood that their individual skills could bring something valuable to the table. She knew from listening to her friends talking about human resource management, which until this moment had been just senseless corporate jargon to her, that it was her job to make sure everyone was happy in their work.

She busied herself from dawn until dusk encouraging and cajoling, lending a hand wherever necessary and suggesting easier solutions. It left her exhausted and unable to spend much time moping. She found that as long as she kept moving that she couldn't dwell on a certain pair of sleepy bedroom eyes and the urgent message they had tried to convey to her in those last few minutes.

She replayed all their moments together like a favourite film, stopping and rewinding the best bits until they were in danger of being worn out by overuse. Then she would pull herself up and give herself a mental shake and tell herself not to be so teenage and obsessive. She knew Tova would be giving her that older sister look which would remind her that at her advanced age she should behave with some kind of decorum and preferably not be cutting out photos of him and sticking them on her dressing table mirror.

She was trying desperately not to plague Quinton with too many questions about his friend even though he was always more than happy to talk about him. She didn't want him to think she was destined for the East Wing like the first Mrs Rochester.

A week passed and the heatwave still refused to break. The fields were parched and turning brown and the lane had dried into hard ruts, the air was heavy with pollen and dust and even the wildlife seemed to be lethargic.

It was too hot to sit outside and too dark and cold inside. She longed for a glass of lemonade or an iced coffee but had to make do with lukewarm small beer.

She continued with the writing lessons for Frances and began to teach her drawing and painting as well; they would take their paints out and sit in the garden in the evenings and paint a little corner of the estate. Benedict and Valentine de Cheverell would act out scenes from a Shakespeare play or shout lines of poetry across the parterre at each other. Constance thought Valentine a little vapid, but he was determined to show that he was a good tutor and worthy of her admiration. She was very careful to give him no accidental hint of returning his affection but hoped that as he had been a witness to Lucas kissing her, he must have a very clear picture now of how the land lay and would certainly have no desire to antagonise the man-mountain that was his employer.

They spent several afternoons being taught archery by Richard Thorne who had kindly offered his services, but it had quickly deteriorated into a competition between boys and girls with the girls proving to be more accurate and not so inclined to rush their shots. Constance, in an unaccustomed moment of competitiveness, didn't let on that she had practiced archery with her nephews, using her father's bow, and won the whole tournament by stealth, much to Benedict's disgust. Frances had crowed in delight, clapping her hands and dancing around her brother just to rile him until reluctantly Constance had to rein them in and give a short lecture on fair play and how unbecoming it was to be boastful. They hung their heads and Frances blushed rosily and apologised. Benedict was then, despite the reprimand, determined to win at every other game they played, whether it was hopscotch or blind man's bluff and Constance noted that there was a certain set to his mouth when he was under pressure that reminded her strongly of his father.

Every so often, when she was between tasks, she would wander idly up to the Long Gallery and stand in front of the painting of Colonel Sir Lucas Deverell and stare longingly at his face. It was a remarkable likeness capturing both his impatience and intelligence and conveying a feeling that he was about to snap at the artist if he didn't get a damn move on. Sometimes she couldn't believe that this commanding figure of a man had lifted her off her feet and ruthlessly kissed her in front of a stunned audience of more than half a dozen people.

She was also waiting impatiently for a letter from Lady Ursula, but the days crawled by with no reply to their begging letter. Quinton reassured her that she would hear eventually but reminded her that communication was not very advanced, every letter having to be transported by either a personal messenger or if you happened to be lucky enough to be on a postal route, by a scarlet liveried postboy, which could take days or sometimes weeks and that was only if the poor unfortunate messenger wasn't set upon by thieves or pillaging soldiers or thrown from his horse into a ditch. Or sometimes the poorly paid messenger would just decide to help himself to the contents of the letters and never be seen again. He told her to be patient and Lady Ursula would respond in her own good time.

This didn't stop Constance from pestering Oates every day to see if he had forgotten to deliver any post. Oates didn't mind. He was quite happy to have an excuse to have a word with his mistress, (as he liked to think of her). He had even had the temerity to speak up for her in the kitchen when Mistress Fitch had forgotten herself enough to say something disparaging within his hearing.

When she took the children on walks across the fields, Oates accompanied them, walking respectfully half a field away but ready for action should he be needed.

Every night she saw the children to bed and heard their prayers which was a whole new experience for Constance. She had to button her lip and not say anything controversial. One night after she had been in bed for about an hour, she heard sobbing and ran along to Benedict's room where she found the poor little soul in the grip of a nightmare. She gently woke him and then held him until he stopped crying and drifted back to sleep. He thanked her in the morning, telling her that he had been dreaming about the house being on fire with them all trapped inside. She had explained about how dreams often meant something entirely different and he had happily accepted that.

News of the war came in dribs and drabs, brought to the house by villagers or passing tradesmen. None of it cheered her heart and she felt they'd be better off with no news at all — at least then they could continue in blissful ignorance.

Then, one afternoon she and Frances were practicing reading on the front steps when there was a commotion at the gates. The wrought iron portals swung open and a lumbering carriage of magnificent proportions drove in, bristling with postillions and coachmen; it was followed by two more carriages which were loaded with teetering stacks of boxes and portmanteaus. They rumbled up the drive and stopped in front of the house. A liveried footman ran around and opened the carriage door. Constance watched in awe as a very smartly dressed lady, in buttercup yellow satin and a straw hat with a curling ostrich feather, was handed down.

"Aunt Ursula!" screeched Frances as she ran in the most unladylike manner to throw herself into her aunt's welcoming arms.

Seventeen

Constance allowed Lady Ursula and Frances to have a moment and then she went to greet their guest. She was very careful not to behave as though she were the lady of the house in case she offended. Lady Ursula caught her eye over the top of her chatting, hugging niece and smiled at Constance. It was such a warm and conspiratorial look that Constance felt immediately that she and Ursula were going to get on just fine. She was even more beautiful than her portrait, alive with understanding and humour but with a decided air about her, as though she would brook no argument; her movements were slow and studied as though she were conserving energy.

Frances, suddenly remembering her duties, drew back from her aunt's embrace and made the appropriate introductions.

"Aunt Ursula, this is our very particular friend, Mistress Harcourt and this is my aunt, Lady Ursula Prideaux."

The two women shook hands politely, a mere touch of the fingers, and Frances beamed with satisfaction at them.

"You may be a little undone by my unexpected arrival, for which I can only apologise!" said Lady Ursula. "Lucas will tell you that I have always been impetuous — as long as it costs me no effort! When I received your letter Frances, I thought, after careful consideration, that it would be quicker to bring you the answer myself rather than send the postboy back to you! So, here I am and travelling light as always! I have only brought a few members of the household with me, as you can see." She looked around at the surprisingly large gathering of servants behind her, "I left most of them in Banbury to care for the house."

Constance couldn't help a little laugh escaping and Lady Ursula, catching her eye, had the grace to laugh as well.

"It is ridiculous, is it not! All this just for one forlorn little female! I would have brought them all with me had we had more coaches. Poor Jacob was always in despair, as you can imagine! Well, I ask you, how is one to do without one's cook? I have reluctantly left him behind because I knew that Mistress Peel would not be willing to share her domain with anyone, least of all a man! Naturally, he was incensed and may be tempted to deliberately ruin my food when I return! He is French and very prone to making overwrought scenes. It is vastly entertaining, but Lucas would heartily disapprove. Where *is* my beloved brother?"

Frances cast Constance a despairing glance so Constance answered, "I'm so sorry but he's been recalled. He left about ten days ago."

"Well, is that not just like him? I wait an age to see him and he escapes!"

Just then, Benedict came hurtling around the corner, followed by his tutor, "Aunt Ursula! It *is* true! Mr Thorne said he had seen a string of coaches go by! Oh, this is famous!" He threw himself at his aunt and gave her a bone-crushing hug, "Did you bring Dash? Oh, I do hope so!"

"I did indeed, young man. As though I could leave him behind. He is in the last coach."

Benedict was already running off, calling over his shoulder, "I expect he is gasping for a dish of water, poor thing!"

Lady Ursula laughed, "In my defence, he is not mine, he belonged to my husband and pays no heed to anything I say to him regardless of the ferocity of my tone! Ah, and here he is! Do not allow him to jump up, he will knock you down and lick your face!"

Dash turned out to be an enormous two-year-old Irish Wolfhound with no manners to speak of and a firm belief that he was still a puppy. Lady Ursula apologised for his behaviour in advance, saying that he was very inclined to chase anything that moved, would eat them out of house and home if you let him and knock furniture and small children over because he was so clumsy. Constance reassured her that she was used to dogs and told her about Badger.

"I'm sure you must be longing for some refreshment, Lady Ursula. Won't you come into the cool and I can make sure that your rooms are prepared at once." She turned to the tutor, "Mr de Cheverell, do you think you could possibly supervise the servants and luggage? It's a lot to ask but I trust you to do it with efficiency and grace." The tutor bowed and stated that he was entirely at her disposal and that it would be a pleasure.

As Constance and Lady Ursula made their way into the house Lady Ursula murmured, "Nicely done, my dear. Is he proving to be a nuisance?"

Constance darted a look at her, "Lady Ursula?"

That lady's eyes gleamed, "He clearly dotes on you. Those great big eyes of his — so expressive! I would wager he writes poetry to the beauty of your eyes!"

"He is very young and a little head-in-the-clouds, but he is very respectful."

"I am delighted to hear it," said Lady Ursula with a warm chuckle.

"Anyway," commented Frances, following hard on their heels, "He would have given up any hopes he may have had when Father kissed Constance in front of everyone," and having delivered this bombshell, she skipped away up the stairs.

Lady Ursula stopped in her tracks, "*Kissed* — ? Well, it seems that I have a *great* deal of catching up to do!" She took in Constance's scarlet face and quickly changed the subject. "Is this heat not completely enervating! When will it ever end? Poor Dash dislikes this weather dreadfully and I have to agree with him — it is unbearable. I only wish I could throw myself down onto the cool tiles like he does!"

Constance laughed and guided their delightful but mischievous guest into the parlour.

Mistress Peel sent a tray of tempting little tarts and a pitcher of lemonade, which Constance, in desperation, had instructed her to make, having become totally disillusioned with the dearth of thirst-quenching beverages available.

Lady Ursula removed her hat with a flourish and made herself at home, washing her hands in the discreetly placed bowl of water on the sideboard. "Ah, that is better. I am a little dusty from the journey but as soon as the rooms are ready, I shall change and brush the grit out of my hair! So, please excuse my appearance for the moment!"

"You are lucky to find me in good order myself; I am usually covered in grass seeds and soil from gardening, with smuts on my face."

"Gardening! Well, I can see you must be a woman of many talents. You must tell me everything. Do you mind if I interrogate you endlessly? I am remorselessly curious. And now I am intrigued by what Frances has so recklessly divulged and am determined to wrest the whole story from you. Lucas told me a little in his letter, and about how you have lost everything because of this dreadful war. I am so grateful that you have ended up here though, it could not be more heaven-sent — for the children." Here she gave Constance a roguish look from under her lashes. "And perhaps for my horribly bear-headed brother?"

Constance felt the heat rising to her cheeks again and laughed awkwardly.

"Ah, I see your chaperone has arrived a little too late!" said Lady Ursula in teasing accents.

"No! Really! I — it was only at the very last minute, as he was saying farewell to everyone — he must have been overcome by the emotion of leaving his family. It struck him very hard."

Lady Ursula raised an eyebrow, "Leaving them has never had that much effect upon him before. It is interesting that he should suddenly mind so much."

"I believe he has been closer to Frances and Benedict, which may have prompted the feelings of regret."

"Feelings of regret? That does not sound like the brother I know. He suffers from feelings of ill humour. He is often overcome by towering rages. But regret no!"

"Oh, no!" exclaimed Constance, "He is not nearly so humourless and disagreeable as everyone says! In fact, he is really quite mellow sometimes and can be very thoughtful and caring —"

"Oh dear," said Lady Ursula solemnly, "I fear I am already far too late to save you."

"Save me?"

"Well, if you have been foolish enough to fall in love with Lucas, a man even his sister finds mostly unloveable, there is no saving you, I am afraid."

Constance's mouth opened and closed several times before she was able to stammer a reply, "N-no, it's not — like that! I — don't think I — you see, he has been so very — "

Thankfully at this point, the door opened and Valentine de Cheverell guided Quinton into the room before politely retreating. Lady Ursula jumped up and went to Quinton immediately, taking his hands in hers and greeting him with affection.

"Quinton! My dear friend. How I have missed you. Lucas has told me all in his letter and I understand we are lucky to still have you with us. Come, sit next to me so I can talk you into a cocked hat! There, that is better. Now, tell me, were *you* a witness to the famous kiss?"

"Oh my giddy aunt," groaned Constance burying her flaming face in her hands.

Quinton let out a shout of laughter, "Ursula! Straight to the point as usual. *Everyone* saw it — apart from me of course, but I was told all about it in glorious detail. If I know your brother at all he will have been kicking himself ever since. That impetuous streak you both have can lead to trouble and may already have induced Lucas to retreat back behind his battlements."

Ursula reached out and patted his hand, "And *you* should know! Always pulling Lucas back from the brink. He must drive a rational man like you quite mad with frustration. I cannot imagine how you managed to work with him all these years. Although you did end up fighting on different sides!"

Quinton smiled knowingly, "We never talk about politics or religion and if ever there is a moment when I fear I may have overstepped I just mention a problem with one of the barns to distract him."

"How cunning. I wish I had thought of that as a child. He was much given to rages when he did not get his own way. Mother just used to laugh and diffuse his anger, but I always seem to make it worse by arguing with him." She leant forward and peered closely at him, "I see signs of powder burns around your eyes and little green spots under your skin. You *have* made a mess of your nice old face, my dear."

"Thank you for pointing that out! Green spots you say? Constance failed to mention that."

"I think Mistress Harcourt has been otherwise engaged and must be forgiven!"

"Lady Ursula! Please! Will I never be allowed to forget this", cried Constance.

Lady Ursula giggled, "Do you *wish* to forget it?"

There was silence for a moment, "No. I don't. I shall *never* forget."

"There!" declared Lady Ursula triumphantly, "She loves him. I am always right in these matters. I simply cannot wait to see my brother! What fun we shall have." She clapped her hands gleefully. "And as we are to be sisters-in-law — "

"Oh, no! Please do not — "

"You shall call me Ursula and I shall call you Constance — or sister!"

Constance felt as though she was being steamrollered by fluffy kittens and ducklings. It was impossible to take offence at Lady Ursula's imperious manner because it was clearly kindly meant but she actually began to understand why Lucas took refuge in anger and the army. She decided to give in gracefully and not battle the whirlwind.

It was not many days before Lady Ursula had settled in and the extra staff had been amalgamated into the household without too much complaint. Benedict was more than happy to have Dash accompany him everywhere; they were very soon hard to separate and after initial attempts to make them sleep in different rooms had the disastrous effect that *nobody* in the house got much sleep because Dash howled downstairs and Benedict upstairs, it was decided, to preserve everyone's sanity, that the dog should be allowed to sleep in Benedict's bedchamber.

Lady Ursula made it abundantly clear, knowing what she now knew, that she had no intention of taking over the running of the Court House; she was keen to see how Constance coped with managing the household and the children. Ursula, by her own admission, was not much enthused by the idea of domestic duties. Her beloved husband had provided her with a plethora of carefully selected servants who made her daily life run smoothly without the disagreeable intrusion of any dreary housewifely obligations. She was inherently idle and not at all inclined to change. As a child she had watched her older brother waste his energy running around, climbing trees, unnecessarily throwing things, and generally exhausting himself for no good reason while she sat and revelled in inactivity. Jacob would laugh at her but lovingly so and tell her that her stillness was one of the things which attracted him to her in the first place. She could be animated if she chose but was loath to become breathless and sweaty if there was another course.

She had liked Constance in an instant, when she held back to give Frances time to greet her aunt, and when she had instinctively defended Lucas when he was under attack. It was quite acceptable that Ursula should demean her own brother, but she wanted whomever he chose to marry to be his staunchest supporter. And when Constance had owned to never wishing to forget that first kiss despite it having caused evident mortification, Ursula was persuaded that this woman would be an ideal wife for her irascible brother. She felt there was something unusual about her and wondered what her whole story was, for Ursula was fairly certain that she had been fobbed off with a fairy tale by her brother. She noted that Constance rarely mentioned anything about her past; the dog, Badger, being a notable exception. On occasion she spoke of her relations, but more often than not immediately changed the subject. Ursula tried gently probing to find out more but found her way blocked each time by a carefully constructed but very polite barrier. Ursula thought it telling that the children were so comfortable with her, especially the notoriously prickly Frances who usually took an age to be at ease with strangers. Also, Dash liked her, which, although not a scientific guide, as he was by nature an indiscriminately amiable hound, gave her another reason to trust this stranger in their midst. It sounded as though it had not taken her usually morose brother long to lose his habitual reserve, throw caution to the winds and to display, for everyone to see, the strength of his feelings for Constance Harcourt.

Something had jolted Lucas out of his perpetual state of detachment, and she had to commend the woman who appeared to have managed this improbable feat.

Ursula loved her brother but would not wish to be married to him for he was as unbending as the oak tree he resembled. She longed for him to return safely from the war so that she could see for herself the effect Constance had apparently had on him.

Ursula had had a monstrous year since Jacob had been killed; it had tested her beyond her limits and once the children had left to return home, she discovered that she was far from happy left in her own company. She became uncommonly restless and easily displeased by the smallest things. Her staff were visibly discontented, and she had to admit to being unhappy when idle because there was nobody there to appreciate her stillness and one day openly acknowledged to herself that she was actually bored! Two days later the beautifully penned letter from Frances arrived begging her to go and stay with them. It was providence! She instructed her maid to start packing her bags immediately and before very long her spirits began to soar. Being at the Court House with her adorable niece and nephew and a charming miracle-worker was what she needed to compel her to stop feeling sorry for herself.

Yes, she thought, smugly, I think this will be the answer.

Eighteen

Colonel Sir Lucas Deverell sat with his head in his hands waiting for something to happen. He was half asleep but still vaguely aware of what was going on around him. Nothing had happened for days now apart from the interminable waiting. All there was to do was stay alive, eat, sleep, and wait. Everything smelled of smoke and horses and blood and gunpowder, sweat and human filth. He had never thought much about it before but now he found it overpowering, almost as though he was, for the first time, fully wake during a campaign. He was tired and disillusioned, his leg wound aching like a freshly broken bone, and it was making him grit his teeth and wish for it all to be over.

The weather had turned unseasonably cold and misty. Fairfax, having besieged Bristol, dug in for the long haul and Prince Rupert, confident that he could hold out until reinforcements arrived, made himself at home. There had been a good deal of sallying to and fro without much success, losing some good men and gaining a few prisoners and intercepting messages but little of any practical purpose. Plague was rife about the city and soldiers and citizens would soon begin to drop like flies if this deadlock continued. Captain Moulton, Admiral for the Irish Coasts, now in the Severn, had expressed his willingness to assist in the storming of the city and after letters for Prince Rupert were intercepted suggesting that the King, marching towards Oxford, was ready to interrupt the siege, there followed many councils of war to determine how to proceed. The city had been set fire to in several places and still its perverse citizens refused to take sides.

Lucas Deverell could not have cared less. He had, as far as he was concerned, done his bit for the cause, willingly challenged the enemy during weeks of pointless skirmishes, watched castles burn and fall, taken hostages and witnessed horrific sights and, given what Constance had told him, for what? In the end it all came down to a ditch or a hedge being in the wrong place or the lane you were charging down being so dusty that you galloped right through the cloud into the main body of the enemy's troops and had to fight your way out or die. His patience was being sorely tried and he was beginning to feel that those at the top were drawing things out for their own aggrandisement. It seemed to him that if they could all just *do* something instead of *talking* about doing something then this could all be over in a fortnight and they could all go home.

Go home. That was a new and worrying thought for him. Before, he had been perfectly content to lead his troops about the country, wherever they were needed, with no thought of home and family in his head. His only desire to do a commendable job in his role as colonel. His troops were paramount, his family a mere ornament in the furthest reaches of his life. Recently those far-off edges seemed to have been moving steadily closer; they were now in sight, within his grasp and yet, maddeningly unattainable.

Home. It was like the Holy Grail. He used to think that his endeavours in the army were what he lived for but there had been a stealthy sea change. There was a time when he could not wait to leave the Court House and ride hundreds of miles in filthy weather and live off scraps plundered from unhappy farmers and face the daily threat of disease and death, friends being wounded and dying in agony before his eyes — this was the life he had deliberately chosen for himself. Seldom did the memory of his children encroach upon his thoughts. Perhaps, he thought now, it had been a way of protecting himself from the harsh reality of a life without loved ones; perhaps he had decided that if he were going to die, then it would be best to die unencumbered, alone and unmourned. He had seen so many fellow soldiers leave this world crying and begging to see their families once more and he thought how miserable, how desperate they had been, and he was determined that he would not die in such a wretched state.

Or perhaps he was really just a cold-hearted tyrant after all. Perhaps nothing could save him. Perhaps this insistent feeling that was growing in his chest was just the result of the terrible food and not a yearning to be somewhere else and with someone else. Perhaps he had caught the plague. Perhaps that was the answer.

Constance tried not to think of what Lucas might be doing at every minute of the day; she found that her imagination, fuelled by the many books and films she'd watched over the years, had provided her with far too much unwanted information about the brutality of hand-to-hand combat and the inevitability of death in wars before the anodyne age of technology. She decided that instead of focusing on his inevitable death and the miserable, lonely life she would lead without him, she would make sure that his legacy, his children and the estate would not be neglected and would, in fact, be a fitting memorial to him. Then she would cry while thinking of him lying bloodied on the battlefield, perhaps calling out for his children in his last moments or maybe even reliving their first and last kiss before those sleepy eyes closed forever.

"Constance! *Constance!*" exclaimed Ursula, shaking her awake. "Wake up, you are having a nightmare."

Constance opened her eyes, which were wet with tears and realised she was sitting in the parlour, a book open on her lap.

"Oh, my dear, you were crying and calling out for Lucas!"

"Oh, no! I'm so sorry. I must have dropped off while reading. So silly. How embarrassing."

"You have been working ceaselessly, it is no wonder that you are so tired. I am worried about you. I am no use to you because, as Lucas would say, he has met nobody in his whole life as idle as me. Jacob used to laugh about it but I see now that it is not a laughing matter. If there is anything you desire me to do, please do not hesitate to tell me."

Constance giggled through the tears, "You're very self-sacrificing, Ursula, and I thank you for the thought but never fear, I shall manage. I've been trying to keep as busy as possible so that I don't think of him, but it seems that he's creeping in by the back door now and haunting my dreams — which is a little unfair!"

"I believe that if you talk about your problems, it will help."

"A problem shared is a problem halved," quoted Constance.

"Well, that is a very succinct way of expressing it, I must say, but yes! Exactly so! Talk to me. Listening is easy for me — it takes no energy whatsoever! I will then tell you what a very pedantic and overbearing fellow he is, and you will see the error of your ways and callously transfer your affections to the beautiful Mr de Cheverell instead!"

"Ah, how I wish I could do that! He'd write me such lyrical odes to my eyebrows and gaze at me adoringly and I'd be very happy. I'm not at all sure that Lucas will ever do that — he's not exactly poetic by nature — or inclined to gaze adoringly — unless you're a barn! Whenever he looked at me, he mostly looked baffled or exasperated! Poor man. I miss him so much — I must be mad."

"Indeed you must! Big old ugly bear of a man."

"I think he's rather handsome in a battered sort of way."

"They do say love is blind," said Ursula, laughing.

*

Two days later Constance managed to leave the house, without Oates seeing her and following her like a faithful hound, and quickly dashed down to the bridge to see if the geocache had anything for her but it was disappointingly silent and empty. She badly wanted communication with her family; she was feeling their loss like a physical pain. Whilst trying to block out those currently missing in her life, she realised that she had deliberately not thought about the idea of how to get home, back to her own time. It was something she could not control, could not face at the moment; in fact, the idea of leaving the Court House threatened to reduce her to tears every time she considered it, so she stopped considering it.

Richard Thorne had informed her that the weather would break soon so Constance decided to make the most of the sunshine and took the children and Ursula down to the river for a picnic and a swim.

"A *swim*?" squeaked Frances, aghast. "What do you mean?"

"I mean, we get into the river and splash about."

Frances looked at Lady Ursula in some shock and then back at Constance, "In the *river*? Like — *peasants*?"

"No, Frances, in the river like sensible human beings who need a wash and some exercise and cooling down on a hot day and some *enjoyment*! I'll teach you how to swim. Bring an extra shift to change into and a drying sheet. I'll ask Mistress Peel for some food for the picnic."

Lady Ursula was gazing at Constance with her lips tightly compressed. "I hope you are not expecting *me* to get wet."

Constance grinned, "Yes, I am and I'm expecting you to enjoy every moment of it too so that the children are happy to learn from your example."

"Dear Lord," said Ursula with deep foreboding.

It was one of those golden days, where the atmosphere was clouded with glittering dust motes and one could almost taste it on one's tongue, where everything seemed to move slowly as though suspended in the soupy air. Doves were cooing rhythmically in the woods and grasshoppers chirruping in the long dry meadow grass. The noise was like a soft symphony which induced a soporific feeling.

Benedict carried the picnic basket and was clearly the only one of the group to be in the least bit excited about the prospect of swimming. He ran ahead with a spring in his step and Ursula had to keep reminding him not to spill the contents of the basket or they would have no refreshment to look forward to. They crossed the low wooden bridge over the river to the bank on the west side and set up their little camp there.

The Dikler wound its way slowly through the valley, a rather refined little river en route to join the Windrush beyond Bourton on the Water; it rolled gently through the meadows and fields and was mostly unhurried and modest with grassy banks and overhanging trees, abundant wildlife and pleasant swimming holes for those long summer holidays. Constance had swum in it from early childhood with her family and friends and was excited to share its joys with others even if they were looking largely unconvinced by her enthusiasm.

The water level was, after a dry spring and a long hot summer, quite low which meant that it would be less daunting for the beginners to start with and made entry into the water a good deal less dramatic.

Constance thought she'd begin with Benedict as he was the only one showing any kind of adventurous spirit. He had brought a long nightshirt to wear in the water and cheerfully changed behind a bush. Frances guffawed at the sight of her brother in his night attire until Lady Ursula silenced her with a frown.

Constance undressed down to her shift and stepped down the bank and into the sandy shallows. The water was pleasantly cool and as soon as she had gauged the depth of the pool, she reached a hand up to help Benedict, but he ignored her and jumped down, landing with a splash and shriek of delight.

"Well done! That's how Rowen would have done it! He's the wild one — always flinging himself into things with gusto! Guy would be sitting on the bank reading his book or contemplating the clouds, like Ferdinand the Bull. And Gabriel would be trying to catch any wildlife unfortunate enough to stray into his path. Right, do you want to go in a bit deeper? I'll come with you and hold you. There's no fear of being swept away because the water is too shallow at the edges of the pool. To reassure you, I am a very strong swimmer and will not allow anything bad to happen."

Benedict shrugged, "But I am not afraid! I will be the best swimmer! Better than Frances."

"Well, as it looks as though you're the only one brave enough to even get into the river, so there won't be much competition."

Out of the corner of her eye, she saw Frances resolutely snatch up her shift and disappear behind the bush.

Ursula heaved a theatrical sigh, "Oh, all right then but if I drown, I shall blame only you!"

"Fair enough. But you won't drown if you do as I say."

"This seems very like activity to me. I dislike activity."

"Oh, Come on Aunt Ursula! It feels nice on your legs! And look! There are fish and wriggly creatures!"

Lady Ursula shuddered and vanished behind the bush to change. Frances appeared wearing her shift and Constance helped her down into the water; on making contact with it, she let out a little yelp and looked as though she were about to burst into tears until Benedict mockingly pointed at her and made a disparaging comment about the feebleness of girls. Riled, she took a deep breath and began to paddle about in the ankle-deep water with every sign of unadulterated enjoyment although Constance could see she was covered in gooseflesh.

"Brave girl," she murmured and received a grateful but nervous smile in return.

While Frances accustomed herself to the water, Constance led Benedict further into the pool until the water was up to his waist. He let out a little gasp of surprise as he ducked under for the first time but quickly masked it so that his sister wouldn't make fun of him. Constance showed him how to float and move his arms in the right way. He was a natural, if a little too reckless, and quickly caught on to the technique. Once she had him able to happily float about and stand up again freely, she was able to turn her attention to Frances.

She could feel Frances shaking with fear and cold but was hugely impressed because she didn't give in; she could actually hear her teeth chattering. Constance kept up an encouraging flow of chat as Frances tried to emulate her more athletic brother. After a while she managed to get her to float on her back and feel more at home in the water. When she had accomplished some kicking and swim-like strokes, she was exultant.

The most entertaining part of the afternoon was trying to get Lady Ursula into the water. Constance suspected that their aunt put on a special show for them to make them laugh and realise just how brave they were. Just getting her to slide down the bank on her bottom caused much merriment and when her toes touched the water, the shriek of anguish she emitted made the children weep with laughter. She then immediately and inelegantly tried to climb back out, but Frances and Benedict ruthlessly pulled her back into the river, assuring her, now that they were experts, that she would soon be swimming like a fish.

Every time some river weed touched her leg, she declared it was a water monster come to devour her and she flapped her hands in distress and the children were jubilant.

They spent a delightful couple of hours splashing around and refining their swimming techniques before clambering out, exhausted, and falling upon their picnic like a pack of half-starved wild animals.

As they lay basking in the sunshine Ursula moaned, "We should be in the shade or we will end up being as brown as walnuts like Constance!" and the three of them laughed uproariously.

Constance pretended to be indignant, drawing herself up, "It isn't my fault that I'm not fish-belly white! I work in the garden and cannot laze about in the shade of a parasol like you good-for-nothings!"

Frances rolled across the flattened grass to Constance and putting an arm about her shoulders, planted a conciliatory kiss on her cheek. Constance was quite taken aback and pleased by this genuine gesture of affection and felt her eyes mist over.

Lady Ursula peeped at her from under her eyelashes and thought to herself that her friend Constance was going to be the perfect stepmother and sister-in-law and she was going to do her very best to keep her here at the Court House for Lucas to come home to.

As they slowly made their way back up though the fields, Constance unconsciously started singing *Morning Has Broken* to herself and Ursula asked her to teach them the words and so, as Quinton Gittings and Valentine de Cheverell were taking a constitutional about the parterre in the late afternoon, they could hear the sweet sound of voices drifting up from the valley like a choir of angels singing.

"What is that tune?" asked Valentine.

Quinton cocked his head and listened for a moment, "I have never heard it before. I suspect it is from Constance's head, she is forever making up new songs."

"She is so accomplished," sighed the tutor.

"Indeed she is," murmured Quinton with a secret smile.

Nineteen

Oates carried a letter in as if it were sprinkled with gold dust and encrusted with diamonds, even though, in truth, it was a bit dog-eared and grubby. He paused on the threshold and looked at the three occupants of the room. He wasn't sure how he was to complete his task without offending someone. He tried surreptitiously edging into the room, but Lady Ursula looked up and seeing him, imperiously held out her hand for the letter.

Oates coughed delicately, "I am afraid, my lady — "

"Oho!" exclaimed that lady, raising her eyebrows, "Is that the way it lies! Well, I am insulted beyond measure."

Oates looked desperately uncomfortable and started to apologise but Lady Ursula let out a delighted giggle, "No! Oates! Please, I jest. Take it to her. I dislike deciphering his childish scrawl anyway. It is too exhausting."

Constance, who had been focused on talking with Quinton, looked up in some surprise. "A letter? For me? But I don't know anyone here — ." She stopped herself just in time, realising that she was about to give away rather too much.

Oates stepped across the room and handed her the letter and then quickly retreated to safety closing the door firmly behind him.

Constance's heart did a weird kind of tap-dance in her chest as she stared at her name written on the front of the folded piece of paper. No stamp, no envelope but sealed with red wax. It was so peculiar. So, historical.

"It will have been sent with other letters for London and Parliament," said Quinton, helpfully, "By army messenger.

It is fortunate not to have been intercepted by Royalist soldiers. His handwriting is famously woeful. You would get a more legible result if you gave a bear an inky stick! I wish you luck."

Constance wanted to take the letter upstairs to her bedchamber and read it by herself, but she knew a letter was an important event and her companions were looking at her with expectant interest. She steeled herself for a missive filled with details about being a soldier or even worse, a Dear John letter: 'Dear Constance, I made a terrible mistake…'

"Heavens, Constance, stop staring at it and open it!" laughed Ursula.

Constance slid a shaking finger under the seal. Unfolded the thick paper. Looked at his writing for the first time. Tried not to cry.

"Shall I read it aloud?" she asked anxiously.

On receiving two affirmatives she took a trembling breath and began, never more grateful for such a poor hand because it meant it was plain writing with few artistic flourishes:

My dear Constance,

We are established outside the City of Bristol, which has been invested. Prince Rupert has the city, and we await the order to storm the walls. We are tired and hungry and most sick of this war. Not least because it keeps us from those we love. The men are certain the Prince will be able to hold the city until reinforcements arrive. We are all wishing for a quick end to the fighting before the weather turns. If it should continue, we must hope for winter quartering and to begin again in the Spring. If this is so, I will return to the Court House. I hope Ursula is with you by now. If she is, you are not to believe all the things she says about me. And make her do some work, she is lethargic and will avoid helping if she can.

"I am so sorry Ursula! I'm sure he doesn't mean that."

Give the children a kiss for me and tell Quinton I am sorry to leave him with so many stubborn women. Please, Constance, be careful and heed Quinton's advice - he is very wise. Richard Thorne will be there to stand guard - trust him. I think of nothing but returning home to you. All else is emptiness. Please stay until then. I have to talk with you. I have to—

She paused —

— kiss you again.

"Oh, my giddy aunt! I'm so sorry, perhaps I shouldn't have read that bit out! How embarrassing. And he finishes with, — "

But the next time it will not be in front of everyone, I swear!

Until that day,
I am your faithful servant,

Lucas Deverell

"I can't bear it," said Constance, in muffled accents because she was weeping into her skirt. Ursula went straight to her side and enfolded her into a gentle embrace.

"My dear girl! If I hadn't heard it with my own ears! For Lucas to be so — eloquent — so openly affectionate! It is nothing less than a miracle. Please stop crying, you are making my shoulder wet and it is very taxing kneeling here on the hard floor."

Constance gave a damp chuckle and severely pulled herself together, "I'm not usually so weepy. It's just seeing his handwriting — knowing he's still — you know — and that he's thinking of us — it's hard to bear. This stupid war!"

"I could not agree more. Although why he should think you might leave, I really do not comprehend. He must be very tired and not thinking straight. Just so that you realise how unusual it is for us to receive a letter from him; the last time I believe was when he was at university and he wrote to beg our parents for more money!"

"Oh," said Constance, "Really? I don't suppose I could write back to him?"

"I fear correspondence going the other way seldom gets through," said Quinton quietly.

"Of course. I understand. It would be hard to direct a letter to just *army encampment, somewhere outside Bristol.* Very likely to go to the wrong person. He says they may go to winter quarters — perhaps then he will come home?"

"Perhaps," said Quinton without much conviction.

"What if he meets someone else!" said Constance.

"In an army camp! I think it unlikely!" he laughed.

Constance was beset by unreasonable fears. So many things might happen to him before he came home. Injury, death, going missing, finding someone better than her, *death.* Or she might be hoovered back through the portal when she least expected it and then she'd have lost him forever and — he'd never know how she felt.

"As I understand it," remarked Quinton reflectively, "Your response to his — er — approach, was most enthusiastic. He is not a stupid man — on the *whole.* I think he will be fully aware of your feelings, as are we all."

Constance blushed, "Oh, no."

"Constance! What on earth did you do?" exclaimed Ursula.

"I — I — " she stammered, "I only kissed him back."

"With, apparently, undisguised fervour," supplied Quinton, trying to keep a straight face.

Constance gave him a searching look, "Quinton! You odious man!"

Quinton Gittings dissolved into laughter while Constance looked on in disbelief and Lady Ursula watched her brother's best friend with unexpected interest. He had a rather attractive smile, she thought with some surprise; it appeared suddenly and made his face crease into sharp angles and his poor damaged eyes light up. How odd that she had never noticed that before.

"Quinton, would you care for a glass of wine? I could send for Oates. I think I shall have one. Constance?"

"No thank you, I don't think I'd better. It'll just make me maudlin," replied Constance.

Quinton agreed that he would like one and to everyone's astonishment Lady Ursula rose majestically to her feet and went in search of Oates.

"Well I never, " said Constance. "That's rather extraordinary."

"What is?"

"Ursula. Going to get the wine. When there was no need."

"Perhaps she needed to stretch her legs."

"No, I think — I think she suddenly had a desire to be helpful for some reason."

"Maybe she had too much sun today and is feeling unwell," suggested Quinton rather unkindly.

"Oh, this is altogether too bad! We are acting as though she has never lifted a finger to help *anyone!*"

"I do not think she ever has."

After a few minutes the door opened and Oates entered bearing a tray, followed by a triumphant Lady Ursula.

"I have brought wine!" she declared happily.

"Just as though she had picked the grapes and bottled it herself!" murmured Quinton. Constance gave a little choke of laughter but turned it swiftly into a cough.

Ursula, seeing this friendly exchange had a sudden and rather unwelcome feeling that came a little too close to envy for her liking and despised herself for it. She was not accustomed to intense feelings of any sort, apart from when she had heard the news about Jacob; then she had been absolutely certain that her life had ended and was deeply disappointed when it continued as though nothing untoward had happened. She found emotions enervating; they ruffled the smooth surface she liked to shelter behind. She had spent her childhood watching her brother be prey to his tempestuous emotions and had found it exhausting. She made a deliberate and dispassionate choice to eliminate any kind of unnecessary sensibilities in case they might cause discomfort or confusion of any kind. This feeling she was having of slight dissatisfaction was most disagreeable. She knew what she was and was at peace with it and to find herself suddenly assailed by a new and unwelcome awareness of other people was far too disturbing to her equilibrium. She was determined to squash it before it ruined her life completely.

Her resolution held for two days. On the third day she was coming in from the garden and found Quinton Gittings about to fall over Dash, who was thoughtlessly sprawled across the floor of the Great Hall, right in his path. Ursula cried out and ran to stop Quinton from stumbling over the prostrate body of the Irish Wolfhound, who remained asleep, despite the commotion.

Lady Ursula grasped Quinton's arm and steered him around the obstacle, "I am so sorry, my dear! The beastly dog is untrainable! He just throws himself down wherever he pleases, no thought for anyone else. A truly selfish creature. I will see if I can persuade Benedict to try to improve his manners. Perhaps if he was bribed with a morsel of beef!"

Quinton laughed, "I am afraid I regularly take tumbles, Ursula. It is all part of my new condition and something I must become used to. Thank you for rescuing me. I must say you were very quick thinking."

"I will have you know that I *ran!* I believe the last time I actually ran was when I was about seven and I saw Lucas help himself to the last cake! I snatched it from his greedy grasp and stuffed it into my mouth before he could do anything! He was livid! He told Mother and I was thoroughly punished for my bad manners and gluttony."

"And well-deserved by the sound of it."

"Oh, Quinton, I thought that knowing Lucas, you would be on my side! How very disappointing."

He patted her hand and she looked at his hand on hers and thought what a fraternal gesture it was, and it shook her that she should recognise it as such. And mind so much.

"Of course, I am on your side. You were only seven and he should have been courteous enough to share the cake with you. However, as you said yourself, you did *snatch* it — "

Ursula gave his hand a light smack. "Now, you are teasing me!" she said with a smile that turned into a frown as she realised once again that he could no longer see her. Each time it dawned upon her, it came as a shock and she wondered if she would ever become used to it.

Lady Ursula had been accustomed to the modest presence of this man, always slightly in the background, overshadowed by the huge force that was her brother. Quinton Gittings was slightly built, medium height, economical of word and movement, with no expansive gestures that might draw attention to him, just a quietly intelligent bearing and an impressive ability to manage Lucas without angering him.

He dealt with everything on the estate; it mattered not how trivial it might be, he treated everyone with the same courtesy and their grievances with equal gravity.

She was beginning to realise just how much they had taken him for granted over the years, not that he would have ever remarked upon it.

She was also coming to the conclusion that her own personality lacked something and wondered if she had been blessed with children if perhaps that might have saved her from becoming this person even she found not very lovable. Jacob had more than made up for her lack of warmth and enthusiasm by being the human version of a puppy — boundless energy, friendly and devoted. She often asked herself what he saw in her. When she asked him, he had replied that she was his anchor. She knew that he meant it in a good sense, but she could not help but think that an anchor weighed one down, a millstone dragging along behind a free spirit preventing escape. What if that was what she was, nothing more than a hindrance; had she prevented him from doing more, *being* more? Was that why he had been so eager to join the army and join the fighting? Had she driven him to it?

"Where were you going, Quinton, when Dash stopped you?"

"To the parlour. I was hoping to listen to Constance teaching Frances her lessons. It passes the time quite pleasantly."

Ursula searched his face for some clue to his thoughts, "I do not suppose you would care for me to read to you for a while as I know that Constance has gone for a walk to the church?"

Quinton Gittings carefully masked his surprise, "If you could bear it, Ursula, that would be delightful."

So, when Constance came back from yet another fruitless walk to the bridge a little while later, she found Lady Ursula sitting beside Quinton, reading in her very pretty voice, from *Arcadia*. Quinton was relaxed in his chair, his chin resting on his hands, fingers interlaced, eyes closed in contemplation and Ursula concentrating hard on delivering the story with as much expression as she could muster. Constance stopped on the threshold, momentarily taken aback by this sight and couldn't help raising her eyebrows in astonishment.

"Do not say a word!" said Lady Ursula menacingly, "Not one word."

Constance mimed locking her lips and throwing away the key. She then backed out of the room and closed the door behind her, leaning against it for a moment while she considered something rather interesting. Her eyes lit up and a playful smile curled the corners of her mouth. So, that's how it is, she thought. How very unexpected. How very — *delicious!*

Once tucked up in bed that night, Constance contemplated the image of Lady Ursula reading to Quinton. It had reminded her of a Victorian painting, a Pre-Raphaelite allegory of romance and poetry. She wished she could paint the memory, but watercolour would not do it justice — it would need a huge canvas and oil paints. Peter Lely would have made a wonderful job of it and it could hang in the Long Gallery with the other portraits.

Other, not-so-pleasant thoughts intruded on her fanciful notions of matchmaking. She had been to check the geocache box to no avail and had then spent a mournful half an hour sitting in the churchyard staring forlornly at the spot where she had first seen Lucas Deverell as though, by sheer force of will, she could conjure him up. And then she wondered about the boys and if they might be able to connect in some way, as Lucas had, if they were in the same spot at the same time.

She had just been about to make her way home when she saw Richard Thorne crossing the field in front of the church. She waved and he strode purposefully towards her, a broad grin on his face.

"Mistress Harcourt! The very person! I was wondering what you wanted done in The Wilderness and up in Bobble Wood? Sir Lucas left no instruction apart from saying I should ask you."

"Really? He said to ask me? Oh. Well, that's nice but a huge responsibility! I will have to rely on your knowledge and skills because forestry is not really my area. I'm just an artist."

"That is probably what he was referring to then; you can tell me how you wish things to look and I can make it possible. He said to me, *I will leave it to Mistress Harcourt to decide She will know what to do and whatever she decides I will like.*"

Constance felt like this was a secret message from Lucas, just for her and it made her heart hurt and the blood pound in her ears. Richard Thorne was watching her with interest, head tilted, still smiling.

"I expect you need time to think about it."

"No, indeed, I think I know one or two things I'd like to suggest. Would you care to sit down, and we can discuss them now?"

He listened keenly to what she had to say and made suggestions about her ideas and what he could do to facilitate them, and they seemed to agree on everything. He was well-informed, articulate, and had easy manners, and Constance enjoyed talking with him; it made her forget her woes for a short while and she could pretend that she had a place here in this unfamiliar world. He made her feel almost normal.

Mistress Fitch, returning from the village, stopped for a moment and stared. A slow smile momentarily altered her habitually sour expression and she muttered darkly to herself before changing direction and making her way stealthily past the church and back to the Court House.

Twenty

A Council of War had been called and on hearing letters from General Goring had been intercepted suggesting the King would be ready to interrupt the siege in three weeks, it was decided the time had come to take Bristol. A detailed description of the proposed storm was presented to the General and approved.

The weather was grim, still wet and misty, turning any kind of charge into a muddied and confused mess, where soldiers could be lost in the curtains of thick mist, never to be seen again. Men and horses were dying because of the atrocious weather and there was little anyone could do to prevent it. Their uniforms rotted on their backs as they never had a chance to dry them and their commanders had to demand higher pay in order to keep the soldiers from deserting in droves.

Prince Rupert sallied out of the city with many hundreds of horse and foot soldiers but was beaten back by Fairfax's troops. It was as though they were all playing an elaborate and deadly game where no-one knew the exact rules, where the weather and the terrain had the upper hand.

Letters were written, very long letters stating terms. A day was appointed. The tenth of September at one o'clock. Then, after some ferocious fighting the city was set alight in several places, and Prince Rupert, having heard no word from the King about imminent relief, sent a trumpeter to request a treaty and, following a good deal more letter writing, the Parliamentarians took Bristol back, it having been lost to the Royalists some months before Prince Rupert and his troops, as stated in the terms were then escorted to Oxford with, as requested, a Parliamentarian guard to protect them from marauding Clubmen bent on revenge for their brutal treatment by the Royalist troops.

By early September it was all but over bar some political manoeuvring and Lucas Deverell's regiment were marching for Bath and, after resting there for a few days, on to the Castle of Devizes and the mighty Basing House.

There was no sign of Winter Quartering on the horizon and he was starting to question his own beliefs. He had had his fill of listening to dusty old aristocrats pontificate over the lives of his fellow countrymen be they for Parliament or the King, casually ordering thousands to their deaths. He had grown tired of waking up cold and wet, his bones aching and bitten by God knows what kind of malevolent insects. One morning he ordered his sergeant to shave off his hair and beard. He'd had enough. Now he really looked like a Roundhead on the outside despite what he was starting to feel inside. He noticed for the first time, that there was, beneath the general swagger and zeal, rumblings of dissatisfaction amongst his men. It seemed to him that every soldier had different motives for fighting, self-interest being the supreme reason; otherwise, religion, profit, loyalty, mistrust of someone or something, or just the love of a good brawl, appeared to be sufficient. Lucas was finding it difficult to sustain his initial reasons for joining up and without that strong impetus he found his incentive and fervour was waning. His respect and admiration for Sir Thomas Fairfax had never been in doubt — he knew a good man when he saw one. A mostly moderate man who with a share of good fortune and truly inspirational leadership had taken the New Modelled Army and honed them into a devastating and unstoppable fighting force. There was a point when Lucas would have followed him to the ends of the earth and beyond but that blind faith in his leaders was slowly being revised.

Now, it was just becoming a question of when would this madness end so he could go home to tie up some important loose ends which were keeping him awake at night.

Constance kept the letter beside her bed. If she couldn't sleep, she lit a candle and reread it. Sometimes she went to sleep holding it to her chest. She'd wake in the morning in a panic fearing it had become creased or the ink had smudged.

The unreasonably hot summer drew to a close and Autumn arrived. The simple everyday tasks became what held life together. Preparing the garden for winter, teaching Frances, working with Richard Thorne, trying in vain to train Dash to come to heel when he was determined to chase anything that moved, making sure Benedict had plenty of exercise to balance all his studying, keeping Quinton amused and healthy, finding ways to avoid being alone with Valentine de Cheverell and his inconvenient devotion, and gently matchmaking for her two friends.

Constance tried not to think of the past or the future; she tried hard to stay present in the present, but it was a struggle. She knew at some point she was going to have to face up to the truth; she was but a leaf caught in the winds of time and, unless she got blown back to her century, would have to make the best of this strange new world.

Although Quinton was as helpful as he could be with the knowledge he had, he couldn't make up her mind for her and even though he stayed as impartial as he could, they were both perfectly aware that he could not be entirely neutral.

Without Lucas there to receive his regiment's regular dispatches, news about the war came intermittently; they eventually heard about the successful outcome at Bristol and Rowton Heath and the fall of Basing House but other than knowing Lucas had been at Bristol at some point, they had no way of finding out where he and his troops had been sent afterwards.

The geocache remained stubbornly silent for several weeks until one day Constance had just passed through the gate on her way back from visiting Amos Carter to see how he was progressing and as she was walking up the path towards the church, she felt the familiar tingling of her skin. She stopped and closed her eyes, the vibrations continued and suddenly she was running back down to the bridge.

She tugged the box out of its hiding place and opened it.

The letter said, in Guy's beloved scrawl,

Dearest Con,

There may be a way to get you back. I have a theory. Not sure it will work but we may as well give it a go. Details to follow. Just be ready. Keep your bags packed! Everything all right here so no need to worry. We love you and miss you.

Your favourite,

Guy.

And that was it. Someone else had made up her mind for her and decided her fate. All she had to do was obey orders and trust in the gods. And yet, she wasn't sure that she did. She trusted Guy, but she wasn't at all sure what she wanted. She just knew she was going to be torn in two whatever happened.

Then, in the middle of the night, during a deafening thunderstorm, she awoke with a start, absolutely certain that she couldn't go anywhere until she had seen Lucas again. Of course, she had no idea when that would be, but she realised that however long it was, she would wait. She *had* to wait. The next day she left a letter for Guy in the geocache box explaining that they would have to wait for a while until she had solved a conundrum and asked him to send the details anyway so that she could be prepared when the time came.

Lady Ursula, agreeing with Quinton, insisted that Constance had some clothes made that were her own and would actually suit her colouring and figure. A local seamstress was employed to create some gowns although the fabrics were hard to come by; they managed to gather together some promising materials, partly from what was hidden away in the various linen chests and presses in the house and half a dozen lengths from the seamstress herself who had some bales of material left with her by a customer who had died before she could make up the required dresses for her.

A good deal of amusement was had as Constance was measured and fitted and the dresses began to take shape. Frances and Ursula joined her in her bedchamber, Frances lying on her bed on her stomach and Ursula draped elegantly in an armchair, each happily giving their expert opinions on how the gowns should look. Constance felt like a shop-window dummy, turned this way and that, pushed and pulled, pricked with pins, and generally ignored by her three more knowledgeable companions. The colours were glorious; rich earth reds and burnt orange, mustard and citrus yellow (apparently all the rage), olive green, peach and coral, and some sober blacks and greys in case they were needed for church or formal occasions. Taffetas and watered silks, velvet and damask, satins and sarcenets. It was all utterly bewitching to Constance who was used to wearing a very limited and dull selection of long cotton dresses or jeans and t-shirts. She remembered dressing up in her mother's clothes as a child and how each garment could change the way one moved and acted and felt. When corseted and cinched into the yards of gathered and pleated fabrics, she found she could almost forget her modern self and become the gracious lady of the manor everyone thought she was. She had always enjoyed a spot of play-acting, often taking a leading role in her school stage productions. This was the biggest production yet.

When the gowns were finally all finished, and she had them all arranged about her bedchamber she found she had not the enthusiasm for wearing them she thought she would. When it turned out the only person she wanted to wear them for was not present, there seemed little point in going through all the trouble and discomfort of being laced into them, when her only admirers were Valentine de Cheverell, who would have thought she looked exquisite in a potato sack, two children, one of whom would only have shown an interest if she had four legs, Ursula, who's admiration she could probably live without and a blind man. She tossed her hair moodily and carefully but regretfully put all the gowns away in the linen press and firmly shut the door on them.

When she arrived at dinner that evening still wearing faded hand-me-downs, Lady Ursula fixed her with a penetrating glare, which reminded Constance a good deal of the missing brother, "What on earth are you wearing that old thing for? What have we had all those beautiful gowns made for if you are not going to — ohhh! I *see*." She shook her head despondently, "Is *that* how it is to be? Really? We are to remain in mourning for my brother until his return? Well, if you do not mind my forthrightness, I think it is a pity for everyone who has to look at these ill-fitting garments and a sad waste of that good lady's sewing skills."

Constance turned a little pink, "I know it may seem silly to you, but I had imagined wearing them — you know — for him. And although I love you all very much, it's not quite the same — begging your pardon!"

"We will strive to overcome our disappointment," said Lady Ursula in mock despair.

Constance smiled, "Anyway, there is always a chance that Dash will jump up and ruin them with his muddy paws or I will get the hem caught on a bramble! It's better if I wear clothes which don't matter for now."

"It is entirely your choice, my dear."

By November they heard that the King had returned to Oxford for the winter but that the New Modelled Army was still intent upon securing the South West despite some wickedly inhospitable weather. This, they all knew, meant that Lucas would now be unlikely to return home before the spring.

Richard Thorne gently reminded Constance to be on her guard as there was a real risk that Royalist soldiers could be roaming the countryside looking for trouble as they would be billeted nearby. He also told her not to forget that he was lodging in the room over the stables so he would be near at hand should he be needed. There was something about him which gave Constance confidence and even a little hope. He had immense belief in his old commander and even though the news was seldom what she wanted to hear, he seemed always able to leave her smiling. She thought with a twinkle, Lucas was quite right to have been a little disconcerted by her teasing praise of the forester. Perhaps if she hadn't met Lucas first…!

Winter came and Christmas. There was a persistent rumour that the Parliamentarians were trying to ban festivals, believing them to be ungodly. Sundays only were to be reserved for the worshipping of God and all other Holy Days were to be abolished. At least, that's what they wrote on paper; it was another thing altogether actually enforcing the law across the entire land.

Reverend Woode, it turned out, was a rather liberal clergyman with surprisingly advanced ideas about the detrimental effects of excessive piety; he was a man who believed in, what Constance called to herself, hippie values, love and peace for all. He was long-haired, extremely tall and attenuated, long-limbed, and hollow-cheeked, as though he seldom ate a good meal and spent his days on his bony knees praying and fasting. This was, apparently, very far from the truth for he was a hearty eater and liked nothing more than cheery chats with parishioners or a game of blind man's bluff with the children. He was an optimistic and generous man who had entered the church to help people less fortunate than himself. His wife, Cassandra, was as wide as he was long and equally amiable. She cheerfully blamed her father for her preposterous name and said she was very far from being a Trojan princess. Her husband gave mercifully short Sunday services, mostly focusing on good neighbourliness and forgiving the sins of others. He was, on the whole, a thoroughly right-on modern thinking man who enjoyed a good joke. When pressed for a definitive answer about Christmas, he smiled sagely and said that everyone should follow their own conscience because God was very understanding and forgiving and would probably have liked a good excuse for a celebration Himself. Constance thought he should have finished the sentence with a peace sign. Much to her delight he was full of tales of Lucas's youthful antics, which he had gleaned from his predecessor and Sir Walter, Lucas's father, and Constance found herself listening with a dopey smile on her face. Cassandra Woode had noticed that smile and remarked later to her husband, in bed, that he might want to prepare himself for a wedding service if Sir Lucas returned safe and sound from the war because she had never seen a girl so evidently in love and could not believe that he would be able to resist her beautiful green eyes and unusually lively nature. The Reverend Woode trusted his wife's uncanny instincts and began to pray in even more earnest for Lucas Deverell to be spared.

Christmas came and went with very little disruption to their daily routine. The house was lightly but defiantly decorated with holly, rosemary and some bay; plum puddings were made and heartily consumed, and small gifts were given. There was some spirited dancing and some surprisingly tuneful singing and Lady Ursula distributed boxes to the staff and villagers as was the custom. The children dressed up in borrowed clothes and ran riot for an evening, reinvigorating The Lord of Misrule customs of the past despite Puritan disapproval, and they were allowed to preside over the Feast of Fools until their exuberance got out of hand and they were sent to bed. Constance couldn't help thinking that this was what Christmas should be like, elegantly understated and about family, but she caught herself and feared she was fast becoming Puritanical by osmosis.

Constance thought longingly of her own family Christmases and although consumerism and hedonism had mostly destroyed the real spirit of Christmas, being with the boys and her sister was what she really remembered with great joy and also, given her predicament, some sadness.

She thought of Lucas, probably sleeping in some cold and wet cow byre so far away from his family, with nothing to look forward to for months ahead except marching over muddy fields, sporadic fighting and an uncertain outcome, and she wished hard for things to be different, knowing deep down that nothing she could do would change anything.

January, raw with frosts and snow, made Constance and her adoptive family retreat further into the house, to stay close to the blazing fire and keep their extremities from freezing. They bundled up warmly in multiple layers of woollen scarves and shawls and any cosy hats they could find that might keep their ears from turning bright pink and mittens, even when in bed; they began to resemble corpulent knitted dormice. Benedict was so worried about Dash catching cold that he fashioned him a coat from a red blanket, which luckily the Wolfhound didn't object to, being a mild-mannered and tolerant sort of creature, and he perambulated about the Great Hall with it dragging behind him as though he were canine royalty.

Then after the snow had melted came February fill dyke, with a biblical deluge of rain and blustery winds which left a trail of damage across the estate. The fields were flooded and the lanes virtually impassable. Venturing out at all was foolish but in long skirts and poorly designed shoes, almost impossible. Constance longed for her Wellington boots and jeans so that she could check the geocache and walk up to the village to see Amos. Anything to get her out of the claustrophobic confines of the house. And then before she had time to even blink, February was almost over.

Her problem was the hours of the day when she couldn't do anything practical, no gardening or walking, no visiting villagers. Nor was she keen on embroidery; she found it a mindless occupation. Worse, the number of books available were limited; there were plenty in the library, but they were mostly of the type only Valentine de Cheverell could appreciate: dusty volumes pontificating in a dreary manner about scientific or religious matters, large bibles, too heavy to even lift or books of out-of-date maps — all seemed deadly dull to Constance, brought up on a diet of exciting and varied modern novels and dramatic television programmes. She had been spoilt and it was frustrating not to have something just right to read when the mood struck.

It was clear to Constance that Lady Ursula was at war with herself. Her natural indolence was constantly in danger of being overruled by an instinctive but unnatural need to make Quinton's life easier for him to bear. Every so often she would rebel against these new and undesirable impulses she had so unexpectedly become pray to and would desperately try to ignore her friend's requirements for a while, but she was always confounded by the fact that he would never ask anyone for help, always striving for independence. It drove her nearly mad. If he had been whiney and demanding she would have been able to consign him to the devil, but he was so phlegmatic, so concerned for everyone else that she couldn't resist going to his aid. It went against every natural instinct and infuriated her so that she often must have sounded less than happy to assist him. And still he would not complain.

Constance talked to them together and separately, delicately leading them along this new and rocky path, without being too blatant about throwing them together. In fact, at times, she found counter measures were more successful anyway. A bit of reverse psychology often seemed to do the trick.

"Ursula, I was thinking that I would take Quinton into the orangery while the sun is still out and let him sit for a while in there; it would do him good, the house is so very dark. You must be longing to have a moment to yourself, why don't you go for a little walk while the weather holds? It would do you good."

Ursula continued to stitch her embroidery in her usual careless fashion, not looking up, "Yes, I might do that. Although, the lane is very rutted and hard on the soles of one's feet. And the wind is particularly biting this morning, do you not think? Perhaps I shall stay in and sort out my needlework box. You should go out. Were you not saying that you needed to see Richard about something — urgent?"

"Oh, well, it wasn't urgent. It can wait. It was only about the beech trees beside the lane. No, it can certainly wait."

Ursula made a few more untidy stitches on her tambour, "Whatever you think, dear. Although, to be perfectly honest I am feeling somewhat enervated, being cooped up inside all this while. Perhaps, I should take Quinton to the orangery? You do so much for him, you deserve a rest."

"Oh, how thoughtful! Yes, that would be ideal. I will go and talk to Richard and see you later," declared Constance with a triumphant gleam in her eye.

Ursula waited until she had left the house and then walked quickly to her bedchamber to dab on a little scent and ridiculously, tidy her hair, and then without looking in the least bit eager, she went to find Quinton who was in the library with Valentine and Benedict.

"Quinton, Constance has ordered me to take you for some sunshine in the orangery. She was so very insistent that I am too afraid to refuse!"

Quinton Gittings smiled serenely at her misty outline and rose to his feet, "Well, we cannot deny her, then. If you can bear it?"

Her ladyship moved to his side and resting his hand on her arm, she led him across the room, "I was sewing. I dislike sewing very much."

Quinton laughed, "So, I am the lesser of two evils?"

"No, indeed, my dear, you could never be evil, you are all goodness."

"I can assure you Ursula that I am nothing of the kind!" said her companion with a sardonic twist to his mouth.

Ursula regarded him, intrigued, "Is that so? That surprises me."

"Oh? You think I am a saint? How little you know me, then."

"Well, you are my brother's best friend, after all. I know only what I have been told by him and what I myself have experienced and Lucas is devoted to you so only has good things to recount. How am I to know if you are concealing a dark side?"

"Hardly dark! I am merely saying that not all my thoughts are of heavenly choirs and rainbows."

"I should hope not! How perfectly *dreadful*!" exclaimed Lady Ursula in mock horror. "Rainbows, indeed! Enough to drive a degenerate man like yourself to drink!"

Quinton gave a shout of laughter and for an all-to-brief moment pressed her hand with his; she considered the gesture and thought a squeeze was slightly better than the fraternal pat. But only slightly.

Richard Thorne, standing in the middle of The Wilderness, a saw in his hand, a pile of deadwood at his feet, greeted Constance with a slight frown, which was so unusual. She knew immediately that something was wrong.

Twenty-One

"Richard? What is it?"

For a moment he didn't say anything, as he regarded her with concern, "I was coming to see you at the house because I have just received some news from a fellow wounded soldier, who was on his way home from the West Country to Stow."

Constance flinched and turned pale, "Oh, no. Please — don't — "

Richard Thorne steeled himself, "He had been first at Bristol with Sir Lucas and then followed him to Basing House and then finally to Torrington a few weeks ago."

Constance had stopped breathing and closed her eyes.

"Mistress Harcourt, perhaps I should wait until Lady Ursula —"

"Just — tell me."

"There was an explosion in the church, killing — "

"No, no, no — "

" — killing many of the Royalist prisoners held there and there were also some casualties on the Parliamentarian side. I am sorry, but Sir Lucas was badly injured but survived and was billeted in a field hospital in a manor house nearby. When recovered enough, he was escorted with others to Taunton and then on to Bath. When last he was heard of, he was in the care of St John's almshouses."

"I don't understand. Why hasn't he been brought straight home?" asked Constance in a suffocated whisper.

"Mistress, I know not. He said they did not know what to do with him — how to cure him and left him there for his own good."

Constance stared at Richard Thorne but didn't see him, her eyes blinded by unnamed terror, "Will they bring him home eventually — when he is well enough?"

"No, mistress, I believe not. The army have already moved on and they cannot carry their wounded with them. It is customary to leave them behind. They still get their regular pay and where possible are left with medical help."

She was looking right through the forester as though in a trance, "Well, then the answer is quite simple. We must go and collect him."

"Mistress? How? We cannot just set forth in the hopes of finding him — "

"No, you're quite right. We shall make an excellent plan and *then* set forth and find him. You and me and that first-rate stable-boy, Will —"

"Will Sparrow! He must only be sixteen or so."

"Will Sparrow, yes, that's the one. I noticed that Lucas always favoured him and, when I asked, he said the boy was diligent and had potential to be something more. That's enough for me."

"Whatever you say, Mistress. Anyone else? We will need at least four if we are to attempt this."

"Do you have any ideas, Richard? You know what we might come across and who would be suitable."

"Someone comes to mind: served with Sir Lucas, lives over in Wyck. Captain Hugh Maitland, injured at Naseby so I know he will be at home recuperating. Just the man to have by you in a crisis."

"That's four then," said Constance.

"Three."

"And me, *four*."

"But — Mistress Harcourt — if you do not mind me saying —"

"Well, I *do* mind. I am quite capable."

Richard Thorne looked a little uncomfortable, "Yes, I am sure you are but — "

Constance's eyes narrowed dangerously, "I'll have you know, Mr Thorne, that I was a Girl Guide. Nobody messes with a Girl Guide."

The forester was baffled but remembering what Sir Lucas had said about certain people's tendencies to be headstrong, he bit back his words until he could find some way of persuading her to give up her hare-brained notion. He didn't like to think about what Sir Lucas would say if he allowed her to ride across the war-torn countryside. He had seen the way Sir Lucas had looked at her and had quickly realised his commanding officer was smitten with Mistress Harcourt. It had secretly amused him to see Sir Lucas at the mercy of his emotions; Richard had seen him in the worst conditions imaginable — under heavy bombardment, facing muskets and pikes, trudging through knee-deep mud in a snowstorm and badly injured and suffering in a filthy field hospital — but never had he seen him so prey to doubt, and it was a revelation to see him entirely unable to control one small woman with beautiful green eyes. Until the very last moment he thought Sir Lucas had not been behaving like himself; he seemed unusually skittish and bad-tempered but when, minutes before leaving he had finally acted and regained some control, Richard had been relieved to see him back in command. But it had not lasted long because Mistress Harcourt's reaction had been unexpected, to say the least — not at all maidenly and he could not help but feel that Sir Lucas had lost that particular skirmish. Now, here he was, in charge of the victor and she was already proving to be a handful.

"I have no idea what a Girl Guide is but I have no doubt that it is something of which to be wary and I have no desire to anger one but on the other hand Sir Lucas left me in charge of your safety and I think that this venture is not suitable for a — "

"If you dare to say *woman* in a disparaging manner — I — I shall plant you a facer!" snapped Constance angrily.

Richard Thorne noted her clenched fists and decided reluctantly to admit defeat. "If you do come then you must promise me that you will listen to reason and not act wilfully or impulsively. Our lives could depend upon it — *his* life could depend upon it. This is not some child's game — it is a matter of life or death. I need you to understand that."

Constance nodded meekly, "I will listen and obey, I promise."

"Do you ride?"

"Ah, I was afraid you might ask that. I do, but not very well, horses are not really my thing. Tova, my sister, loves them. I'm more of a cat person."

"Cats? As long as you can stay in the saddle, we should be all right — although you will probably get a little saddle-sore. The journey should take about three days, following the old Roman road, the Fosse Way. We will be sleeping under hedges."

She smiled knowingly, "You will not put me off that way either. We camped out under the stars many times — and sang songs."

"There will be no singing."

"All right. When can we start?"

"The day after tomorrow at the earliest. I must find Captain Maitland and explain. We must prepare horses, provisions, maps, weapons — and you will need some kind of disguise."

"Disguise? Like a servant? I could borrow some clothes from the kitchen maid."

Richard Thorne looked at her pensively, "I was thinking more, like a young boy, from a good family. The long hair would work well, and it would be easier for you to wear boy's attire whilst riding and you would be hopefully safer."

"Splendid! I'll call myself Humphrey."

"I find it is always better to stay as close to the truth as possible. You shall be called Conn. Can you put on an Irish accent?"

"Yes, I can."

"If stopped, we will say we are going to find your injured father."

"He won't like that."

"We won't tell him. Now, we need to find you some clothes. You are of small build — Benedict's might fit you?"

"I'll see what I can find."

"You have no objections?"

"None at all. I am quite used to wearing breeches."

The forester gave her a quizzical look, "Somehow I am not surprised by that."

Two days later they were prepared, and Constance was eager to leave. Richard Thorne was doing a last-minute check, in his methodical and military fashion, driving Constance to distraction with his lists and counting, packing and repacking.

Will Sparrow had been beside himself with pride and joy when asked if he would join the rescue party and his skinny chest had been puffed up ever since.

Captain Hugh Maitland had immediately agreed to the mission because he was an out-and-out military man, trapped at home with his family, and desperately needing a project to give him an honest excuse to leave for a while. Constance could see why Richard had recommended him. He had an air of capability about him, a decisive walk; something about the way he clicked his boot heels into the ground gave one confidence. Not above average height, lean, square jawed and with a clipped and authoritative voice, and unexpected dimples when he smiled, Constance instantly trusted him and was glad he was going with them.

They each had a horse of their own and the three men were to lead three others, two packhorses and a suitable mount for Lucas Deverell. Richard had chosen Tulip, a steady looking dapple-grey mare, for Constance and made her ride around the stable yard several times so that he could be sure they were a good match.

Constance rummaged through Benedict's press and found some of his cast-offs which almost fitted her with a few hastily done alterations. The toes of his boots had to be stuffed with rags because they were at least two inches too big for her and she stitched a thick band inside his hat so that it didn't keep sliding down over her eyes. By the time she'd finished, she thought she made a very creditable youth.

Frances, who had helped her dress, stood back to appreciate their hard work and nodded, satisfied with the result, "That should fool most people. Although you do look rather effeminate, maybe you should have a false beard?"

Constance laughed, "I think I'll just be a late-developer and hope for the best. I wouldn't want your father's first sight of me to be too off-putting."

Frances's face lit up, "You think you will find him then?"

"Of course! I'm certainly not going to give up until he's apologised for his appalling behaviour."

"I wish I could go with you."

"After a few nights spent under a dripping hedge with rats and foxes, I think you might change your mind."

"I suppose you are right," said Frances with a half-hearted smile, "But I dread you not being here. What if — ?"

Constance went to her and took her in her arms and held her tightly, "No, we will not have what ifs! We *will* find him, and we *will* bring him home. You'll be safe here — you have Mr de Cheverell, Mr Gittings, and Oates. And I can assure you nobody would dare to challenge your Aunt Ursula! She is indomitable. And you also have Dash to scare away intruders."

"Oh, Constance! He is completely useless — unless he could deter them by licking them to death!"

Constance was given a flintlock pocket pistol with an ivory handle and a dagger in a sheath to tuck into her boot. Richard gave her some lessons in loading and firing and he pronounced her quite a decent shot.

Mistress Peel, whilst in a bit of a lather about all the comings and goings, gleefully took on the task of supplying provisions for the expedition, "Just as though," remarked Lady

Ursula, "the King himself had ordered a banquet for all his most esteemed courtiers."

Richards looked askance at the various baskets and packets of food and flagons of drink filing past him, "We only have two damn packhorses," he muttered darkly but still they kept coming.

Constance, trotting down the elegant staircase in her boy's garb for the first time actually felt slightly awkward especially when she caught Mistress Fitch eyeing her disapprovingly.

"That woman could sour milk with just a glance!" she growled at Quinton Gittings, who was waiting by the door to see them off on their journey.

"Ah, you will be talking about our dear housekeeper. She must be torn between wanting her master returned and the need to keep you away from him. Poor confused woman."

Constance gave an unladylike snort, "I can't understand why he keeps her on."

"He is relentlessly loyal and underneath the harsh exterior he has a good heart."

"Pah! He's going soft."

Quinton smiled, "Possibly. Have you heard from Guy?"

"There was a message a few days ago agreeing to wait before attempting my return to — my own time. And, I have written to let him know that I'll be away for an unspecified amount of time on a mission. There doesn't seem to be any rhyme nor reason for the workings of the geocache — it's a mystery. It just either works or it doesn't. I wish it were easier to regulate. It's so random. It's a bit like the Internet."

"The — ?"

"Oh, dear friend, I wish I could explain but I don't even understand it myself! Nobody does. Now, by the looks of things, I think the time has come. Will is on his horse already and Captain Maitland is mounting up. Richard is looking at me impatiently and Benedict is about to cry. Farewell and good luck managing this unruly lot! Be kind to Ursula, she's not nearly as tough as she makes out and she'll need support."

"That suggests that I do not always give succour where it is needed."

Constance laid a gentle hand on his arm, "Quinton, you can sometimes be a little abrasive with her. I suppose it must be a case of familiarity breeding contempt. You've known her so long that she's become part of the furniture. While I'm away I'd like you to work on what we'd call your *people skills*. Be nice! Ursula appears to be lazy and imperious but it's just a carefully constructed mask. She doesn't want people to guess her true feelings, to see that she has weaknesses."

A slight frown appeared between his sightless eyes, "I — had not thought — but I see that you are right and I — have been careless in my treatment of her. I swear that I will try to do better. Thank you for your guidance."

"You're so welcome. Now, I really must be on my way or Richard will have a seizure!" and she gave him a warm hug which he returned with gusto and went out to join the little cavalcade waiting in the thin winter sunshine.

Oates was holding Tulip, ready to help her up into the saddle. Frances, Benedict, Valentine de Cheverell, and Lady Ursula were gathered in a knot at the bottom of the steps. Benedict's eyes were round like saucers and shimmering with unshed tears and his bottom lip was trembling. Constance went to him first.

"It'll be all right — we'll bring him home. I'm depending on you to keep an eye on your sister and aunt please and Mr de Cheverell and Mr Gittings will, in turn, keep an eye on you. This way I will know that you're all safe and sound."

He nodded, his mouth pressed firmly into a determined line. She then hugged him and everyone else and with a speaking glance for Ursula she allowed Oates to assist her onto the patient Tulip.

It felt very strange sitting high up on a horse, looking down at all the anxious faces looking up at her. She suddenly felt rather tearful and afraid.

Frances held up her hand and Constance clasped it, fighting a surge of emotions, " Constance — I — " her cheeks turning pink.

Constance squeezed her hand, "I know. Me too. We'll be back."

As they rode away, the tears were streaming down her face. She turned back once as they passed through the gates and waved. She couldn't see them through the blur of tears.

They headed West into the valley in order to join the old Roman road at Northleach. Richard Thorne thought they could cover about twenty miles a day; he wanted to ease both people and animals into it, allowing time for resting and for setting up their first camp at Duntisbourne Rouse.

Once they were up on the virtually treeless rise above the Windrush Valley they were quite exposed to the weather and after the weak morning sun had disappeared into low cloud, the temperature dropped, and the wind picked up. Constance was glad to be wearing breeches and a thick leather doublet; she wrapped her heavy cloak around her and pulled Benedict's hat down over her face, while Tulip plodded on steadily. The only noises, the thumping of the horse's hooves on the turf, the metallic rattle of the bridles, the creak of leather and the occasional whicker or snort. The humans were oddly silent, concentrating on getting some miles under their belts and concerned about the task ahead.

Eventually, it was Will Sparrow who broke the silence. They were passing the village Constance knew as Farmington when the young stable lad cleared his throat, "My aunt lives in Thormerton," he said.

"In — this village?" asked Constance guessing it was the old name he was using.

"Aye."

And that was it for another few miles. Nobody seemed inclined to chat. They were crossing softly rolling hills which were grazed by sheep and gentle curved wooded valleys, the occasional hamlet or farmhouse and smallish rivers and streams. Every five miles or so they would get down to walk for a bit to allow the horses to cool off, graze, and rest. Richard was a stickler for this, explaining that horses were brave beasts but could be fragile if overworked. If they cared for their mounts they would be amply rewarded by their steadfastness.

They stopped around halfway for food and to water the horses in the River Coln, near Fossebridge, where the steeply sloping hills were hard for both horse and rider. The sky was beginning to darken by the time they reached their first day's destination, Duntisbourne Rouse. The winter days were short and riding in poor light was too dangerous with an inexperienced rider like Constance amongst them. The men were very considerate about her needs and uncomplaining about the slow progress.

Captain Maitland was encouraging, "You will become used to being in the saddle after a few days and the soreness will abate. You are doing remarkably well, Mistress Harcourt."

"Thank you, I don't feel like I am, and I can't help but think I'm a terrible burden because of my poor riding skills."

"No, no! Richard would make us go at this pace anyway! He is very particular, as I am sure you have noticed."

Constance smiled, "He is extremely thorough. Captain, please would you call me Constance?"

"With pleasure! It does seem a little strange to be so formal whilst in this unusual situation. Call me Hugh."

They were skirted around Cirencester in order to avoid any pockets of soldiers, of either persuasion; Richard was adamant that they should do their best to stick to the back roads. Constance couldn't help a slight knowing smirk as she compared back roads in her mind. Back roads here were little more than sheep tracks. The village of Duntisbourne Rouse was surrounded by woods and the church, where they were setting up their camp, a short way north of the tiny settlement, was sheltered by steep wooded slopes. Richard and

Hugh quickly and efficiently raised two wedge tents, a slightly smaller one for Constance and the other for the three men to cram themselves into. Constance felt guilty for making them share such a confined space, but they were sanguine, saying they were soldiers and used to such conditions. Will Sparrow bustled about the horses, unsaddling, brushing down, feeding and watering them, and then hobbling them for the night. A fire was built and lit in the blink of an eye and before long there was water boiling and a freshly trapped rabbit roasting. Potatoes were thrown into the hot ashes and a flagon of ale was opened and distributed. Richard foraged some logs for them to sit on and they settled down for their supper in some comfort, even though the cold was biting. At least they were sheltered from the worst of the weather. Constance thought that the food was particularly tasty after a long day in the saddle and as she tucked into her potato with a hunk of strong cheese, followed by a rather wrinkled apple, she thought about all the tasteless packaged food she had eaten in the future and wondered if things had really improved at all.

After supper they chatted for a bit around the fire. Will talked about horses and his four older brothers, Hugh Maitland spoke of his life in the army and his wife and two daughters, and Richard was mostly silent. Constance guessed he was worrying about the journey ahead and in what state they were going to find Lucas.

When she eventually turned in for the night, she found that Richard had made her a pretty decent looking bed and she knew that she was so tired that sleep was a certainty. They all slept in their clothes for ease and added warmth and even though Constance had the tent nearest to the fire, it was bone-chillingly cold sleeping on the ground with only some canvas for protection.

She awoke a few times in the night when she heard the cry of an animal or Richard tending the fire.

The blue light of dawn filtered through the trees and she was awake and scrambling out of her blankets, eager to get going. They were one day closer to finding Lucas and that's all she could think about.

Twenty-Two

Time passed in a sluggish manner, made up of monotonous routine and odd little bits of excitement, a river to cross, slippery slopes, and the ever-changing weather; Constance did everything she was told with a mute obedience which would have made Tova raise her eyebrows in disbelief. But Constance knew that any ripples she made would just slow them down. She didn't know anything about his circumstances except that something was preventing Lucas from being sent home. Neither Richard Thorne nor Captain Maitland could expand on the information they had been given and she could tell by the sudden closing of the shutters that it was best not to delve too deeply into the reasons.

South of Cirencester they rejoined the Roman road and followed it past Malmesbury until camping again just south of Sherston. They had met nobody but a farmer and his son and their waggon-load of pigs, who stopped for a chat and in conversation it was mentioned that just south aways, near Grittleton, there was an encampment of Royalist soldiers who, according to locals, were making their leisurely way back to Oxford for winter quartering after months of fighting in the West Country. Richard Thorne and Captain Maitland put their heads together and made some adjustments to their route. Hugh was fairly certain that if it had just been the three men, they could have managed but with Constance, even in disguise, it was a risk not worth taking.

They decided between them that they would skirt around Bath and enter the city by the West Gate and from there it was a direct route to St John's Hospital where Lucas had been taken. They would have been happier to leave Will and

Constance outside the city, but she was obdurate, saying if they didn't take her, she would go alone. They had no choice.

The journey to the gate was uneventful and they passed through with no trouble. Inside the walls the city was gentle hustle and bustle, a market town going about its business. Constance found herself rather taken aback by the medieval look of the place, staring up at the half-timbered buildings as though they'd dropped from outer space; in her mind's eye it was still the golden Georgian city she had often visited.

Towering above the jumble of roofs was The Abbey, dwarfing the surrounding buildings with its magnificent height and commanding presence. Constance longed to explore this version of Bath and, now on foot with Tulip beside her, had difficulty walking without bumping into passers-by because her eyes were on the architecture and looking in amazement at the crowds of ordinary seventeenth century people milling about. The streets were surprisingly clean although the smells were strong and Constance couldn't help wrinkling her nose in distaste at the human and animal waste, rotting food, and other not so easily described smells. A young street sweeper was busily keeping the crossings clean for the noble ladies who tip-toed across in their pattens and inconveniently trailing gowns looking like exotic birds. There were alehouses and stables and people selling their wares, calling out in loud voices and stray dogs and cats wandering about in the hopes of some scraps.

Richard had to keep an eye on her in case she got left behind and she realised she was behaving like a typical tourist, dawdling in the middle of the road, careless of the traffic.

"Conn! Keep up with us and stop drawing attention to yourself!" he snapped, losing patience with her lack of concentration.

Constance closed her gaping mouth and pulled herself together. Captain Maitland said that St John's Hospital was just off Westgate Street and she lengthened her stride, in what she hoped was a manly fashion, as she guided Tulip through the throng. They left Will to hold the horses in the main street so they could more easily negotiate the narrow alleyways which led to the hospital.

With Captain Maitland leading them with a military watchfulness they soon came upon the place, set in a medieval courtyard enclosed by half-timbered houses, with their diamond-leaded windows, crowded in elbow to elbow, like nosy neighbours. At the main door, Captain Maitland instructed Richard and Constance to wait just inside the hallway while he went to speak to the clerk.

Constance's heart was racing, and she felt a little shaky with anxiety and anticipation. She watched Hugh talking to the clerk and observed their body language with mounting dismay.

Hugh returned to them, his face solemn, "He says that they had a Colonel Sir Lucas Deverell here for a while, but they could not provide treatment for him — he was not the type of patient they usually accommodate. Apparently, he has been removed to Shepton Mallet." He paused and put a firm hand on her shoulder, "I am afraid he has been taken to the prison there."

"Prison!" whispered Constance, her throat constricting as though she were being strangled. "He's — not here?"

"They had to move him. Come, we will set out at once. It is just a day's ride."

She could barely cope with the disappointment and frustration. Another day in the saddle, another night under canvas before she'd be reunited with him. She was fighting back the tears.

"Tomorrow, Conn, we will find him tomorrow."

"Never jam today — " said Constance wretchedly.

Richard and Hugh exchanged concerned glances and gently steered her back to Will and the horses.

They followed West Gate Street into Staule Street and left the city with something of a sigh of relief by the South Gate. They were soon back on the Roman road and making their way across the Mendip foothills, but this time Richard was happy to push them a little, keeping up a slightly faster pace.

They avoided the villages and made the steady climb up to Shepton Mallet. As they finally neared their destination the Captain questioned a cheery parson trotting past in a pony and trap, who was happy to give directions and advise them where to camp for the night. They found a sheltered spot in Harridge Woods near Nettlebridge and made camp. It had rained most of the afternoon, making the riding uncomfortable and the riders miserable. Constance was quiet and paid little attention to the desultory conversation around the fire and after eating a token supper, she bid the gentlemen goodnight and retreated to her tent, where she sat for a good half an hour crying soundlessly.

Not finding Lucas in Bath had woken her from her stupor, a sort of anaesthetised state which had helped her endure the hardships of the journey and the nervous tension that was slowly building inside her. She hoped never to see another horse as long as she lived and would never go camping again if she could help it. From now on it would be five-star hotels all the way.

She wanted to take off her sodden clothes but knew that would be a mistake; they may be wet but at least they were warm. She lay down and wrapped herself in her blankets and noticed that there seemed to be an extra one; someone had given up their blanket for her. She fell asleep with tears sliding down her frozen cheeks.

Shepton Mallet Prison was a bleak looking place from the outside, high blank walls and tiny, sightless windows; a pall of hopelessness hung over it like a sinister fog. It had clearly been neglected for many years and was in a state of disrepair. There was a moment when they all just stood and stared, wondering how they were going to storm this intimidating citadel.

Then Captain Maitland squared his shoulders and jaw, "I have a scheme — it is not much of a scheme, but it is all I have. In prisons like these the gaolers are not paid a wage, they get their money from providing the prisoners with luxuries such as edible food and clean water. I believe the wardens will be open to a bribe. How much money does everyone have? I have about seven pounds and a few shillings."

Richard and Will emptied their pockets and Constance handed over the purse that Ursula had pressed upon her when saying goodbye. She hadn't even looked in it.

The Captain tipped out the coins and counted up their bounty. "I think we have more than enough. Richard and I will go into the prison and you two will stay with the horses. In the event that anything goes wrong, I am trusting you, Will Sparrow, to get Mistress Harcourt to safety."

"Aye, Captain, I will make sure no harm comes to her," said the stable lad briskly.

"But — " began Constance.

"No," said Richard firmly, "You will obey, like you promised you would. It is too dangerous. If it were discovered that you were a woman — it would be disastrous and jeopardise the whole rescue mission. You want to see Sir Lucas again? This is his best chance."

Constance looked at him mutinously but nodded. She knew he was right.

Richard and Hugh adopted forceful military guises and entered the prison by the impressive main entrance. They were greeted by a testy guard who demanded to know what they were about. Captain Maitland, in his best army voice, informed him that they had been sent to collect a prisoner for trial at the Assize Courts in Devizes.

The guard regarded them blankly, "Devizes? An' what prisoner might that be?"

"Colonel Sir Lucas Deverell. Parliamentarian. He was mistakenly transferred here from Bath. He was supposed to be in hospital. We have had to make an unnecessary journey and it has already delayed us. Time is of the essence. Now, where is he?"

The guard folded his arms across his chest, "An' who might you be, sir?"

"Captain Maitland, Fairfax's New Modelled Army. Deverell is wanted for desertion." Even as he said it, it made his guts churn, it was so far from the truth. But he kept his face rigid as he waited for the stupid man to think things through.

"I ain't heard nothing about this. You got papers?" demanded the guard.

Captain Maitland shook his head in despair, "You think our commander-in-chief has time to write personal letters to all and sundry? Think again, fool! He has better things to do. Now, stop quibbling and take me to the prisoner at once!"

The guard gave him a knowing look, "You goin' to make it worth my while, then?" he asked with a sneer.

Captain Maitland sighed and held out his hand to Richard Thorne, who dropped the purse into it. "This should help grease the wheels and make up for the burden of looking after him. As much again, if we find him fit to travel."

The guard shook the coins out and counted them slowly. He was clearly more than happy with the quality of the bribe and pocketed it quickly before any of his fellow workers could see it. He led them down a corridor and into one of the prison wings. A long line of cell doors and walkways reeking with the smell of death and disease and the desperately unsanitary conditions made even the two seasoned soldiers choke. The noise of the inmates grew steadily louder as they went deeper into the building. The one sound above any other which made their blood run cold was the crying of infants and women mixed in amongst the cacophony of male voices.

They came to another smaller wing and eventually the guard stopped outside a cell door. He unlocked it and stood back to let them enter.

Captain Maitland paused on the threshold, "God damn your souls to hell," he muttered.

It was drizzling and Constance was pacing along the outer walls, talking to herself while Will Sparrow walked the horses so they didn't get chilled. Richard and Hugh seemed to have been gone for ages and she was beginning to fear the worst. What could be keeping them? Part of her wanted to march in and see what was going on but she remembered the look in Richard's eyes and took a shaky breath. She must be a good, obedient female. She ground her teeth and kept pacing.

A slight commotion in the doorway alerted her and she turned to see Richard and Hugh coming out of the portico. Between them they were part carrying, part dragging, someone in a state of collapse.

Something inside Constance broke.

She found she couldn't move. She stood at a distance and watched them as though in a dream.

There he was, just in front of her, after all this time. And she was frozen to the spot.

Richard glanced at her, "Take the horses, Conn. Will, come and help."

Constance ran to the horses and took their reins. The young stable lad went to help carry his master and lie him down on the bank opposite the prison entrance. He was then instructed to go and cut two stout poles to construct a litter. Constance buried her head in Tulip's warm neck and tried, in vain, not to think. She knew she would have to face up to the truth eventually, but she wanted to remain insensible for as long as possible. She had caught a glimpse of his beloved face. Constance was frightened. The truth was plain to see. This was a man broken by war. She had seen it before on news reports, in documentaries. There was no mistaking shell shock or PTSD as it would one day be called.

They quickly and efficiently made a litter, from the poles and a couple of blankets, to drag behind one of the packhorses and strapped it to the saddle. They lay their patient down on it and bound him so that he couldn't fall and covered him in blankets.

When he was firmly fastened and the others were mounting up, Constance made herself go to him. She squatted down beside the litter and reaching out, stroked his face. He opened his eyes, but she knew he could see nothing, there was no recognition, no understanding in those familiar, hooded eyes.

"You stupid git," she whispered, "You couldn't just come home to me could you! You had to go and get yourself all messed up. Well, if you think this is going to put me off, you're very much mistaken. It may be a major hiccup, but I'm made of bloody Kevlar. And, if you think this is going to save you from an almighty bollocking, think again, mate!" She leant forward and kissed his battered forehead. "Fuckwit," she added for good measure.

The journey to their first campsite for the night was slow and painful for everyone. The litter was fine on the muddy tracks but harder to manage on steep slopes and when crossing water. It had to be unstrapped and then bodily lifted over obstacles and it took precious time and energy to accomplish. Constance wasn't strong enough to help, so she was relegated to holding the horses. The first night they camped in the crook of some hedges, facing away from the prevailing wind and it took some time for Richard to get the fire going because everything was wet. They set up the tents as usual and then there was a moment when they had to discuss which of the three men would be sleeping out by the fire, to make room in their tent for the patient.

Constance waited until there was a gap in the discussion, before saying quietly, "There's really no need for anyone to suffer! Lucas can sleep in my tent."

Captain Maitland's face was a picture of shocked disapproval, "Constance, that would be most inappropriate!"

She made a dismissive sound, "*Really?* In his state? With you three within shouting distance — whispering distance actually! I think I shall be perfectly safe, and I want to keep an eye on his condition anyway."

Richard sighed heavily, "She is right. Look at him. Some-one will be on watch."

It was agreed and the patient was manhandled into his bed in the tent. Constance tried to get him to eat something, but he was unresponsive to all her cajoling. In the end she gave up and thought that he had at least started off with enough bulk to be able to last a while without sustenance.

When all was quiet in the camp and she had wrapped herself in her blankets and wriggled down in the narrow space left for her, she turned on her side and stared at her companion. He was sleeping like the dead.

She studied him, wondering when he'd had his hair shorn and why. His face and body showed the signs of the impact from the explosion, he had some deep gashes that needed stitches if he wasn't to be badly scarred for life. He looked very different without the long curls and Van Dyke beard. Harder, even less approachable and more like the stereotyp-ical Roundhead. She thought she could probably get used to it but having always liked long hair on men, she felt a ridicu-lous sense of disappointment. Here he was, suffering from massive mental and physical trauma and she was fretting about the length of his hair. She wondered if she wasn't per-haps a bit traumatised herself. She couldn't resist running her hand softly over his head, to feel the mole-like nap of his buzzcut. He didn't stir.

She had nothing but questions and nobody to supply the much-needed answers. She tried to recall what she had seen about shell shock and it amounted to very little. She knew it hadn't really been recognised as a proper thing until the First World War and that treatment to begin with had been cruel and primitive. The sufferers had been considered cowards and treated as such They'd been given brutal electric shock treatment and doctors had tried to bully them back to sanity, while the government had wanted the whole embarrassing thing just buried and forgotten. And that's how it was until an army psychologist called Rivers found a more humane way to effect a cure. Constance now wished she'd paid more attention to the details. What she did know was that she had to coax him to talk, to make him feel safe, and to reassure him that this state did not have to be permanent.

The journey took an extra two days which meant that they ran out of food and were living off the land and what they could beg from farmers. Richard was a dab hand at shooting squirrels and rabbits and Will seemed to know what roots they could eat without poisoning themselves. An old lady saw them trudging past her cottage and insisted on loading them up with some potatoes, a couple of very good pies, some wrinkly apples and two flagons of ale. She said her sons would never miss them and anyway, being God-fearing boys, they would be only too happy to have helped some strangers, be they for Parliament or the King. She said that in the end God would find a way to resolve the arguments. Constance inwardly rolled her eyes but thanked their benefactress profusely for the supplies.

The old lady gave her the glad eye, "Handsome boy," she said appreciatively.

Captain Maitland chuckled for about a mile afterwards.

Late in the afternoon on the fifth day they finally limped home. Tulip came to a standstill in front of the house and Constance, too tired to move, just sat slumped in the saddle staring up at the house. Every muscle and bone ached, her hands were split and sore from being constantly wet, she knew she probably smelt to high heaven and her clothes were a uniform muddy brown. And her hair — her *hair!*

Richard and Hugh were dismantling the litter and preparing to carry Lucas into the house when a joyous bark heralded the arrival of Dash, galloping at full tilt, around the house. He was followed by Benedict, running, who skidded to a halt, took in the sight before him and suddenly hurtled at Constance, who had just slid from her horse onto the ground and found to her dismay that her legs weren't holding her up very well. Benedict collided with her and she was knocked back against Tulip's sturdy flank.

"Constance! Oh, *Constance!* You are back!" he exclaimed loudly.

Constance held on tightly to him, for fear of falling to the ground in an exhausted heap.

The barking and shouting brought the others. Ursula and Frances flew down the steps and straight at Constance who was now sobbing uncontrollably. Through the hiccupping wailing she managed to warn them, "We — have him. But he isn't himself. You must be prepared — he needs time to recover."

Frances, wiping away tears, turned to peer over her shoulder at the man lying so still on the litter. Constance watched proudly as the girl immediately went to her father and knelt beside him, burying her face into his shoulder. She met Ursula's eyes and then she was in her arms and Ursula was crying into her neck and Constance was trying to still her shaking knees.

"Well, what a glorious sound," said Quinton Gittings from the top of the steps and Valentine de Cheverell escorted him down to join the welcoming party. Ursula broke away to see her brother and Constance was impressed that the only sign of distress was that she turned a shade paler. Ursula followed the litter as it was carried in by Hugh, Richard, Will, and Oates and as they disappeared into the house Constance wrapped her arms about Quinton and attempted to just breathe evenly to steady her heart rate.

"Tell me," said Quinton.

"I think he's suffering from something called shell shock or battle fatigue. It looks like he'll never recover but — I think there's a way to bring him back. We — learn a lot — over the centuries about the treatment of such mental disorders."

"The symptoms?"

"I'm by no means an expert but from what I recall, anything from confusion and nightmares to amnesia and tremors. Episodes can be triggered by loud noises or trauma — it's distressing for everyone."

"We will prevail, my dear, I have faith."

"Faith in what?"

Quinton smiled, "Faith in your love for him and his for you."

Twenty-Three

Lady Ursula, hands on hips and frowning. Constance, mutinous, mouth petulantly downturned, like a toddler being denied her favourite sweet.

"You need to wash and change your clothes, Constance Harcourt."

"I *will.* Just not right *now.*"

"You have been saying that since yesterday. It is time, my love. I will sit with him while you go and remove those — clothes. You cannot keep wearing breeches and a doublet now you are home. And you not only look like a stable lad, you smell like one! There is a bath waiting for you in your bedchamber full of steaming hot water and orange flower water, just as you like it. *Go*, Constance! If he wakes, I will call you."

Constance sighed theatrically and leaning over her inert patient whispered, "In the immortal words of that great actor and politician — I'll be back. Don't do anything silly while I'm gone. By the way, your sister is unbelievably bossy!"

"Thank you," responded Ursula, "After growing up with me, I am sure he is already well aware of my imperfections."

Peeling off her boy's costume was actually a relief; it was stiff with dirt and starting to chafe. As she dropped it onto the floor, she wondered what Tova would have made of her wearing the same clothes for over a week. Her sister was fastidious and usually showered twice a day. Laughing to herself, Constance slid gratefully into the hot water and closed her eyes. It wasn't the usual hip bath, more of a wide trough, but she had decided that although she shouldn't mess with timelines, she really couldn't endure a life without bathing.

These people had some pretty archaic and silly ideas about getting wet and she was damned if she was going to give in. This week of washing avoidance was just an aberration.

Getting dressed again in clean petticoats and skirts was oddly comforting and she wondered if she was starting to suffer from Stockholm Syndrome or whether it was merely a case of inevitably integrating into your surroundings and circumstances.

As soon as she had rubbed her hair dry and twisted it into some kind of suitable arrangement, she eagerly returned to her patient.

Ursula looked up from her sewing and smiled, "There! Do you not feel better? You certainly look better and smell more fragrant!"

"You were right, annoyingly. I do feel refreshed. Has he — ?"

"He has not moved at all. You have missed nothing. I do think that you should have a rest this afternoon. You did not sleep at all last night. I am going to have Oates make up a truckle bed for you in here as I know you will not leave him."

"That would be wonderful! I want to be here if he wakes. I need to be."

"I can sit with him while you sleep. You want to look like yourself or he will mistake you for Mistress Fitch!"

Constance laughed, "Cruel! I passed her last night in the corridor and she pressed herself against the wall as though she might catch my depravity! I very nearly said something but then thought better of it."

"Very wise. She can twist things and I sometimes fear that she could very easily allow herself to be swept away by her prejudice. You should be cautious around her. Lucas only kept her on out of pity and guilt but now he cannot keep an eye on her and rein her in should she need it."

Constance looked at their patient, "It's one of his worst and best qualities. We'll have to clean him up too and see to those wounds, there are several that need stitches."

"Captain Maitland has already sent for an army surgeon he knows, from Donnington. He should be here this afternoon. The Captain says he is entirely trustworthy before you start doubting his credentials."

"I *wasn't* — no, you're quite right, again, I was! If Hugh approves of him then that is good enough. Shall we get Lucas washed and ready for his visit?"

Ursula agreed and went off to find Richard to help. Constance pulled the chair closer to the bed and sat, leaning on the edge, as close as she could get to Lucas. She watched for signs of his waking, stroking his face and telling him about their journey and repeating amusing things the children had said then she leant her forehead on his shoulder and waited.

Richard Thorne proved to be as efficient at bed baths as he was at all forms of forestry, shooting small mammals, and kidnapping prisoners. Ursula tried to persuade Constance to leave them to it as she felt it would be unseemly for an unrelated female to assist in such an intimate procedure.

Constance dismissed her concerns, "We've already slept together, so it's too late to save my virtue!"

Lady Ursula was not amused, "Constance! You must *never* repeat that to anyone! I know it was necessary at the time, but it could be misunderstood. Your reputation would be ruined. Lucas would not approve."

"I know — he's such a killjoy. I honestly can't think why I like him. Right, let's get on with it. Pass me that cloth!"

Doctor Horatio Spry reminded Constance of a wire-haired fox terrier. He had a bristling grey beard and bushy white eyebrows which hung over his dark beady eyes and a shock of unruly ginger hair which followed no particular style. He was the oddest-looking fellow with a stiff-legged walk and very small hands which were constantly fidgeting. She could tell, by the way he greeted everyone in a brisk manner and then without further ado moved swiftly to his patient's bedside, that he was a man on a mission.

Constance couldn't help watching him for signs of poor medical habits but, to her surprise and relief, he even demanded a bowl of water to wash his hands in and then rolling up his sleeves, donned a clean apron and, considering what he could have been like, behaved in an exemplary fashion throughout, although he did talk briefly about the merits of bleeding and the application of leeches. Constance desperately wanted to update him but managed to keep her newfangled ideas to herself.

Richard held Lucas steady while Constance stood by with clean linen and an oil lamp for extra illumination. She was not normally squeamish but watching Doctor Spry stitching into Lucas's skin very nearly made her faint and she was grateful when Ursula slid a chair behind her and shoved her into it without ceremony.

"You are looking a little pale, my dear. It would not do for the doctor to have to stop what he is doing to assist you. You are feeling the after-effects of your journey and should be resting."

The doctor cleaned and stitched half a dozen of the worst gashes and removed some imbedded splinters of metal and wood. He seemed happy that the other wounds would heal without stitches. He had a discussion with them about his general care which Constance again was unable to argue with and he said he would return at the end of the week to check on him and to make sure there was no signs of infection. He suggested giving him nourishing bone broths and oatmeal when he was ready to take sustenance and not to despair, for he had seen many miraculous recoveries on the battlefield and at least here he had the very best of care.

It was at four in the morning that Constance was awoken from a fitful sleep. She sat up in her truckle bed and peered into the darkness. There was another sound. She quickly threw off the covers and grabbed the lit candle from the table, lighting the others from the flame.

She tiptoed to the bed and perched on the edge of the chair. And listened.

There was a change in his breathing. It was barely noticeable, but Constance had been measuring its rhythms for days now and heard the subtle difference. She had no idea if it was a good or bad sign.

"Lucas?" she whispered, "Lucas, it's Constance." Don't push him, she thought impatiently, let him come to you at his own pace. However much you need him to be the man you love, you need him to be healthy first. God, she thought, all he did was change his breathing pattern and I'm already getting ahead of myself.

She sat back in the chair and closed her eyes.

She must have nodded off, just for a moment.

Her eyes flew open and she looked at Lucas.

He was staring at her.

She leaned forward and put her hand on his arm. "Lucas? You're at the Court House — your family home and you're safe. You're going to be all right."

He continued to stare at her, unblinking, as though only seeing the darkness. She moved a little closer. His focus changed and she could see that he was able to make out some kind of shape in the gloom. His eyes travelled around her face, but she was fairly certain he remained unable to identify her. Her disappointment was bitter, but she was determined not to start crying again because her waterworks were really beginning to annoy her.

"I'm going to get you a drink. Stay there!" she ordered. Then as she got up, she shook her head despairingly and mouthed, "*Stay there!*" to herself as though she was losing her mind. Like he was going anywhere! She found a beaker and filled it with the water she had asked the kitchen maid to boil earlier in the day.

"Here, I'm going to just sit you up a bit," she said as she rearranged pillows, then she slid her hand under his shoulders and put the beaker to his mouth.

A good deal of the water went down his neck, but some went into his mouth and she was triumphant.

"That's bloody brilliant!"

The dawn light was just peeping in through the curtains when Ursula arrived, still in her night robes, to find Constance fast asleep on the four-poster bed, curled up like a little girl, next to her brother, who was staring blankly into space.

As she approached the bed, his eyes found her and followed her movements but there was no recognition.

"Good morning, dear brother. Have you been keeping poor Constance up all the night? I think, as you are awake, I shall go and warn Mistress Peel and she can heat you up some bone broth for your breakfast — it will do you good."

It was very odd to receive no answer; they had always been able to argue about anything as children, bickering about who had whittled the best stick or whose pet snail was the fastest. She would give anything for him to disagree with her now, to tell her she was being childish, to hear him complaining about her laziness. She had a little barter with God, promising that she would never be idle again, if He would just cure Lucas.

It did not seem so very much to ask.

Constance awoke to find that she had snuggled up to Lucas in her sleep and that someone had covered her with a blanket and that his sister, fully dressed, was sitting beside the bed mending a hole in a scarlet stocking. Ursula looked up and smiled, "You looked so comfortable and you needed to sleep, so I left you."

Constance raised herself up on her elbow and peered a little blearily at Lucas. He was asleep. "Did he wake at all?"

"His eyes were open when I came in, but I would not exactly say he was awake. He did not know me. He has shown no expression or emotion but — and prepare to be *very* impressed — I did manage to get him to take a little broth."

Constance sat right up, "Oh, Ursula! That's wonderful. How clever!"

Lady Ursula graciously inclined her head and then laughed out loud, "I do not think I would have made a very good mother! He ended up with more on his pillow than in his mouth!"

"I got water all down his neck! And you would have been, and still could be, a splendid mother. Frances and Benedict adore you."

"Oh, they *have* to! I am their only aunt. It is their duty."

"Children cannot be forced to love. Any more than we can — even less so, because they cannot reason in the same way. They just love or they don't. It's simple."

Ursula raised her eyebrows, "You have nephews but no children of your own?"

Constance smiled but it didn't quite reach her eyes, "Yes, I have three. Giants with good hearts. And, I have no children of my own. I was always busy with my — painting and never met the right man." She looked down at the still figure beside her, "Until now. And it may be too late."

"Did your parents not try to arrange a marriage for you?"

"Lord, no! They'd never have even thought of it! Oh, Ursula! I'm sorry, of course — Lucas and your parents — !" She blushed furiously, "I'm such an idiot."

"No, do not fret! Lucas's marriage was not a good example, but my parents had a long and happy life together. It shows it can work sometimes."

"Your marriage was not arranged?"

"Not arranged — although expected. Jacob was the son of my father's best friend, Sir Geoffrey Prideaux. They were at school and Oxford together. Inseparable, apparently. I think our mothers always hoped but it was already a foregone conclusion. Jacob and I always knew, even when we were children, that we were supposed to be together. It was a perfect fit, you see; we never argued, we just made each other happy. Being without him is like losing a limb. I feel incomplete."

"Oh, Ursula, I'm so sorry. I wish I'd met him. He sounds very — lovely."

Ursula laughed, "You were going to say *long-suffering!* I know! Everyone thinks he must have been driven to distraction by my terrible character flaws, but he always said he loved all of me and without those traits my family found so impossible I would not have been the girl he fell in love with," she sighed, "He was certainly remarkably good-natured. He would have been such a good father."

"You tried for children — ?"

"Yes, but I had two miscarriages and the last one made me very ill. Jacob became extremely alarmed and could not be persuaded to try again. And then the war came."

There was a gentle tapping on the door and Frances and Benedict came in, both wide-eyed and stony-faced. Constance knew this was going to be very difficult for them, but she felt that in the end it would be good for the children and it might make all the difference to Lucas.

"Come in! Don't be afraid. He's been seen by the doctor and is much stitched and bandaged now but he still looks a bit of a mess. He has been awake although he's not quite with us yet. Come closer if you want."

The two children shuffled a little closer to the bed, but she could see they had the very understandable disconnect young people have when faced with old age or ill-health — a desire not to acknowledge the horror of human frailty. She thought of Rowen, who had had to overcome his morbid fear of old people. "I'm going to explain to you what has happened to your poor father and what we need to do to help him come back to us." She took their hands and held them firmly, "He's been in a very bad explosion, which has damaged both his face and body. It's also injured his mind. Sometimes, when things are too much for us, our brains just stop working, in a way to protect us from the horror of what we're facing. Also, a violent explosion can cause parts of the brain to be shaken so badly that they cease to work for a while — they need time to mend. Do you understand?"

The two children nodded and held onto her hands with fierce grips.

"So, what we all need to do, is to anchor him here with us, to make him understand that he's going to get better and to make sure he knows that we all love him. Together I believe we can heal him."

Benedict was trying valiantly to keep the tears at bay, sniffing and wiping his face on his sleeve; Frances was dry-eyed and tight-lipped.

"We have each other. The most important thing is — talking! We must try to encourage your father to talk and we must all talk to each other — that way the sad feelings we will all have can't get bottled up inside and hurt us. Does that make sense?"

More nodding.

As Lady Ursula was listening to this, she was thinking about what this would have been like had Constance Harcourt not fallen into their lives. She tried to imagine looking after the household and the children by herself. Her heart quailed. Ursula was no fool, she knew what her limitations were, and she knew her strengths. She knew that she was able to remain calm in a crisis because she was far too lethargic to allow herself to become agitated — being agitated took energy. She also knew that she was not naturally maternal but, without meaning to, she found she was learning a good deal from Constance, who had a way of talking to children as though they were small adults, which appeared to work well. Constance was an emotional creature, swinging violently, Ursula thought, from misery to joy and back again, without ever worrying about the consequences. She watched her hugging the children as though they were her own, as though those embraces were what sustained her. What a peculiar woman. What an oddity! Lady Ursula suddenly realised that she loved this oddity with all her heart. It came as something of a shock to her as she was not inclined to spread her affections far and wide. She had loved her parents, of course, felt fondness for her brother and a kind of dutiful love for the children but other than the devotion she had had for Jacob, there was nobody else — unless you counted the strange and hopefully fleeting affliction she was suffering from at the moment due to Quinton — she was exceedingly sparing with her love.

A thought occurred to her. Perhaps it was not Constance who was the oddity. Perhaps it was her.

This idea took her breath away.

Suddenly she was kneeling next to the children and Constance and had her arms around them all. She felt Constance start with surprise and laughed out loud.

"You are a very bad influence upon me!" she said. "I shall soon be hugging Dash and inviting him to sleep on my bed! There is no telling where this may end!"

Constance hooted with laughter and that set the children off and in a second they had collapsed into a giggling heap; the strain of the last two days finding an outlet in the ridiculous.

A gentle movement from the bed brought it to a sudden end. They all scrambled to their feet.

Lucas was looking at them, his slightly bloodshot eyes moving from one face to the next. His scarred and stitched face, blank.

"Lucas?" said Constance, hopefully.

His eyes met hers.

His mouth moved and she leant closer eager to catch any sound.

"I think he might be thirsty. Ursula could you pass the beaker please?"

She propped him up and this time managed to get most of the water into his mouth. When he'd had enough, he turned his head away. "Benedict could you be a sweetheart and run down to the kitchen and ask Mistress Peel for some more of that wonderful broth please? Frances could you go and find Quinton please and ask him to come up?"

After they had left the room Constance and Ursula changed Lucas's nightshirt for a clean one. Constance had split them all at the back, so they were easier to remove and replace. Undignified but necessary. He made no sound and put up no resistance which Constance found distressing and unnerving. She would rather he railed against them to show that somewhere inside he was still the bad-tempered Lucas of old. This silence and stillness felt like he was dead inside and that she could not bear. She needed a sign.

Ursula suddenly remembered something she had to do and hurried from the room. Constance suspected it was to tidy her hair and dab some scent on, as Quinton was about to arrive. She smiled, thinking she must begin her matchmaking campaign again and see if she couldn't somehow make Quinton understand that Ursula was trying hard to change. There seemed to be some kind of obstacle that was making him shy away when Ursula got too close.

Valentine de Cheverell arrived guiding Quinton and stayed just long enough to say an encouraging word to his employer and to bat his eyelashes at Constance whilst fulsomely praising her heroic efforts. She managed to politely stop him mid-flow before he started to quote poetry at her and he retreated from the room with a besotted smile on his face.

Quinton chuckled as Constance assisted him to the chair by the bed. "That boy! He needs to find a nice girl his own age and settle down. He read me some of his poetry the other day and quite frankly, it was some of the worst balderdash I have ever had the misfortune to hear. And mostly about some magical creature with eyes the colour of the first leaves of Spring!"

"Oh, my lord! How very tiresome. I cannot apologise enough. Although I've done absolutely nothing to encourage him, I swear!"

"He needs no encouragement. He is so certain that you are his muse, I doubt he would cease even if you grew warts and a third eye! Anyway, you called for me? Can I be of assistance?"

"I was wondering if you might talk to Lucas for a while. A man's voice might make a change for him. I feel if we ring the changes a bit it might kickstart — revive — his brain. His mind is sheltering him from the trauma he has suffered. This is something we've discovered in — my time. The brain is a complicated thing and can defend itself but with time, can be healed. This is what I'm hoping. But while you talk to him, I want to run down to the bridge and see if Guy has left anything in the geocache."

"You go ahead, my dear. I will do my best to bestir my friend. Take care though. Because the King is quartered in Oxford there are stray soldiers about and when they are idle, they can be dangerous, as you know."

Constance dropped a kiss on the top of his head, told Lucas not to do anything rash and dashed from the room.

Twenty-Four

Even though she had thrown on her warmest cloak and rammed one of Lucas's hats on her head, Constance was soaked through within minutes. It was raining heavily from a leaden sky, she felt as though she could reach up and touch the clouds just above her head. But she didn't care — she had to see if Guy had written. She was desperate for some kind of contact with her family. She put her head down and raced along, splashing through puddles without caring about the hems of her skirts or the state of her boots.

As she approached the gate her skin started to prickle. She slithered down the bank and wrenched the box from the wall. She was shaking. She stood under the shelter of the trees and pulled her cloak around her so that the rain couldn't damage the contents.

A letter. Two packages and a book. She quickly shoved them into her pockets and replaced them with the letter she had written earlier.

As she hurtled through the door into the Great Hall, she ran straight into Mistress Fitch, almost knocking her over in her haste to get out of the cold rain.

"Oh! I'm so sorry! Are you hurt?" she exclaimed.

The housekeeper brushed herself down as though ridding herself of parasites. "You should look where you are goin'! So careless." She fixed Constance with a sly look, "Been out to the stables?"

"No," replied Constance, "Just getting a quick breath of fresh air while Mr Gittings sits with Sir Lucas for a while."

"Not been with your new swain then?"

Constance frowned, "My new — ?"

Mistress Fitch curled her thin lip, "I seen you. You sweet on him? While the cat is away — !"

Constance looked confused, "I'm not sure I understand — "

"You can play the innocent with them — but you are not foolin' *me!"* she pushed her face closer. "I *seen* you! Whenever you think nobody's lookin' — off you go to meet him. Disgustin' behaviour and Sir Lucas so poorly as well. Shame on you!"

"Do you know what, Mistress Fitch? I've absolutely *no* idea what you are talking about! Have you gone quite mad?" snapped Constance irritably.

"I am not the mad one! You and that new forester always together, not carin' who might see you. So brazen! Makes me sad for those poor children."

"*Mr Thorne?* You *must* be insane! Not that I need to justify myself to you, but I *have* to talk to him about the estate while Sir Lucas is recovering and when we were away, *rescuing your master,* we had two others with us *at all times!* I think you had better return to the kitchens before I say something I regret."

"Sir Lucas must be blind not to see that you are a heartless leech. A harlot. You will *never* replace Lady Esther — she was an *angel.*"

"Well, she certainly is *now* — so you'd better learn to move on because she's dead and she's not coming back!" As soon as she said it, she could have bitten off her tongue. The housekeeper looked so stricken. Constance was so horrified that she almost reached out to her but before she could the woman had spun on her heel and stormed away.

Constance watched her go with a feeling of creeping terror. She knew she had just cooked her own goose and would now have to watch her back. She stamped upstairs smouldering with rage and slammed into Lucas's bedchamber before she recalled she should be quiet. Quinton looked around with a start and raised his eyebrows, "Constance?"

She pressed her lips together trying to prevent the torrent of words from gushing out. She paced the room making annoyed puffing sounds.

"You sound like an infuriated dragon. What on earth has displeased you so?"

"Oh! If you only *knew!* That *woman!* God, what an evil *witch!*"

"I surmise that we must be talking about Mistress Fitch. In which case you need to be very cautious, she can be utterly poisonous."

"She's a snake! She's a — scorpion!"

"Perhaps you need to calm down and tell me exactly what has occurred, my dear. I cannot work with epithets alone."

Constance exhaled an exasperated sigh, "She thinks — outrageous! She thinks that I'm dangling after Richard! *Richard!* Because she's seen me with him a few times — discussing the estate! At the same time, she thinks I want to replace Esther! She's crazy. Totally off her rocker."

There was a slight pause before Quinton continued, "Well, to be fair, you would like to — er — be with Lucas, so she might infer that you were trying to take her beloved mistress's place. No, do not explode. But I can quite see that you would be insulted by the suggestion that you were, as you say, dangling after Richard. It is, of course, ridiculous and we need to put a stop to her scandalmongering at once or things might spiral out of control. I think Ursula should have a word with her and see if she can pour oil on troubled waters."

"God, I'm so selfish! I haven't even asked about Lucas. Has everything been all right?"

Quinton gave a small chuckle, "He has listened to all I have to say with great forbearance, and I am pleased to reveal that he has not disagreed once with anything I have said — which is highly unusual."

"I wish he *would* argue and get angry. It's this nothingness which is killing me. Maybe I'm wrong about his treatment."

Quinton shook his head, "Everything you have said sounds like sense to me. We can but try anyway. You saw what would otherwise happen to him — prison! This is an infinitely better choice. If he cannot heal here amongst those who love him what chance does he have anywhere else?" He felt for her hand and gave it a comforting squeeze, "Did you find anything in the box? You have not said."

Constance jumped and started searching her pockets, "God! I completely forgot. Yes, look, a letter and two packages and a small book on, oh, for god's sake! — lunar and solar eclipses. How — odd. And the packages — " She unwrapped the first, "Oh, even odder, sunspots. Strange boy — when have I ever professed an interest in sunspots? And the second one — The Laws of Time Travel. Hmmm. I think he's trying to tell me something."

"I think he sounds like a very wise young man and I think they desperately want you back with them. He has gone to a good deal of trouble. And the letter — ?"

Constance opened it and read it out loud,

"Dearest Con,

I hope you solved your conundrum. I've sent some helpful information — please read carefully. We need to co-ordinate dates and times accurately, so I have enclosed a watch for Lucas. I believe that your Crossover happened during a lunar eclipse and an unusual long-term event where there were very few sunspots. This is significant because it's proven that during times like these there are always inexplicable happenings. Like disturbances in the weather patterns, the Thames freezing over, failing harvests, wars, civil unrest, Witch Hunts, the Plague and so on. I've been Googling like mad! Honestly, I think I'm onto something. All we have to do is line everything up with the next Lunar Eclipse - unfortunately we've just missed one on January 31st. The next one is July 27th, 1646. This, at least, gives you plenty of time to plan and tie up any loose ends and knowing you, I'm sure there will be plenty of those!

The kids send their love and Tova says she misses you.

Hugs,

Your favourite,

Guy

P.S. Not sure how the damn geocache works though! Think it may be emotional or something unquantifiable like that. Weird.

There was a moment's silence.

Quinton cleared his throat, "So, you will be leaving us? I suppose I knew you would have to in the end. It seems a cruel trick though, to make us all love you and then to lose you. July is not that far away."

"Don't, Quinton. I can't bear it. I just need to concentrate on getting Lucas back for now. Then, I'll face whatever is coming."

"You know, you have made an enormous difference. You have changed us all. For the better."

"Please stop. I've started to feel like I've been here forever and that my other life is a dream. It's surprising how quickly things fade — not the love but the colours and the realness."

"It sounds like being suddenly blind. Your memories of how things once looked begin to change. You are not sure anymore about the truth. Then your memory becomes more about a feeling rather than a picture."

"That's it."

Lucas muttered something in his sleep and his two companions stopped breathing for a second to listen. Constance put her hand on Quinton's shoulder, "Did you catch what he said?"

"Something about prisoners, I think. Maybe he thinks he is still in prison?"

"Well, at least he sort of spoke. That's an improvement of sorts. Every little bit helps. I'm going to change out of these wet clothes and then I'll be back to take over from you."

"No need to hurry. He is very undemanding."

Their days fell into a sort of rhythm, each of them playing their part, understanding that it would take effort and patience. Frances read to her father in a small sad voice and even Benedict spent some time every morning before his lessons just sitting on the bed and idly chatting about the sort of things all young boys enjoy, firearms, horses, and Dash's exploits. It made Constance smile to listen to him because it could just as easily have been one of her nephews despite the intervening centuries. One would never have guessed that Lady Ursula was not keen on exerting herself because she did her share and more. Every time Constance turned around or felt she was failing, Ursula was there with a hug or an encouraging word, ready and willing to do her stint at the bedside. Quinton filled in the gaps with slightly more erudite conversation and humorous anecdotes about the family and life at the Court House. Valentine de Cheverell came every evening to read his poetry, which Constance mused, would be sure to make Lucas want to leap from his bed and declare he was fully fit. Captain Maitland visited every few days just to see how they were going on and brought news of the war and gossip from the village. He also told them that his wife, Elizabeth, had offered to help if they needed an extra hand. He assured them that she was extremely proficient in the sickroom, having nursed both her ailing father and great aunt. She also offered to have the children to stay with them in Wyck Rissington should things become too taxing for everyone, their own children being not much different in age. Richard came daily to discuss estate matters with Constance, but she made sure that Quinton or Ursula was with them at all times to prevent the housekeeper's malicious gossip from taking hold. She had also had a word with Ursula about the altercation she had had with Mistress Fitch and Ursula had promised to see what she could do to arrest the smear campaign before it spread too far. She had been shocked to hear about the argument, fearing that the woman had somehow become a deadly enemy living amongst them and pondered the merits of turning her out of the house. Constance felt that would only make things worse but promised to make sure she didn't add any more fuel to the fire. She understood Ursula's implied disapproval of her retaliating and causing an even greater divide.

Constance kept a close watch over Lucas hoping for even the smallest sign of improvement. There was very little to encourage her. He drank a little and ate minuscule amounts when almost forcibly persuaded but she could see his weight was dwindling and felt powerless to help him. Doctor Spry came regularly and seemed to think that they should be grateful that Lucas was still alive but not to get their hopes up for a complete recovery, although, as he kept adding, as a comforting rider, miracles did sometimes happen.

Quinton reassured her, "If he had remained in that prison, he would already be dead. You have to remember that. You have, at the very least, given him a fighting chance."

"*We* have. I hope you're right, but I feel I could be doing more. I've asked Guy to do some research for me, to see if there is any better treatment. I must check to see if he has replied."

Guy supplied information which confirmed that Constance was thankfully on the right track. He said talking, a healthy diet, and daily massage were recommended. She had already organised his diet, making sure it was as nourishing as possible and he was talked to throughout the day whether he liked it or not, so massage was next on the list.

She found some of the lavender oil she and Frances had made at the end of the summer and began a twice-daily routine of massaging Lucas's battered body. She started with his hands and arms and when she eventually felt comfortable, she progressed to his legs and feet and then his face. If Ursula was in the room she stuck to the extremities and concentrated on keeping his muscles in good working order, she didn't want them to waste away. When Ursula left them to attend to something elsewhere, Constance gradually gained in confidence and began to work on his torso, which despite the damage done by bomb-blast, inactivity, and lack of sustenance, was still fairly solid. She smiled, thinking he was lucky to have been built like a brick outhouse in the first place. There were definite signs of wastage, bones where before there had been solid bulk and she could see some of his wounds were healing nicely but one of them looked a little inflamed. She didn't want to use the antibiotics she still had unless it was absolutely necessary so kept on with the lavender oil, which she knew was good for speeding up healing wounds and disinfecting. He didn't seem to be in any obvious pain, but she feared his mind was protecting him for the time being. He occasionally became restless, mumbling in his sleep and had taken to thrashing his limbs about which everyone found distressing. Constance found that a massage with the lavender oil calmed him. Whenever Ursula allowed it, Constance slept on the truckle bed in his room and was able to soothe him during the night if necessary. She actually preferred it when he moved about and fought her, it was far more encouraging than the blank emptiness.

One night she heard him moaning and jumped up to tend to him, but he grabbed her by the throat, strangling her; she was choking and fighting for breath, but he wouldn't release her. She had no idea why, but she suddenly deliberately went limp in his grasp, feigning death and as soon as the fight left her, it also left him, and he let her go. At other times she had the feeling he thought he was buried under something and couldn't escape, then she stroked his face gently while humming a lullaby to him which seemed to soothe him. It was all a steep learning curve, if some method didn't work, she'd try something new.

Often, she would wake in the morning to find she was curled up against him, holding onto his arm, and Lady Ursula would be primly sewing or writing a letter in the chair beside the bed. Constance knew that although she accepted some of her more outrageous behaviour that there was a deep seam of puritanism in Ursula which meant occasionally they were at genteel loggerheads but it was always over quickly when Constance pointed out that she would never do anything to disgrace the family.

Ursula already knew this. She just could not help the ingrained strait-laced streak rearing its ugly head every now and then, even though she no longer welcomed it. Even though she knew that Constance meant no harm and would have a ready explanation for her behaviour. Even though she was oddly comforted by the sight of this strange woman lying with her brother, part of her was also scandalised. She had noted the fingermarks around Constance's neck and said nothing, knowing that if she had wanted to tell her, she would.

Constance had decided not to tell Ursula about the strangling incident; she didn't know how to. *Oh, by the way, your brother tried to kill me?* No, some things were best left unsaid. She'd seen Ursula's gaze slide to the telltale bruises and away again. There was no need to mention it.

Twenty-Five

By the end of the second week Constance thought they were functioning like a well-oiled machine, each of them an important cog in the works, striving together towards the same goal. She was really quite proud of them. She continued with the massaging and introduced some simple stretches, to keep his limbs in good working order and found that she actually enjoyed the intimate contact with him, even though he didn't seem to be aware of what was happening. Mistress Peel had taken on board the need for special food and it brought out the competitive side of the cook's nature, although she clearly thought some of Constance's menu ideas were outlandish.

Richard had told them a little more about the explosion, having heard more news from another soldier. In the dark of a miserable night, the Parliamentarians had confined two hundred Royalist prisoners in the parish church at Great Torrington, without realising they had stored eighty barrels of gunpowder there. A stray spark ignited it, the explosion being so great the ground shook, the shock waves being felt for miles; all but a few of the prisoners were killed, many of the Parliamentarian guards killed or maimed and a good deal of the houses in the town were damaged, some beyond repair. Sir Thomas Fairfax was nearly killed by flying lead from the church roof and the streets were littered with bodies and body parts. Sir Lucas, according to witnesses was running towards the church at the time, after his horse had been shot out from under him but was cut down by the explosion and buried under falling masonry and bodies. It took some while to dig him out. When they finally rescued him, he was unconscious and in a bad way and they feared for his life. He had been taken to the field hospital in a local manor house and treated for his wounds, but he showed no signs of recovering his senses, so they carried him with other injured troops to Bath, where he was left with the St John's Hospital but as they were unable to cope with the seriousness of his mental state, they were reluctantly forced to send him on to Shepton Mallet Prison.

Constance could now fully understand why Lucas had retreated into this fugue state. He had suffered not only the impact of a devastating explosion but been buried alive under the mangled bodies of his fellow soldiers. It was no wonder that his brain had crashed.

It became even more urgent to try to gently prise him out of the darkness and guide him back to them.

"You are exhausted, Constance. This cannot go on," said Lady Ursula in commanding tones, "You look awful."

"Thank you! I haven't washed my hair for a week which doesn't help." And I'm missing my concealer, thought Constance miserably. She'd seen the dark circles under her eyes that morning and despaired.

"What about sending the children to stay with the Maitlands? Elisabeth is very keen to have them. It might ease your burden a little."

"God! They aren't a *burden!* I love them being here, although I worry that this is too much for them and that perhaps I'm being a selfish cow keeping them here."

"I wish you would not say *cow*. It is not at all becoming in a lady."

Constance laughed, "The things that offend you never cease to amaze me!"

"Your inelegant choice of words never ceases to amaze *me!* You must never say these things in company. Or lift up your skirts and run as you do, or sing so loudly, or be so free with your embraces! You shocked poor Will Sparrow to the core the other day when you hugged him."

Constance made a face, "I know but he was so sweet to bring me a posy of Kingcups. I just gave him a little squeeze."

Ursula rolled her eyes, "You must not hug the servants, Constance. It really is not acceptable."

"All right. I'll try to behave as I should. But it's very hard."

Constance rolled over in her sleep and found something warm and solid in her way. Solid but shaking so violently that the bed was moving. By the light of the candle, she could see that although Lucas appeared to be asleep, he was being assaulted by terrifying tremors. His whole body trembling convulsively. She had no idea how to treat it, but her instinct was to just calm him as best she could, so reached for the massage oil and kneeling beside him on the bed, began to gently massage his upper body. She talked to him in a soft voice, reassuring him. She let her hands get into a rhythm, back and forth, back and forth, slow circular movements, until even she started to feel a little mesmerised. She remembered calming Rowen when he was a baby, whispering into his ear and humming until he was hypnotised into sleep. She leant forward and put her lips to Lucas's ear and started whispering to him. She told him how she felt about him and that he had to stop messing about and get better. She sang *"I Will"*, an ancient Beatles song. But the opening lines made her sob into his neck, which she felt was probably counter-productive. She sniffed and straightened up to continue the massage. As she laid her hands on his chest, she noticed the tremors had diminished slightly. She peered at his face and found his eyes were open.

"Lucas?" she breathed, trying not to startle him. He turned his head slightly and his eyes found hers.

"Lucas? It's me, Constance."

She took his face in her hands and tried to will him to recognise her. He just stared. His gaze travelled around her face but so blankly that Constance wanted to shake him out of his stupor.

"We're all just waiting for you to join us, y'know. You've been away such a long time. We're all doing our very best, but I do feel you could put a bit more effort into this. You're being a bit of a slacker. Just lying there. Look, your wounds are healing nicely, even that one on your forehead and the bad one under your ribs. Your ugly old face looks almost respectable. I mean, it's never going to win any beauty contests but I kind of love it anyway," she trailed a finger down the side of his face, over his cheekbone and down to his mouth. "You have quite a grumpy mouth really but when you smile, it's a *very* different story. You look, almost handsome. Well, no, perhaps, not handsome, exactly, but tolerable. If you were in a band, you'd have to be the drummer — right at the back," she chuckled. "Lord, you'd never fit in the twenty first century! You're such a man of your time. I suppose I have an unfair advantage knowing how history works, having read all about it. You know nothing about the future. You only know me, which could be considered something of a disadvantage!" She frowned at him, "Your sister doesn't always approve of the things I do. I bring out the Puritan in her. But I do love her. You were wrong when you said she's nothing like you — you're actually quite alike, obstinate and opinionated, and so moralistic. Oh, wait! You remind me of Guy!" She laughed rather too loudly and covered her mouth with her hand, "God, I don't want to wake Ursula, she'll come scurrying in, her nightcap all askew, expecting to find Sodom and Gomorrah in here! I'm not sure she trusts me with you. I can't *think* why! I've been perfectly well behaved, haven't I? I haven't compromised you. Oh, my giddy aunt! *Listen* to me! Banging on like the Duracell Bunny! The boys would be complaining about me being too garrulous and they'd be joking about herds of donkeys with no hind legs — " She stopped dead in her tracks. "What?" She leant closer to him. "*Lucas?* Did you say something?"

Colonel Sir Lucas Deverell closed his eyes and took a deep breath.

Constance saw his lips move slightly again.

She put her head closer to his and listened with every fibre of her being.

His warm breath caressed her cheek.

"Speaking — in —tongues," he sighed, his voice no more than the faintest exhalation.

Constance's heart was thumping so loudly in her ears she couldn't think clearly. She couldn't catch her breath. She thought she was going to faint.

"*Lucas! Lucas! Lucas!*" she wept at him incoherently, stroking his face in wonder. "You spoke! Oh, my god! This is mind-blowing! Of course, the first thing out of your mouth *would* be a bloody criticism! But I don't care! Don't stop talking! Say something else! Oh, Jesus, now I'm pushing you too hard. Don't say anything—just rest. You must be exhausted. I thought — I'd started to think — "

She stopped and gazed down at him, tears pouring down her face, she just looked at him as though he might be snatched away from her at any moment, trying to fix his face in her memory, trying to hold on to him. She took his face in her hands and leaning forward planted a gentle, chaste kiss on his lips.

"Goes against all nurse-patient protocol in every nursing manual — but I really don't give a damn. Oh!"

Lucas had reached up and put a shaking finger to her lips.

"I'll be quiet. Sorry. *Oh!*"

She found herself being pulled closer to him. She eyed him in astonishment. "Lucas?"

His lips met hers. His rough beard grazing her skin. She could feel that he was still trembling in spasms. He was watching her from his sleepy grey eyes. She kissed him back tenderly, revelling in his lips against hers, whilst, at the same time, berating herself for being so weak as to assault a vulnerable patient in her care. If she really were a nurse, she'd be struck off.

She pushed her hands against his chest, pulling away from the enticing warmth of his body.

"I shall be sensible for both of us. If Ursula found out — ! Look, I want to just kiss you all night long, but you've been really ill — *are* really ill. It would be irresponsible of me," she said in very resolute tones. "But I need you to know that I want to kiss you all over, every bit of you! Until you beg for mercy! This is going to hurt me more than you. I'm really not good at restraint. You're a sodding Puritan — it's in your blood." She reluctantly slid off the bed. But as she did, his hand reached for hers and held on. She stopped and stood with her back to him, "So tempting, so *very* tempting but no, one day you'll thank me for this." His fingers tightened on hers. She could tell he was not at full strength because she could have so easily pulled away, but she returned the pressure for a long moment, whilst contemplating sinking even deeper into depravity and never finding her way back.

She let him go and went to wake Ursula.

Lady Ursula was all smiles. Frances was leaning on the bed and chattering at her father without pause like an over-excited little bird. Benedict was sniffling into Constance's chest while she stroked his hair, as much to calm herself as him. She was starting to wonder why he cried so much — it seemed unusual.

Lucas, she noticed anxiously, had retreated again. He had returned to the blankness and mostly kept his eyes closed, although he did manage a weary smile for his family as they crowded around his bed. Constance allowed them to have a few moments with him and then shooed them out of the room to go and get dressed and ready for breakfast.

Ursula lingered, "What do you think woke him?"

Constance laughed, "He just wanted to tell me to shut up! I was talking at him like a crazy person. I think he just wanted some peace and quiet. It might have been when I started to sing to him — !"

"Oh, no! Constance! You sang? My poor brother. How could you?"

"Ha ha! Very funny. It's not that bad. Although to be honest, it was exactly at that moment — oh, no! It *was* my terrible singing. *Lucas!*"

Lucas opened one drowsy eyelid and looked at her. She could see the laughter in it.

"Oh, my god," she said, "I love you so bloody much. But I swear I will make you pay for this."

His mouth twisted into the slightest of smiles and within minutes, he was asleep again.

Constance watched his breathing slowly steady and heaved an exhausted sigh. She pulled Ursula to the other side of the room, "This is excellent progress, but I fear there are bound to still be setbacks. He has been through so much. The shock of it all, the force of the explosion, being buried and then the horror of seeing — it's no wonder he has battle fatigue. It's too much to ask of any man."

"Was he pleased to see you?"

Constance couldn't help a slight smirk, "I would have to say he seemed, once I stopped talking, to be *very* pleased to see me!"

"Constance! Did you — ?"

Constance giggled, "I may possibly have kissed him. But he owed me a proper kiss with no audience! Honestly, I think I've waited long enough."

"You are incorrigible. And really quite wicked."

"I couldn't help it — he looked so sleepy and defenceless! I took advantage because I may never get another chance."

"Shameless. So, how do we proceed? More of the same treatment, as it seems to have worked?"

"The next thing is to get him up and moving. Which, even though he has lost weight, is going to be quite a feat in itself — he's so tall. We will need help from Richard and maybe Will or Hugh. I really don't fancy lifting him. And I think Valentine is a little too delicate for manual labour!"

"He could recite his lamentable poetry to encourage them while they work," Ursula said with a malevolent smile.

There was an undercurrent of excitement and relief quivering through the house; everyone had a spring in their step and there was an air of barely suppressed celebration, which Constance, trying to remain pragmatic, thought might be a bit premature. She gently warned the children that anything could happen and that it was best to be prepared to prevent disappointment, but she wasn't at all sure that they wanted to understand.

Lucas began to show small signs of improvement. His appetite increased and he was awake for longer, sometimes an hour or more at a time. Eventually Doctor Spry took the stitches out of his wounds and announced that they had all healed remarkably well. Ursula redoubled her efforts as chaperone, but she couldn't be in attendance all the time, so Constance just bided her time.

Quinton Gittings had heard the news with a rush of joy and found the emotion to be quite overwhelming. Lady Ursula had told him of the miracle as soon as he came downstairs and when he showed signs of being overcome, she gently guided him to his chair and stayed with him while he processed the information.

"Is there permanent damage? Has his brain been impaired, do you think?"

"Constance says he is still able to kiss very well!" declared Ursula with a wicked look her companion missed.

"I beg your pardon?" exclaimed Quinton, not at all sure he had heard correctly.

"It seems that the first thing he did was return Constance's kiss. So, some parts of him are working perfectly, apparently."

"I am delighted to hear it," said Quinton rather austerely.

Ursula laughed, "You would think as a Royalist that you would be a bit more — tolerant. I must admit that I was rather shocked but that is to be expected. I am very small-minded." She watched his face keenly.

He frowned, "I would not describe you as small-minded."

Ursula narrowed her eyes, "How *would* you describe me, Quinton?"

Quinton Gittings sensed he was tiptoeing towards some kind of trap and prevaricated, "I have always believed you to be an extremely good-natured — "

"You have *not!* You think I am spoilt and selfish and idle."

And there was the trap, thought Quinton, a bear-trap right in the middle of his path. He knew it was there but did not know how to avoid it. He had also known it would come eventually. He had hoped to side-step for longer. He had hoped to continue without having to hurt anyone. But happiness was infectious, and Lucas's recovery was going to infect everything. Everyone would want to share in the joy and would begin to find their own lives wanting. Human beings had an insatiable appetite for happiness and once they tasted it, they would always want more. But now, with the trap set, he had no choice but to try to let this wonderful, impossible woman down as gently as he could.

"I think nothing of the kind, Ursula. These last few weeks have proved to anyone who may have doubted your potential that you are stronger and braver than they could have possibly thought. You have been a tower of strength and none of us could have coped without you. I know I would have been at even more of a loss had you not been here."

"Which does not really answer my question though, does it? I am not unattractive, or so I have been told. I am still fairly young and am an independent woman, thanks to Jacob, who saw fit to provide me with every comfort. His endowment is beyond generous. I have no children and my only dependent is Dash, who much prefers Benedict anyway. I think that adds up to a rather enticing marriage prospect, do you not?"

Quinton could not help a wry smile, "It does indeed."

"And yet, Quinton and *yet*, you do not find me in the least alluring, do you?"

He felt the floor begin to give way under him, and the panic rise. “You are the sister of my very best friend. My employer, in fact. I am bound by — ”

“Oh! You *know* it is not that! Those are just excuses, because you are afraid! You are an intelligent man. You may have lost your sight, but your faculties are unimpaired. If you cannot *see* — !”

The door suddenly burst open, crashing back against the wall, and Benedict rushed in, stopped in confusion and blurted out, “Mr Thorne says that Lord Astley is on the march to join the King at Oxford!”

Twenty-Six

It appeared that the Royalist cause was losing momentum, having lost Hereford, Chester, and Lichfield in quick succession. Lord Astley had managed to raise some troops and was marching to Worcester but was to be delayed by Parliamentarians at Gloucester after Colonels Birch and Morgan joined forces. After evading his pursuers Astley crossed the River Avon and marched into the Cotswolds with the intention of reaching Oxford. They were further delayed by skirmishers but, according to Richard Thorne and Hugh Maitland, it looked as though there was going to be a confrontation before very long. The household was put on alert, provisions were collected and stored just in case and every weapon available was cleaned, oiled, primed and loaded, and hidden about the house. Richard and Hugh supervised the addition of some new bars on the downstairs windows and padlocks and chains for the gates. Hugh arranged for some retired local soldiers to patrol the estate and even Will Sparrow, to his complete delight, was given a pistol but with a stern caveat that he was only to use it in a real emergency and not for shooting squirrels. The forgotten priest hole under the library, accessed via the fireplace was renovated and well stocked.

Constance heard Lady Ursula leave the sickroom, tread down the main staircase and into the parlour. She was worried; it seemed as though Quinton and Ursula had had a serious falling out and were being so icily polite to each other it was painful to witness. They were like the little wooden couple in an Alpine weather house: one came in, the other went out. Constance didn't know whether to interfere or not. She had no desire to make things worse but at this rate things were not going to end as she hoped. She had a feeling that Quinton had shied off, despite her having had words with him before she left for Bath. And Lady Ursula had become withdrawn and uncommunicative. Constance compressed her lips and squared her shoulders; she was determined that her plan should bear fruit. She would just have to be even more devious.

As soon as the parlour door had shut behind Ursula, she tiptoed along the corridor from her bedchamber, where she was supposed to be resting, and slid quietly into Lucas's chamber. Valentine de Cheverell was sitting at the table scratching away with a quill.

"Mr de Cheverell, I've come to sit with Sir Lucas for a while, until Captain Maitland and Richard arrive to help take him for a walk. You must be longing for some quiet for your composing; please don't let me detain you."

The tutor leapt to his feet, "But, I have only this minute arrived, Mistress Harcourt!"

"Oh, how very confusing. I must have my timings in a muddle. Well, never mind, I'm here now," and she fixed him with a warm but inflexible smile. He reluctantly took the hint and bowed his way out of the room.

"Unscrupulous wench," murmured Lucas.

Constance laughed and flew to the bed, diving on to the empty side so that she could lie next to him; she wriggled closer and flung an arm around him. "I have urgent needs," she whispered, her cheeks colouring.

Lucas looked down his crooked nose at her, his grey eyes darkening dangerously, "Hussy," he said hoarsely.

"You're nearly well enough to — to — "

"To — *what,* Mistress Harcourt?"

She grinned at him and happily burrowed her head into his neck, "I couldn't possibly say!"

A frown drew his dark brows together, "I am sorry about last night. I have no control over the seizures when they happen. Did I hurt you?"

"Lord, no. I'm becoming proficient at dodging the worst of it. I have very good reflexes. Anyway, I don't mind," her hand went unconsciously to her throat.

His frown deepened and he moved his head away to get a better look at her face, "Constance? Have I hurt you?"

She found it hard to meet his penetrating gaze, "It was nothing. It — was when you were at your worst. It wasn't your fault."

"What did I do?"

"Um, you sort of tried to strangle me. But it wasn't really you, it was the result of the shell shock. I was fine, honestly. I played dead. You were easily fooled!"

Lucas turned pale, his fingers found her face and traced a line from her jaw down to her collarbone. "I would not hurt you for the world. I would die rather."

"Don't you dare bloody die! I've only just got you back. And I've discovered that, worryingly, I can't actually live without you."

"You were what kept me alive under — the rubble. In the hospital. In the prison. You. I had to keep living so that I could return to you and explain."

"Explain what, exactly?"

"To beg your forgiveness for making a spectacle of you in front of everyone. I do not know what came over me."

"It wasn't *totally* one-sided! I added fuel to the fire."

He gave her his slow lazy smile, "I also wanted to come back to finish what I started."

"Go on then," breathed Constance, her heart thumping in her throat, where his fingers were still idly tracing patterns on her skin.

"I can feel your heartbeat, I am not sure any more excitement — "

Constance reached up and pulled his head down and when it was within inches, she just looked at him.

He kissed her, gently at first and then, quite forcefully, as though his famous iron control was finally lost, pulling her hard against his still healing body. He did not care about the pain it caused him, he did not care if his sister walked in, he was consumed with a burning need to make this woman understand that, whatever happened, it was not just his control which was lost, his heart was lost.

Constance emitted a surprised little gasp as she was ruthlessly man-handled into the embrace she had so longed for. Bloody hell, she thought blissfully and swung her leg over his hips. She felt him start but then, not without some immense physical effort, he dragged her up and across him, so that they were face-to-face, he was then able to get both his arms around her and she, to her utter delight, had the upper hand. Although, she could feel that the effort of lifting her had taken a toll, he was starting to shake and knew, in that moment, that she was being selfish and needy.

She flopped forward, her cheek resting against his broad chest, "Oh, hell and damnation," she sighed, "I am going to be a grownup again and save you from certain injury. But I want you to know that I shall now retire to my bedchamber and cry into my pillow for a good while."

Lucas tightened his arms about her, "Stay. I am all right. The tremors will stop."

"You're not strong enough. Yet. Anyway, Hugh and Richard will be here soon and if you've used up all your energy on — on — other activities, they'll have a terrible job getting you out of bed and it'll be all my fault. Imagine what Doctor Spry would say if he could see me straddling you, with no thought for your wounds! He'd be outraged! *I'm* outraged on your behalf. Honestly how could you allow yourself to be so easily seduced?"

"Did you just say *straddling?"* said Lucas feigning disapproval. "Say it again!" he chuckled.

She put her mouth to his ear and whispered the word again.

He groaned deep in his throat and closed his eyes, "Perhaps, you *are* right. You are a very bad influence."

Constance giggled and gave him a lingering kiss, finishing with little butterfly kisses all over his face. Then, hearing a sound outside in the corridor, she leapt off the bed and threw herself into the chair, just having time to arrange her skirts and smooth down her hair before Ursula marched into the room. Lucas, spying Constance's abandoned shoes on the bed, quickly concealed them under the covers, away from his sister's keen scrutiny and Constance tucked her bare feet out of sight under her skirts.

"I just met Mr de Cheverell in the Great Hall and he tells me that you threw him out when I had expressly bidden him to sit with Lucas!"

"I — I — ", faltered Constance lamely, desperately looking to Lucas for help.

"I am afraid I could not abide any more of his prosing on, Ursula. Constance was kind enough to rescue me," explained Lucas, his face a picture of virtue.

"Oh, I see. He can be a bit prosaic sometimes. Well, I expect you have things to do, Constance?"

Constance got to her bare feet and meekly shuffled towards the door. Ursula went to the press to take out some clean linen and while her back was briefly turned, Lucas retrieved the shoes and shied them at Constance, one at a time. She snatched them deftly from the air and bolted from the room.

Richard Thorne and Hugh Maitland managed to get Lucas out of bed, walk him around his bedchamber, then down the corridor and back again to sit in the chair beside the fire for a while. Constance pleaded with Ursula to be allowed to go and see him out of bed and Ursula graciously acquiesced. Constance was permitted to sit in the opposite chair and make idle chitchat, with her hands primly folded in her lap. Every time she caught Lucas's eye though she had to bite her lip quite fiercely to stop herself laughing. His heavy eyelids drooped down to hide his amusement from his sister who was patrolling the room like a guard dog. Then, there was a moment when the laughter died, and they were just looking at each other. Just seeing each other. Just breathing at the same time. Constance's heart rate slowed down, and she felt as though she were floating. When Ursula suddenly interrupted with some inane comment about the weather, they were both startled out of their trance.

Talk inevitably turned to the war when Benedict joined them after his lessons, he was excited about the action coming so close, without having any real idea of the gravity of the situation. He wanted to ask his father about what had happened to him in Torrington but with Lady Ursula and Constance hovering, he felt awkward. He was fascinated by the explosion and how it had happened, and he wanted to know why his father had been running *towards* the church at the time. He should have been running away. He was reflecting on the wisdom of asking his father for information when Lucas took his hand in his, "What do you want to know, Benedict?" he asked softly. His son stammered some sort of muddled reply and Lucas spent the next half an hour describing what he remembered of the incident. He left out the gory and horrific details and focused on the enormity of the explosion and how it had lit up the night sky, shaken the ground like an earthquake and destroyed half the town, and then he spoke a little of what he could recall about the aftermath, which was almost nothing until, he had felt compelled to wake up because Constance was singing to him and would not stop talking. That made Benedict laugh, and he said he had heard Constance singing and did not wonder that he should want her to stop. Lucas met her eyes over his son's dark curls and raised an eyebrow, "I think her singing is the most beautiful thing I have ever heard in my life," he murmured, "But if the song is sad it makes her cry and that I cannot bear."

Constance's face crumpled and her eyes shone with unshed tears.

Benedict cast her a despairing glance, "Females do cry a good deal too much," he said, and Constance opened her eyes wide but said nothing about his own alarmingly frequent bouts of weeping.

His father frowned, "I think, young man, that until you have suffered what they have suffered, you are in no position to criticise."

Benedict straightened up, "No, I suppose you are right. Constance was very brave to march off like that to rescue you. Not many ladies would do that. And Mr Thorne says that even though she was very afraid she was determined to find you and bring you home. He said nothing would have stopped her. Not *even* a pack of ravening wolves."

Lucas looked across at Constance, sitting so serenely in her chair, her gentle face giving no clue to her inner strength and courage and wondered what he would do if she was forced to leave him. He was not ready to face that hurdle yet.

"Father? They said you were running towards the church where the explosion was! Why did you do that?"

There was an awkward silence as Lucas avoided Constance's baffled gaze, "I overheard someone say that they were storing the gunpowder in the church. I thought I could prevent exactly the sort of accident that blew it up. I was too late."

Constance glared at him, "You stupid fool! Why would you do something so reckless? You were very nearly — !"

Frances came running into the bedchamber, "Oh! Good afternoon, Father! That is good, you are in a chair! Oates says he has seen soldiers in the village! Royalist soldiers! He says they were up to no good. Although, I do not know what he meant by that. Constance, when are you going to wear one of your new gowns?"

Lucas raised his eyebrows, "Constance has new gowns?"

Constance laughed, "*That's* all you got from what Frances said? *Gowns?* What about the up-to-no-good soldiers?"

Lucas's lips twitched, "I would much rather think about you in your new gowns or even — "

She gave him an admonishing look, "*Lucas!*" she hissed.

He grinned at her, "Yes, Constance?"

She glanced furtively at Lady Ursula who was perched on the edge of the bed, pretending not to listen.

"I think children we should call Mr Thorne and Captain Maitland back to help get your father into bed because he is becoming unruly! Could you please go and ask them to come and help?"

The two children raced off, fighting to be the first out of the door and then hurtling noisily down the stairs.

"Well," said Lady Ursula, "I believe we need to have a discussion about appropriate behaviour."

"I think, dearest sister, that I am old enough and ugly enough to be able to court whomsoever I please and it pleases me greatly to be able to court Constance. If you so heartily object there is always an answer."

Constance held her breath. Court? Really? She was being *courted?* She thought her heart was going to burst.

Lady Ursula cleared her throat, "It is not that I object, you understand. I would like nothing better than to have Constance in the family, but I am very afraid of what people will say. She is not a relation — she is unwed and living here with us unchaperoned and therefore open to criticism and gossip. And you will admit she is inclined to be wilful and careless of conventions! She should not be alone with you. I am fearful that Mistress Fitch will stir up trouble. She has a vicious tongue and cannot accept Constance. Her obsession with Esther is dangerous."

Her brother's expression hardened, "Again, a simple solution. I will let Mistress Fitch go, with a generous farewell gift."

"But I am worried that any such action will just inflame the situation," said Ursula anxiously. "She is already convinced that Constance is dangling after Richard! I have had a word with her about it and she seemed to accept what I said but I think she just wanted to appease me."

Lucas narrowed his eyes at Constance, "*Dangling?*"

Constance lowered her gaze and looked chastened, "Well, in my defence, he is remarkably attractive."

"*Is* he indeed? No broken nose and badly stitched scars?"

"And *such* an engaging smile! And so very good-tempered into the bargain."

Lady Ursula looked from one to the other in some confusion, "Are you joking? I can no longer tell! Are you angry Lucas? *Does* Constance dangle after Richard? I wish someone would enlighten me."

"I most certainly do not dangle after *anyone!*" exclaimed Constance, not daring to meet Lucas's interested gaze.

"I beg to differ," he remarked, with an evil glint in his eye. "I would say there had been — "

"Lucas, if you say one more word I shall — I shall be forced to inform Mr de Cheverell that the one thing that soothes you is the sound of him reading his poetry!"

"You would not dare! In my weakened state? I might suffer a relapse."

Lady Ursula threw up her hands, "I am beginning to think that I am missing something. Will you stop behaving like naughty children and include me! I do not like being on the outside."

"If you promise to trust me not to compromise Constance with my er — unruly behaviour."

"Oh, all right. I will try. Although I cannot help feeling that it may be Constance's errant behaviour which needs curbing not yours! But, Lucas, you must do something about Mistress Fitch before it is too late."

"Agreed. Tomorrow I will send for her. Stop worrying, Ursula. I am already improving, apart from the odd attack of shaking; I will be able to resume my normal duties in a few days."

Ursula flicked Constance a questioning glance and received the slightest shrug in response.

Richard Thorne and Captain Maitland were on hand to assist Lucas back to his bed, but both agreed that, considering his injuries and the previous precarious state of his mind, he was doing remarkably well. Hugh declared that he had seldom seen such a miraculous recovery and although he understood Constance's reservations, he suggested that she should be advising Parliament or the medical profession, at the very least.

"Massage, mindless chatter, and entrancing singing should be recommended to all military forces in the country as a dependable cure for all ills," said Lucas, straight-faced.

Captain Maitland frowned, "I am not sure that would be — oh, I see — you were speaking in jest — no, I think I understand!" He flushed pink with embarrassment and put his head in his hands. "Elizabeth says I am often far too literal!"

A gentle knock on the door heralded the arrival of Quinton Gittings and the prompt departure of a stiff-necked Lady Ursula Prideaux, who swept from the room without a word.

Richard and Hugh made their excuses and left, and Quinton sat down for a comfortable talk with his friend about the estate. Constance kept an eye on her patient, who was looking a little pale and tired and warned Quinton to not stay too long and wear him out with too much excitement about barns.

Lucas threw her a darkling look and Constance hastened from the room in giggles.

Twenty-Seven

War came to the Cotswolds. For the residents of the manor houses, farms and villages, it came stealthily at first and finished with a violent flourish in the square at Stow on the Wold. It didn't seem like much of a place to end the first Civil War, just an unremarkable, cold and windy hilltop village, more used to sheep trotting up the streets than regiments of Royalist and Parliamentarian troops intent on conflict. The last battle of the First English Civil War started just outside Donnington by dawn's first light and ended in Stow square by the ancient cross but not before much blood had been shed and lives lost. It would end with Royalist garrisons surrendering around the country, triumphal processions, and confusion.

For a while the countryside was teeming with deserters and the wounded, who were generally abandoned in the local area, left for others to bear the burden of care and the inevitable and unwelcome cost. The troops moved on, disbanded, and dispersed. Warring brothers and uncles and sons were reunited with their families. Mothers, daughters, sisters, and aunts welcomed them home, praying there was an end to the fighting at last. Mass graves were dug and filled, over and over; a shroud for every soldier kept the weavers in business. Pensions for the legions of wounded soldiers were eventually established, too late for many. For a while things were back on an even keel, the ship was righted, and life took a breath and began again. The Court House took in half a dozen stray soldiers from both sides, billeting them in the stables until they were well enough to return to their homes. Constance, Lady Ursula, Richard Thorne, and Doctor Spry cared for them as best they could, until they were finally able to send them on their way with a clean bill of health.

When the armies came so close to the Court House you could almost smell them, and Colonel Sir Lucas Deverell became restless and Constance sensed his desire to be with his troops. He constantly asked Richard and Hugh for news and seemed distracted.

It was around this time that he and Constance had their first proper fight.

Lady Ursula and the children had come to say goodnight and Benedict had asked for a pistol like Will Sparrow's, so that he could protect the house from the soldiers. His father had promised that as soon as he was able, he would show him how to prime, load, and fire one safely and then maybe they would see about him having his own. Ursula had objected strongly to this and said so in no uncertain terms. Lucas had taken umbrage and Constance had had to usher the children quickly out of the firing line. She had returned to find them still arguing and had quietly sided with Ursula which had not gone down well with a usually active man confined to his bed and at the mercy of two strong-minded women.

In the end Ursula had stormed from the room in a rage and Constance was left to try to explain to Lucas how they felt about him offering to give a gun to a child and his general high-handedness. Constance then couldn't resist flinging his obvious yearning to be off getting killed with his regiment in his face at the same time. She felt a little hurt when she realised his thoughts were elsewhere and, considering what the war had done to him, she was hard-pressed to comprehend why he should want to leave her and return to the horror of the battlefield.

He had fallen silent, his eyes hooded and cold, his mouth grim, while she quickly became angry and incoherent. When she eventually ran out of steam, he glared at her, "Have you quite finished?"

She nodded, suddenly realising that she could make him ill again by getting him so riled, "Yes, I have. But you are being very unreasonable." She noted his grey pallor and cursed herself for being so careless with his still fragile health. "But, you see, in my time, young boys steal guns and kill each other and the idea of Benedict having a gun is just terrible and — ", she faltered.

She could see he was only just holding onto his temper, "And you think that I would just let Benedict have a gun and shoot people? You think I am such an incompetent father?"

"No, no! But you said — "

"I said that I would show him how to use a gun safely and we could talk about him having one of his own. I did not mention when."

Constance bit her lip, "No, you didn't — I — I'm sorry. I shouldn't have shouted. I should have trusted you. I'm an idiot." She backed away towards the door. "I'll tell Ursula to come back. I'll see you in the morning. I'm really sorry." She opened the door and was halfway out when she heard his voice.

"Constance."

She stopped and looked back.

He was holding out his hand to her.

She paused for only a moment and then flew back to him. He took her in his arms and held her, his lips against her neck.

"We will always argue. It makes no odds," he said softly, "I am not easy to live with. But you must know that if I have been distracted it is not because I want to re-join my men, although I do feel guilt for not seeing it through to the end. I want nothing more than to be here with you. You are the reason I breathe. I want you always by my side. I desperately need to keep you safe but at the moment, while I am confined to this damn room, I am unable to do that which makes me frustrated and probably unreasonably bad-tempered."

Constance slid her arms around his neck and lay her head on his chest, "Lucas? When you say you want me by your side — ?"

"Good God, woman! Ursula will probably come back in a minute! Have you no shame?"

She sat up, "None," she admitted, giving him a wicked look from under her eyelashes. "And when you think that in *my* time, I am considered to be exceedingly strait-laced! You've had a lucky escape really, mate. Crikey, when I think who you might have had to deal with! I'm swiftly coming to the conclusion that life is too short for shame and regrets. When you don't know what may be around the next corner — "

Lucas pulled her back to him, "We will come through this somehow. I cannot help but feel that there must be a reason for what has happened. It cannot just be arbitrary."

"You don't think it's just the Universe having a laugh at our expense?"

He gave her a quizzical look, "No — *if* I understand you correctly, and I am beginning to worry that I *am* starting to understand your peculiar speech correctly — I think we are like lodestones."

"You mean we have magnetic fields? I think we may be talking about a Flux Capacitor!" laughed Constance.

"Hmm. I may have spoken too soon! Speaking in tongues."

"Never mind. It's a silly Time Travel joke. And, by the bye, I like my men rather stupid."

Lucas pushed her away and held her there, "Perhaps we need to talk about your — men! *Plural!* How many exactly?"

She started counting up an imaginary amount on her fingers, "Five, six, seven — Ouch! I'm *joking!* One and a half! One proper boyfriend and then sort of half of one. I was a late developer." She studied his face anxiously, "Why are you looking so cross? Oh, hell and damnation! You're not *jealous?* I said one boyfriend not a dozen! You were bloody *married!*"

Lucas clenched his teeth and took a calming breath; he knew he was being foolish, but he had not previously properly considered that she may have been with other men. It came as rather a shock to his Puritan soul. "I was trapped in an arranged marriage with someone I did not love and who did not love me. It was no more than a civil contract."

She sat up again and contemplated him incredulously, "Do you expect me to believe that it has only ever been Esther? Your whole life? What about, you know, camp followers? Ladies of the night? You're a soldier! You must have —"

He shook his head, "As a boy I was taught that the pursuit of pleasure was the road to damnation. Perhaps you would rather have a Royalist? They are known to be libertines."

"I would hardly say Quinton was a libertine!" she said with a slightly concerned smile. "Lucas? Do you think I'm a — loose woman? Does my behaviour shock you?"

He thought for a moment about evading the truth but her beautiful green eyes were searching his face with an almost childlike expression, "Sometimes, of course. We come from such different worlds. Surely I must exasperate you when the puritanical side gets the better of me."

"Not really. I see it as something of a challenge. And I rather like it — for some perverse reason."

"So, this other man — ?"

Constance made a face, "Are you sure? Well, if you insist. He sold paintings — "

"Ah, a *shopkeeper!*" said Lucas, gratified.

"In my time it is considered to be a very superior occupation, owning a gallery. Anyway, he was amusing and charming and sophisticated and I was quite flattered that he seemed to like me. However, after a while I realised he was only amusing when he drank rather too much and only charming when he didn't. And sophistication, I soon discovered, is vastly overrated."

"A boorish drunkard. You choose well. Did he treat you honourably?"

"Mostly. Although he could be a little — thoughtless."

Lucas knew from what she was holding back that, if he ever met this man, he would kill him without compunction.

"Handsome?"

Constance took his battle-scarred face in both her hands and brushed her lips against his, "Very. But I prefer irascible, ugly men with good hearts."

"You loved him?'

"Never."

"Have you ever loved anyone?"

"My nephews — "

He growled, "You know exactly — !"

"I have only ever loved one man," said Constance.

Colonel Sir Lucas Deverell, leader of men, intrepid soldier, felt his damned heart miss a beat and wondered what the hell was wrong with him.

He tightened his arms about her and pulled her close, "Tell me. I can bear it."

"You're such a blockhead," she whispered and buried her face into his chest, "It's *you,* of course."

He lifted her head up and forced her to look at him, "*Tell* me."

"I love you, Lucas, I love you. *I love you*."

He tilted up her chin and kissed her rather roughly and it completely took her breath away, making her heart race and the blood pound in her head. She suddenly nipped his bottom lip with her teeth and stifled a giggle when he protested.

"Constance!"

"You have something to say to *me*?"

"You *know*. I would die for you."

"I don't want you to bloody die for me, you dolt. I want you to live for me," said Constance crossly.

Lucas cocked his head, "I would do anything for you. I love you."

"*Do* you? Do you *really?* I thought maybe you just, you know —"

"No, I do *not* know! You thought I just wanted to *bed* you!"

Constance blushed furiously and turned her face away from him.

"I sometimes forget that you're not like the men I knew. You see, my — boyfriend had an affair with my best friend. It's made me a little wary. I tend to expect the worst now. Until I met you, I thought that I had finished with men altogether; I was going to concentrate on my work and the boys and keep my heart from being broken. Tova said I was hiding from life because I was scared of getting hurt and therefore not really living at all, which is probably right. And now look what I've done! I've fallen in love with a grumpy old Roundhead from a different time. It couldn't be any worse! I must be mad. I can't see this ending well. But there was a moment back there when I thought we wouldn't get you back alive and I'd never be able to explain how I felt about you and I was so filled with fear and rage that I realised that it didn't matter about the pain; all that mattered was the time, *whatever* time we have left — I want to spend it with you. Even if it's only a minute. So, I'm prepared for the pain and heartbreak to come because I've had these moments with you. And, frankly, I don't even care if you do only want to *bed* me — I'll take that. I'm not proud."

He was looking at her, his grey eyes shadowed, and his dark brows drawn together in a frown. He pushed a stray curl of hair back from her forehead and traced the outline of her face with a long finger, then stroked it across her mouth, like a kiss. "Constance Harcourt, when I was lying under several feet of masonry and I thought I was dying, you were all I could think about and when I had moments of lucidity in the field hospital and in the prison, I saw you and you held out your arms to me and called my name and I knew that if I could find you everything would be all right. Ever since the moment I first saw you I somehow just knew. I fought it because I did not understand. You are the love of my life and I will fight anyone who tries to take you away from me. Do you hear me? I will love you to my dying day."

Constance, sniffling into his neck said in muffled accents, “I do wish you’d stop banging on about dying, it’s really starting to piss me off.”

Lucas laughed and lifted her across his body and rolled her onto the bed beside him, where he kissed her very thoroughly, much to her satisfaction.

After a few minutes, he drew back and took a deep shaky breath, “I think you had better leave now before it’s too late,” he said, his voice ragged.

“Oh, don’t you want to bed me after all?" she murmured huskily and trailed her hand down his chest to his waist and then was about to slide it further down when he grabbed it very firmly and returned it to her.

“You are playing with marked cards, Constance. Go to bed.”

“Oh, all right, you killjoy, I’m going. But only because I don’t want to be blamed for tiring you out and making you even more irritable than usual.”

For a while the country was a little subdued, as though momentarily stunned from its recent efforts. Even the tiny domain around the Court House had suffered during the fighting; injured locals of every persuasion returned home, unable to work, some a great burden to their families, some changed forever by their experiences and returning to wives and children who no longer recognised them. Some never coming home at all, because they were rotting in a mass grave, or a water-logged ditch or had just wandered away, their memory obliterated by the violence and ugliness of war.

Quinton Gittings, still in charge of the workings of the estate despite the loss of his sight, made sure that their employees and their families were well cared for; Doctor Spry was sent to all the relevant houses to ensure that each soldier was given the best medical treatment available and Quinton, under his employer’s strict instructions, provided generous pay packets and food parcels. Constance and Lady Ursula visited the families and discreetly observed what was needed and would send clothes for the children, fuel for their fires, provided by a very hard-working Richard Thorne, candles, clean bandages for dressing wounds or anything else they might desperately need. Widows and orphans were comforted and supported, Reverend Woode was sent to pray with them, which seemed to help some and antagonise others, and Cassandra Woode was called when they especially needed someone to listen to them — she was a very good listener — and to hold their hand while they wept and reproached God for deserting them.

Lucas continued to improve but would occasionally have inexplicable relapses. He suffered from intermittent bouts of dizziness and fatigue and would often have a long night where sleep eluded him or he was beset by nightmares, which sounded to Constance like not unexpected flashbacks and he could become distressed by what he was seeing. The worst manifestation for Constance were the night-time terrors which usually ended or began with terrifying paralysis where he was unable to speak or move his limbs and followed by attacks of tremors which rendered him helpless with their ferocity, his uncontrollable movements shaking the bed violently. Richard Thorne would come and help Constance hold him down until the worst was over, so he couldn't hurt himself. He remembered little of these episodes but knew from the residual effects that something had happened. He became morose after the attacks and Constance had to work hard to make him believe that it didn't change how she felt — that it was merely a symptom of what he had suffered and not actually the man. But being a large, mostly unreconstructed alpha male, she found he was inclined to rail against his diminished physical powers and had an overwhelming desire that she should not be allowed to see him in such a weakened state. She just informed him he was being a total dick and ignored him.

Often, she would be called in the night, by whomever was on duty and she would sit beside him while he was in the midst of one of these attacks and she'd hold him and talk to him. Every time the tremors dissipated, and he was left exhausted but unharmed, she would watch his eyes come slowly back into focus and would know he was seeing her properly again and she would breathe a sigh of relief. Sometimes he would smile weakly at her and squeeze her hand, other times he would turn away, unable to look her in the eye.

During the day he was able to get downstairs without help and could wander about at will, although he tired quickly and would fall asleep in a chair for a few hours until his strength was replenished. His wounds had healed but the terrible scars that remained would have scandalised a modern-day plastic surgeon. Constance ran her finger over the one on his forehead which was as ridged as a ploughed field and still an angry red. She told him that they made him look piratical and extremely attractive and he remarked that she was a very unnatural female.

As he followed this insult with a deeply erotic kiss that left Constance craving more, she didn't take umbrage.

Twenty-Eight

March melted swiftly into April and life returned to some kind of recognisable pattern, although the bars stayed on the windows and the muskets stayed primed and loaded. Lucas reminded everyone that despite the armies having mostly disbanded there would inevitably still be stragglers and small bands of dissidents and those intent on making the most of the turbulent times to make their fortunes, although they usually just ended up being arrested or murdered for their troubles.

One of the many problems with a country at war was that the disruption and uncertainty stirred up repressed emotions and gave them permission to be dragged into the light. It gave otherwise ordinary people an excuse to take their revenge on those who had slighted them, and this feverish hysteria could spread as quickly as a fire in a hay barn.

In the East of the country the self-appointed Witch-finder General, Matthew Hopkins, was making life extremely uncomfortable for women who lived on the margins of society as well as the elderly, the poor, the young and vulnerable, and those of unsound mind.

Even though he had stern opposition from influential people he still managed to make a very good living from accusing and taking women to trial for what he and his helpers labelled witchcraft. Reasonable people were naturally afraid to confront the unreasonable in case they too were accused. Women and some men lived in fear, never knowing if their neighbours were going to find fault with their behaviour and accuse them.

Then, one late April afternoon, a sound, unrecognisable at first, it being so unusual, shattered the tranquillity. The sun was shining but it was chilly and there was a nippy breeze which scurried across the hills towards the Court House as though in a hurry to get somewhere important.

The children were sharing a lesson with Valentine de Cheverell in the library and Quinton Gittings was listening in. Lady Ursula had stolen away to have a sneaky nap while everyone else was busy. Sir Lucas and Richard Thorne were out on a gentle bit of estate business and Constance was in the Great Hall arranging some cherry blossom in a vase. She heard the commotion getting gradually louder and went to peer curiously out of the window.

Amassing at the foot of the steps was a vociferous, rag-tag crowd of people, some she recognised but many she didn't. Puzzled, she opened the front door and stepped out into the pleasant sunshine.

"There she is! That is her!" shouted an anonymous voice.

Constance looked around at the faces and saw Mistress Carter and several others that she regularly visited in the village; she smiled warmly at them, but their response was one of embarrassment which was confusing. There was Agnes Fitton, Jane Kench, and Robert Shoesmith. Right in the front were a group of strangers, in Puritan clothing, who seemed to be in charge. Constance scanned their faces and settled on one who clearly thought he was the leader of the motley bunch. He was short and stocky with a large head and small dark eyes which reminded her of a shark. He was staring at her intently and the others were looking to him for confirmation. She moved forward to the front of the terrace and looked down at him unflinchingly even though she was quaking inside. There was a cruel twist to the corner of his fleshy mouth and a confidence to the set of his shoulders that made her immediately uneasy.

"Good afternoon. I am Constance Harcourt, and you are — ?"

The man's cold smile widened, "Reverend Sayer Crane."

"And how may I assist you, Reverend Crane? You seem to have come with a very definite purpose in mind."

"We have come to take you into custody."

"Is that so? How interesting. And may I ask, why you feel the need to do this?" asked Constance calmly.

Another sly smile, "You have been accused of being a lustful daughter of Eve and a witness has seen you committing lewd acts in public."

Constance wanted to laugh out loud, but she knew this was a deadly serious situation and that she had to keep her wits about her. She'd seen a mob in action before on news reports and knew it only took one wrong word or movement and everything could go haywire.

"May I know who is accusing me of this heinous crime?"

"No, you may not. You must come with us."

Constance glanced quickly around the sea of faces, "I believe I know the instigator of this nonsense. Is she brave enough to be here amongst you or is she hiding her Janus face from me? Mistress Fitch?" Seeing the Reverend's slight start of surprise, swiftly masked, she knew she was in deadly trouble. She had no choice but to play for time and hope that someone in the crowd would begin to see sense. She already suspected that some of the villagers were there just out of curiosity and others because their lives were governed by the Church and its ministers.

"She has confessed!" cried a voice from the back of the crowd.

"Yes, she admits Mistress Fitch has seen her lewd acts with the forester!" shouted another.

Reverend Crane held up his hand to still the growing noise. "Quiet. We are taking you to a Special Court, where you will be tried by judge and jury."

"No, really I don't think so. I'm not going anywhere with you."

Constance was suddenly aware that some of the people were staring at something behind her.

She looked around and saw Benedict standing a few paces from the door, he was directing a wobbling musket at the Reverend and looking like he was going to be sick.

"Benedict! Put that gun down! It won't do any good if you shoot someone."

He shook his head, "*No!* I will kill anyone who tries to harm you."

There was a gasp of shock from many in the mob.

"And if he misses, which is unlikely at this range," declared Frances, in a clear voice, "I will put an arrow through the next person to move. And I can assure you, I am a *very* good shot."

"Frances! Benedict! I am very grateful, but this is too dangerous. You must both go inside at once."

"Constance, *you* must go inside and bolt the door," said Lady Ursula appearing, slightly dishevelled, behind the children. "Take the children. I will deal with this."

"I'm not going anywhere. This is my fight."

"This is *our* fight," said Quinton Gittings from the doorway, Valentine de Cheverell at his elbow.

An uneasy murmur ruffled the air, a few of the villagers began to shuffle awkwardly. A lone female was a very different matter to a group of belligerent people with weapons. And now, there were men as well. This was no longer looking quite so simple.

Around the corner, from the stables, came Will Sparrow brandishing his newly acquired pistol, followed by Oates, looking menacing with a pitchfork.

Constance started to breathe more easily.

Reverend Crane glanced around and saw that his support was beginning to collapse, and he realised he was losing ground.

"What about the witchcraft she used to cure this man?" he demanded, his voice penetrating the sounds of shame and regret emanating from the crowd. "She used her powerful magic to cure him of the typhus and now, to heal her master! Only a sorceress could do that. She is in league with the

Devil. Who knows where she came from? Nobody! She just appeared from nowhere and has beguiled this poor family so that they no longer have control over their actions. See how these unfortunate children would kill for her? They are possessed."

"They are not possessed. They love her, as do we all," said Valentine de Cheverell unequivocally.

Quinton tapped his way out onto the terrace, "You must be a very stupid man to think that one woman would be able to accomplish all this and still have time for all her good work. I wonder how she has time to sleep! Perhaps you are just afraid of women in general?"

"The witch has taken possession of your soul too. We can believe nothing you say, she is speaking through you. She is the serpent in the Garden of Eden. You are corrupted by her and cannot be trusted."

Lady Ursula Prideaux stepped forward and surveyed the gathering with cold disdain, "You have seen Mistress Constance Harcourt frequently in the village, visiting and helping those in need; I do not remember any of you complaining about her being a witch then. Mistress Carter? Did she not cure your husband just by suggesting he ate some citrus fruit? Hardly the work of a witch! You should be ashamed. Robert Shoesmith, it is interesting that you should be here. Should you not be in gaol for stealing cheese? I am *sorry*, I cannot hear you! Did you say that Mistress Harcourt wrote a letter, so compelling, that the judge was persuaded to release you? You may *well* hang your head! And, I have no doubt you have all heard that she rode to Bath and effected the rescue of my brother from prison and through her ministrations he is now much recovered. It seems to me that you are all just following Reverend Crane like sad little sheep."

One or two of the villagers were shuffling to the back of the group and melting away toward the gates and safety. There were still some hostile faces, especially the ones at the front who looked as though they were determined to have their moment.

The Puritan leader curled his lip, "Women are weak and make empty vessels for Satan."

"Weak! I would like to see a *man* go through childbirth!" remarked Frances with unexpected worldly wisdom.

"*Thou shalt not suffer a witch to live*," intoned Reverend Crane.

At this, as though triggered by a signal, ten or so of the burly strangers nearest the house suddenly sprang forward and began to mount the steps as one.

Constance pulled the children to her and started to back towards the door. Benedict turned and whispered in her ear. She nodded. He then wrenched himself out of her grip and aimed his gun at the crowd. Frances was at full draw, her arrow aimed at the Reverend's chest.

Will Sparrow and Oates pushed in from the side and some of the crowd saw them and scattered.

The zealots advancing up the stone steps with increasing aggression seemed unimpressed by the opposition and kept moving forward. Benedict turned quickly to Constance and snapped an order at her. As he lifted his gun and fired, she picked up her skirts and ran.

Benedict's musket ball flew harmlessly over the heads of the crowd, people ducked and then tumbled over each other trying to get out of harm's way.

Reverend Crane took another step up but stopped in his tracks, looking rather taken aback. He looked down, perplexed, to find an arrow sticking out of his chest. He grabbed it and crumpled to his knees as though about to pray. His eyes goggled at Frances who, although shaking from head to toe, returned his gaze resolutely. He tried to mouth something at her. She moved a little closer, "You should not have likened me to an empty vessel. That was *very* stupid when I have a bow in my hand." She watched him slip sideways and fall to the ground in a heap. She backed away and ran into her aunt's open arms.

At this unhappy moment Lucas and Richard arrived at a run, having heard the sound of a gunshot reverberate down the lane.

Colonel Sir Lucas Deverell assessed the situation in a second and told Richard to get Ursula and the children into the house; he ordered Will Sparrow to aim at the remaining Puritans, with manifest intent to shoot anyone who showed the least dissent and asked Oates to kindly show the villagers to the gates with the aid of his trusty pitchfork.

Lucas went to look at the Reverend dispassionately while asking Quinton for an explanation of the incident. "The arrow?"

Quinton had no choice but to tell him, "He annoyed Frances. She had already notified him of her intentions, but he was not in the mood to listen."

"The gunshot?"

"Benedict fired a warning shot over their heads, which gave Constance a chance to escape. They were becoming a little hard to contain."

"Constance? Where is she?"

"Benedict told her to run and she did. They had come for her, — to take her to trial."

"Trial? For *what?*" snarled Lucas.

"Witchcraft. Mistress Fitch has been spreading her poison abroad and this was the result. She had informed them that Constance had committed — lewd acts with — I am sorry, Richard and when that failed to work, Reverend Crane said she had used witchcraft to cure us. Ursula did a magnificent job of talking some of them into leaving. She was — indomitable — a veritable Valkyrie!"

The crowd had almost entirely dispersed, quietly returning to the village and forlornly hoping that their presence at such a terrible spectacle would be overlooked. Oates took great pleasure in poking some of them in the rear with his pitchfork to encourage them to move faster.

"When all is said and done, Ursula is a Deverell," said Lucas with a frown.

Richard appeared at his side and gave the unfortunate preacher a bruising kick with the toe of his boot to see if he was still alive, "Shame. Not dead. Shall I — ?"

"No, I think that might be going too far but if you and Will could remove him and make sure the Judge is informed, that would be good enough. Now, I shall go and speak with Ursula and my children."

"One at a time! I cannot understand you when you all speak over each other. Now, you say Constance met with the crowd first?"

"Yes!" said Benedict, "She must have been very scared. But she kept talking to them — "

"Of that, I have no doubt," muttered Lucas grimly.

"And I heard them outside making a dreadful din so Frances and I found our weapons and came out and Mr de Cheverell brought Mr Gittings out with him and That Man called Constance a serpent and then Aunt Ursula told everyone how wonderful Constance is and then That Man said women were weak and Frances said she would like to see a man give birth and That Man called her an empty vessel which probably was not wise and Those Men charged at us and I fired a warning shot and Frances shot That Man with an arrow, which was splendid! And then you came."

Lucas ruffled his son's hair, "You are both very brave and I am proud of you although we will need to have a word about the proper use of weapons. Now, what happened to Constance please?"

"Oh, when I thought she was sure to be taken I told her that I would fire to distract them, and she should run."

"Where did you tell her to run, Benedict?" asked Lucas as patiently as he could while aware that his heart was pounding uncomfortably in his throat.

"Oh, come here — ", said Benedict and whispered in his father's ear.

Lucas smiled at him and flicked his cheek with a finger, "Of *course,* clever boy!"

Benedict puffed out his chest with pride and watched his father limp away through the parterre.

In the Great Hall, Lady Ursula was sitting with her head in her hands trying desperately to stop the terrible waves of trembling which shook her body. She was making little gulping sounds, although no tears came, just dry gasps that hurt her throat, as she attempted to come to terms with what had just happened. She had never been so afraid in her life. Their faces would stay with her forever; their ugly, maddened, unreasonable faces.

"Ursula?"

She shook her head and kept her face covered.

Quinton put a gentle hand on her shoulder, "Please."

She shook her head again and turned away.

Quinton carefully got down on his knees beside her. "Ursula. Listen to me." He felt for her hands uncertainly, "You were so very brave. And I could not help you because of my damned eyes. I wanted to protect you. I am so sorry."

The dry sobs diminished a little and Ursula looked down at him in astonishment, "But you did help me. Just knowing you were there was enough. Oh, Quinton, what if — ?"

He reached up and found her face and caressed her cheek, "It is over now. Everyone is safe. No what ifs! We all stood together, and their madness could not vanquish us. When I heard your voice and knew you were in danger I could not bear to think of our ridiculous argument. How trivial it all seemed in that moment!"

Ursula put her hand over his, "I know! It is too terrible to contemplate. But, Quinton, I have to ask — when I practically threw myself at you — you rejected me. I must know why! Am I so repulsive?"

"Oh, God, Ursula! Can you not — *see?*"

Her face crumpled and she shook her head, which he felt rather than saw, "No, I cannot understand! I tried so hard to be someone you might learn to — bear — but you spurned me out of hand and gave me no reason."

Quinton leant forward and laid his head upon her lap, "I cannot ask you to marry me because I am utterly beneath you! I am your brother's estate steward. I am a servant. And I am blind. What do I have to offer you?"

"For a clever man you are remarkably stupid," said Lady Ursula, rather timidly stroking his hair, "A woman does not expose her vulnerability in such a manner unless she has come to realise something very important — that she would risk everything for a particular person. I have no illusion about what I am, Quinton — you would be getting the worst of the bargain. In you, I see everything I am not. You are diligent, honest, kind and loyal. My brother does not suffer fools gladly, he would never employ someone who did not reach his exacting standards and you have always been his best friend into the bargain."

"But, Ursula, my eyesight."

She tossed her head, "Oh, pooh! What do I care for that? It means I can grow old without a care and you will always remember me as I am now. I am very vain, you know!"

Quinton Gittings raised his head and found her face with his hands, "I would treasure every line. Every silver hair."

"Silver hair! God forbid! I shall wear a coif. Quinton?"

"Yes, Ursula?"

"Do you think you might kiss me now?"

"I am not sure we have agreed — "

"Quinton! We are agreed! Now, kiss me before I lose my temper!"

"Very well, my love."

And he did and Lady Ursula Prideaux found it to be even more enjoyable than she had so frequently imagined.

Twenty-Nine

The Wilderness was quiet. The only sounds, faint dry rustlings and the whispering of soft new leaves; in the deep dark heart of the wood not a bird sang, or an insect stirred. It was as though the trees were listening and waiting and wondering. The air smelt of fresh green buds and leaf litter, the old world decaying and earthy, and the new one, verdant and alive.

Lucas's boots hardly made any noise on the damp woodland floor as he weaved his way through the trees. He found the ladder, which he noted had been mended in several places and climbed up into Benedict's treehouse. He squeezed through the boy-sized doorway and into the half-light of the carefully constructed wooden room.

With a sigh of relief, he saw the huddled shape on the straw-filled mattress and just paused for a moment to subdue a slight rush of panic. She was lying very still and for a second he thought the worst but then saw she was breathing.

He crossed the small space and knelt beside her, looking down at her, curled up like a dormouse, folded in on herself as though to protect herself from the anger and violence.

He gently touched her shoulder but even though it was only the slightest pressure, she flinched.

Suffocated by fear, her only instinct was to retreat from the danger.

She was like the injured turtle dove he had found as a boy. It had a broken wing and he first had to win its trust before he could mend the wing and nurse it back to health.

He just laid his hand on her arm and let it rest there for a while before very slowly sliding it down to her wrist. He took her hand in his and held it. Stroking the back of it with his thumb. He could feel her pulse under his fingers and waited until it had slowed before continuing to try to coax her from the stupor she was swaddled in. He understood where she was. She had hidden herself away just as he had. In the shadows there was a kind of solace; there were no sounds and no pain or fear, just oblivion. The problem with oblivion was it could be so compelling to those who are damaged that it could become an addiction. There had to be a stronger reason to fight your way out than the reason keeping you in.

Like he would with an unbroken horse, he kept gentle contact with her until she stopped flinching and retreating from his touch, gradually increasing the time he held her until he could feel she had relaxed a little.

Then, he very slowly lay down next to her, easing himself into a position so that he could cradle her, sliding an arm under her shoulders and the other around her waist. He waited, almost not daring to breathe. Her breathing altered. There was the slightest sigh. He pulled her a little closer until her back was pressed against his chest.

And then he held her while she slept, binding her into his world.

She slept as though unconscious and he listened to her every breath. Breathing with her. Until he couldn't tell them apart.

He had no idea how much time passed. He didn't care. He just knew that she needed him.

The sun was setting. It was getting cooler. Constance stirred in her sleep. She took a deep shuddering breath and turned in his arms so that she was facing him. She nestled her face into his neck like a kitten, nudging at his jaw. He looked down at her, committing to memory the dark line of her sooty eyelashes, the curve of her cheek, the soft sighs coming between her slightly open lips.

He wondered if perhaps she *was* a witch and had enchanted him; why else would he feel this way about someone? He smiled to himself and thought if she were a witch, he didn't really care either, he was content to be under her thrall.

The sun disappeared and the temperature dropped.

Constance wriggled in closer to him, seeking warmth. The straw-filled mattress rustled.

Suddenly he knew she was awake. A change in her heartbeat, the rhythm of her breathing, her body subtly altered. He pressed his lips against her hair and breathed in the sweet scent of her.

Then he realised she was crying, the tears sliding silently down her cheeks. He shifted his position so he could see her face and kissed away the salty tears, the taste of them like the sea. He rhythmically rubbed the small of her back and gently rocked her in his arms.

She started to shiver. To share his warmth, he reached down and lifted her leg over his, pushing his knee between her thighs, her voluminous skirts a barricade.

He had to grit his teeth together hard when she pulled him closer by hooking her leg around his hips. He closed his eyes for a moment and gathered all the resistance he could muster.

He felt her lips on his eyelids and opened his eyes and looked into hers. In the fading light, they just looked at each other.

"Are they all right?" she whispered.

He nodded and kissed her forehead.

"They were so brave."

He kissed the end of her nose.

"I shouldn't have left them."

He pressed his mouth against hers and felt her shivering intensify. He pulled away and looked down at her quizzically.

"It's not the *cold* — " she breathed.

He smiled, suddenly rather more sure of himself.

He smoothed the tangle of hair back from her face and kissed her deeply until she let out a soft moan. He laughed quietly.

"Lucas?"

He pulled away again.

"Don't *stop!*"

He looked at her with laughing eyes and kissed her ruthlessly.

She came up for air, "Bloody hell, *Lucas!"* she gasped.

He propped himself up on his elbow and frowned at the row of decorative bows on the front of her stays. He tried undoing them while Constance looked on impatiently.

"It's laced at the *back*."

He groaned. Then without warning, he flipped her over and started to unlace her gown. He got the laces snarled and lost his temper. She started to laugh until he grabbed the laces and just ripped them out.

"Oh, no! It's *new!* It's so beautiful. I wanted you to see me in it. It's a lovely mustard yellow taffeta — "

"I do not care! Get the damn thing *off!* I do not want to see the gown, however beautiful it may be. I will buy you a dozen more! I want to see *you!*"

"Lucas Deverell you really are a barbarian! Stop *ripping* at it like a bloody bear! Heathen!"

Constance sat up and began to struggle out of her clothes, until she was down to her underskirt and shift. Lucas watched her with a glint in his eye.

"Now you, Sir," she commanded in husky accents and began to help him out of his doublet, but he became even more impatient and suddenly she felt his hand sliding up under her petticoat.

"What do you think you're *doing?* Lucas! Oh, dear *Lord* — "

"Just lie still will you! Stop wriggling! Let me do this for you!"

"*Oh!*"

He stopped her mouth with kisses and then there was silence, apart for the odd ecstatic moan from Constance who had no idea that life in the seventeenth century could be this rewarding.

She didn't even mind the sound of rending material, she found it deeply satisfying. She found everything satisfying and then it just got better.

When she wrapped her legs around his waist, she knew he was taken aback, looking down at her in the gathering gloom with wonderment. But, when he started to withdraw, she held him fast and told him to sodding well carry on and finish what he'd started.

He was happy to gratify her wishes.

They lay together on the straw-filled mattress, in the dark, Lucas with his head resting between her breasts, his finger idly drawing patterns on the sweaty skin of her midriff.

"Constance Harcourt, you are the most glorious hussy. Will you please marry me so that we can do this every night for the rest of our lives?"

"We don't have to get married to do this!"

"Yes, we do. It goes without saying that I am extremely old-fashioned. I would rather keep you all to myself. As you have already noticed, I am tyrannical."

"Well, in that case — gladly." She ran her fingers over his thick, cropped hair, "But could we please just do it again now? And then maybe, again — ?"

"Harlot. They will be missing us at home."

"I'm sure Ursula will come up with a plausible excuse for our absence. The children will be in bed. It'll give Quinton and Ursula a chance to be together and sort things out."

"Ah! So that is what you are up to! Poor helpless Quinton. What a life she will lead him."

"Oh, it's quite clear they are meant to be together. He brings out the best side of her; he makes her strive harder to be considerate. And he will take care of her in his own way, curbing her excesses with a kind and thoughtful word. It's perfect."

"Good. I am glad your scheming will bear fruit. But can we stop talking about my sister please? It is not helping! I would rather discuss what you would like me to do next. For instance, this — ? Or — *this?*"

"Oh, that, *please!*"

"What if they — ?" said Ursula, pacing the parlour and fretting.

Quinton sighed, "*No news is better than evil news.*"

"Oh, really? You are quoting at me at a time like this? That is *very* fine!"

"Your brother is perfectly able to command a regiment of unruly soldiers. I think he will manage to find Constance and work things out satisfactorily."

"But where can they have gone? They have been away for hours now! And Constance was so scared!"

"If something had happened, we would have heard by now. Leave them be," said Quinton firmly.

Lady Ursula cast him a startled glance, opened her mouth to say something and then closed it again. She crossed the room, knelt in front of him and drawing his head down, kissed him.

"That will not work with me, my lady!" laughed Quinton.

Ursula chuckled, "Yes it will, my love, yes it will!"

After another long moment, Ursula sat back on her heels, her hands on his knees, "Oh, I wonder — you do not think they are — ?"

He smiled, "Yes, I do and that is why I think you should stop worrying and we should retire for the night and in the morning, they will be back home and looking a little pleased with themselves."

"I cannot wait to tell them our news!"

"You will allow them to enjoy their moment first, Ursula, and not overshadow them."

"As *though* I would!"

Quinton lifted her hand to his lips and kissed it, "My beloved."

Later that night, just as dawn was breaking, long after everyone had gone to bed, two dishevelled figures let themselves quietly into the Court House like thieves, one wearing nothing but his breeches and the other, a badly torn gown. Holding hands and giggling like wayward children. They reluctantly parted company on the landing outside her bedchamber, after a heated moment with her pinned up against the wall, her feet off the ground.

"Oh, Lord! You *must* let me go!" she mumbled into his searching mouth, "Or we'll look like hell in the morning and everyone will guess."

He abruptly dropped her, and she slipped to the floor with a thump. "*Go* then!"

She gave him a saucy look and slid through the door into her room.

Lucas Deverell stood for a moment with his forehead pressed against the door, trying to catch his breath and get control of the aching in his loins. He was shattered but had never been happier.

"Another beautiful spring day," remarked Ursula, in relentlessly cheerful tones.

"It is indeed," replied Quinton, with a wry smile.

The breakfast table was unusually subdued, the children were monosyllabic; Constance, her cheeks flushed with a rosy pink, barely looked up from her plate. Lucas arrived late and discussed with Quinton and Valentine de Cheverell the previous day's incident, asking what had happened after he had left and if the Reverend had been safely delivered to the judge.

Benedict looked up at his father, "Is That Man all right?"

"Yes, he is. He will survive the wound, it did not go very deep, fortunately."

"*Un*fortunately," said Benedict.

"I wish it had killed him dead," muttered Frances through clenched teeth, "He deserved it. If I had been a better shot, I could have shot him in the eye. That would have worked."

Ursula looked shocked, “Frances, my dear, I do not think it is at all respectable to be so bloodthirsty.”

“I have no wish to be respectable, Aunt Ursula. I want to be like Constance.”

Lucas made a choking sound and the colour in Constance’s cheeks deepened to scarlet.

Ursula looked from one to the other with interest, “I think, Frances, that you might want to choose someone else to emulate!” She could see her brother’s shoulders shaking, “So, where did you two disappear to yesterday? You were away so long!”

“Ursula Prideaux!" said Quinton with something of a snap.

Lucas pushed his chair back and stood up. He cleared his throat, “I have an announcement to make,” he said with a sly look at Constance, “Mistress Constance Harcourt has done me the honour — ”

“I *knew* it!” exclaimed Ursula, clapping her hands.

“ — of agreeing to become my wife.”

The children leapt to their feet and danced around the table, hugging everyone and babbling excitedly. Ursula embraced her brother and her future sister-in-law with real joy and Quinton made a little speech about true love and how trying times could sometimes bring change for the good.

Constance peeked up at her betrothed from under her eyelashes and bit her lip hard to stop herself from crying, but it didn’t work and as tears flowed, she found herself crushed against his broad chest.

“You will be our mother! Oh, this is beyond *anything!"* cried Benedict happily.

The only person who did not look quite so joyous was Valentine de Cheverell, who had to bravely school his stupefied face into a smile as he congratulated his divinely beautiful Constance, who, in his humble opinion, was throwing herself away on his employer who, although a very fine and upstanding man, was far too prosaic to be a suitable spouse for his muse.

Lucas released his beloved, who was now looking very overheated and disordered after a rather fierce embrace and he smoothed her hair away from her face with such an uncharacteristically loving gesture that his sister burst into fresh tears and threw herself into Quinton's arms.

This stopped everyone in their tracks, and they stared in astonishment at the wholly unexpected sight.

"Aunt Ursula! You are *hugging* Mr Gittings!" exclaimed Benedict, his eyes like saucers.

His aunt said something too muffled to understand and Quinton laughed. "What Lady Ursula is trying to say is that while you were away last night, we came to an amicable understanding."

Lady Ursula made an explosive sound of derision, "Oh, for heaven's sake! What a typically turgid way of putting it, Quinton! What he is trying to tell you is that I love him, and he has agreed to love me back because he is too afraid to say otherwise!"

There followed a stunned silence.

"Well, this seems to be the day for surprise announcements," said Lucas with a wide grin. "May I offer my blessings to you both? I could not be happier. Quinton, my dear friend, are you *sure* you know what you are doing?"

"I am absolutely positive. I have been cowardly but after yesterday I am convinced that although I have had and still have some reservations, they are unimportant when one is faced with a volatile situation such as the one we just encountered. And Ursula assures me that she is about to become a changed woman, so I have no fears on that count!" His smile faded away and a frown appeared, "Lucas, do I have your permission?"

"You do not *need* my brother's permission! I am a widow with my own means! I can do what I like."

"Ursula, allow me to speak. I would nevertheless like to have your permission Lucas, not permission to address your sister as a prospective suitor but permission to remain your friend despite marrying her. For marry her I will, with or without your consent."

Lady Ursula cast a self-satisfied glance around her assembled family, "He is surprisingly imperious for such a mild-mannered man, is he not?"

"He is going to need to be," remarked Lucas sardonically.

Constance felt life was becoming even more surreal. It had gone from high drama and imminent danger to utter bliss and on to quiet contentment. To see Ursula and Quinton together completed her happiness. The children were fizzing with excitement and making plans. She found it thrilling to take a secret peep at Lucas and find him gazing at her with a look that made her heart leap and other parts of her behave quite improperly. She found it difficult to continue with her daily chores with the same enthusiasm as before because she was always daydreaming about him, like a teenage girl, wondering when she could find him alone so that she could smother his battered face with kisses. She had to give herself a stern shake and a talking-to. Frances was overflowing with questions. When did you first know you loved him? Why do you love him? How does it feel to love someone?

Constance answered every question with honesty and patience, happy to talk about Lucas until the cows came home, but one ear was always listening out for his halting footfall.

Lucas Deverell found he was drifting in and out of conversations about the estate, news of the war, now indefinitely stalled, and the uncertain plight of some of his employees, as visions of a night in a treehouse kept intruding and distracting him. Even barns had lost much of their fascination for him, apart from when he was imagining Constance lying back in the warm, dusty hay, wearing a torn mustard yellow gown —

He rubbed a hand over his tired eyes and asked Richard Thorne if they could continue the discussion the following morning as he was feeling a little weary.

Richard, who had heard the family's good news and had that morning found, to his amusement, a discarded petticoat near the treehouse, smiled and agreed.

Lucas then went in search of his betrothed because he hadn't seen her for a few hours and needed to talk to her about — he groaned to himself — about kissing her again. This just would not do! He had to get control of his emotions and desires. He was supposed to be a Puritan! He knew he was already on the road to damnation; perhaps there was no use trying to save their souls. Perhaps they were already lost. He could not think of anyone he would rather be lost and damned with than Constance. Where the hell was she?

Constance was just skipping down the main staircase when Lucas strode purposefully into the Great Hall. She saw the look on his face, muttered "Uh oh!" under her breath and turned and made her way quickly back up to the landing, her stomach doing excited flip-flops. He found her in her bedchamber and slammed the door behind him. She backed away towards the bed, chewing her lip, as he advanced towards her, his eyes dark and his breathing a little rapid.

"I'm not sure that daytime fornication is a good idea! I think we should — !" She tumbled backwards onto the bed laughing and pulling up her leaf-green skirts. "Or maybe not! Did you lock the door? Lucas! No *ripping!* I *love* this gown!"

There were several inevitable repercussions from the day of the Witch Hunt or as Constance liked to call it, Treehouse Day.

One was that Mistress Fitch was officially dismissed although, as she never returned to the Court House after her machinations had failed so disastrously, nobody had their cathartic moment of triumph, watching her forlornly haul her baggage away down the lane.

Another was that Reverend Sayer Crane was arrested for inciting a riot and spreading false rumours but because he claimed Benefit of Clergy, was turned over to the Church, which was, particularly for Frances, a deeply disappointing result. She had been hoping for, at the very least, imprisonment or a public whipping. She muttered darkly for days about the unsatisfactory judicial system in England and said she hoped his wound festered and he died in agony. Eventually her aunt took her on one side and told her that if she continued in that vein, she would be forced to devise some kind of punishment to fit the nature of her poor behaviour, which, she suggested slyly, to Frances's disgust, might be no more archery lessons. So, she obediently buttoned her lip, her eyes sparking fire.

And some of the villagers who had been present at the rout, were too ashamed to receive either Ursula or Constance in their homes despite being reassured that both women understood the reasons for their actions.

The final one was that there were two weddings to be organised.

*

It was only when there was a lull in the feverish excitement after the announcements that Constance had time to think about July twenty seventh.

April was now May and she knew that before she could say Jack Robinson it would be June and they would be hurtling towards July. She had told Guy in the last geocache communication that she would be ready on the specified Lunar Eclipse date for whatever he had planned but she was now torn between trying to return home to her family and staying with Lucas and the children.

She was caught with her feet in two camps and in her waking hours she could pretend she was so busy that she didn't have time to consider all the possibilities and ramifications of her plight but then her nightmares would show her some of the horror which lay ahead, and she began to dread going to sleep.

The idea of never seeing her sister and the boys again made her go cold with dread. She couldn't imagine life without their incessant noise and fighting and silly jokes, their bruising hugs, and loving disrespect. To never see them all grown-up, to miss out on all the important moments in their lives; how could she reconcile with that? And how on earth was she to tell Lucas? She would try every so often to bring the subject up and then balk at the last minute and the longer she put it off, the more difficult it became.

Lucas had said he thought there must be a purpose to her being there with him, but she couldn't help thinking it was just a giant cosmic joke. Some bored Supreme Being, in an idle moment, between sipping nectar and eating ambrosia, had decided to have some harmless fun and this was the result. Chaos.

Her life, perfect and in ruins at the same time. She preferred not to think about it. She preferred watching Lucas limping towards her with a wicked gleam in his eyes, a mountain lion intent on pouncing on its prey. She liked being the prey. Or to be diligently working in the garden trying to think only about what she was doing but finding herself lifted off her feet and swung around in the air, just as though she weighed no more than thistledown. Or to be just drifting off to sleep and hear her door creak open and the bed give under a heavy weight, an arm circled her waist and then the sound of his even breathing as he slept. Or the time when she had searched for him everywhere and unable to find him, even in the barn, had sat down amongst the hay to indulge in some panicky self-pity and then an afternoon nap, only to wake a short while later to find him standing over her, an odd little smile twisting his mouth.

"A dream come true, except you are not wearing the yellow gown," he said obliquely and then proceeded to make her forget her woes for most of the afternoon.

She noticed, with relief, that the symptoms of shell shock had mostly abated, and he was able to go for maybe a week or more without any signs of it recurring. Nightmares were still a slight problem, but her hearing was good, and she was a light sleeper so she could usually get to his side and soothe him before he woke. The tremors were now mild and infrequent, and he no longer suffered any attacks of dizziness. She felt that they were winning some kind of battle with an invisible foe. Doctor Spry, when he called to check up on his patient, was clearly impressed by his progress and asked curiously about the sort of treatment he was getting.

Lucas told Constance that being distracted by love and lust was a great healer and thought he should recommend it to the army surgeons.

And then one morning in the middle of June, she knew for sure.

She woke Lucas from a deep early morning slumber by sliding into bed next to him and staring intently at his sleeping face until he sensed something was amiss and roused himself.

He peered at her a little blearily, "Constance?"

She just looked at him. Her eyes questioning.

He adjusted his position, "What is it?"

"Do you love me?"

"A remarkably stupid question," he responded, frowning.

"*Do* you?"

"God, Constance! You know I do! More than life itself."

"I need to be certain."

He quickly sat up, the frown deepening, "Are you leaving me?"

"No, we're not leaving you."

"God, I thought — I have been dreading — *we?*"

She smiled, "Yes, my beloved Neanderthal. *We.*"

He stared at her for a moment as the truth dawned slowly.

"Are you — how is this — I cannot — ", he faltered.

She looked at him anxiously, "Lucas? Are you angry?"

She was abruptly folded into his arms and found it rather hard to speak or breathe for a while.

"Mind? This is — I have never been — I cannot believe — !"

"Are you ever going to finish a sentence again? I seem to have broken you!"

He planted the gentlest kiss on her lips, "I love you. *Both* of you!"

"Well, thank God for that! I thought for a minute that I was about to be thrown out into the snow with no references!"

"You *still* mistrust me?"

She tilted her head, considering him for a moment, "No, I trust you implicitly. It's not that. I suppose I hadn't really considered the implications for us both. For the children."

"They will be enchanted and we — sadly we will have to avoid — union — now," he said gloomily.

"*Union!* You mean sex? Fornication? Making love? Bonking?"

"Constance! It is not a laughing matter."

"Well, you can try to avoid it if you like but this lady is not for avoiding!" she declared and went into peals of laughter.

She saw he was not sharing her amusement and wiped her eyes on her shift, "Oh, I'm sorry! It's just that, luckily for us, that particular folk-tale has been thoroughly disproved."

"A mother's passion can affect the baby."

She took his face in her hands, "No, it can't. Doctors in the future know a lot more about pregnancy and giving birth and I swear to you that we will not damage the baby in the slightest by having regular and passionate sex! So, stop looking so downcast! In fact, I can prove it to you right now, if you'd like! Or are you going to need time to get used to the notion?"

He grinned at her, "I am a remarkably quick apprentice. I believe you!"

With a giggle, Constance slid deftly out of her nightshift but was stopped by Lucas who bent down to press a reverent kiss upon her belly.

"You're so sweet," she said, with a watery sniff, "But I feel it's only fair to warn you that I fear I'm going to be one of those irritating females who when expecting, become highly emotional and make the fathers go insane."

"I really do not care. You can do what you like."

"We'll see if you're still of the same opinion in a few months' time! Why are you just lying there?"

His eyes lit up, the corners creasing into laughter lines, "I believe I have done my work, Mistress Harcourt. It's your turn," and he put his arms behind his head and gave her a challenging look.

"Oh, my! So, that's how it's going to be, is it? You're just going to lie back and think of England! Lazy git."

She pulled back the covers and laughed, "Sleeping naked, again, sir! Well, that makes everything a whole lot easier," and she slid her leg over his hips, straddling him, with a throaty giggle. "You are always so gratifyingly pleased to see me!"

He just lay supine, his eyes gleaming, "It can make everyday business quite — uncomfortable — if I see you in the distance, or you brush past me in that provocative way you have!"

"I'm not being provocative! I'm just walking!"

"Well, I find your walking provocative! Kindly be careful when you do it."

"You're ridiculous. You know, this is not the behaviour of a gentleman."

"I keep trying to tell you that I am not a gentleman. Are you just going to sit there all day looking beautiful?"

"You think I'm beautiful?"

Lucas cast his eyes up, "Constance Harcourt, you are the most entrancing creature I have ever set eyes upon."

"Oh, that's nice of you to say so."

"I tell you every day."

"I know."

He took her hand and placed it against his chest, just over his heart, "Are you worrying about later?"

Constance blushed, "I know it's silly but — my sister was absolutely enormous when she was pregnant! She looked as though she'd swallowed a goat. She could barely walk. All her boys were huge babies and now they're giants. What if — ?"

"You think I will find you unattractive?"

She nodded and then slumped forward against him, stomach to stomach, chest to chest, skin to skin.

"I must say I had thought you quite an intelligent female, but I am starting to wonder. The idea of you carrying my — *our* child makes me feel protective, proud, happy, and very excited. You could swallow a herd of goats and I would still want you. It makes no difference. I am but a simple man with simple needs."

"That's one of the things I love about you. Although I would call you uncomplicated rather than simple. Black and white. I wasn't doubting you. I just needed reassurance. Oh, we cannot tell anyone our news until the twelfth week, and I think this must be week seven as I am absolutely certain this baby was conceived in a treehouse! We have learnt that the first three months are the most unsafe. Now, please stop distracting me, I have a point to prove!"

Lucas chuckled, "I thought you had forgotten all about me."

"Never!" she said and wriggled slightly to get into a more comfortable position. Then, feeling the instant reaction this got, she slid slowly down his body in a deliberately provocative manner until his breathing became satisfyingly uneven.

A little while later, Lucas was lying half-asleep, his arms around her, her head nestling against his chest and he smiled into her very tousled hair; she was sound asleep, exhausted and emotional and he thought about what lay ahead of them and he silently promised her that he would keep her and their baby safe. She stirred, moaning softly in her sleep. He stroked the small of her back until she relaxed again. The weight of her against his body, the slick of sweat between them, the gentle thump of her heart, the way she trusted him, fought for him, the way she loved him — this was his reason for living.

Constance rushed into the Great Hall, a little late for breakfast, she greeted everyone, patted the children on their heads as she passed and quickly slipped into her chair. She reached over and squeezed Quinton's hand, nodded and smiled at Valentine de Cheverell and Lady Ursula and took a deep steadying breath. She then took a peek at Lucas, who was looking at her from under his sleepy eyelids. They exchanged a glance. The merest glance.

Lady Ursula, who was observing them, let out a little gasp which she swiftly turned into a cough and excused herself, saying a crumb had caught in her throat.

Her eyes widened and she thought to herself that they had better hasten the wedding arrangements, because otherwise dear Constance would not fit into her wedding gown.

"I have asked Reverend Woode to preside over the troth plighting ceremony," said Lady Ursula in tones which brooked no argument. "In two days' time," she added.

"That seems rather — hasty," murmured Constance.

Ursula couldn't meet her eyes, "I think it is best."

"So, the troth plighting is followed by the official wedding sometime later, I understand?"

Ursula swallowed, "That would certainly be the usual practice, yes."

Constance eyed her anxiously, "But, this is not a *usual* wedding?"

"Well, of course, it is! I was not suggesting — no, it is *perfectly* usual. I think that we could have the wedding in a few weeks' time, before Summer is over. Yes, that would be fitting. We must arrange for your gown to be made. You could wear the chocolate brown silk for the troth plighting and then I was considering a new gown of deep periwinkle blue for the wedding? You look so very beautiful in that particular shade of blue."

Constance smiled, a slow, understanding smile, "You're so very good to me, Ursula and I love you to bits. But, although I'm happy to go along with the accelerated timing of the wedding, I would really like to wear mustard yellow for the ceremony, if you think that would be acceptable?" She watched her future sister-in-law's expressive face with interest, "I have a *particular* fondness for it."

"Mustard yellow? Well, it is not what I would have chosen but if that is what you desire! Do you not already have a gown in that colour?"

'Yes. It was very beautiful too, but it suffered a terrible accident and is irreparable, sadly."

"Wait! Were you not wearing it the day the witch-hunters came? Surely — ?" Ursula stopped and put her hand to her mouth and then flushed scarlet to the roots of her hair. "*Oh!*"

Constance laughed, "Ah ha! I thought so!" She took Ursula's hands in hers, "My *dear*, sister. You know, don't you? Well, I'm glad! That night — the gown annoyed your brother very much and I'm afraid it will never be the same again. However, that was the night that you became an aunt, as I think you have already cleverly surmised!"

Lady Ursula Prideaux threw her arms around Constance and wept copious tears. "An aunt! I knew it! As soon as I saw you and Lucas at breakfast — I just knew! Hence the haste with the wedding. Oh, this is wonderful. Although sinful," she added quickly, frowning.

"*Very* sinful," said Constance, stifling a giggle.

"Constance!"

"I'm sorry, Ursula. But who knew your brother — !"

Lady Ursula clapped her hands over her ears, "Do not say more! I forbid you!"

Constance doubled over with laughter and eventually Ursula had to smile and admit it was all quite ridiculously funny.

"Have you and Quinton — ?"

"Certainly *not!*"

Their eyes met and they collapsed together in uncontrollable giggles, their arms about one another.

Lucas and Quinton entering the parlour at this moment, paused on the threshold.

"Ladies? Can we ask what has sent you into such paroxysms of mirth?" asked Quinton.

Ursula wiped her eyes, tried to say something, failed and started laughing again.

Constance couldn't meet her beloved's eyes. "It was — just — a silly thing — too trivial to explain."

A gleam lit Lucas's eyes, "My darling, do share it with us. Nothing is too trivial between us."

Constance bit her lip, "No, indeed, it was — just a female thing — of no importance — just — amusing — "

"Quinton and I could do with a little humour," he said with a malicious smile. "Is it to do with the wedding perhaps?"

Constance made a choking sound and sent him a ferocious look.

"I think," said Quinton moving forward towards his chair, "that you should stop torturing them now, Lucas and behave in a more gentlemanly manner."

Lucas narrowed his eyes, "But, as I keep reiterating, I am not a gentleman, I am merely an oafish soldier and therefore very little in the way of good manners should be expected."

"On the whole your manners are perfect," said Constance, innocently, "Apart from an occasion recently when you behaved in a rather uncharacteristically selfish manner and left me to do all the hard work."

Lucas raised a fiendish eyebrow, "Frankly, my love, there was very little work to be done by then as I had already done the *hard* bit — "

Constance let out a little shriek of dismay and fled the room.

Thirty-One

The day of the troth plighting arrived, and the house was gently buzzing. It was a gloriously sunny July morning, the sky a deep cobalt blue and not a cloud in sight. Reverend Woode arrived with his wife Cassandra and the excited staff gathered outside in the parterre.

Lucas, in black leather doublet and black silk with bronze ribbons, looked severe but elegant and Quinton in dark grey, with Ursula, on his arm wearing a silvery blue silk gown, with bows of chestnut brown waited impatiently on the terrace. The Reverend was making idle chitchat about the harvest and the weather, which he felt was his duty, while his wife complimented Frances on her gown of rose-pink silk and asked if she was looking forward to the wedding.

"Oh, very much! It is the best thing that ever happened — even better than shooting That Man with an arrow!" She saw Mistress Woode's face and blushed, "I should not have said that! I am so sorry. It is just that That Man was so very bad and wanted to hurt Constance, so I had to shoot him. You see?"

Cassandra Woode, who had five quite poorly behaved children of her own, gave the girl a comfortable hug, "Yes, I do see, my dear. If anyone tried to hurt my family, I would probably also want to shoot them with a bow and arrow. You were very brave."

"No, I was not. I was angry and scared and perhaps I should not have *actually* shot him, but he had evil eyes and Constance is a good person not a witch. And I doubt you would have shot him, you would have prayed for him, because you are a nice person. Oh, look, here she comes!"

Constance Harcourt, stepped out into the sunshine, blinking a little in the bright light and looking around for a pair of hooded eyes to reassure her. She found them and caught her breath. For a moment there was only the two of them, as he came towards her with his halting gait and took her hand, kissed her cheek and looked down into her green eyes.

"At last, my love, I have waited all my life for this moment."

She smiled at him, her eyes sparkling like peridots, "I'm so happy it's you. It could never have been anyone else."

And he led her to Reverend Woode, who performed the simple ceremony with humour and wisdom and, thankfully brevity, which very much pleased everyone there.

He asked, at one point, if they were to exchange gifts and Lucas beckoned to Benedict who stepped forward, looking hugely pleased with himself, and handed his father a small mother-of-pearl box.

Lucas took out two simple gold bands and showed them to Constance. She read the inscription engraved inside the ring, *"What God has joined together let Time not put asunder."*

"And mine says the same," he said sliding the ring onto her finger. She then did the same for him and he kissed her hand and kissed away a tear from her cheek. Frances gave her a delicate posey of forget-me-nots and leant on her with her arm about her waist.

Constance bent and whispered in her ear, "Time will never keep us apart," and Frances buried her head against her.

Constance caught Lucas's hand with her free hand and pulled him towards her, "The rings?"

"When I was a boy, my father gave me an old wooden chest which contained some treasure my great, great grandfather had dug up when he was a boy. There are coins and a battered chalice, an amulet, some rings and strange carved figures and amongst all the very fine things, a rough lump of gold. Father told me that one day I would find someone worthy of it. And so I have."

"I can't believe it — they're so beautiful. It feels so right on my finger, like it belongs there." She raised her eyes to his, "But I have nothing for you!"

He leant down and kissed her mouth softly, "Yes, you have. You have given me the best thing of all." He took her hand and held it over his heart, "You have given me *you*."

She bit her lip, "Stop making me cry! It's not fair."

"Come, then, we must go and feast. Mistress Peel has laid out a veritable banquet in the Great Hall and if we do not do it justice there will be daggers drawn!"

The servants had a sort of day off although they still chose to help and as there were only a very small number of invited guests, the Woodes and Hugh and Elizabeth Maitland and their children, the party was quite jolly and informal. Dash caused a slight stir when he sank his teeth into a large capon and dragged it from its embossed silver platter, disappearing underneath the long refractory table with it, where he growled at anyone who tried to wrest it from him, in the end he was left to his own devices, but the sound of slobbering and crunching kept making Benedict and Frances snort with laughter.

There was an awkward moment when Valentine de Cheverell insisted upon reading a sonnet written to the beauty of Constance's eyes, but it was quickly dispelled when Lucas told the poet that he heartily agreed with every word and wished he could write so eloquently; this was high praise indeed and brought a tear to the young man's eye.

There was a little flurry of dancing when at the end of the evening Richard Thorne sang some cheery folk songs in a very mellifluous tenor and Constance who, was by then, quite squiffy, because in her excitement she had forgotten that she shouldn't be drinking, grabbed her betrothed and showed him how to slow-dance.

"You know, Quinton," Ursula confided, "Sometimes I wonder at all the strange things Constance says and does, it is as though she is from another country. Maybe Germany or somewhere. This manner of dance! I have never seen anything like it. It is really quite shocking."

"Could you describe it for me please?"

"They are crushed together with no space between them and they are just — swaying from side to side. I would not really call it dancing. It looks too intimate to be done in public."

Quinton felt for her hand and lifted it to his lips, "I would rather like to try it with you," he murmured.

She gasped, "You are such a Royalist! So depraved. I am not at all sure that I can marry you for fear of my soul being lost!"

"Even Cromwell likes a dance apparently!"

"I may have been somewhat forward recently in my endeavours to engage your attention, but I do not think I am entirely lost to all propriety."

"More's the pity," said Quinton mournfully.

"My darling wife to be, I think you have probably had enough wine now. I think you might be better off safely tucked up in bed before you scandalise everyone beyond repair."

"Bed," said Constance happily.

"Say goodnight to your guests. I am going to take you upstairs."

"Oh, goody! 'Night everybody! Love you all! I'm going to bed now. Not with Lucas — *obviously* — because that would be — very very *sinful* — but to my own lonely bed — because we're not properly married yet — and really I shouldn't be drinking at all because — "

Ursula gave Lucas a fierce warning look and he swept Constance up into his arms, bid everyone a laughing goodnight and bore his still rambling betrothed up the wide staircase to her bedchamber.

He dumped her on the bed and stood looking down at her, "You really should not drink. It makes you behave very badly. Reverend Woode had to avert his eyes. As for your dancing, I am not at all sure we are prepared for that yet."

Constance smiled at him, bleary-eyed, and held up her arms to him, "Stop talking and kiss me!"

"You need to sleep."

"I need to sleep with *you*."

"I could not possibly take advantage of you."

Constance sat up very suddenly which made her head swim, "Well, then I shall go and find someone who appreciates my fine eyes! They're the colour of sunlit leaves apparently!" she giggled, "And *unripe acorns!*"

"At the moment they are more red than green, but still very beautiful," said Lucas, trying to maintain control of the situation. "I thought you said alcohol was bad for the baby!"

"Everything in moderation, they say. Except sex. No moderation there please," she patted the bed, "Look! Plenty of room for you. Lie down with me, I promise I won't touch you."

Lucas sighed, "That would be desperately disappointing."

"All right then, I promise I *will* touch you!"

Lucas sat down on the bed and pulled off his boots and stretched out next to her. She immediately nestled into him and kissed his neck.

"When we are married, Mistress Harcourt, you will be expected to behave with decorum and be a good example to our children and the staff."

"I promise."

"And to be a diligent housewife."

"I promise."

"And to obey me in all things."

She stopped kissing his neck and frowned up at him, "*That's* not going to happen!"

"I will admit that I was not very hopeful," laughed Lucas, tightening his arms around her, "But, I have a feeling that if I withdraw certain privileges, I might be able to hold sway over you!"

"Ah, that is a truly dastardly scheme, but will probably work."

"Lucas?"

"Mmmmm?"

"I don't *mean* to be so awful, you know."

"I know."

"Will you still love me when I'm old and grey and moody?"

"Undoubtedly."

"Even if, after the baby, I get really fat?"

"All the more for me to love."

"You're perfect, you know."

"I know. Go to sleep."

"Yes, my liege."

Constance threw up her hands in despair, "The twenty-seventh? *Really?* It has to be on *that* particular day?"

"What does it matter what day it is? We have no other engagements."

"But, Ursula, it could be any other day. Why does it have to be that one?"

"Reverend Woode suggested it and I agreed. We cannot change it now — it is all arranged."

"Where is Quinton? I must speak with him?"

"I think he is in the orangery," replied Ursula, anxiously. Constance had turned quite pale and become visibly distressed and it would not be good for the baby. "Calm yourself, Constance, I am sure it will all be all right. We will talk with Lucas."

"No! Don't say anything to him! I must find Quinton," and with that she raced away, leaving Ursula quietly fretting.

Quinton could hear the alarm in her voice and sensed the rising fear, although he could hardly make head nor tail of what she was saying, "You have not *told* him? But Constance, surely that is the answer? Just tell him and he will understand."

Constance buried her face in her hands and groaned, "He'll think I'm leaving him. He won't understand. I should have told him ages ago, but I couldn't find the words. How am I to tell him now that on our wedding day there is a good chance that Guy will open up the portal or whatever the hell it is and — and I will want to return to them? He will think I've deliberately lied to him."

"You have very little faith in him then. My dear, he is not a particularly scholarly man, but he is intensely loyal and whatever happens will always stay true to you — although he may lose his temper and rail first, as is his custom. Like a summer storm, you have to just wait for it to pass. You simply have to trust him."

She raised her head and looked at him hopefully, "You truly think he will understand?"

"I know he will — once he thinks it through."

Constance dropped a kiss on top of Quinton's head and hurried out of the orangery to look for Lucas.

She discovered him coming back from The Wilderness with Richard at his side, deep in conversation. Glancing up, he saw her waiting for them by the garden wall. He nodded to the forester and continued limping towards her. She was wearing a green silk gown which was billowing in the gentle breeze, but she wasn't smiling. She looked apprehensive. He clenched his teeth and braced himself.

"What has happened?" he demanded.

"No, everyone's all right. I just need to talk with you. It's important."

He took a breath, "Here or in the house?"

"Oh, here will be fine. It's something I should have told you a long time ago, but I didn't know how."

"Come, sit on the wall, you should not be standing."

She perched on the top of the low wall, while he remained on his feet.

"Lucas? Please will you listen first before you say anything and *try* not to get angry?"

He frowned and nodded, "You are making me exceedingly nervous Constance."

"I'm sorry," she looked up at him pleadingly, "Ursula has arranged for the wedding to be on the twenty seventh of this month." He opened his mouth to respond but she held up her hand, "No. Wait. You see, we had just got you back and you were gravely ill, and Guy told me that he had a scheme to get me home. Don't *say* anything! He said that it had to be on the twenty seventh of July because of the moon, or some such thing. I don't really understand but he wanted to see if it would work; he has a very questing nature. I was so tired and worried about you at the time that I sort of agreed with him and now it's the same day as our wedding."

Lucas was shaken. He felt as though the ground he was standing on was not secure. She had called the other place *home*. She was talking about leaving. He tried to focus. He could not bear her looking so afraid, it twisted his stomach into knots. This was a test of his strength. He knew that the way he reacted now would have a profound effect upon them.

"If Guy's idea worked, would you want to go — home?"

She flinched, "I didn't mean — *home,* exactly — it was just a word. No, — I mean — oh, I don't know! You must see? I'm here and there and *nowhere*. I don't really belong anywhere anymore. I'm caught between two worlds — one foot in each."

"And you are being pulled in both directions. I understand. It seems to me that unless we reach some sort of conclusion, we will always be wondering what might have been, had we taken a different path. I have no wish to make you stay with me if you are going to be forever looking over my shoulder," he lied.

"So what shall we do?"

He hardened his heart, "We will get married on the twenty seventh as arranged and that way, whatever happens, we will be bound together, and we can face the consequences — together."

Constance slid off the wall and straight into his arms, "Together. That's it. We can face it together. I thought you'd be so angry. I was a little frightened."

He held her away from him, frowning at her critically, "Frightened? Of me?"

She cast her eyes down, "Well, not precisely of you but of your reaction. You do lose your temper quite readily over the smallest matters."

"I am trying to be less volatile. You know I would never hurt you?"

She reached up and pulled his head down to kiss him, "I'm not an idiot. You may be shouty but you're really just a big teddy bear."

He cocked his head on one side, "Speaking in tongues."

"Teddy bear? It's a child's plaything, looks like a big fierce bear but just likes cuddling. A gentle giant."

"I am not sure I like being compared to a harmless toy."

She grinned at him, "I didn't say you were *harmless!*"

"Good. So we are agreed? The wedding proceeds as Ursula has ordained — come what may."

"Agreed."

They walked back to the house, hand in hand, the warm setting sun on their backs.

Thirty-Two

The twenty seventh of July started with some inauspicious drizzle, which made Constance furious and was not an ideal start to the day.

She was also feeling rather queasy, which she didn't know whether to blame on morning sickness or wedding day nerves. Ursula brought her a cup of fresh mint tea with homemade honey which helped a little, but she was spoiling for a fight.

She was still in her nightshift and pacing the bedchamber like a caged tiger.

She managed to pull herself together when Benedict and Frances popped their heads around the door to wish her good luck but then grumbled at Ursula about having to wear stays and glared at the maid who brought up the hot water for the hip bath. She was about to hop into it when she just lost it.

She stormed out of her bedchamber, the door smashing back against the wall and stamped along the corridor to Lucas's room where he was still lying drowsily in bed.

His grey eyes narrowed, and he battened down the hatches.

"Constance?"

She stood, arms akimbo, face flushed, eyes sparking.

"I have morning sickness. My belly is sticking out like a bloody football. I have to wear stays! It's drizzling. I'm going to tell the children about the baby this morning and they'll probably hate me. And I want to stay in bed with you all day and have long, lingering sex. This is all your fault."

"You are right. It certainly *is* my fault. I cannot do anything about the first four things on the list, not having any control over our child, lady's fashion or the weather. I can help you tell the children, who could never hate you, and I can most certainly help with the last part. Although, as we have guests coming, I think spending all day in bed is not entirely feasible."

"Oh, isn't that just like you! Being bloody reasonable! It's so irritating."

His lips twitched, "Did you not say it was bad luck to see the bride before the wedding?"

"In her *wedding gown!* As you can see, I am only wearing my horrid nightshift."

"And very alluring you look too."

"Don't be ridiculous! I look huge and shapeless. And it's drizzling!"

Lucas dared to smile, "Constance?"

"Yes," sulkily.

"You know that I would like nothing better than to lie with you all day, but I want to wed you and make you mine. No! Do not bridle! I know I am old-fashioned, but I will not feel happy until today is done. You are not huge and shapeless, but I would not care if you were. You are nervous and the baby is making its presence known because you are distressed." He shifted over on the bed, making room, "Come. Lie by me and I will help soothe you both."

"God. I *hate* you," snapped Constance crossly as she arranged herself on the bed with her back to him.

He wrapped his arms around her and put one hand on her belly. "Yes, I know. Take deep breaths." He gently stroked her stomach and pressed soft kisses behind her ear.

"That's nice," she whispered, "Very nice."

"Do not talk. Just lie still."

"I'm sorry I shouted. I was feeling agitated. I told you I would be highly emotional."

"I do not blame you. There are a good many reasons," he murmured into her warm neck, "Now, I think the baby has had enough attention, it is time for you to have a share," and he slid his hand down between her thighs.

"Lucas! I should be having a bath not — not — oh, I forgive you for *everything*," she sighed.

Before breakfast Constance, feeling a good deal calmer and more at peace with the world, called the children into the parlour, where she and Lucas were waiting.

"Your father and I have something to tell you. It may come as a bit of a shock, but I want you to know that it won't change what we have together or the way we feel about you. In fact, it will hopefully make everything even better." She took their hands, "Your father and I have made you a brother or a sister. I am going to have a baby."

Constance had been secretly afraid that the announcement would be poorly received by the two children who might very well resent having to share the attention, but it was met with unadulterated joy. Their only caveat was that Frances hoped it would not be another boy because she had had enough of having her hair pulled and Benedict begged Constance not to have another girl because it would ruin his entire life. Constance laughed and hugged them to her, smiling at their father over their heads.

After they had run off to have breakfast, Lucas held Constance back for a moment, "There was no need to worry. Have you heard any more from Guy? Did he answer your last message?"

"No. When I told him about the wedding, he said that he would think of something. He seemed to think though that once this lunar event is over then there may not be another way back. But he's still working on his theory. He's very clever."

"So, you are happy for the ceremony to continue?"

"After this morning? Yes, I am!" She looked at him shyly, from under her eyelashes, "Thank you for not getting angry with me and for well — you know — er — calming the baby down. You are very good at — soothing."

"I very much enjoy soothing you," said Lucas, entranced that she would still blush when talking about such things. She was such a strange mixture of brazen and demure and he found it utterly mesmerising. He never knew which Constance he would encounter but was happy to see either. Brazen Constance was a challenge to his seventeenth century ideals and made him question everything he believed in. Demure Constance, he wanted to shield from anything that might possibly pose a threat to her. She was also brave and ferocious and maternal and wanton. He spent a good deal of his time in a state of blissful confusion. It was exhausting and unsettling but having lived in a sort of tedious limbo until she was thrown into his life, he welcomed the glorious turmoil with open arms. He could no longer really remember what his life had been like before and could not imagine a future without her chaotic presence in it.

Constance was joined by Ursula and Frances in her bedchamber to assist her into her wedding gown. She was delighted with the gown; it was so like the original, mustard yellow taffeta that hushed as she moved, very simple in design, with a falling band around her shoulders and voluminous sleeves with ivory silk cuffs. Ursula dressed her hair into soft ringlets on either side of her face and Frances decorated it with forget-me-nots, love-in-the-mist and heads of wheat. When they finished they stood back to admire their handiwork.

"The yellow is most unusual," said Ursula, "But it suits you admirably. I think the traditional silver gown would have been too insipid for your colouring. And temperament!"

"I think you look beautiful," declared Frances hugging Constance so hard that the row of little pearl buckles holding together the front of the gown dug into her, but she didn't mind at all. From underneath her petticoats her newly cleaned tennis shoes peeped out, with the addition of more pearl buckles. She had had to override Ursula's vociferous objections, saying she knew they were peculiar, but she wanted to be comfortable on her wedding day and not left with blisters on her toes and it was Ursula who had insisted on adding the decorations.

There was a knock on the door and Quinton entered bearing a gift from Lucas.

Constance opened the silk bag and pulled out two pretty blue garters, which Ursula tied just above each knee.

"It is traditional," explained Quinton, "Blue for luck. They will be collected later by Hugh and myself — as is the custom."

"Constance knows about that, Mr Gittings!" said Frances, witheringly.

"Yes," murmured Quinton, "I was forgetting."

Constance thanked him under her breath and smoothed down her skirts.

"Well, I think I'm as ready as I'll ever be."

"Oh, my giddy aunt. He's wearing his uniform! That's not very sporting, I won't be able to concentrate. If I drift, give me a nudge Ursula! Bloody hell, *look* at him!"

"House of God, Constance!" reminded Lady Ursula as they paused for a moment in the doorway, so that everyone could admire them.

Lucas, standing next to Quinton, looked up to see Constance enter the church. Quinton heard a sharp intake of breath and smiled to himself.

"That damn gown," muttered Lucas, shaking his head.

"I understand from Ursula it is very striking."

"It is a message for me alone — a teasing reminder."

He watched her walk slowly towards him, not taking his eyes from hers.

When she reached his side, she looked up at him with a mischievous smile, "Fancy seeing you here! Do you like my gown?"

"You know I do. I am looking forward to removing it, again."

"Tsk tsk! House of God, Lucas!"

As they came out into the churchyard, the drizzle continued unabated, but Constance didn't notice it. She was holding hands with her husband and nothing else mattered.

Entirely unbidden, a thought rudely intruded into her bliss and her smile slipped a little. She thought she had masked it swiftly enough, but Lucas observed any slight change in her and caught the fleeting moment of disappointment that crossed her beautiful face.

He flicked her chin with his finger, "My love. My only love. My wife. My only wife. Nothing that came before you matters to me."

She smiled faintly, "I don't know why it even occurred to me — so silly."

"You are highly emotional at the moment and very likely to suffer from such intrusive thoughts. It is hardly surprising. Fortunately, I am here by your side to shield you." And he tightened his grip on her hand and was relieved to feel a squeeze in response.

Around them, their family and friends; Quinton Gittings, the Maitlands, Woodes, Richard Thorne, and Valentine de Cheverell, threw wheat grains and rose petals at them and there was much joyous laughter despite the dismal weather and when Lucas swept his bride into his arms and kissed her enthusiastically, there was loud cheering.

Constance pulled the children into the embrace and kissed them all soundly. "Five of us all together," she said happily.

"Five! It is so thrilling to be one of such a large family!" declared Frances twirling along the path ahead of them, a blur of rose pink.

Lucas glanced down at his wife and found her to be frowning and staring at her wedding ring in some astonishment.

"Constance?"

"My ring — it — it's burning my finger! Like on fire. How very odd!"

He reached out and touched it and it did indeed feel hot to the touch.

She tried to pull it from her finger, but it wouldn't budge.

Then, as though compelled, she looked back over her shoulder towards the church gate.

She somehow wasn't surprised at all to see that the drizzle, as it fell in a grey veil, was shimmering like a heat haze in one small area near the gate.

She turned and took a step towards it.

Lucas held onto her hand.

Frances stopped her pirouetting and stared, open-mouthed.

"What *is* it?" shouted Benedict, which brought all the guests to a sudden halt.

Through the glimmering mist they could see shapes emerging.

Constance moved closer, her arm at full stretch back to Lucas.

"*Guy?*" she whispered.

The abstract shapes resolved into figures, into three boys.

"Rowen! Gabriel!" cried Constance, tugging hard at Lucas's hand.

He held fast for a moment and then relented, and they approached the apparition, although he was still firmly holding her back.

"Con! We've come to get you!" yelled Guy's voice from within the rippling air.

"They've found me, Lucas. They're here. Oh my god! Look how they've grown! Gabe's a giant! Gabriel!" She was crying and laughing and reaching out to them.

She caught a glimpse of Guy's face quite clearly through the distorting curtain. He looked absolutely terrified.

She stopped pulling and turned to look at her fingers so firmly clasped in her husband's large hand. She looked up at his ashen face and her heart shattered into a million pieces.

Just as she was about to take a step back towards him, Lucas let go.

He just let go.

She looked at her empty hand. She was mystified. His face was blank. Empty, like her hand. She reached for him.

But he was fading.

Her hand was melting before her eyes.

"*Lucas!*"

Then there was nothing and he was gone.

She didn't have more than a split second before she was being crushed until she thought her bones would be ground to dust.

There was a babble of voices, exclamations, explanations, and triumphant laughter.

She was feeling dizzy and queasy. Her eyes couldn't focus properly.

Guy's shaking voice said, "Let's get her to the bench before she collapses!"

And she found herself sitting on the bench, in the churchyard, in her own time, with her own nephews all staring at her like she had just dropped from the sky.

"That's a pretty impressive dress, Con!" said Rowen, who always noticed things.

Con looked down at the crumpled yellow taffeta and remembered his face as he released her hand. He let her go. She had, in that instant, made up her mind and he let her go.

"Con? Are you feeling all right? I've brought a bottle of water and Rowen brought orange juice in case you need sugar to stabilise you."

She pointed and Rowen handed her a bottle.

Gabriel was sitting next to her, his hands firmly clasped around her arm, as though to prevent her from flying away.

"Thank you," she said hoarsely, "How did you manage it?"

Rowen laughed, "We're not quite sure! Guy did the maths. And the science. And the astronomy. The *worrying*."

"We missed you, Con," said that particular genius.

"I missed you too, like you wouldn't believe. Where's your mother?"

The boys stepped back and pointed.

Her sister was standing some way away, half hidden behind the trunk of a large tree. They beckoned to her and she approached them with such trepidation it actually made Con smile faintly.

"It's all right," said Con, "I'm not radioactive!"

Hearing her voice sounding so normal, if a little strained, made Tova fly to her and fling her arms about her and sob on her neck.

"I thought you might come back all melted or in bits!" she wept. "That's such a pretty dress. You look like Titania."

"I think we should get her home, she's looking really pale," said Rowen. "We have the car round in the carpark. It's not far. We'll help you."

Being in a car again was quite an experience for Con. Firstly, trying to bundle the voluminous gown into such a small space and then the noise. She hadn't heard an engine for a year. Or been on anything faster than Tulip.

In the next few hours, she was to find the noises almost too much too bear. Every so often she would put her hands over her ears to muffle it. Then, it was the lights, which hurt her eyes. She felt like she had been in solitary confinement for years and released suddenly into a barrage of camera flashlights and people demanding to hear her story in loud grating voices.

In reality, everyone was very quiet and considerate. They kept the lights low and their voices lower. They made no sudden movements and tried desperately to ease her back into the twenty first century without scaring her. They kept Badger away unless he became over-excited and barked too loudly.

Con refused to change out of her wedding gown and sat in an incongruous cloud of mustard yellow taffeta amongst all the usual technological debris that followed three teenage boys around.

Tova hovered. She was uncertain about the look in her sister's eyes. She looked haunted. Every so often she joined them for a while, would smile and laugh and talk and then she'd drift away again.

Then came the swapping of stories, the different perspectives, her initial terrifying moments in another century, the people, the astonishingly three-dimensional people. Frances and the shooting of Reverend Sayer Crane went down very well with the boys, they thought she sounded totally *righteous* and Gabriel wanted to hear more about Dash and his antics. They marvelled at her abbreviated tale of rescuing Lucas and thought that Lady Ursula sounded awesome but a bit scary. Valentine, they considered sad but in a funny way. Sad-funny.

Tova noticed that lengthy descriptions of Lucas were missing and that when questioned about him, Con became visibly anguished.

She came to the morning of her wedding and began to describe how she felt but the words just wouldn't come out and she faltered into silence

Tova leant over and put her hand on her sister's, which she found to be trembling, "You don't have to tell us, Con. Why don't you go to bed now? You look absolutely done in."

"I'm pregnant," said Con.

Thirty-Three

There was complete silence. The kind of silence that has its own moon, or a force-field; it was so deep, you'd have got the Bends if you came out of it too fast.

"Twelve weeks pregnant. It was after the witch-hunt. I was wearing this dress or at least, one very like it but Lucas — it really annoyed him and he — he — so I thought it would be nice to wear it for the wedding and he knew straight away — like I knew he would and he — he thinks I wanted to leave but I didn't — I wanted to stay — but he let me go. *He let me go.* Because he said he couldn't bear for me to be looking over his shoulder all the time, but I *wouldn't!* I had decided. Now, he's there and I'm here and he thinks I wanted to leave but I didn't — "

Tova cast Guy an anxious look, "I think it's bed-time for you, Con. You're going round in circles. Rowen will make you a nice cup of mint tea — "

"Mint tea! Ursula! Oh, my god. She will know now. She'll think I'm a witch! Mistress Peel will be beside herself if they don't eat the food! It'll all go to waste! Oh, no! What will Hugh and Elizabeth think? And Richard? Poor Valentine, he'll be so confused — it doesn't take much to confuse him — "

Tova turned to Gabriel, "In the kitchen cupboard. My sleeping pills. They're mild and one won't hurt her, better than being so stressed." Gabriel dashed away to do her bidding, glad to have something practical to do as listening to his aunt have a breakdown was not really his sort of thing. "Rowen, make mint tea!"

Tova felt immediately better once she was issuing orders. The situation had just become extremely complicated and she needed some space to sort things out in her head. She was a straightforward, practical woman, good in a crisis but she hated to be rushed. This was all getting a bit weird for her. Although, considering they were basically dealing with the logistics of Time Travel and the seventeenth century, being made pregnant by a Roundhead was not really that exceptional. She was happy for the boys to know all the details however odd; they'd had a tough time this last year and deserved to be treated like adults as they'd mostly behaved like adults, with the odd exception — mainly Rowen and the vodka incident but that was to be expected. Guy had started to really concern her as he desperately fought to work out a way to get his aunt back from the past. She could see his bedroom light on late at night and he was beginning to look frayed around the edges, which for a usually healthy boy of his age was hard to bear. Being teenagers, they had readily accepted the strange fact that their aunt had disappeared with a dodgy-looking Roundhead. They watched so much fantasy on their devices that it must have seemed as though life was just melding with their online lives, especially as it all started with a game of Pokémon Go. For Tova, it was a very different matter; she not only had to look after her boys and their daily needs and make sure that they didn't suffer from any ill-effects, she had to keep working as a nurse and on top of all that, worry about what was happening to her sister. She hadn't been blessed with much of an imagination so accepting the deranged truth of her sister's disappearance was a tough ask. She had missed her so much. Now, having got her back, she was beginning to relax but the tortured look in Con's eyes was making true contentment an impossible dream.

An hour later, she was tucking Con into bed, the yellow dress was hanging where her sister could see it and she was becoming a little slurry from the effect of the sleeping pills.

"He's just a big Neanderthal teddy bear. He can be so stupid and shouty like a Vogon and then — so tender and sexy and he loves me so much and he ripped that dress off me in Benedict's treehouse and it was so — so wonderful — and — I love him so much — so *very* much — and I've taken his baby away from him — he'll be so hurt — I can't bear to think about him all alone — he needs me because he's such an idiot — "

Tova stroked her hair, which with the drizzle and the tossing and turning had lost some of the glossy ringlets and was looking a little bedraggled. She had removed the flowers and put them on the dressing table but was still picking wheat grains and rose petals out of it.

"Go to sleep, Con. We'll sort everything out in the morning. It'll all be all right. You're home now."

Con woke up screaming.

Tova, who had not slept well and was awake and fretting, was at her side in seconds.

She supposed Con was bound to have nightmares after all she'd been through. She knew her sister had held back on some of the incidents, leaving out details which she felt weren't suitable for their sensitive modern ears. Pregnant. That was beyond belief for someone who had so readily given up on men. She had one bad experience and had promptly tarred their whole sex with the same tainted brush. It sounded to Tova as though this Lucas wasn't exactly politically correct; he sounded like just the sort of male Con would have crossed the road to avoid in the old days. Tova felt the intensity of their situation had brought them together, as though being in a war zone and away from everything familiar had triggered something untamed in Con which had previously been locked away, out of sight. This man, this unreconstructed bruiser, seemed to have the key. It sounded like a combination of basic chemistry and magic. Tova found she was quite envious, although the idea of living in the past did not appeal at all, being a thoroughly modern woman who liked her hairdryer and iPhone. Con had always been a hippy chick, happier barefoot, and with a penchant for historical novels and costume dramas and long flowing dresses.

Con settled back into sleep and Tova sat and watched her for a while. She may not be happy being back with them but at least the child would be born in a nice clean hospital with doctors on hand should anything go wrong. The child. Mother: Book illustrator, Father: Roundhead soldier.

Con stretched her aching limbs and rolled over in bed, still slightly caught up in her pleasant dream. She smiled and opened her eyes and then remembered; the memories crashing into her brain like a multi-car-pileup, one after the other with no cessation. She sat up and covered her eyes, but nothing would stop the endless images, a video on fast re-wind. A fairground ride to hell.

Guy came running.

"Con! What is it? Oh, Jesus! Are you all right? What can I do?"

Con tried to pull herself together, not wanting him to see her like this. "I'm fine. It's just the transition, it's proving to be a little — hard to bear. It'll stop soon, I expect."

Guy took her hands in his, "I'm so sorry! This is all my fault. I shouldn't have tried the stupid Moon-Portal thing. I didn't really think it would work but something weird happened and it did."

"Guy! You are not to blame for this. Nobody is. It's all entirely beyond our control. You did what you could to bring me — home."

A frown knit his brows, "Yes, home. You see, we didn't know if you were in dire straits or what! We had no way of knowing to start with and even with the geocache postbox, it was so intermittent, we were still not sure you were all right. Unknown quantities. We're basically mixing up algebra with chemistry, physics, and astronomy and getting like, a huge Gallic shrug! This is uncharted territory. You can't Google it. You can't factor in love either, or unborn babies. It's Cosmic Soup!"

Rowen strolled into the room bearing a tray, "Decaffeinated coffee with oat milk, freshly squeezed orange juice, and Mummy's healthy granola! Delish." He arranged it on Con's lap and plonked himself onto the bed, nearly upsetting the drinks. "Oops! Soz. Don't let Guy drive you crazy with his pontificating. He doesn't mean to be a dreary science bore but for the last year it's almost all he's thought about. He's been like Badger with a bone, relentless and really annoying."

Con looked at her eldest nephew, "I'm so sorry. There was nothing I could do."

Guy knelt by the bed, "Con? You wanted to stay with Lucas?"

Her eyes filled and she impatiently dashed away the tears, "I — hadn't had time to really think about it, I was so caught up in their lives. And then, in that last moment, something called me back to him, I don't know what it was. I just *knew*. But — he let go of my hand. In the end the decision was taken out of my hands. Oh, there was something rather weird, though. Just before the portal thing appeared my wedding ring heated up. It burned my finger."

"That's kind of interesting. Can I see?'

Con took off the ring and handed it to Guy.

"Real gold. Good thermal and electrical conductor. This is a very fine ring. Oh, *nice* inscription!" He cast her a searching glance, frowning heavily, "Does Lucas have one of these too?"

She nodded, not trusting her voice.

"Ah. Same inscription? Interesting. I don't suppose you know where the gold came from?"

"He said it was a large nugget that his great, great grandfather found buried along with some other treasure — coins, carved figures an amulet, of some sort. I didn't see it. He had the rings made from the nugget. He devised the inscription all by himself. Fat lot of good it did."

"Well, actually — we'll see. You know I feel bad for tearing you away from him but I'm awfully glad to see you."

"Me too," said Rowen drinking her orange juice. "You gonna eat this granola?"

"Yes, I am. Get your own breakfast! I've been longing for your mother's granola. The seventeenth century's no place for a vegetarian! Everything is based around meat of some kind and when I suggested to Mistress Peel that more salads might be a good thing, you'd have thought I was advocating having the Devil over for tea! But I suppose you can get used to anything in the end." She sighed, "I thought Lucas was a thumping great pillock when I first met him, but I changed my mind pretty damn quickly. Pillock, by the way, means penis in those days, which was a bit embarrassing."

"Two worlds separated by the same language. You must have managed quite well though because you're so immersed in the olden days anyway. All those books that you've filtered through your brain. And you practically cartwheeled every time they made a new Jane Austen series. And Poldark! Maybe that's why you were chosen, because you were basically born in the wrong century."

"Or," said Rowen, "maybe it was just some kind of magnetic attraction between the two of them. Between Con and Lucas. Like the universe made an almighty big mistake and was trying to rectify it."

"That's not a very scientific theory, Ro. I don't think you're going to be awarded the Nobel Prize for that!"

"But I like the sound of it," said Con, wistfully.

"Of course you do. Science was never your thing, was it? *We are all magnets; like attracts like. You become and attract what you think.* That's not science by the way, just something I read on one of those self-improvement websites."

"I wish it were that easy. Did it say anything about being separated by three centuries? Sort of messes things up a bit doesn't it?" said Con gloomily.

Tova arrived with a mug of steaming coffee in her hand, "What's going on? Family conference? Eat your breakfast Con. You're eating for two."

"He said he wouldn't care if I got fat," repined Con.

"You're kidding! Does he have brother?" laughed Tova.

"No, just Ursula who is so wonderfully — high maintenance. Poor Quinton, he's going to have such a hard time now that she's seen me — go *poof!* I mean, can you imagine the explaining that's going on? Hugh and Elizabeth, Richard and Valentine, and the children, they all have to be told now. There's no denying it anymore. They saw with their own eyes. Oh, poor Lucas. And on his wedding day too." She looked at the yellow taffeta dress hanging on her mirror. "He was so looking forward to taking that off! Again. The first time he — "

"Well, boys, I think you all have prep to do? Off you go. I know it's summer holidays but you've still got to hand in some work at the end of it. We'll get takeaway for supper as a welcome-home treat." They rolled their eyes but left the room.

"Takeaway," said Con dreamily, "The closest we came to takeaway was when Richard shot a rabbit or a squirrel."

"When you were *en route* to Bath?"

"Yes, it was like the weirdest camping trip ever. I hate camping but I just had to find him. We were wet all the time and so cold. And, can you imagine, I was on a bloody horse. It was grim. They wouldn't let me go into the prison, but you could tell by the state of him that he'd had an unspeakable time. He said he saw me in his dreams, and I called his name."

"Jeez. Like in Jane Eyre. When Rochester calls to Jane after the fire."

Con cocked her head to one side, considering, "Just like that I suppose. He's not unlike Rochester, bullish and a bit angry, and inclined to mood swings but I would never want to tame him like Jane did. I love him when he gets all shouty; it makes me laugh and reminds me that he's just a big kid, wearing the uniform of a Roundhead soldier. Okay, he's done and seen some pretty terrible things and it's marked him. Not just physically but mentally; he was in such a state — couldn't speak, the tremors. I thought for a while we wouldn't get him back. And you should have seen his poor face after the explosion at Torrington. He looked like Frankenstein's monster for a bit. I mean, he's no great beauty in the first place! Even when he was young, in the painting, but you'd see what I meant if you saw his eyes. They're sleepy and bedroomy and laughing. And his smile is so beautiful and creases up his face. Ugh. I sound like a teenage girl."

"You sound like a woman in love."

"Why did he let me go, Tova?"

"Think about it. What would you have done in his position? Would you have held onto him and forced him to stay? Of course you wouldn't. You have to let things go to avoid losing them."

"Blimey, since when did you become all hippy-dippy?"

"Since my favourite — only — sister was spirited away to the seventeenth century."

"Sorry. I didn't think. I forget how it must have been for you."

"I have to say I had a hard time at the beginning. I felt as though I was trapped in one of those cases of mass hysteria. But I knew my boys couldn't possibly all lie about such a thing. Besides, Gabriel is a shockingly bad liar as you know! Instantly looks guilty. Caves at the slightest resistance. He'd make a terrible politician. He stood up to my interrogation though like a real trooper. Looked me straight in the eye. And I would rather have believed that than think you had willingly just abandoned us. I'm not saying I didn't have my doubts, of course I did — *many* sleepless nights. I thought about calling the police or some kind of exorcist because that was all I could think of, but it wasn't an exorcism it was a *retrieval,* and nobody talks about that. I even contemplated, for about 30 seconds, calling our vicar but I honestly think she'd have fainted."

Con had finished her breakfast and handed Tova the tray. "Your granola was worth the three hundred year wait," she grinned.

Tova was just pleased to see her eating and smiling.

"I've made you an appointment with your doctor for tomorrow. Just to get you checked out. No argument."

"I'm happy to go. I want to make sure the baby is all right after all that travelling and also, I may have drunk a little too much on the night of the troth plighting. I wasn't thinking straight."

"Oh, dear, *not* good for baby. Did you disgrace yourself?"

"A bit but he didn't seem to object! I think he probably thinks I'm mad but loves me anyway, despite himself, despite his strict religious upbringing. He can be quite prudish sometimes, which I find funny because he looks like a rugby prop.
"

"He sounds like quite a handful, but he must be all right if he loves you."

"Tova! Don't be so mushy! It's really unsettling."

Guy put his head around the door, "Had a thought. Gonna pen a letter to put in the geocache for Lucas. Do you think he'll remember to take a peek every so often?"

Con's eyes lit up, "Of course! I'd forgotten. He might do, if he stops sulking long enough to think straight. Oh, what will you say?"

"You know, safe and sound and sad. I'll explain. He can read, can he?"

Con shied a pillow at his head, "Of course he can bloody read! He's a Colonel in Cromwell's New Model Army!"

"*Mamma mia*! We learned about them in history. Very progressive for the time but ruthless. Especially in Ireland."

"Well, he won't be going to Ireland because he's been so damaged by the explosion, he's ended up with shell shock. Hard to believe it was even more misunderstood in the First World War than during the Civil War. But thanks to the information you sent Guy, we were able to help Lucas find his way out of it. I mean, he'll always be a bit fragile but on the whole he's able to cope now. Well, until this last catastrophe, of course. Who knows how he's managing now."

"I'll go and write the letter. Anything you want to say?"

"Yes. Tova, give him a spray of my forget-me-nots. Put those in the box, please. Tell him we're safe, the baby and me, but missing him. And tell him I will write as soon as I am on my feet and that — I said he's not to be a pillock."

"K. I'll post it ASAP. Sooner he knows you're okay the better for his mental well-being," and he disappeared again.

"That boy — "

"I know," said his mother smugly.

Thirty-Four

Lucas twisted his wedding ring round and round his finger and stared vacantly into space.

His sister eyed him anxiously from across the parlour, her stomach tying itself into unaccustomed knots. She had no idea how to proceed. The room seemed hugely overcrowded and everyone was looking to her, as though she might have some answers, their faces a mixture of confusion, dismay and suspicion. She needed time to try to understand what she had just seen and even Quinton's hesitant but lucid explanation was not helping. She felt as though she'd fallen into a long dark tunnel and was still falling. Lucas was being no help whatsoever; he seemed to have withdrawn into his previous stupefied state, so she was expecting no imminent rescue from that quarter.

Elizabeth Maitland was weeping into a very small lace handkerchief while her dazed husband absent-mindedly rubbed her back.

Valentine de Cheverell had turned a worrying shade of grey and was sitting with his head in his hands, unable to think of even one coherent poetic thought.

Quinton was wishing he could help Ursula cope with this moment but could think of nothing more to say which could possibly be constructive in such a fraught situation.

Benedict was sniffling into his sleeve and Frances was sitting in the window-seat, staring blindly out into the garden.

Richard Thorne cleared his throat, "I know it is not my place to say anything, but it is clear to me that *something* needs to be said." Encouraged by the lack of response and the palpable sense of stupefaction in the room he continued, "We have just witnessed some kind of miracle, whether it be the work of the Devil or of God, is, as yet, unclear. But, putting aside everything we do *not* know and thinking about what we *do* know — Mistress Harcourt has been spirited away. Whether she left of her own volition, we do not yet know, but I think I can safely say that none of us here wished her to leave. Mr Gittings has explained, as best he can, how she came to be here in the first place, and we all know that while she was here, she became indispensable to us all. We now know that she is carrying Sir Lucas's child which makes getting her back all the more urgent. The question in my mind is, can anything be done to help bring her home?"

"Thank you, Mr Thorne for that and I am sure everyone heartily agrees with your sentiments. As to bringing Constance home, I am hoping my brother will have some ideas," said Lady Ursula, relieved to have the stunned silence broken at least, "Lucas? Do you have anything at all to say?" She looked at him without much hope.

"When she saw them — I knew. She wanted to be with them," he said, almost to himself.

"Oh, for God's sake, Lucas! Of *course*, she wanted to be with them! It would not have been natural if she had not! They are her nephews. She adores them. Do you not *see?* How could she choose? In the end you chose *for* her. Benedict will you stop *sniffing* please!" she snapped and then when he started to cry again in earnest, she went to him and pulled him into an impatient embrace.

"Aunt Ursula, I do not understand what is happening. Where is Constance? Why did she leave us?" he asked in muffled tones from deep within the hug.

"I wish I could answer that, my dearest but none of us really know. As Quinton tried to explain, it seems that Constance is from a time yet to come, which is extremely hard to comprehend and she has had to return there even though she did not want to go." She directed a scowl at her silent brother, "You know, it does not really matter where she came from or where she has gone — what matters is that we love her, and she loves us. We must remember what is important and not get lost in despair."

"She said time would never keep us apart and to never forget that," said Frances, her eyes wide, her cheeks ashen.

"That is it, my love! Remember that."

"But it is as though she knew what might happen and was preparing me. Do you think she always knew she might not stay with us?"

"I am sure she would have had suspicions that her life here with us might be temporary, but you will admit that she certainly never allowed it to affect anything; she was always so considerate, putting everyone else first and doing her very best to make sure everyone was happy. Whatever happens, you must remember that while she was here, she was part of the family and now, even though she is somewhere else, she and the baby are still family and always will be."

"But why did she not say anything to us?"

"Well, of course, your father and Mr Gittings knew, and I expect she thought we would not believe her. It is not easy to believe," said Ursula as calmly as she could, tiptoeing through dangerous territory, "Even Constance would have had a difficult time believing such an impossible thing. It makes no odds where or when you come from, what we have witnessed is not at all usual. It is beyond our imaginations. But strange things happen. After all, do we not believe in a God we cannot see?" She rose majestically to her feet, "Come, let us go and eat some supper before Mistress Peel leaves us too! Did you see the size of that pigeon pie?"

And she ushered them all out of the room deliberately leaving Quinton to talk with Lucas.

Quinton took a breath and braced himself to be thoroughly exasperated, "Lucas, dear friend. I cannot imagine what you are feeling at the moment. This must be torture for you. But you must take courage because the children suffer. They need someone to tell them how to go on. They need reassurance — as do we all."

"I have none to give. I see no way out of this hell," said Lucas, rubbing a hand over his blank, tired eyes. "I just see more hell to come. How can I help the children when I cannot help myself?"

Quinton stood up and turned to face his companion, "You are being pitiful, Lucas. This is not the man I know! God, if Constance could only hear you now! She would probably plant you a facer! Break your nose again. You certainly deserve it. When she saw the state you were in after Torrington, did she give up? Did she throw up her hands and walk away? No, she never left your side, and she did everything in her power to bring you back home. She fought tooth and nail for you."

"There's nothing I can do."

Quinton ground his teeth, "Well, I must say it is fortunate she did not say that when you were imprisoned in Shepton Mallet! You would still be there."

He knew he was being brutal, and that Lucas's mental state was not yet as it should be, but he was hard pressed to recognise this disconsolate creature before him and was beginning to wonder how they had ever become such firm friends. The real problem was that the only person who had the slightest chance of talking him out of this mood was Constance herself. No amount of censure from him or anyone else would penetrate his armour.

"We will talk about this in the morning. You need some food and then sleep. Today has been — challenging, to say the least. But, Lucas, for pity's sake give the children some comfort. They need you to give them a little hope."

"Lie to them?"

Quinton swallowed the angry words which rose up and slowly made his way to the door, "If that is what you have to do then most certainly. You are their father. They have nobody else now, having lost Constance. She was like a mother to them."

Lucas put his head in his hands, "She was. She loved them."

"Loves them still, wherever she may be."

"Quinton! It is too much for any man to bear! I saw her face as I let go of her hand. She thought — she thought I — oh, dear God! She thinks I wanted her to go."

Excellent, thought Quinton, this raw anguish was far better than the emotionless barricade he had been hiding behind. "If you think that, then you are even more of a fool than I thought! That woman knows you love her, above anything; she may be confused for a while but that will pass, and she will remember. You mark my words, Lucas, she will remember. Now, come, my stupid friend let us go and speak with Frances and Benedict."

Lady Ursula looked up as they entered the Great Hall and thought to herself that her betrothed was a very clever and patient man. He was arm in arm with her brother, as Lucas led him to the table.

Before he sat down, Lucas rapped on the table with his knuckles, "I have an announcement to make," he waited until everyone was paying attention, "Frances? Benedict? Your father is unfortunately, as Mr Gittings has just kindly pointed out, a fool. I forgot for just a moment that Constance is now a Deverell and that means that nothing, *nothing* can separate us. Whatever happens, she will always be your mother and my wife. If there is a way, she will find her way home. Remember what she said to you Frances, she said time will never keep us apart. That was her way of telling us that should the worst happen then not to despair."

Frances smiled, "It was like a secret message for when she could not be here to tell us herself."

Quinton suddenly stood up, his chair grating loudly on the floor, "Damn it, Lucas! The box in the wall!"

Lucas stared at him for an uncomprehending second and then laughed, "You are right, I *am* a fool! But there would be no point in looking now, she will not have had time — but there may be a chance tomorrow. Quinton, you old scoundrel! What would I do without you?"

"You would be well and truly lost."

"Box in the wall?" queried Benedict, perking up.

The following morning Lucas organised a small expedition and took the children and Dash to the bridge to introduce them to the mysterious box.

As he approached the wall, the hairs on the back of his neck stood on end and he felt a strange chill. He removed the box from its hiding place and the three of them sat on the grass bank as he opened it, while Dash enthusiastically searched the field for rabbits.

"A letter!" exclaimed Frances joyously, "Oh, look! She has sent forget-me-nots! That is a message for *me!*" She took the flowers and tucked them into the front of her bodice. They were looking a little worse for wear.

Lucas took the letter out and with a loudly thumping heart, read it out loud,

Dearest Other Family,

No idea when or if you will get this but Mummy and Baby are doing well and are going to the doctor tomorrow for a check-up. Obviously Con is distraught and weeping a lot and talks about nothing but Lucas and Frances and Benedict! It's already quite annoying! Also, Lucas, she says she will write as soon as she is back on her feet. And try not to be a pillock — her words, not mine!

We're taking good care of them and doing our best to find a solution to this peculiar predicament we find ourselves in.

Do not despair!

Love and hugs,
Your step-nephew-cousin,
Guy

P.S. Congratulations on marrying my wonderful aunt! You're a lucky man.

"She is distraught," said Lucas with a faint smile.

Frances frowned at him, "Which is *not* a good thing!"

"No, indeed. You are quite right. But if she is weeping —
"

"It is not something to *smile* about."

Chastened, Lucas reread the letter and this time tried not to smile. Constance was safe, she was with family who loved her, their baby was well, and she was missing him. That would have to be enough for now.

"May I please write back to her?" asked Frances. "I want her to know I am practicing my letters."

"Of course, we can all write. Although we do not know when she will receive the letters. The box seems to be — a law unto itself."

"Enchanted."

Lucas put a hand on his daughter's shoulder, "We must be very careful about this; talking of enchanted boxes will very likely bring the witch-hunters back to our door. Do you understand?"

The children nodded, terrified.

Lucas groaned, "I do not mean to scare you. I swear I will not allow anything bad to happen to either of you. Just be sensible. Do not speak about the box or Constance disappearing to anyone other than those who saw what happened. Others will believe the worst and may become angry because they do not understand. Ignorance is dangerous, you cannot argue with ignorant people."

"Like Mistress Fitch and That Man?"

"Exactly so."

"Best to shoot them, then," said Frances.

A week later, Constance found their replies.

Rowen discovered her lying on her bed with a pillow over her head, to muffle her sobbing.

"Yeah, that's not really working, Con. Unfortunately, I can still hear you." He removed the pillow and sat on the edge of the bed, looking down at her flushed and tear-stained face, "'Sup?"

"They wrote."

"That's a good thing, no?"

"Frances says she's spent enough time apart from me now— in the most beautiful copperplate and Benedict says Frances is being really annoying. Lucas — Lucas says — his writing is so awful — that life without me is unbearable. That's brilliant."

"That his life is unbearable?"

"Well, no, obviously! But he's missing me. That's good. Although, it's also bad."

"You're not making much sense, love. You know, you shouldn't feel bad about wanting to go back to them. We understand. I mean, we're pissed but we're okay with it, sort of. It's such a crazy situation anyway one has no choice but to suspend one's disbelief and just roll with the punches. Life is short. Life is a roller coaster. Love is a battlefield. That enough metaphors now?"

"More than enough. But thank you."

"Last one. Hope is on the horizon."

"Good one to end with."

"Always end on a high note."

"Ro."

Tova was starting to relax. The doctor's appointments were going well. Constance was looking healthy and the baby was growing at the correct rate and due at the end of January. The nurse in her was satisfied. Autumn was here. Things were looking good. Then, Guy threw a spanner in the works.

"No lunar events. No astrological activity at all. Nothing."

"But I don't understand. What does that mean?" said Tova apprehensively.

"I'm not entirely sure because I can't be certain what actually worked in the first place. I think it was a combination of circumstances, like all the tumblers in the universe lined up and the safe clicked open. I do have a theory about the return journey though, if you're interested?"

"Return? Back to the seventeenth century? No, not interested. It's better for them if they stay here."

"Better for you?"

She glowered, "Better for everyone."

"I don't think you're being honest with yourself, Mum. And I don't blame you but someone in this cosmic equation has to lose out."

"I don't see why it should be us! She's already been away a whole year."

"Do you recall when Whatsisname did the dirty and then dumped her? She disappeared for a while, not physically but mentally. Just vanished and when she came back, she wasn't the same. She'd put up all those protective barriers. You must have noticed though — when she talks about Lucas? When she forgets they're separated and just remembers. Barriers all gone. It's our Con again. She positively radiates happiness. She doesn't want to leave us, but she wants to return to Lucas. She wants everyone to be happy. But we know that's not possible. And there's the baby to consider. Safer here, for sure — but happier? What if its mother becomes depressed and it never knows its father? What if it finds out that we kept it from its family? There are so many questions, so many permutations, so few solid answers. I couldn't live with myself if we did what Lucas accidentally did — made up her mind for her, taking away her choices. It wouldn't be fair."

Tova stared at her eldest son with a mixture of respect and loathing, "I know you're right. But I hate it. Sometimes you're just like your bloody father. Sometimes one doesn't want to hear the truth. It's too cruel. So, say she wants to go back, how does that happen if there are no upcoming astrological events to hang this on?"

"I'm still working on that. There's a lunar eclipse but not until the end of January. But I have a not very convincing theory that we lost her in the first place when our timelines aligned because a weakness was created by a collision of unusual events — the Maunder Minimum, the lunar eclipse, and quantum mechanics. Then, add to that, some kind of powerful human magnetism, a dollop of destiny and as Rowen pointed out so succinctly, the universe trying to make up for being a gigantic arse, we have accidental time travel. Although there is also the interesting phenomenon of her wedding ring heating up as the portal opened — that might be significant. On the other hand, maybe our mistake is trying to work out why it happened in the first place and how it might happen again, and we should just be trusting our primitive instincts. It happened. It will happen again. Everything is cyclical. We just have to be ready. We have to build our Stonehenge. Simples."

"I'm so glad we spent so much on your education."

"Google, Mum, not the physics master, Mr Rowntree!"

"He was so dishy! I like to think a little of the money we spent has made a difference."

He gave her a patronising hug, "Of course it did. I learnt how to use a computer."

"Oh, Guy!"

"Oh, Guy, what?" asked Con, coming in from the garden with Badger at her heels and a huge bunch of pink and white phlox in her arms.

"He was just saying he learnt everything he knows from Google."

"He's teasing you, Tova. Most of what he learnt has come from all those books he's read. His brain is like the British Library only with bleached blonde hair. Must say Guy I love the new look. I wish I had the courage to do that to my hair; it'd make washing it so much easier. Imagine how quick I'd be in the morning! But I think Lucas would kill me if I chopped this lot off. He likes my hair."

Tova and Guy exchanged loaded glances.

"What? Why the look? Something you're not telling me?"

Guy twisted his mouth to one side and then back again, "Con? Do you have any, like, plans?"

"What now? I was going to arrange these in a vase."

"No, I mean like more wide-ranging, long-term plans that might include a big ugly Roundhead dude."

"I was waiting for you to come up with some sort of scheme. But I — want to — oh, I don't know!" said Con anxiously.

"Yes, you do. You just don't want to upset anyone. What do you want to do?"

There was a moment's silence while Con wrestled with her demons.

"I want to go back to Lucas," she whispered. "I'm *sorry* Tova!"

Her sister dashed away the sudden tears with the heel of her hand, "Oh, don't be silly! Of course you want to go back! I mean, he doesn't care if you get fat! What's not to love! I knew all along you wanted to be with him and although I couldn't do it, I don't blame you. So, where do we go from here, then?"

"I'll leave that to Mr Rowntree's favourite student. Didn't he ask you out once, Tove?"

Tova rolled her eyes, "Oh, God, so he did! At the school dance. I was so tipsy I kissed him, and he asked me for a date. So embarrassing."

"Obviously a weakness that runs in the family!"

"Mum, you must never do that again. Gabriel would never go back to school!"

Tova laughed, "I promise! So, what about the baby?"

"I think I might have it here just in case it takes after its Dad and is the size of a brick shit-house!"

"Oh, brilliant. Then, when you're back to fitness, we can load you up with a crate load of medicines and disposable nappies and send you back."

"I'm not taking landfill back to the seventeenth century with me! But Guy, do you really think there's a way back?"

"I have absolutely no idea."

Thirty-Five

Turn more to the light. To your left. Now, do a trout pout," said Rowen, grinning from behind his camera.

"I will not!" said Con, firmly. "I'm not sure this is a good idea anyway. It might just upset him. He can be a bit of a bear when he's upset, and I don't want the children to suffer."

"How can he not like a photo of his wife and the increasing bump, taken, if I may say, by a total genius? It's traditional. He can stick it on his fridge."

"Oh, haha. This can't be good for him though. Too much tension and stress might trigger his shell shock again. I don't suppose it will ever really be gone for good. I've been reading up on it. He's lucky though — he could have been permanently damaged. Some of the victims during the First World War ended up as tramps on the street or abandoned in asylums. They really had no idea how to treat it. Thought it was just cowardice and swept it under the carpet — stiff upper lip and all that. They'd 'cure' the patient with inhuman treatments and as soon as he could string a sentence together, they'd send him straight back to The Front. Hugh says that at least Lucas won't be called up again — now they've broken him. Weirdly, though he'll get some benefits — eventually; they have social welfare, of sorts, for maimed soldiers. Not that he needs it."

"Filthy rich, eh?"

"I guess so. Inherited. His family must have been rolling in it back in the day. He could have just lounged about but instead he joined the army and has been an exemplary landlord and master to his tenants and workers. You'd like him.

I think even Guy might be able to overcome his intolerance of anything remotely un-PC because despite his rigid Puritan upbringing and the teachings of the time he is remarkably open to new ideas. Not always, but he can be persuaded with a little — bribery!" she said with a reminiscent smile.

"Ugh. Con! Stop! Too much information," said Rowen, screwing up his face in disgust. "You really have to stop over-sharing."

Constance laughed and then, as usual, felt guilty for laughing.

"Don't *do* that!" said Rowen. "Don't stop your laugh half-way through. It won't help Lucas."

"I know. But I feel disloyal. Like we're on a see-saw — if I'm having a nice time, he must be having a terrible time. Ridiculous."

"This whole thing is pretty ridiculous. It's like when you're watching a film and you can't get into it because it's just too far outside your own limited experiences; you have to either switch it off and do something more productive or knuckle down and concentrate. I've always been of the knuckling down variety. Somebody, we're not quite sure who yet, has gone to a good deal of trouble to write this weird script and we might as well sit back and enjoy the ride. You just have to know that somewhere Lucas is walking with Dash across the same fields or staring at the same sky and thinking about you. He sounds like a practical kind of guy though — I doubt he's just sitting around moping. He'll be doing guy stuff. Shooting and fishing and mowing."

"Hmmm. I rather think they may be a little moping going on. He's probably driving Quinton loopy."

"Can I ask why you fell in love with him in the first place?"

"His smile. Well, not just the smile — it was what was behind it. I suppose you could say, he could *see* me. There's also an immense attraction just knowing someone thinks you're his world. He sort of grew on me. After initially thinking he was just a gigantic bruiser with his knuckles grazing the ground, I saw he needed looking after, needed someone to translate for him. Although he acts like a military dictator sometimes, marching about barking orders, that's just a disguise. We all hide behind masks. For protection. Once he let the mask slip, I could see he was as vulnerable as — well, Benedict, who thankfully hasn't yet learnt to mask his feelings. It's a cliché but under all that metaphorical and physical armour Lucas is just a gentle giant, who, admittedly has had to do some despicable things in his time. It's always going to be tough to understand. We do what we have to in the circumstances. I think I would have killed to get him out of prison, without hesitation." She sighed, "And when he loves, it's as he said himself, he's a simple man with simple needs, he really *loves!* I think he got a bit lost after his wife died. Probably guilt played a part because he wasn't able to love her and he felt no grief for her loss and then the war gave him a valid excuse to leave the children and any uncertainty behind. Nice and neat. Simple, go destroy stuff. It takes your mind off things."

Rowen was scrolling through the photographs he'd taken, "I get it. You have to walk a mile in someone's shoes to understand them. Ah, look, that's the one. Vogue cover." He showed her the screen. "I'll print it for you."

"Thanks Ro, it's a beautiful photo. I hope it doesn't upset him."

"Hey, no man's gonna be upset seeing his wife doing a bit of soft porn."

"Unless, of course, he's a Puritan."

"Fair point."

Lucas lifted the lid.

"What have they sent?" demanded Frances, craning her neck to see.

"They have sent some pictures. They are like little paintings. I cannot recall what she called them. Here is one of, oh — good God!"

"What is it? Can we see? Let me see!"

Lucas, feeling a little hot under the collar, did a swift sleight of hand and slid the first photograph out of sight. "Yes, look, there is one of Constance and her nephews," he said with some relief, "And the dog, Badger."

"I like the dog," said Benedict. "Constance is very fat now."

Lucas, who was taking a surreptitious peek at the other photo and thinking he would cheerfully wring his wife's neck, murmured something vague at his son, while his disordered thoughts wandered.

"I wish she would come home now. I miss her so much," said Frances miserably.

"I know. But they say it is better for the baby this way. And we must prepare ourselves for the worst. She may not be able to come home. There is a possibility that — how did Guy put it? — that the door between our worlds is now locked again and there is now no way back."

"I think if we pray hard enough, the door will open," said Benedict with the unquestioning confidence of a child.

Lucas wished he could be so sure. He had been battling insomnia for a few weeks and found the only cure was to sleep in the treehouse. He could find a little peace. There, high up above the battlefield, he could gain the hill and the wind and avoid the fire and smoke from the skirmishing below. He could think a little more clearly and maintain a level of calm which meant the days were less likely to end in him losing his temper over some paltry matter and shouting at everyone. Quinton seemed to sense when he was on the edge of the abyss even though he was unable to actually see the signs and could pull him back from the brink with some well-chosen words. Ursula was finding looking after the children quite a trial this time around and everyone lived in fear of an unjust scolding from her. She refused to talk much about Constance because it usually ended in her crying angrily and then she was inclined to take it out on anyone who happened to be close by. Valentine de Cheverell had sunk into a fit of the sullens from which he would not be coaxed. He spent his spare time writing melancholy verses about rejection and languishing about the place looking exquisitely beautiful but hopeless.

Almost the only person Lucas could bear to be with for any length of time, apart from Quinton, was Richard Thorne, who said little and provided companionship without trying to make him talk about anything other than practical matters. Hugh and Elizabeth Maitland were regular visitors, partly because they wanted to discuss what had happened with the only people who could possibly understand their consternation and curiosity. Fortunately, for their own sanity, their children had only seen the aftermath of the event because they had already run ahead of the churchgoers and only returned when they heard the ensuing commotion. Their mother had quickly conducted them away from the scene and given them what she hoped was a plausible enough explanation to stop them asking interminable questions about Constance and her strange disappearance.

He found his own children relentlessly inquisitive and it was a strain. He did as Quinton ordered and tried to give them hope but as his had worn thin the moment his wife had left him and dissembling was not his strength, he stumbled along without much of a clue as to how he was going to get through the next few hours, let alone reassure his children that all was going to be well.

Quinton had told him he was pitiful, and he knew it. He also knew that Constance would tell him the same but probably using more brutal language. His friend had also told him to beware of hiding in his misery. It had taken him a while to work out what he meant.

Then one day Frances begged him to practice archery with her before the weather turned and made it impossible and when he declined, she had looked at him almost with contempt, "If Constance could see you now, she would be so disappointed and wonder why she chose you to be father of her child! Perhaps it is better if she does not return to us after all," and she had stalked away leaving her father furiously mulling over her words and finally coming to the conclusion that his fourteen-year-old daughter was wiser than he was. It was mortifying.

He found her in the parlour talking with Quinton. He stood on the threshold, feeling strangely awkward.

Having just listened to Frances pour out her woes, Quinton smiled, "Would you like me to leave?"

"No," said Lucas gruffly, "I deserve to have you hear this." He closed the door behind him and stood for a moment looking at his daughter, who, almost without him noticing was turning into a beauty like Esther, but with more spirit; he also noticed, for the first time, that she was no longer a child.

"Frances Deverell," he said taking a deep breath, "You and Mr Gittings are quite right. Constance would definitely have broken my nose by now if she were here. I have been wallowing in my own misery. She would give me that look."

"Oh, *this* one?" said Frances doing a very creditable impersonation of her stepmother's disapproving expression.

"That one exactly!" replied her father, laughing. "Quinton, all I can say is that it is an expression which would quell the most savage of beasts! And yet — I miss it. I miss her. I would give anything for her to be here and quelling me with that look!'

Frances flew across the room and into his arms. He looked down at her shining dark golden curls in some astonishment.

"I wish you talked about her more, Father. I like to hear about the things she said and did and how much you love her. It makes me feel happy inside," said Frances, mumbling into his chest.

"We will talk of her, I promise."

"Con? We need to talk logistics," said Guy.

"All right, go ahead. You look worryingly serious. Is everything okay?"

"As far as it can be — when we are basically messing with the laws of the universe with our fingers crossed as our only guarantee. "Okay" is hard to quantify. I mean, I could say it's not exactly rocket science, but it is, although, obviously with no rockets."

"Thanks, Guy, so reassuring and lucid. Now, what's the problem?"

"Okay, we have several. No, don't panic! The main one is the baby."

"Oh, dear god."

"Yes, it's possibly a problem. The question is, how do we know the baby can Time Travel when you and it are separated? And, as it'll be so small, how do we know if it'll be able to stand up to the journey itself? We are dealing with powerful magnetic fields, quantum gravity, entangled states, and Schrödinger's cat."

"Could you just explain it in words I might actually understand? Although I did understand the word *cat*."

"How does one explain the unexplainable? Does Time Travel even exist? Do *we* exist? If this is an entangled state maybe you're here and there at the same time. Or maybe time doesn't exist at all. You see?"

"Are you joking? Do I see *what?*"

"Okay, to put it more simply — Time Travel is an unknown quantity despite all the films you see and everything you read. You can line it up with whatever natural phenomena you care to choose and throw cats at it, but it will still be utterly and nonsensically random and unknown — *unless* — it has nothing to do with physics and everything to do with the human beings triggering the event. My very flimsy theory is that during some unsettling natural disturbances the — er — fabric of time became fragile, like any material when under stress and at the point where it was at its weakest, an aperture appeared. Now, the absolutely crucial part of this fascinating and yet, easily refuted hypothesis is that you and Lucas were in exactly the same point at the same time only in different centuries. And like two human magnets, you needed to be together — you literally had no choice. Although, it seems that it's not just a one-way system, it seems to work for the return journey as well. I think that your wedding ring wasn't heating up because you were being drawn *into* the portal, it was because you were being drawn *away* from Lucas. See? Simples."

Constance stared at her nephew with narrowed eyes, the green so dark they looked like deep pools, "You mean, and do please correct me if I'm wrong — you *mean*, that all we'd have to do was to be *near* each other for the portal to work?"

Guy shrugged, "How long is a piece of string theory? Possibly. When I said hypothesis, I actually meant the result of an obsessive teenager with a computer, an embryonic knowledge of physics, and a calculator adding two and two and getting a very dodgy three. Now, whether you trust me enough to test my theory is another whole fandango."

"Let me get this straight! If he were in the churchyard *now* — I could go back right this second?"

"Well, you'd have to be in the churchyard too — "

"Guy!"

"Theoretically." He shrugged again, "Obviously you'd have to give him some warning through the geocache box, he'd have to find it and then write back to confirm — it's going to take a while to organise. But the big question is are you going to wait to have the baby here? I mean, you're pretty close now to your due date and we're still not sure the baby has a passport."

Con frowned, "Four weeks. Okay. We organise this. I pop out baby. We go."

Guy put his arm around her, "Sure?"

"Sure."

"The thirty first of January at eight minutes past six in the morning," said Lucas, faintly.

Frances and Benedict were looking up at him wide-eyed.

"That is when they are going to attempt it. I have to be in the churchyard at exactly that time or it might not work. There is apparently a full lunar eclipse then which may or may not help."

"Constance is coming back to us?" whispered Frances.

"We hope she is. With our baby. But there are risks which they cannot control."

"They may get hurt?"

"Guy does not know."

Benedict sniffled, "I do not care if our baby is a girl anymore as long as they do not get hurt. Can we say a prayer for their safety, Father?"

Constance looked anxiously at the clock. "That's five minutes."

"Ah, well, it doesn't exactly have a calendar in there," said Tova, her hand on her sister's huge stomach.

"But it's three and a half weeks early."

"I think someone is a bit eager — must have heard you're going on a trip of a lifetime and didn't want to miss it! No worries. I will get the car. Rowen take her overnight bag. Guy, stay with Gabriel, I will phone when we know what's going on and you can call a taxi. Right, let's get this show on the road."

"I think Benedict is destined to become a clergyman," said Lucas with a wry smile, "Which, for someone who likes to shoot things as much as he does, is a trifle ironic."

Quinton laughed, "He will more than likely grow out of it and join the army where his marksmanship will be of more use."

"I hope he does not join up. It is no life for anyone with any sensibilities. He would hate it."

"This has been a very hard year for a boy of his tender age, Lucas," said Ursula, "Think of all he has had to endure! Quinton being so terribly ill and injured, a complete stranger appearing from nowhere and moving in with us, you, dear brother, having to be rescued from prison and being so unwell, the war coming so close and intruding on his life, a wedding cut short when his mother disappeared before his eyes — even we, as adults, are finding it hard to cope but imagine being a child and not fully understanding what is going on around you. A terrible time for him. Frances has a better grasp on everything being a little older."

"And wiser," said her father, not without some pride.

"And a girl," said Ursula.

"It's a girl," declared the nurse happily and having wrapped the howling baby in a cloth, she handed it tenderly to the weeping mother.

"A girl! Benedict is going to be so disappointed," sobbed Constance, who throughout the labour had yelled for Lucas, alternately raining curses down on his stupid head and then wishing he was there to witness his child being born and then back to cursing his loins for being so fruitful. She had gripped Tova's hand like it was the last lifebuoy on the Titanic and swore to get even with her lustful husband for making such a colossal child.

The nurse had weighed the baby and smiled, "It's fortunate that she came early! She's a whopper! You're so slight, is the Dad big?"

"Bloody enormous. Like a battleship."

"Shame he couldn't be here. Is he in the Forces?"

Constance laughed, "He was. Permanently furloughed after being injured. Otherwise, he'd have been here."

"Do you have a name for Baby?"

"Oh, god! We didn't really have time to think about that before we were separated. Tove! What shall we call her? Oh, I wonder if he has some family names he'd want used. His mother was Cicely."

"That's a pretty name. Cicely Deverell. A nice ring to it. Old-fashioned," said the nurse and wondered why her words caused more laughter.

"Cicely Frances Deverell."

I'm not going to tell Lucas yet. I don't want him to start worrying about it before he has to. He has enough on his plate at the moment without that."

"It's entirely your choice. You're the only one who knows. It's not long now anyway and by the time he gets the letter and writes back — it'll be time to go. It really is Snail Mail."

Constance looked around at her nice house and her lovely sister and wondered what the hell she was doing. She looked down at the sleeping baby in her arms and wondered what the hell she'd done. Not so long ago she had a very pleasant life, no real worries, no scares and alarms. Just a normal, humdrum life. It was absolutely perfect bar one large detail — it didn't contain Lucas Deverell.

Cicely was a scrunched up little thing with dark downy hair and a good set of lungs. "Those, my child, I'm sorry to say, you get from your father! He can be very loud, especially when he's cross about something. Dark hair from your brother Benedict and that worried frown from your sister, Frances. What a mix. Hopefully you'll get my placid nature and ability to Time Travel!"

"Placid nature!" scoffed Tova.

"It will be dark at that time in the morning. We can take that lantern that Guy sent. Benedict you must put it in the sunshine for a while, then it will be ready. And you must make sure you have warm clothes — it will be very cold."

"Aunt Ursula says I can borrow her fur-lined cloak."

"That would be perfect. But, children, you must be very quiet, and do as you are told at all times. It is very important."

"Yes, Father," they chorused in unison, keen not to give him an excuse to leave them behind.

"You must also remember that she will be very upset about leaving her family, so do not tax her with endless questions and demands."

"Of course. We will be as silent as the grave."

Their father made a rueful face, "I am fairly sure that will not happen!"

Quinton was listening for a certain light footfall. He always had one ear cocked. When Ursula entered the room, he was interested to feel his blood course a little faster through his veins. It was fascinating to him that anyone could make one's body alter in such a way. But he had his work cut out for him at the moment as she tried to come to terms with all the new and wondrously strange things which were happening around her. She was not a woman who could let her hair down with ease. She had always been formal to the core and had, through necessity and neglect, become even more remote since Jacob had died. He had recently sensed signs of that icy protective layer thawing a bit but noticed when she became distressed over her lack of control, she retreated behind the forbidding barricades once more.

"I have come to take you for your perambulation around the garden," she said, sounding alarmingly like his old nurse.

"Thank you, my dear, you are too kind. However, I would much rather you sat with me for a moment," he said in caressing tones.

"This bodes ill," she declared with a brittle laugh but nevertheless drew up a chair next to his.

He reached out and felt for her hand, "Ursula. Firstly, I must reiterate, that I love you beyond measure. No, do not interrupt! I heard you take a breath for speech. I love you and I am fairly sure, after your determined pursuit that you love me. But I must risk your displeasure by drawing your attention to the fact that I am merely blind and not in the slightest bit enfeebled. All my limbs are in good working order, my mind still functions as it ever did, and my heart is strong; strong enough to cope with anything you care to throw at it. I will not keel over and die if you should happen to touch me. You are, thankfully, not my much treasured but annoyingly bossy old nurse. We are betrothed and neither of us are in our first flush of youth, so I believe we are wise enough to the ways of the world. I find it charming that you should wish to mother me, but I have to warn you that I have no need of cosseting and am likely to become quite agitated if this regime continues. I have a very urgent desire that you should treat me like an ordinary man who is brimming with love and — I am not ashamed to admit — *desire* for his betrothed."

There was silence and he waited rather anxiously for her response, wondering if he had gone too far. There was the slight sound of movement and he felt her shift a little closer and then her cool hands on either side of his face and to his relief and delight, her lips on his, in a gentle kiss.

He chuckled, "That is a start, but I assure you that I am in *every* way still perfectly robust," and he took her in his arms and kissed her without restraint, which, he was happy to note, left her speechless.

"Well!" she said when he had released her and her powers of speech had returned, "Mr Gittings!"

"Yes, my darling?" he murmured and silenced her again.

"I reckon if you cram it all in a rucksack and wear the rucksack then it has no choice but to go with you. What are you planning on taking?"

"I have no idea really. Meds. Nappy rash cream. A breast-pump. Books on child rearing. Some baby clothes? Would they be noticed by anyone? Maybe if I cover them with lace embellished shifts or something! I must say the idea of dressing her in all those stiff clothes is not very thrilling. How is she supposed to run around freely when she's imprisoned in all that rigid fabric? Stretchy materials are not a thing in the seventeenth century. Still, we'll manage, as many millions have done before us. We will improvise and adapt."

"Huh," said Rowen, "Says the least adaptable person I know!"

"I'll have you know that Necessity is the Mother of Invention and you'd be astonished at how quickly I settled into their way of life. Salads were a bit of a stumbling block but I'm fairly sure I can change that, and I do get a little tired of the endless pastries, syllabubs and damned currants in everything, but Mistress Peel is susceptible to flattery, so I feel that I'll be able to win her over with my new-fangled ideas in the end. I'm thinking I might steer Lucas into investing in coffee or some other up and coming commodity. His father made his money in spices, so he's already had a whiff of trade in his life and won't be able to turn his beautiful broken nose up at the thought." She sighed, "God, I can't wait to see him. I can't believe it's only two days now. It seems like forever." She saw a look flicker across his expressive face, "I'm not happy to be leaving you guys though. I miss you dreadfully. Not being with you is like a constant ache that can't be cured."

"We get it. It's a hard choice — three of the finest beings known to Man slash Woman or one knuckle-headed Roundhead. No contest. You *total* weirdo."

"I know. But Cicely deserves to know her father. And I deserve my bloody wedding night! I missed out!"

"Ugh," said Rowen putting his hands over his ears. "Old people."

Lucas looked with some satisfaction at their bedchamber. It looked very welcoming. Ursula and Frances had filled it with evergreens, ivy and rosemary and juniper; it looked verdant and smelt fragrant like a forest. Ursula had dug out the best quilt and spread it on the bed and Richard Thorne had somehow found the time to make a beautifully carved oak rocking cradle and that had pride of place at the end of the four-poster bed. Ursula had cobbled together a small quilt from scraps of material she'd found in various chests around the house and although the workmanship wasn't up to much, she was quietly pleased with the result. New homemade beeswax candles had been placed in every sconce and they had moved one of the finer rugs from the library upstairs which covered more of the elm floorboards and made the bedchamber a little warmer. Applewood logs were already set in the grate and Oates was just waiting for the signal to get out the tinderbox.

"Has there been another communication from Guy? No news about Constance or the baby arriving?"

Lucas knit his brows in a fierce line, "Nothing. Only the instructions for tonight and this — timer, as they call it. It is strange. But as we know there are many dangers. Perhaps —"

"Do not even think such things! Guy would have said something, and did you not say that they are more advanced in their knowledge about birthing? Anyway, babies seldom follow orders. It will arrive when it is quite ready."

"Of course, you are right, dear sister but not being with her is — more painful than I am willing to admit."

Lady Ursula laughed and impulsively put her arms around him and embraced him with real affection, something she had not done since they were children. He was startled and then returned the embrace.

"I am sorry that I have turned your normally ordered life upside down, Ursula."

"I would not want it any other way, I was bored out of my mind", she replied. "Now, we had better at least pretend to sleep for a while before we all have to traipse out in the cold and dark to meet Constance."

Constance was looking slightly askance at her daughter, who was screaming her head off, her tiny face purple with rage.

"You look just like your Daddy. And that is *not* a compliment. Did you really have to inherit his vile temper instead of perhaps, Guy's sweet nature? You had better have your Daddy's laughing eyes or I might just leave you behind. Oh no, I didn't mean that! You must have a bit of wind. I don't care how old-fashioned he is, this is going to be his job in the middle of the night. It's going to be a steep learning curve for Colonel Sir Lucas Deverell, I can tell you."

"Everything packed and ready?" asked Rowen, who, as the practical one, had taken it upon himself to organise his aunt and little cousin.

"Yup, ready. Cicely will pipe down in a minute I expect and then we can head off. I'm so excited I can barely breathe."

Gabriel was eyeing his new cousin with a measure of disgust, "Babies are gross," he said and then belied his words by planting a kiss on her forehead. "I'll be seeing you when you're hopefully a lot less shouty, kid!"

"Are we taking the car?"

"Probably best as it's so cold. We can probably all cram into it if Gabe sits on someone's lap."

"He's not sitting on mine," said Rowen, "I value my legs."

Lucas Deverell awoke with a start, like the soldier he still was, he was alert immediately and swinging his legs out of bed. It was time. He had gone to sleep in his clothes for expediency, he quickly grabbed his boots and pulled them on. Then paused, something was not right.

He listened. Nothing. No sound at all coming from the house.

Then, he realised what it was. He could smell smoke. He leapt to his feet and snatching up his pistol ran for the door.

The door would not budge. It was jammed shut. Locked or blocked in some way. Faint ribbons of smoke were snaking under the door.

He tucked his pistol into his belt and threw his shoulder against it in the certain knowledge that not even a battering ram could break it down.

He lit candles and looked at the watch Guy had sent. He picked up a chair and smashed it against the door. He stopped for a moment and took a breath.

"Calm down. Think clearly."

He went to the casement and opened the window. Two storeys. Onto grass, but he was a heavy man, and the window was narrow. He had no choice. He climbed onto the window seat and eased himself through the gap, feet first and turning around with great difficulty, he lowered himself as far as he could, holding onto the mullion. As he let go, he pushed himself away from the wall and bent his knees as he hit the ground. It made no odds, he still smashed into the ground like a giant oak tree. Searing pain blotted everything out for a second and he had to shake his head to clear it, something had given way in his leg, but he had no time to sit and try to work out what he had injured, he staggered to his feet and limped around to the front of the house.

Smoke and flames were belching out of the parlour windows. He mounted the steps and tried the front door. Locked and barred from the inside of course. He ran to the library windows and without even considering, smashed the beautiful stained glass with a stone. The library was thankfully not aflame. But it was dark, and he had to fumble about trying to find a candle and light it from the still hot ashes in the fireplace. Eventually he got one lit and opened the door into the Great Hall. No fire there either. So far, it seemed to be contained in the parlour. He hobbled up the main stairs to the first floor and along the corridor. He passed his own door and saw a metal bar had been shoved through the handle. As he turned the corner, he saw a ghostly blue light coming towards him.

"Father!" cried Benedict, his voice shrill with terror. "I smell smoke!"

"Good boy. You have Guy's lantern, well done. I want you to wake Frances quickly and leave by the back stairs and the kitchen door. You stay outside whatever occurs, do you understand. I am going to wake the others. Now go!"

Benedict ran off to his sister's bedchamber. Lucas turned and limped along to the other end of the corridor, where he met Valentine de Cheverell leading Quinton, followed by Lady Ursula.

"What has happened? Where is the fire?" demanded Ursula.

"At the moment it is only in the parlour, but it will spread quickly. Go down the back stairs and through the kitchen. Valentine, as soon as you get them safely out onto the lawn, raise the servants and the stable lads and get them round here with buckets. I am going back down to see what I can do to stop the fire spreading."

"But Lucas! What about *Constance?* It cannot be long before you should be by the church! We were all up and ready. You must not tarry! Valentine run now and alert the servants — I can get Quinton downstairs."

Valentine de Cheverell glanced at his employer and on receiving a curt nod, he dashed away to find help.

There was a crash from downstairs and Lucas gestured to the back stairs and watched only to make sure his sister and friend were heading away from the fire before limping down to see what could be done to save the house.

In the back of his mind, he knew he did not have long before Constance and her nephews would be trying to unlock the portal, but he had to make sure everyone was safe, and the fire was under control. He recalled the moment when Constance had accidentally made it known that the Court House no longer existed in her time and he had a sense of dread that this could possibly be why. If Constance had not arrived here, if they had not already been in a state of readiness, if they had not smelt the smoke until too late —

In the Great Hall he could see the pulsing orange glow in a fiery line all around the parlour door, the smoke was chokingly dense, and he was coughing, his eyes smarting.

He suddenly caught a glimpse of some movement outside and peered out hoping to see the stable lads but through the pall of thick smoke drifting across the garden he could see a woman eerily lit by the glow from the fire. She was dressed in a severe black gown, with a white coif covering her hair. Mistress Fitch. She was smiling malevolently up at the house. Her eyes were wild, reflecting the red of the flames. Lucas didn't have time to address the cause of the fire, he had to focus on the result of her terrible obsession.

Then suddenly the stable lads and Oates were there along with members of Ursula's entourage and Richard Thorne was organising them. Lucas unbolted the front door and let them in.

He looked at Guy's watch again.

They parked the car behind the church and made their way around to the south side. Cicely was wrapped up against the cold, like a fat sausage roll. The boys were buzzing with excitement and Tova was silent. They looked like a cluster of fireflies with their torches all flickering in the dark.

"Of course, this may not work," said Guy, starting to feel that maybe some blame may be heading his way. "It's all conjecture. I mean, there are no guarantees."

"It's all right, Guy. No need to panic. If this doesn't work, we will find another way. You can only do what you can. I think I am fully prepared for anything."

"Well, fingers crossed."

"What's the time?"

"About four minutes later than the last time you asked."

Lucas pulled the curtains down and then he and Richard beat at the flames with them. Stable lads were dashing to and fro with buckets of water trying to douse the fire. Their faces covered in soot and their hair full of debris. Will Sparrow led them with his usual wiry tenacity, urging them on in a loud voice, not letting them slacken their pace. Oates and Valentine de Cheverell worked side by side, poet and footman in perfect harmony, bucket after bucket, back and forth to the spring in the courtyard. Lucas wiped the smuts out of his eyes and watched as one of the smouldering tapestries was carted past by two of the housemaids, who had all volunteered to help.

He looked at the watch, which glowed curiously in the dark.

"It's time, Con."

"Oh, lordy." Con found herself being suffocated in a group bear hug, "Mind the baby!" she yelped from within the scrum.

One last embrace from her sister who was valiantly trying not to sob too loudly, and she moved towards the church gate, a rucksack on her back and Cicely cradled firmly in her arms.

"Okay, good luck! Safe trip," said Guy. "If this works, we'll be in touch via the geocache and I'll keep working on exit strategies."

"Thanks Guy, for everything. You'll take care of this awful shower, won't you? Don't let Rowen drink too much. Make sure Gabe does his prep — "

"*Really?* This is what you're saying in your last few minutes? Not very profound!"

He looked at his watch with a little frown.

"What is it?"

"Nothing. It's a minute past time now."

Frances and Benedict, with Dash at their heels, came running around the side of the house, followed more slowly by their aunt and Quinton.

Frances was getting jittery, "Father! We must go! We will be too late!"

Richard Thorne removed the bucket from his employer's hands and pushed him out of the door. "We can manage. Go."

Lucas hobbled down the front steps towards his children.

He had just reached them when something flew at him from out of the darkness.

Con slumped down onto the cold wet grass, her legs refusing to hold her up a second longer.

"He's not coming," she said, burying her face into the warm bundle in her arms.

"Con — "

"Something's happened. I can feel it. Something's not right."

Lucas reeled backwards from the force of the blow, pain shooting up his injured leg. He held out his hands to fend off his assailant, but it was putting up a frenzied and ferocious attack. He felt his pistol being dragged from his belt and was suddenly facing a maddened Mistress Fitch, primed pistol in hand.

"Children get back." he said calmly. "Mistress Fitch, please put the gun down. You have done enough damage. I am sure you do not want to injure anyone."

"You filthy traitor! Lying with that whore! You were never decent enough to be with my Lady Esther! She was too good for you. And that witch, she tried to take her place. Now, you will all be sorry — " and she deliberately aimed the pistol and cocked it.

There was a loud report, a flash of white-hot light, sparks shooting through the air, the acrid smell of gunpowder and then a stunned silence.

Will Sparrow looked down at his smoking pistol and made a face, "I think this counts as a real emergency."

Richard Thorne stepped forward and gave Lucas a shove, "You need to *run!*"

Lucas Deverell set off, trailing various members of his family and an over-excited Wolfhound. He didn't even glance over his shoulder at his home. He thought to himself as he ran, it's only a damn house — just as long as everyone was safe.

"Con, get up! Here, take my hand."

"He didn't come. He must be in danger. Anything could have happened."

"Will you please get off your arse!" snapped Guy, pulling her to her feet. "Now, just hold your horses. He's a big lad and can fend for himself, he'll be okay. We can try another day."

"Try another — " began Con crossly, then looked down at her daughter who had opened her eyes and was staring at her mother. "Now, what's the matter with you — ? Cicely?" The hair on the back of Con's neck was standing on end, "*Guy!*"

She looked to the space behind her nephew. Near the gate. In the light of the blue torches, there was a disturbance in the darkness.

"Interesting," muttered Guy, "Maybe it's just *them* — "

Con kissed her baby's grumpy little face, "Daddy's here," she whispered.

Tova held her hand as she moved nearer the portal, "Don't forget us."

"Oh, very funny."

"Look!" yelled Gabriel unnecessarily loudly, "It's Uncle Lucas!"

And there, emerging from the shadows, was the faintest glimmer of a human shape.

Con reached her hand through the shimmering dark and Lucas grabbed it and held on tightly.

She could hear Dash barking wildly and someone sniffling and then she was being dragged through the rippling air and into her husband's arms.

For a long moment they stood as one. And then there was an indignant bellow from somewhere between them.

"*Constance?*"

"Ah, yes, my love, I've been meaning to tell you — um — I'd like to introduce you to your daughter Cicely Frances Deverell. She's a bit pissed off."

"*Frances!* You called her after me!" cried Frances as she desperately tried to see her namesake.

"Oh, Benedict! Do stop *snivelling!*" said Lady Ursula wiping tears from her eyes.

"Cicely," murmured Lucas, his face buried in his wife's sweet-smelling hair, "After my mother. Very apt. Mother had a fiery temper too."

Constance tilted her head away from his shoulder where it had happily been resting, "Why do you smell of *smoke?* And your face — it's all covered in — Lucas! What's been happening? Oh, I knew something was wrong, I just *knew* it!"

He laughed, "It is just a small matter of the house being on fire, but it is nothing to worry about. All that matters is that you are back. For a moment I thought — "

She looked up at his soot-blackened face, "I will always come back to you. You can't escape."

"I have no desire to escape. I am happy to be your prisoner. Here, Benedict, take the bag from your mother's back, it looks heavy. Frances, take Cicely! I need a few moments alone with my wife."

The little crowd of friends and family melted discreetly away into the darkness by the church, leaving just two people standing in the shadows. Dawn light was filtering into the sky in the east above Bobble Wood and somewhere a cockerel crowed.

"Lucas?"

"Yes, Constance?"

"She came three weeks early. I didn't want to alarm you."

"I understand."

"She is quite noisy for something so small. I fear she has your temper."

"Constance?"

"Yes, Lucas?"

"I need to kiss you now."

"Yes, Lucas."

And he picked her up in his arms, crushing her to him and kissed her very thoroughly indeed.

When there was a slight pause, she let out a contented sigh, "I've missed you so much. It kept me awake at night, just longing for you."

"I had some difficulties sleeping too so I removed myself to the treehouse."

Constance chuckled into his neck, "Oh, how often I relived *that* night! It quite wore me out!"

"My darling, I would carry you all the way back to what is left of our house, but I fear that jumping out of the first-floor window just now has aggravated my old injury and so you will have to walk."

"Oh, put me down at once! Why didn't you *say?* You big dope," she looked at him lovingly. "How did *our* house catch fire?"

"I am afraid it was Mistress Fitch. I should have realised her rage was not so easily arrested. She must have broken into the house — she knew the place so well — and barred my bedchamber door."

"Oh, my god! You might have all been — "

"But, you see, we were all awake and alert because we were waiting to see you again. If it had not been for you, she may very well have burnt the house to the ground, and it would have been no more, just like you said. But nobody was hurt. Well, apart from Mistress Fitch."

"Oh? What happened to her?"

"Young Will Sparrow shot her with his trusty pistol. I shall have to have a stern word with him, he was rather too pleased with himself."

"I'll bet! He was longing to use that gun! Poor woman, I fear she was quite mad."

It took them rather a long time to make their way home because they had to keep stopping. As they came to the gates, the smell of smoke was strong but there was no fiery glow to be seen coming from the house and although they could hear voices in the distance, they no longer sounded panicked.

"It looks like the fire might be out," said Lucas, gently manoeuvring his wife up against the stone pillar. "But not *this* fire."

"Oh, my!" said Constance breathlessly. "Here? Someone might see!"

"If we go into the house everyone will naturally want to talk to you. It has been nearly half an hour now. I would say that deserved some reward. I have been remarkably patient."

"The patience of a saint," she laughed. "Oh, my giddy aunt! Lucas! Be careful of your injury! Knickers. I'm wearing knickers! Sorry! Wait! Oh, dear lord! Must you always be in such a tearing hurry! You're going to cost us a fortune in clothing. No, don't *stop!*"

"Constance Deverell, I love you more than life itself but if you do not stop talking, I shall be forced to silence you."

"Go on then, you have my permission." said Constance happily.

Epilogue

So, basically, what you're trying not to say," mused Rowen, "Is that I was right all along?"

Guy grimaced, "You could say that, but you know you just got lucky. You can't conduct scientific experiments just using random guesswork."

"I think you'll find it's just been proven that you can. So, what does this mean, in the grander scheme of all things Time Travelly?"

"I'm not entirely sure but I have a sneaking suspicion that their connection is so strong that not much else is needed to activate things. Although, their wedding rings — "

"So, that means — ?"

"Mamma mia! I don't *know!* It could mean nothing at all but I have a theory — "

"Your theories are well dodgy," said Gabriel, taking the last pancake.

The Great Hall seemed very crowded, everyone was there to welcome Constance and Cicely home. Some were a little surprised and confused and others were beside themselves with joy. Valentine de Cheverell let it be known that he had penned a short poem in their honour and Frances wouldn't allow anyone else to hold her sister; she was already, in just half a day, an expert in all things baby.

Constance looked around, taking in the soot stains on the ceiling and the stacks of rescued furniture and singed wall hangings in the corner, to the gathering of servants who had come to see the new baby. Quinton and Ursula were holding hands under the table and she thought they were both looking rather smug which made her think that dear Quinton had stormed that particular citadel with some success. Hugh and Elizabeth Maitland were there along with Reverend Woode and his wife, Cassandra, who had, of course, witnessed her sudden and spectacular departure after the wedding but were never to mention it again as long as they both lived. Richard Thorne and Will Sparrow, Oates and Mistress Peel full of cheer and good wine, all expressed their unqualified delight.

Apart from some serious smoke-damage and the residual sour reek of smoke and wet cinders, the parlour was thankfully the only room which had been destroyed; most of the linen-fold panelling, the furniture and the wall-hangings were in ashes, but Lucas said it was nothing. He said things could be replaced.

He cast a glance down at his wife and found her green eyes looking at him steadily. His heart thudded forcefully in his chest and he smiled.

He stood up and addressed the joyful congregation, "I could make a long speech about being thankful and friends and family and loyalty, but I can see that my wife is tired and needs to be in bed. So, I will just say, thank you and goodnight."

And to a chorus of cheers, he swept Constance up in his arms, despite her feeble protests about his injury and bore her out of the room, saying over his shoulder, "Frances, you are in charge of Cicely!"

"Shall I bring her up now?" asked Frances, jumping up at once but her aunt put a firm hand on her arm and held her back.

"Not now, my dear, we will somehow manage."

"In front of *everyone!* What will they think of us? Poor Reverend Woode! Have you no shame?"

"None. He has five children, so I am fairly certain he will understand."

"But — Cicely!"

"You have already fed her, and she is sleeping peacefully. Ursula is in charge. No harm can come to her." He carried her up the staircase and along the corridor and shouldered open the door to their bedchamber.

"Oh, *Lucas!* Did Ursula and Frances — ? It's beautiful! It's like being in The Wilderness!" Still in his arms, she buried her head in his neck, "I feel I must warn you that having just given birth I look a little different to that first night — "

"It makes no odds to me. You are perfect."

"Oh, don't make me cry. I swore that if we found each other I would never cry again. I spent the last few months just crying, it was very tiresome."

"I am sorry to admit that I was happy to hear that you were crying — Frances reprimanded me, but it meant you were missing me. Now, I can wait no longer, I am going to make love to my wife, for the *first* time, officially, in our own bed!" He kicked the door shut behind him and booted a chair up against it. He then lowered her gently onto the bed and stood looking down at her.

"Masterful," murmured Constance.

"I am your lawfully-wedded husband and according to the law of the land, you are now my chattel," he said with a crooked grin.

His wife frowned at him, "Oh, I *do* wish Guy could hear you say that! He'd be having kittens! Well, Sir, as long as you don't mind a chattel who pays no mind to anything you say and swears a lot and makes you get up in the night to see to the baby and laughs at you when you're being ridiculous and hugs your servants and flirts with the forester and —"

"Talks incessantly? Constance? This is our second wedding night and I mean it to be memorable but for very different reasons. I love you more than I will ever be able to tell you. Not being an accomplished poet like Valentine, I will have to *demonstrate* just how much! And, be assured, that I will never willingly let you go again." He lifted a corner of her skirt, "Do you like that gown?" he asked huskily, but with a malicious glint in his eye.

"Oh, yes, I do! I'm *particularly* fond of it, as you know full well. There are very precious memories attached to it. And it's such a very lovely shade of mustard yellow! Lucas, wait, I'll remove it. You'll enjoy it just as much, if not more, I promise! See? Look, I'll unlace the bodice slowly and oh, well never mind, I've gone all seventeenth century again anyway, I find it's so much more energy-efficient when your husband's such a rough and rude Roundhead — !"

There was a moment's silence.

"Heathen!" whispered Lady Constance Deverell blissfully.

The End

HISTORICAL NOVELS BY CAROLINE

Set in the years shown

A Very Civil War (1645)
Dark Lantern (1755)
The Widow (1782)
Out of the Shadows (1792)

A VERY CIVIL WAR (1645)

Con's life in the small Cotswold village, where she spent an idyllic childhood, is nothing out of the ordinary, which is good because she likes ordinary. She likes safe.

Her three boisterous nephews have come to stay for the summer holidays, and she's determined to show them that life in the countryside can be fun — she has no idea just how exciting it's about to get.

Whilst out exploring with them in the fields near the village, they find themselves face to face with a Roundhead colonel from the English Civil Wars and, due to some glitching twenty-first century technology, Con is suddenly transported back to 1645 and into a world she only recognises from books and historical dramas on television and finds hard to understand. She reluctantly falls for the gruff officer, who is recovering from injuries sustained in recent hostilities with Royalists but has to battle archaic attitudes and unexpected violence in order to survive.

With no way of getting back to her family and her nice secure real life and unable to reveal who she really is, for fear of being thought a witch, she struggles to acclimatise to her new life and must fight her growing feelings for Colonel Sir Lucas Deverell and deal with the daily problems of life in the seventeenth century and the encroaching war. When she intervenes to save a dying man, suspicions are raised and she begins to fear for her life, with enemies on all sides. Constance Harcourt discovers a love that crosses centuries and all barriers, but which could potentially end in heartbreak. Can the power of True Love overcome the power of the Universe?

This is a time-slip story filled with passionate romance, the very real threat of persecution and war, the beauty of the Cotswolds and touches of Beauty and the Beast.

Dark Lantern (1755)

An unexpected funeral, a new life with unwelcoming relations and a mysterious stranger who is destined to change her life forever. Martha Pentreath has been thrust into a bewildering and perilous adventure.

Set in 1755 on the wild coast between Cornwall and Devon, this swashbuckling tale of high society and secretive seafarers follows Martha as she valiantly juggles her conflicting roles, one moment hard at work in the kitchens of Polgrey Hall and the next elbow to elbow with the local gentry.

Then as dragoons scour the coast for smugglers, she finds herself beholden to the captain of a lugger tellingly built for speed. Unsure whom to trust, Martha soon realises that everything she thought she knew was a lie and people are not what they seem.

With undercurrents of The Scarlet Pimpernel, Cinderella and Jamaica Inn, this is a story of windswept cliffs, wreckers, betrayal, secrets, murder and passionate romance.

Martha fights back against those who would relish her downfall and discovers the shocking truth about her own family. But she will find loyalty and friendship and a love which will surprise her but also bring her heartache.

Caroline Elkington's first novel powerfully evokes the landscape she came to love when visiting her grandparents' home on the Rame Peninsula. With her passion for all things Georgian, this heart-warming romance is adeptly interwoven with the events of the time and draws the reader into every scene with insights into the lives of eighteenth-century country folk

THE WIDOW (1782)

Nathaniel Heywood arrived at Winterborne Place with no intention of remaining there for longer than it took to conclude a business proposition on behalf of his impulsive friend Emery Talmarch.

Impecunious, cynical and world-weary, he is reluctant to shoulder any kind of responsibility. Nathaniel was just looking for an easy way to make some money to save Emery from debtor's prison and possibly worse. He had no idea that he would be offered such an outrageous proposal by his host, Lord Winterborne and find himself swiftly drawn into a web of intrigue and danger. He wants nothing more than to escape and be trouble-free again.

Above anything else he wanted his freedom.

And then he meets Grace.

OUT OF THE SHADOWS (1792)

In this deeply romantic thriller, Out of the Shadows, an inebriated and perhaps foolhardy visit to London's Bartholomew Fair begins with an eye to some light-hearted entertainment and ends with a tragic accident and Theo Rokewode and his close friends find themselves unexpectedly encumbered with two young girls in desperate need of rescue and as a result their usually ordered lives are turned upside down as danger stalks the girls into the hallowed halls of refined Georgian London and beyond to Rokewode Abbey in Gloucestershire.

Sephie and Biddy are hugely relieved to be rescued from the brutal life they had been forced to endure but know that they are still not truly safe. Only they know what could be coming and as Sephie loses her heart to Theo, she dreads the truth about her past being revealed and determines to somehow repay her new-found friends for their gallantry and unquestioning hospitality but vows to leave before the man she loves so desperately sees her for what she really is.

Her carefully laid plans bring both delight and disaster as her past finally catches up with her and mayhem ensues, as Theo, his eccentric friends and family valiantly attempt to put the lid back on the Pandora's Box they'd unwittingly opened that fateful night at the fair.

This story is loosely based upon a real case which occurred in 1767, Elizabeth Brownrigg, a respected midwife, was given custody of several female children from the Foundling Hospital to use as servants but one, Mary Clifford, was so badly tortured she died before she could be saved. Neighbours finally reported the midwife, and the other girls were rescued, and Brownrigg was eventually executed for her crimes and the laws were changed to provide more safety for the foundlings.

ABOUT CAROLINE ELKINGTON

When not writing novels, Caroline's reading them - every few days a knock on the door brings more. She has always preferred the feel — and smell — of a real book.

She began reading out of boredom as she was tucked up in bed by her mother, herself an avid reader, at a ridiculously early hour.

In the winter months she read by moving her book sideways back and forth to catch a slither of light that shone through the crack between the hinges of her bedroom door.

Fast forward sixty years and she's someone who knows what she wants from a book: to be immersed in history (preferably Georgian), to be captivated by a romantic hero, to be thrilled by the story, and to feel uplifted at the end.

After a long career that began with fashion design and morphed into painting ornately costumed portraits and teaching art, she has a strong eye for the kind of detail that draws the reader into a scene.

Printed in Great Britain
by Amazon

60468288R00234